SHE WAS A CELESTIAL IMAGE, A PICTURE OF PUREST BEAUTY

Leith's heart seemed to still in his chest. Naked, she stood upon the silken sand—like a goddess revealed to him alone.

Hard need gripped him with sudden urgency. Primitive yearning twisted in his gut.

Shadow and light limned her delicate form, hiding and enhancing. She stretched, lifting her slender arms toward the moon, reveling in its magical light.

He stepped forward, drawn by invisible bonds . . .

Other **AVON ROMANCES**

FOREVER HIS *by Shelly Thacker*
A GENTLE TAMING *by Adrienne Day*
KENTUCKY BRIDE *by Hannah Howell*
PROMISE ME HEAVEN *by Connie Brockway*
SCANDALOUS *by Sonia Simone*
TENDER IS THE TOUCH *by Ana Leigh*
TOUCH ME WITH FIRE *by Nicole Jordan*

Coming Soon

THE LADY AND THE OUTLAW *by Katherine Compton*
VIKING'S PRIZE *by Tanya Anne Crosby*

And Don't Miss These
ROMANTIC TREASURES
from Avon Books

CAPTIVES OF THE NIGHT *by Loretta Chase*
CHEYENNE'S SHADOW *by Deborah Camp*
LORD OF FIRE *by Emma Merritt*

Highland Jewel

Lois Greiman

AVON BOOKS ◆ NEW YORK

HIGHLAND JEWEL is an original publication of Avon Books. This work
has never before appeared in book form. This work is a novel. Any sim-
ilarity to actual persons or events is purely coincidental.

AVON BOOKS
A division of
The Hearst Corporation
1350 Avenue of the Americas
New York, New York 10019

Copyright © 1994 by Lois Greiman
Published by arrangement with the author
Library of Congress Catalog Card Number: 93-90644
ISBN: 0-380-77443-7

First Avon Books Printing: March 1994

AVON TRADEMARK REG. U.S. PAT. OFF. AND IN OTHER COUNTRIES, MARCA
REGISTRADA, HECHO EN U.S.A.

Printed in the U.S.A.

RA   10   9   8   7   6   5   4   3   2   1

To the Dream Team—
Cary, Jane, Nellie, Nora, Sharon, and Susan,
who help me celebrate the joys,
mourn the disappointments,
and believe in the dream.

Chapter 1

The Year of Our Lord 1491
St. Mary's Abbey, England

The grave marker was hewn from quarried stone. Arched at the center, it was slightly tilted and infested with gray-green lichen that shadowed its surface like the untended beard on a warrior's craggy face.

The tombstone beside it showed little variance from the first and although Leith Forbes had no need to read the inscription, he did so nevertheless, feeling a dull ache of pain at the knowledge of the child's passing.

Touching the etched words for a moment, he tightened his jaw before expelling his breath and settling back onto his heels. He'd traveled a long and winding course to come to this spot, had left his kinsmen and home for a quest that granted no more than a view of this weathered tombstone and a sympathetic word from a holy woman.

Leith clenched his hands about the small bundle of tartan the abbess had given him.

"*For you,*" she'd said simply. "*Perhaps it will lighten your old lord's sorrow some small whit.*"

But it would not, of course. Only the girl could ease their troubles—only the girl, live and whole.

Leith dug his fingers into the soft baby's blanket. It was red and blue plaid, barely large enough to

1

cover Beinn's saddle, and inside the woolen was the brooch with its amethyst jewel set into the unmistakable double-knotted scroll of the MacAulay clan.

It was the brooch the MacAulay had given his lovely English bride. The brooch she had taken with her when she'd fled Scotland with her infant child.

A single obscenity slipped from Leith's lips. He rose abruptly. Perhaps it was unseemly to curse on hallowed soil. But sweet Jesu, he had endured much—only to find that both mother and child had died seventeen years earlier, before the lass' first birthday.

Damn it to hell! He clenched his fists again. *Damn Elizabeth MacAulay*, he cursed silently, then rubbed a hand across eyes smarting with the dry pain of disillusionment.

Turning stiffly, he strode a short distance away.

Blue-petaled harebells grew in scattered clusters, and he paced to the nearest, plucking a few to grip them in calloused hands and stare at their incongruous cheerfulness.

Damn Ian MacAulay, the wily old bastard who had sent him on this quest, promising his own daughter as Leith's wife, promising peace between the clans. Damn the hot Scottish blood that flowed in his people's veins.

And damn himself for failing them!

Turning back, Leith walked slowly to the child's grave and bent, gently laying the blossoms before the mossy stone.

"I canna blame ye for yer own death, wee one," he murmured grittily, "but I would that ye had lived." For a moment his shoulders slumped with the weight of heavy responsibility. "Betwixt us two," he added, touching the grave marker reverently, "we could have vexed yer sire greatly."

He remained a moment longer, but straightened finally. It would do no good to mourn a babe who had died long ago, a babe he had never met. And yet the thought of a true-born Scot dying far from her homeland wrenched his soul. None should endure such a fate.

And neither should he tarry here. Hardly did England welcome its Scottish neighbors with open arms. Even with King James IV's efforts for peace between the countries, it was unsafe. James was a new king, a better king, striving to improve the lives of his countrymen—even the lives of the Highlanders. Indeed, he spoke the Gaelic, a fact that set him apart from the former monarchs, a fact that made Leith believe now was the time to press for peace, to join efforts with the king himself to create a difference in his Highland clan.

Turning his face from the gravesite, Leith noticed the pink-stained sky on the western horizon. There would be little enough daylight left to travel by. They should leave immediately, yet he felt some indefinable urge to remain for a time, perhaps indeed to mourn the passing of the babe who might have spared much bloodshed.

Walking down the verdant slope, Leith allowed himself a moment without conscious thought, letting his weary muscles relax. It was warm and still beneath the shelter of the trees and he drew a heavy breath, noticing for the first time the fresh green of spring.

Birds sounded their familiar cries—the flute-like whistle of a golden oriole, the penetrating call of a nuthatch issuing from dense upper branches. The slope became steeper and a lochan appeared finally, the water of the small lake dark and waveless in the diminishing light.

He rested here, settling wearily upon the weather-softened leaves to stare at the lochan below. It was a bonny spot, where he could well imagine he was yet in the Highlands, listening to his sister's fair voice as she sang. Before her death, before the feud between the clan Forbes and the MacAulays.

There had been a time when the two tribes had been united in spirit, when a Forbes need not fear for his life should he cross to MacAulay soil, but that peace was no more. It had been shattered by Eleanor's death.

Dear Jesu! Leith tightened his fists, letting his eyes fall closed as he remembered.

He had harbored such hopes for this quest—had longed to right the wrongs, erase the pain. But there was no hope now.

Long ago he had met the mother of the lost child. She had been English and new to the way of the Scots and the MacAulays. Even as a lad Leith had been left speechless by her beauty, awed by her regal demeanor. But there had been a sadness upon her, a melancholy he could sense and still recall.

She had hated Scotland, hated the loneliness, hated the marriage that brought her there. And so she had escaped, finding her final resting place here.

Would the daughter have felt the same? Would she have preferred death to Scotland? Or would she have been the bond needed to heal the hatred?

It was dark when Leith awoke, and the air was still, like the muffled memory of a dream. Awareness shifted into his senses and he opened his eyes.

The lochan below lapped quietly at its sandy shore, moving restlessly and glittering in silvered points of moonlight.

It seemed a magical place, soothing somehow, but he had already spent too much time here.

A movement arrested Leith's attention and he turned his gaze.

It was a woman. Or was it? She was dressed in purest white and beside her was the sleek, dark shape of a . . .

He shook his head tentatively, trying to clear his mind, but the scene did not change. Still the woman remained upon the sand, and at her side was a wildcat.

Sweet Jesu, it could not be. Wildcats were not pets, but independent fighting beasts, revered for their strength and ferocity. Indeed, they were the very symbol of the Forbes.

A noise issued from below, rumbling up from the sleek cat as the woman placed her hand gently to its head. Purring! Sweet Jesu, it was purring and rubbing close against its mistress' robed leg.

Leith felt the magic like the sizzling shock of nearby lightning.

Never had he seen a *bean-sith*, but this must surely be one. In his youth he had heard many tales of the fairy people. Long had it been since he had hoped to view one in the flesh.

She spoke.

He could not hear her words, for they were meant for the cat. Her tone was soft and melodious, like a dove's dulcet cry through the fog of morn. Leith straightened slightly, letting the magic sear his senses as he endeavored to see more clearly through the foliage before him.

The moon had slipped above the uppermost

branches of the trees, casting its gilding light upon the unearthly creatures by the lochan. He saw the fairy lift her robes. Her feet and legs were pale and bare, shapely and mesmerizing as she touched her toes to the water.

Cold! It would be cold as winter on a windswept mountain, Leith surmised. Yet the figure did not draw immediately away but walked for a while through the water, lifting her robes high enough to expose her knees and a scant few inches of lovely thighs, and beside her, through the glassy liquid moved the cat.

A fairy woman and her familiar. Eerie and frightening. Yet Leith was not frightened, for the magic seemed to surround him too. He clenched his fists, feeling an instinctive desire as old as time. Indeed she was of the fairy folk for she drew at his senses, seeming to wrestle his will from him. Need reared its insistent head. Too long had he thought of naught but his people, too long had he neglected that which made him man.

Not drawing his eyes from the gilded fairy, he sat silently upright. Little more than ten strides separated them, but the distance was crowded with leaves and bracken and she failed to notice for she spoke to her familiar and raised her hand.

The cat lifted its head, listening, and then it was off, bounding through the water to disappear into the darkness.

Stepping from the silvered lochan, the fairy looked quickly about. With one smooth motion she pulled the wimple from her head. Masses of burnt-crimson hair cascaded down her back in wild abandon, catching light like moonbeams on rubies.

Leith felt his breath catch in a hard knot. She was a celestial image, a picture of purest beauty, and he half-expected her to be joined there by a unicorn of ivory hue and deep-chested power.

The rope about her waist fell away. Her hands lifted.

Sweet Jesu! Leith's heart seemed to still in his chest. Naked, she stood upon the silken sand—like a goddess revealed to him alone.

Hard need gripped him with sudden urgency. Primitive yearning twisted like a well-placed dirk in his gut.

She was as straight as a reed, as supple as a sapling, caressed by hip-length hair and illumined by enchanted moonbeams. Shadow and light limned her delicate form, hiding and enhancing. Her back lay like a smooth glen that sloped down to the curve of twin hillocks, and when she turned he saw the sister peaks of her taut breasts.

She was a supernatural being, but did legend not say that the Highlander had sprung from matings with such creatures in the dawn before time? *'Twas an honored tradition*, said his unconscious mind.

She stretched, lifting her slender arms toward the moon, reveling in its magical light. Inviting him to come to her?

Yes. Of course. In all his six and score years he had never been granted a view of a fairy. But now, at his darkest hour, she was revealed to him. It was destiny. On some primal level he felt her call to him, entreating him. Begging him to take her. As one in a trance he rose. She held his future in her magical hands and he had been led here to join with this mystical being—to let her cure the ills of his clan, to heal the wounds that he could not.

Aye! She was the answer.

He stepped forward, drawn by invisible bonds.

A branch scraped against Leith's doublet, causing the fairy to lift her face. It was pale as moon-light in the darkness; her gasp was sharp and startled.

Do not fear, Leith wished to tell her, for he would not harm her. Destiny moved him, drawing him onward, but a snarl from behind him jerked at his attention.

He tried to push the sound from his mind, to concentrate on the fairy, but the snarl sounded again, closer now and more deadly.

In one swift movement he turned, dropping a hand to the bone handle of the dirk at his side.

A dark shadow crouched not far away. It snarled again, its fangs just visible in the darkness. Leith steadied his stance, gripping his weapon, every sense focused on the battle he would wage for the fairy goddess.

But from below a rustling noise brushed up from the sand of the lochan and running feet pattered speedily away. The dark shadow of the cat rose, twitched, and was gone, like nothing more sub-stantial than the furtive whisper of a frightful dream.

Drawing a deep breath, Leith forced his muscles to relax and turned slowly. The fairy was no longer there.

On the pale, crescent stretch of beach, footprints were frosted onto the sand. Near the water's edge the glitter of metal caught Leith's eye. Pacing to it, he squatted. Finding a coarse chain, he scowled, lifting it slowly to let it drift through his fingers until he felt the rough wood of a small cross bound in brass wire.

"Sweet Jesu!" He whispered the words aloud, his gaze caught fast on that humble symbol of Christianity. It was the distinctive cross he had seen on the ladies of Saint Mary's Abbey, the cross each of them had worn about their necks.

Leith's gaze lifted to follow the gilded footprints.

So the enchantress was not a fairy.

She was a nun!

Chapter 2

God's toenails! Bloody hell! Damnation!

Rose Gunther sank silently to her knees. After she'd spent half a night in open-eyed terror, the day had been no better. Pure fatigue had made her late for morning prayer. Pure terror had stretched her nerves to the breaking point.

Beside her, eleven pious women prayed in silent devotion. Rose prayed in abject desperation!

How had she lost the cross of St. Mary's Abbey? And why in heaven's name hadn't she noticed it right off? Not that she could have returned to the lake anyway. For what if her instincts had been true? What if a stranger had indeed been lurking in the dark woods—watching her shameful disrobing?

And what of her dreams? What of the dark, masculine figure that had haunted her sleep? He had seemed so real. So close. So disturbing and yet alluring, like a forbidden fruit.

She shivered, wondering at the eerie feelings that had invaded her peace. Had those frightening moments on the beach been no more than a product of her too-vivid imagination? But no—Silken had snarled as he always did if a stranger approached. The wildcat had been waiting by the lake, almost seeming to know she would come. But of course he could not know. She had not even known herself. Probably Silken spent many nights by the lake and it had been mere coincidence that brought them there together. Whatever the reason, it had been so very good to see the cat again and ever so lucky for her that he had warned her of another's presence.

But what now? Even if, by some miracle, the abbess didn't notice her loss, someone was bound to find the cross. What would happen when the goose girl wandered along the lakeshore, as she was wont to do, and found a fat gander pecking irreverently at the wooden cross bound with brass wire? What then?

It would be a simple matter of elimination. What lady of St. Mary's was missing her cross? And why had it been found taking a dip in the cold water of the nearby lake?

Why indeed?

She should have stayed safely within the confines of the stone walls, should have spent her time in fasting and prayer. Rose opened her eyes to narrow slits, studying Mary Katherine, who had a strange habit of swaying back and forth as she prayed. Her rosary hung securely by her hip and upon her sturdy chest rested the unique cross of their order.

Rose bit her lip, remembering her Uncle Peter's amazing sleight of hand. He could have whisked that chain from Mary Katherine's neck without . . .

God help her! Rose crossed herself with speedy desperation. She was devil's bait. That's what she was. Considering pinching a sister's cross! It was scandalous. Still . . . She slitted her eyes again, watching the little cross sway seductively with Mary Katherine's movement.

But surely the theft of a cross would be frowned upon, both in heaven and here in their humble abbey, for in truth the Lady Abbess had yet to forgive

Rose for her sojourn onto the roof. It had been a harmless little jaunt really, though perhaps she should not have tried to scale the side of the abbey, even though the squirrel had ventured down that way. The animal had been the most peculiar color—almost white with just a patch of red in the center of its chest. It had sorely piqued her curiosity and she had seen no harm in investigating such a unique creature.

She'd been within arm's length of the pale squirrel when she'd lost her grip on the crumbling stone and fallen—smack into the shaded kitchen garden. Sister Ruth had shrieked in the most high-pitched tone imaginable. Sister Frances had fainted dead away.

In truth it had been the most excitement they'd seen in years. They should have thanked her for the diversion. Instead, she'd been sent to her cell with no supper.

Rose's stomach rumbled at the memory. She bit her lip again. If her cross was found by the lake, she'd be lucky to be allowed so much as a whiff of food between now and the Lord's next coming.

She'd have to find the cross and pay penance for her shameful behavior. After all, she'd promised her mother on her deathbed that she'd become a nun. And God damn it—Father forgive her—that's what she'd do.

She'd be a model of decorum, stay discreetly out of the way, and hope the good Lord would have mercy on her, a pitifully poor sinner. But why hadn't the Lady Abbess chastised her for her tardiness to morning prayer? And how had she failed to notice the absence of her cross?

There were visitors in the village, Rose knew— two large men on fine, powerful steeds. They'd spoken to the abbess. Perhaps they'd kept the lady's mind too occupied for her to consider Rose's less-than-exemplary conduct. Perhaps it was the divine providence of God.

That was it. The good Lord had taken note of her earnest attempts at pious devotion and was about to give her the opportunity to retrieve her cross without the abbess' knowledge of any wrongdoing.

Rose said a sincere prayer of thanksgiving.

It would be simple enough. She'd slip out her window after they'd been sent to the isolation of their cells. It'd take her only a moment to scale the wall and not much longer to vault the outer enclosure. She wouldn't tarry by the lake as she so wished to do, but would come back straightaway.

She scowled again, pulling her lower lip between her teeth. It was true that she'd promised the Lord never to sneak from the abbey again. But was it not also true that the Almighty knew her weaknesses? Therefore He must realize she would be unable to keep such a vow—for He knew all things.

Rose nodded once, content with her sound reasoning. The Lord knew her weaknesses and therefore counted her feeble attempts at piety more favorably than the seemingly much grander piety of the sisters.

Likewise, the Lady Abbess must forgive her also.

The bell chimed. Rose crossed herself and straightened rapidly, made hungry by her feverish rationalization—and bumped messily into Lady Sophie, the abbess.

"Oh! Mother!" Rose gasped, grabbing the Lady Abbess' frail form to keep her from tumbling over backward. "I didn't see . . . I'm . . . " She gulped, wondering suddenly at the woman's unexpected presence. " . . . sorry." Her knuckles, she realized, were rather white as she gripped the elder woman's robes in a somewhat irreverent clasp. "So . . . so sorry," Rose mumbled, finally dropping her hands to brush gently at the wrinkles she'd pressed into the other's robes.

Their eyes met, Lady Sophie's calm but patiently exasperated, Rose's wide and unmistakably panicked as she remembered the lost cross.

"So, so sorry," she repeated, wondering dismally if she should admit her loss and craft a likely alibi for the cross' strange disappearance, or pretend nothing was amiss and hope to God the abbess wouldn't notice.

"I wish to speak to you in the parlor," said Lady Sophie evenly.

"Speak . . . " Rose knew her voice cracked when she said the single word, which was quickly accented by the deep rumble of her stomach, set to panic at the thought of another missed meal. "Speak . . . "

The abbess nodded and turned.

"Yes." Rose gulped again, trying to achieve the proper stoic demeanor. "Yes, Lady Abbess."

The parlor was a sizable room. It was divided by heavy, cast-iron grillwork which reached from ceiling to floor and separated the sisters from any visitors they might receive. Rose had spoken to Uncle Peter there, before he'd been accused of stealing the neighbor's cow and thought it best to remove himself from the immediate vicinity.

She wished she would find him there now, his round, jolly face watching her through the bars, but the far half of the room was blanketed in darkness, lit by only one sputtering candle.

The Lady Abbess occupied the lone chair. The chaplain was there also, unsmiling and silent as

Rose stepped into the room. For a moment all bravery abandoned her and she was tempted to flee, but she swallowed hard and prayed, pulling the creaky door shut behind her.

Why was the chaplain here? It wasn't that he frightened her. Indeed, despite all her misfortunes during her years at the abbey, he had been the one to plead for the sisters' patience and understanding on her behalf. After all, he'd reminded them, Rose was young, and so full of life. She was sure to sometimes fall short of their expectations.

Had she fallen so far short this time that she was about to be expelled?

Panic gripped her. Despite how it might seem to the sisters, she truly tried to emulate their actions, to attain their contentment, but there was so much life outside these walls. There was so much to see and do and consider, that sometimes she felt as if she would burst if she did not escape for a short while.

Generally though, she was content enough, Rose reminded herself quickly. It was true that the hours of prayer became long and tedious, but she had learned much in the way of healing in the past five years. Much that she would not have learned had she been allowed to remain with her parents on their small plot of land. But the Lord had taken them so quickly, allowing the fever to sear away their lives and leaving her unharmed.

"You wished to . . . speak to me?" Rose asked, clasping her hands behind her back and feeling the cool sheen of panicked perspiration on her palms.

"Yes, my child." It was the chaplain who spoke, his soft, even voice sounding worried and slightly sad.

Rose braced herself, clasping her hands harder.

They knew! Or did they? Best to confess to the lesser of her crimes first.

"I'm sorry for my tardiness at morning prayer. Please forgive me," she began speedily, but the abbess lifted one fragile hand to stop her words.

"It is not that which concerns us just now," said she, rising slowly, her expression solemn.

Dear God! They did know. But of course they would. "Oh!" Rose backed away a step, hitting the wall with a muffled smack, her face going pale. "That! Well . . . " she mumbled nervously. "I can explain. It's really quite simple. It was so hot, you see, and . . . " Rose brought her hands forward to clench them in front of her simple robe. "I know it was wrong. And I promise not to do it again if you can but forgive this one slip. I didn't mean to . . . "

Her voice lapsed into silence as she recognized the identical expressions of surprise and uncertainty on her superiors' faces.

"Didn't mean to—ah, disgrace . . . " She sucked in her lower lip, her eyes going wide as her gaze skittered from one aged face to the other. Well, hell, she realized with mind-numbing relief, they didn't have any idea what she was talking about.

"Perhaps you should take that up with our Lord, my child," said the abbess, her pale eyes seeming to mildly chastise Rose for whatever violations she had perpetrated this time. "Just now we need to discuss another matter with you."

"A-another?" Rose stuttered, her emotions flung hither and yon with each word spoken. Had she done something even worse than losing the cross? It was possible, she supposed, for it seemed she was forever sinning in new and creative ways she'd never even fathomed were sinful. The time she'd used her rosary to tie the barn door shut, for instance. But the rope had been missing and . . .

"Perhaps you know we've had visitors here at the abbey?" began Lady Sophie.

"Well . . . " Rose hedged, not quite certain if she should admit her knowledge. After all, it was a sin to be too preoccupied with the business of others. Wasn't it?

"The fact is, we *have* had visitors," continued the abbess. "Two men from Scotland."

"Scotland?" Rose's eyes widened even further as she allowed her hands to drop to her sides. "Barbarians?"

"Perhaps we are all barbarians in the sight of God," said the chaplain quickly.

"They have come looking for their kindred," explained the abbess in her usual gentle tone.

"Here? In England? But why . . . "

"It seems they have come a long and hard way, in search of an English lady and her Scottish-born child."

Rose frowned, her mind working quickly. "I know nothing about . . . "

"The lady came here long ago, Rose. And died soon after of much the same fever that took your parents."

"Oh." The awful fever was a greedy thing that showed no mercy. Already Rose could feel her eyes fill with tears at the haunting memory. "I'm sorry," she whispered. "And the child?"

For one tense moment there was silence, then, "Dead also, I fear," stated the abbess, gripping her own hands now, as if Rose's worry was a contagious thing. "Both buried in our gravesite."

Rose cleared her throat, pushing back the pain of remembering and filling her mind with the present. She'd read the inscriptions on all the tombstones in the small cemetery and sometimes felt drawn there, as if an elusive peace beckoned to her from amongst the silent stones.

"It seems the Scotsmen have come at the request of a dying lord," continued the abbess. "It was *his* wife and child who came here those many years ago. Not knowing the two had died, the Scotsmen traveled here to find them. But . . . " Lady Sophie shrugged, looking old and worn. "I told them of the grave markers and—"

"What were their names?" Rose interrupted distantly, an eerie sensation gripping her chest as the hair on her arms rose slightly.

The abbess watched her silently, as did the chaplain.

"They were of the MacAulay family, I am told," said the Lady Abbess at last. "The mother was named Elizabeth. The babe—Fiona."

"Fiona," Rose whispered, feeling oddly breathless and supposing it was part of her strangeness Papa had sometimes referred to, and Mama had always shushed him about. The strangeness that made the hair on her arms stand on end and her mind see shadowed, unexplained images. The strangeness Rose had promised never to mention to another living soul.

The abbess cleared her throat now, moving a step closer. "When the Scotsmen acknowledged the deaths, they were most distraught. It seems the old lord had set his heart on seeing the child again."

"After all these years?" asked Rose weakly, trying to draw her mind from the unnerving sensations that haunted her.

"Sometimes a man can only see what is important in life after he has lived a good deal of it," said the chaplain wisely.

The abbess nodded. "The old man is gravely ill."

"And in great pain," added the chaplain.

"The Scots fear he will die, or linger in agony if he is not attended to."

Realization began to dawn slowly in Rose's mind, but she said nothing and waited.

"They have asked that we send someone learned in healing," admitted the chaplain finally.

The room was silent for a moment.

"Me?" Rose's single, startled word surprised even herself.

"It would be a long journey," said the abbess gently. "Fraught with danger."

"But I . . ." Rose lifted her hands in open supplication. "I promised my mother I would live out my days in this house. I promised myself to the work of the Lord."

"This too is the Lord's work," reminded the abbess. "Tending those who suffer."

"There are other healers," Rose said, suddenly frightened by their expressions, their intentions. They wished to send her away. Because of her poor conduct? "More knowledgeable healers than I," she blurted rapidly. "Surely . . ."

The chaplain shook his head slowly. "There are none as gifted as you, my child." He drew a deep, weary breath. "Even Lady Mary, rest her soul, was not so gifted as thee. And you are strong—that strength will be needed for the journey."

Rose was silent for a moment, remembering the heat of her mother's hand as she gripped hers with desperate strength, begging for her promise. "If it's my past sins . . ." began Rose abruptly, "I will make amends. I will do better." She took a step nearer. She had promised her mother and her Lord that she would live out her days in this abbey. "I can be like the others. Truly—"

The abbess raised a blue-veined hand. "It is not because of any shortcomings on your part, child.

Although . . . " She smiled gently, her pale, patient eyes steady. "I doubt at times that the Lord wishes you to be . . . like the others. Still, it is not for me to command you to go. The decision is yours."

"Then I must stay." Rose stepped quickly nearer, taking the Lady Abbess' hand in her own. "I made a vow."

"I believe the Lord would understand, should you see the need to go," said the Lady Abbess.

But the vow had also been to her mother. *"Promise me you'll seek the peace and safety of the convent,"* she'd begged. *"Promise me you'll never speak of the things you see in your head."* Her voice had been only a whisper. *"Do not dwell on them. Do not think of them. People would not understand, would not accept. Go to the abbey, Rose,"* she'd pleaded. *"Do the Lord's work. You'll be safe there."*

Sometimes in the quiet of prayer time or during the darkness of night Rose would consider that. Safe from what? Were the images that sometimes appeared in her head evil things?

"I must stay, Lady Abbess," she said, guilt wearing heavily on both sides, worry making her voice soft. "I must keep—"

"And let me auld laird die?"

Rose gasped, dropping Lady Sophie's hand to find the source of the voice that came from behind the iron grill.

"This is one of the Scotsmen. Come to plead his cause," explained the abbess, but Rose failed to hear her words, for her entire attention was riveted on the large, dark shape of the barbarian behind the wrought-iron rail.

God's whiskers! It was the dark image from her dreams! Breath stopped in her throat while her heart seemed to have gone stone-cold in the tight confines of her chest. "Who are you?" she whispered, knowing her words were rude and failing to care.

Quiet held the place.

"I am called Leith. Of the clan Forbes."

His burr was as thick as morning fog—and as chilling. Rose felt a shiver take her, frightening her with its intensity. "I can't go with you." She whispered the words, as if saying them too loudly might awaken some evil demon.

"Canna?" The Scotsman gripped the grill tightly, the flat of his broad nails gleaming pale in the light of the lone candle. "Or willna?"

"Please." She drew back quickly, not knowing why, but feeling the frightful power of his person, the terrifying knowledge that he had appeared to her in her sleep. He was a large man, perhaps the largest she'd ever encountered. Or was she allowing the shadows and her own too-vivid imagination to frighten her?

Lifting her chin up slightly, Rose clasped her hands before her chest, drawing upon inner reserves she was supposed to possess. "Do not ask me to break my vow to my God," she pleaded weakly. But within, she questioned her true motives for refusal. Fear?

"Ye vows dunna urge ye to help a man in need?"

The Scotsman's tone was somewhat jeering, she thought, and lifted her chin higher. "My vows urge me to follow my conscience and not the brutish insistence of a man with no understanding of my faith."

He was quiet, but his eyes held her in cold perusal. "And me, I thought we shared the faith of Christ. But na. *Me* God calls for bravery of spirit."

He'd called her a coward, she thought in silent shock. The man dared enter the hallowed walls of the abbey and imply she was less than godly! He had the manners of a boar in rut! In fact, she'd met boars in rut who were more becoming, she decided, refusing to acknowledge the fact that her own manners and thoughts were far from a model of purity.

"Regardless of the fact that you think me spiritless," she said, breathing hard and raising her left eyebrow in stern condescension, "I shall not go with you." She turned stiffly away, feeling his hot gaze on her back and trying to still the tremor in her hands.

"Na even if I return what is yers?" he asked huskily, his voice so soft only Rose could hear.

She froze in her tracks. Her heart had risen suddenly into her throat and now refused to beat. "Mine?" she breathed, managing to turn toward him.

"Aye." He nodded.

She watched him in breathless panic, seeing one corner of his mouth lift in a devilish smile.

"Found near the wee lochan yonder," he murmured.

Chapter 3

Her cross! Rose clenched her hand over the empty place where it usually lay against her breast. Air rushed into her lungs in one breathy inhalation. God's toenails! The barbarian had found it!

Behind her the abbess and chaplain were silent. Did they know?

"If ye could find it in yer heart to come . . . " The Scotsman slipped one hand neatly into the pocket of his dark doublet, his voice quiet. "There'd be na need for discussing—last night."

Her gasp was audible now. Her hand rose to where her throat was covered by the coarse wimple, as if to shield herself from his eyes. Had he seen her nakedness then, or just found the cross?

With a concerted effort Rose drew the shattered remains of her dignity about her, but her hands shook near her throat and she wondered if he could see. If the abbess learned of her shameful behavior of the night before, she would surely banish Rose from the abbey—or worse. She swallowed once, thinking fast and hard. But there seemed to be very few choices, for through the fabric of the barbarian's pocket she was sure she could see the telltale outline of her perfidious cross. "Your . . . " She cleared her throat, trying to sound concerned and sympathetic, but the single word squeaked rustily, so that she had to clear her throat yet again.

"Your lord is very . . . ill then?" she breathed.

"Verra ill." His smile was gone now, replaced by an expression she could not discern in the dimness.

"And he has a . . . Christian soul?" she asked weakly.

He hesitated only a moment. "Aye. He does."

"Then . . . " Her fingers curled emptily near her chest as she lifted her chin a bit. "It is my duty to go."

She'd said the words stiffly, with not the least bit of feeling, and Leith raised his brows silently. "Ye've a heart of gold, lass," he murmured, but his tone held no more sincerity than hers had.

"You will find a companion to travel with her," commanded the abbess softly. "Someone from the village perhaps."

The Scotsman nodded, his gaze shifting to Lady Sophie.

"And you will vow to protect her," added the abbess.

"Aye, lady," he promised solemnly. "With me life."

Rose noticed with some irritation that the tone he used for the abbess was vastly different than the tone he used with her. There was no sarcasm now, no quirking of the lips that would make one wish to slap him. Only sober, quiet respect as he spoke to that lady.

"And return her here—if she wishes—after you have no more need for her skills."

"Aye," Leith promised, then shifted his deep-set eyes, so that they clashed abruptly with Rose's. "I will return her when I need her no longer."

Rose would have paced but there was no room in her cell. Instead she sucked her lip and wrung her hands.

The man was Satan personified. She was sure of it. Who else would be sneaking about in the woods in the midst of the night? she wondered, dismissing the fact that she herself had been there. Who else would ransom the cross of a poor postulate of the Lord to gain his own ends?

And what were his ends exactly? For all she knew there might not even be a dying laird.

Prayer time came and she prayed—with a vengeance. They would leave in two days. Enough time, he'd said, for her to gather her belongings and say her good-byes.

Leith had not slept the previous night, kept awake by visions of a fairy princess. A fairy princess with auburn hair and fawn-like eyes. A fairy who was not a fairy at all but the answer to his prayers. A woman of flesh and blood who could as easily as not be the daughter of the old laird of the MacAulays. She was enchanting, just as the Lady Elizabeth had been. And with the amethyst-jeweled brooch and wee plaid the abbess had given him, there would be no way for the old laird to be sure she was not his daughter. Aye, Ian MacAulay would accept her as kin, for he would want to believe it was true, and sick as he was, this would be his last chance to find her.

"She's a fine, bonny mare, brother," said Colin, leaning casually back against a post near a small herd of horses as he interrupted Leith's thoughts.

Leith issued an irritable grunt, wanting to lose himself in his musings again, but Colin was not to be ignored.

Shifting the weed between his teeth, and glancing toward the nearby barn, Colin raised one fair brow and added, "She is indeed the best of the lot."

Another grunt.

"She'll bear the long journey home well."

Silence.

Colin narrowed his eyes. "But why, I'm asking meself—why the best of auld Harold's mares when the others are worthy-enough steeds?"

Leith straightened, paced to the mare's left hind, and bent again, running one hand along the trim cannon bone. "She'll cross well with Beinn Fionn."

"Aye. That she will." Colin nibbled for a moment, watching the other's careful examination before breaking the silence again. "But yer stallion has a full score of bonny lasses awaiting his return. While ye . . . " He stopped on a thoughtful note, grinning crookedly while his brother could not see. "Tell me of this wee nun that's to travel with us."

"Ye will meet her soon enough," responded Leith evenly.

"Is she young?"

"Na so young as ye," said Leith, straightening to caress the mare's glossy hindquarter.

"Bonny?"

No answer came as Leith moved forward again to examine the mare's teeth.

"Is she na bonny?" repeated Colin, deliberately keeping a straight face now as his brother scowled.

"She is na likely to blister yer delicate hide should ye glance her way, if that be yer concern, lad," growled Leith.

"Ah." Colin nodded sagely, causing the ragged weed in his teeth to bobble with the motion. "A hedged answer from my liege is like the highest words of praise from another. So she's a bonny lass." He strode quickly forward. "Dark hair? Fair? What of her eyes?"

"Canna ye find sommat to do?" snapped Leith.

"Is there na a thing to occupy yer time?"

"Na, brother," said Colin with a shrug. "Na a thing. The quest is at its finish. Failed—the child long gone from this world."

Leith turned away, ducking under the mare's delicate jaw to her far side.

"And yet ye seem na unduly troubled," continued Colin thoughtfully. "And after all the struggle to arrive here. If I were na such a trusting man and did na ken ye so well, I would think ye were keeping sommat from me. Why, I ask meself, would we take this wee nun to our homeland? To heal the MacAulay?" He snorted loudly. "Methinks na. Better to run a dirk through his black heart and be done with it. So why—"

"Go fetch a companion for the lass," ordered Leith suddenly, straightening abruptly on the far side of the black to glower over her glossy back.

"A companion?" asked Colin dubiously. "Mayhap I could find her a feather mattress too. We could tote it along in a fine carriage so that she wilna bruise her backside on the hard ground at night."

"I promised the auld abbess she would have a companion," said Leith. "Ye will find a suitable female."

"Suitable?" Colin questioned glibly. "Suitable for what?"

"Suitable for acting as chaperone!" Leith exploded suddenly, his patience at an end. "With legs strong enough to keep her astride a mount for the long journey home. I am certain ye can judge the strength of woman's legs by now, brother."

"Aye." Colin laughed readily. "That I can, me liege. But it's the wee nun ye've chosen that interests me most."

"Sweet Jesu!" swore Leith angrily. "She is a woman of God. And best ye na forget it."

"Me?" Colin lifted a quick hand to his chest, his expression registering shock. "I willna forget, brother. I can have me pick of the lasses," he declared, then scowled momentarily. "When Roderic is not about that is," he amended. "But one canna be expected to compete with one's identical self born into a separate body." He shook his head. " 'Tis difficult to believe the three of us be brothers in truth. For fair Roderic and I are constantly pressed upon by female attention, while ye . . . " He tipped a hand toward Leith. "Ye keep yerself to yerself like a monk."

"I only thank the good Lord I did leave yer devilish twin at home," vowed Leith. "Now go before I pummel some sense into yer flea-bitten head," he added, and, reaching across the mare, seized a fistful of the lad's doublet.

Laughing, Colin lifted his hands as if to ward off violence. "It is na me fault ye canna attract a lass, brother. Perhaps if ye quit yer scowling they would na be so scairt to look on yer scar-riddled—"

The sound of a door slamming interrupted his words, catching both men's attention. Leith dropped his hand and Colin raised his brows at the dark beauty who approached from the nearby house. "Ah, there," he murmured with appreciation. "A woman. And English, so surely she is desperate for a true man. Quit yer scowling now, brother, and give her a try."

"Quit yer yippin' and show some respect," rejoined Leith as he straightened.

"For the lady?" quipped Colin.

"For me, ye dolt," growled Leith before rounding the mare to greet the newcomer.

She was a bonny woman with perhaps a score of years to her life.

"I've come to bring you a bit to drink," she said, raising the tray of sweating pewter mugs so they could be clearly seen above the rough-cut rails of the fence. " 'Tis very hot—for so early in the season." Her gaze settled for a moment on Leith's somber face before turning downward to the mugs.

"Aye," Leith said shortly, and Colin grinned, fully appreciative of his brother's characteristic lack of banter.

"Verra hot," Colin supplied, then added, "and verra kind of ye to think of us, lady . . . "

"Widow," the woman said softly, lifting her gaze finally to Colin's. "Widow Devona Millet." Her eyes, Colin noticed, were an amber color, her features delicate, and her mouth utterly kissable. "I am told you are Scots."

Leith turned his attention to the mare again, seeming to dismiss the woman.

"We are indeed Scots," said Colin, his brows rising as he noticed the widow's low neckline and his brother's blatant lack of interest. "And about to travel back to the land of our clansmen." Leith had been laird of the Forbes too long if he could not appreciate such a fine display of bosom, thought Colin. But perhaps the widow was just the thing to break the monotony of the journey home, as well as pull Leith's mind from his ever-present worries.

Yes. Colin's smile widened as he forced his gaze from the widow's chest. "But we are in great need . . . " He let the statement fall flat, thinking of his own needs for a moment before remembering his brother's. "We require a companion for the lady we will take back with us."

"A lady?" the widow asked.

"A nun," explained Colin, wondering for just a

moment if he heard disappointment in the woman's tone.

"From the abbey yonder?"

"Aye," supplied Colin. Turning to Leith, he asked, "What of *her*, brother? She looks strong of leg—don't ye think, me liege?"

"Methinks ye talk too much," said Leith as he straightened to glare at his brother.

Colin only laughed. " 'Twould be too much to hope that ye might be free to travel with us as a lady's companion," he said.

"All the way to Scotland?"

"Far into Scotland, in fact. To Glen Creag in the Highlands. But ye would be well paid for yer troubles, and carefully ..." His gaze dipped to her bosom again for just an instant and his breath caught in his throat. " ... carefully ... guarded," he said roguishly.

Her cheeks colored prettily and her eyes lowered. "I am not needed in the house of my husband's family," she said softly.

"Then ye will come?" Colin asked, surprised by his good fortune and well aware of the rousing effect she had on him.

"Why do you take the nun to your country?" she asked. "And what would be expected of me at the journey's end?"

It was what was expected *during* the journey that interested Colin most, for if Leith wasn't intrigued by the possibilities, he certainly was.

"She is na yet a nun," corrected Leith evenly. "But a novice, and one said to be a skilled healer. We will take her to the MacAulay who is gravely ill. Ye would but keep her company and return here after our arrival."

"Oh." For a moment Devona's gaze flitted from

Leith's to Colin's. "And you would guarantee my safe passage?"

"Nothing can be guaranteed," said Leith soberly. "But we will do all that is in our power." His hand went to the dirk at his side. "And that is a considerable amount."

She was silent, watching him, seeming to measure the man. "I will go," she said suddenly.

Colin grinned.

Leith nodded, giving the mare one last pat before striding away to duck between the rails and unwind his white stallion's reins from the post. "Buy the dark mare," he said to his brother. "Make arrangements with the widow."

"Arrangements?" Colin asked, pacing toward Beinn. "Does that mean ye are interested?"

Leith was in the saddle in a moment, but bent low to speak directly into Colin's face. "I am not an auld milk-fed maid who needs the help of her witless brothers to make a match. The widow will come as a companion and nothing more."

"And if she wishes for more?" asked Colin evenly.

"Then ye have my blessing," said Leith, and turned his stallion away.

"Well . . ." Colin turned back to the widow with a grin. "It seems we have much to do."

Devona blinked, lowering the tray slightly as Colin bent to step between the rails and straighten again.

"Me apologies for me brother," he said quietly. "He is the laird of the clan Forbes and doesna take time for pleasantries."

"I'm certain he has much to occupy his thoughts."

"Aye." Colin smiled. She was indeed a beautiful

woman. A woman unspoken for, and a woman apparently not desired by his brother. It would be a shame to waste such an opportunity, especially since she was a widow, a woman in whom the spark of sexual desire had once been lit and had now dimmed, left unfulfilled. "We dearly appreciate yer offer to travel with us," he said. " 'Twas indeed generous."

Devona lowered her eyes with a blush. "Perhaps not so generous as you think. I fear I have my own reasons for wishing to be gone."

"Indeed?"

"There is no purpose for my presence here," she explained, resting her eyes on the mugs. "Since my husband's death I feel . . . " She shrugged.

"Unwanted?" The word slipped unbidden from Colin.

"Yes." She nodded slowly. "Unwanted."

Sheer instinct propelled Colin across the short distance between them. "I want ye." The statement came out as a husky caress.

Devona's mouth fell open.

Suddenly he gripped the wooden tray between them.

"But I . . . I don't know you."

"Ye will," he breathed. "In yonder barn."

The widow's eyes opened wide. "The barn?" she gasped.

"Aye, lass. I burn for ye. Let me take ye to the barn and ignite—"

Her palm hit his face with enough force to rattle the mugs atop the tray in his hands. "How dare you?" she cried.

Colin's jaw dropped. Apparently he'd employed the wrong methods. "I did na mean to insult ye. I only meant to lay with—"

"How *dare* you?" she repeated, sounding even more offended.

Colin's brows lowered as the unsated edge of his desire burned on. "There are those who have na been so insulted by me offers."

"And there are those who sleep with pigs," she hissed. "But I am not one of them."

"Pigs!" Colin exclaimed, but already she was striding stiffly toward the house, leaving him to hold the tray in angry bewilderment.

"You will care for her?" asked the chaplain solemnly.

"I will," Leith said, looking down into the man's worried eyes.

Dawn had come and gone. It was past time to be off. Beside him Colin stood unspeaking, restraining his mount, the newly purchased black, and a horse which was packed with their belongings. Just behind him, the Widow Millet silently sat a mousy-brown mare with heavy bones and narrow eyes. Leith kept his gaze on the chaplain, wondering again at Colin's choice for the widow's mount. It was a sturdy-enough steed, but homely and bad-tempered.

"And you will be patient with her?" asked the chaplain.

"Patient?" Leith was momentarily intrigued by the question. Aside from the fact that the girl had not yet arrived, why should he need to be patient?

"Rose . . . " the chaplain began slowly with a single shake of his head, "Rose Gunther is a . . . special child."

Leith glanced toward the north, wanting to be off. "Special?"

"Gifted."

Leith narrowed his eyes, shifting his gaze downward. "How is she gifted?"

"She has gifts of God."

"Canna ye be more clear, Father?" asked Leith impatiently.

But the chaplain only shrugged. "You will learn her worth soon enough, I think."

Leith scowled. When questioned, the people of Millshire had spoken freely of the lass' ability as a healer, granting him a perfect excuse to take her to Scotland. Now, however, he did not believe the chaplain meant her gift of healing.

The door of the abbey opened. Leith raised his eyes.

She stood there, looking small and young, overwhelmed by her pale, voluminous robes and concealing wimple. And yet there was something about her that drew his gaze—or was it his memory of her by the lochan that intrigued him?

"Protect her," said the chaplain quietly, his expression somber. " 'Twill not be a simple task."

Leith watched in silence as the chaplain turned away. He passed the girl at the door where he spoke a few words to her before disappearing into the abbey.

She approached finally, her steps slow and uncertain, her hands tucked demurely into her sleeves, her eyes reddened. From tears? For a moment Leith wondered if he'd been mistaken, for surely this small innocent could not be the bold, enchanting fairy princess he had seen by the lochan.

His fingers fell unconsciously to the pocket of his doublet, feeling the irregular form of the purloined cross through the fabric as she stopped before him.

Silence settled uneasily between them. Leith tightened his grip on Beinn's reins. She was little more than a child, he reasoned uneasily. And he was a deceitful bastard.

"*Kill me, Forbes, and have done with it.*" The tortured words yet echoed in his head, though he tried to shut them out.

Deceitful bastard or not, he would do what needed doing. He would use Rose Gunther to heal the wounds he could not mend alone.

"Come, lass," he said, pushing back his dark memories. "The black mare I call Maise. Great Beauty," he translated. "She is yers. A gift for yer trouble."

Rose turned her gaze to the mare, seeming to note the wide-set eyes and clean limbs, but soon dropped her attention to the ground at her feet. "I cannot accept her."

Leith scowled. He'd planned quickly but carefully and could not afford to waste time. He was not a patient man, but he was determined and he *would* be charming, for he needed to win her over to his way of thinking.

"Ye canna walk the long journey to me homeland," he said, keeping his tone gentle. "Take the mare. I give her freely."

"I cannot."

Leith swore in silence, gripping his hands to fists and feeling his jaw harden. He did not like delays. He did not like bickering, and he did not like women who failed to take orders.

Charming, he reminded himself irritably. He must be charming.

"I chose the black meself. She will give a soft ride. Will ye na—"

"No!"

The force of Rose's refusal surprised him, but it was her eyes that rooted him to the ground. Sweet Jesu! He had been unable to tell the color at their earlier meeting, but he saw now that they were violet in hue—as bright and sharp as precious jewels. So it was not only her deep—auburn hair and bonny features that resembled the old laird's deceased wife. It was her bewitching eyes also.

But Leith Forbes would not be bewitched. Nay. He would keep his head. She would ride the mare. And he would make her his wife.

Chapter 4

"**Y**e canna pray all night," Leith said, squatting down beside the small, kneeling figure swaddled in woolen robes.

They had ridden all day, stopping only for the nooning meal before hurrying on.

Rose Gunther had not spoken or eaten, and now she knelt in the darkness, looking not at all like the enchanting *bean-sith* he had seen by the magical lochan, but more like a bedraggled martyr with pale face and waning spirit. Where had the bewitching little fairy princess gone? The unearthly, moon-gilded goddess who had ignited his imagination and inflamed his hope, had made him believe in miracles, had made him certain she had been sent as a precious gift from the very hand of God Himself, destined to bring peace to the clan of the Forbes.

He'd been sure such a creature could not be happy in the strict confines of an abbey—had convinced himself he would do nothing but good in taking her to Scotland. But perhaps he'd misjudged her. Perhaps it had only been a vision by the lochan, and this woman did indeed belong within the cloistered walls of a musty abbey.

But blood stained Leith's hands. The blood of his own people and of the MacAulays. Blood that would be washed away once Laird Ian accepted the wee nun as the daughter of his own loins.

'Twas true that Ian MacAulay was a wily bastard. But he was also old, and tired of the feud, tired enough to offer his only child as the wife of the Forbes, if Leith could bring her back to Scotland.

Leith tightened his jaw. He had indeed found her—beneath an aged mound of dirt in an English graveyard. But his dreams had not died there. Nay, they had found new life in the pale, nubile form of an unclothed novice.

A strange way indeed for the Lord to answer his prayers, but Leith was not one to deny a sacred gift. Rose Gunther was that gift. He knew it, just as he knew Ian MacAulay would accept her. Just as he knew she would be the bond that once again united the tribes torn assunder by Eleanor's death.

"Come," he said, retrospect making his tone hard. "Eat before the food cools."

Her face did not lift. Her hands remained folded. "I am fasting," she said in clipped tones.

Damn it to unholy hell! Fasting! Out here in the wilderness where all the girl's feeble strength would be needed just to stay alive. Leith scowled. For a sacred gift of God she certainly was stubborn. He had no time for her martyred antics. But neither would it do him any good to take an unwilling lass to Glen Creag.

Perhaps Colin was right. Perhaps he was wont to frighten the lasses with his dour looks. Leith Forbes, however, had little time for courtship or flattery. He was a man with the heavy responsibilities of his clan on his shoulders. And just now those responsibilities weighed like a stone about his neck, for he saw the possibility of great changes for his clan. Changes that would cauterize old wounds and forge lasting bonds—if only he could charm the kneeling woman before him.

Leith took a steadying breath, remembering his promise to the chaplain, and settled back onto a hip and a palm. "Why do ye fast, wee nun?" he asked quietly.

"Atonement for my sins," she said stiltedly, her head still bowed.

"And what sins are those, wee Rose?" Leith asked, his tone as gentle as he could make it. "Surely ye are too young and frail to have transgressed too grievously."

Silence settled into this sheltered spot in the woods. In the darkness, Leith thought he saw the girl's jaw clench and when she finally lifted her face, her eyes flashed with a less-than-godly light. To his amazement Leith found he had not imagined their size or depth. They were indeed as wide and unfathomable as the deep, dark waters of Loch Ness.

"Do you presume to know the extent of my sins then, Scotsman?" she asked finally, her small mouth pursed.

"Nay," answered Leith, his burr soft and heavy. "I but think such a wee lass as yerself canna have many."

She was quiet again, her pale hands folded reverently, but when she spoke finally her tone was sharp, her eyes bright. "You think your sins more important than mine?"

Leith shook his head, carefully quelling the grin that threatened to lift the corner of his mouth. Without a doubt she was the most interesting and contrary nun he had ever met. "Shall we move to the fire, lass, and compare sins?" he asked, his voice low.

Her mouth was a firm, puckered mound of disapproval above her peaked little chin. "I see nothing amusing about sin."

"I meself find most sins to be quite disturbing." He leaned closer, resting a broad wrist on his knee. "But yers, now, lass—they seem most . . . entertaining."

Her eyes, if possible, became even larger in the darkness. "Dare you speak so lightly of my sins?"

"Dare ye tell me what they are?" he challenged smoothly.

He was close. Far too close, Rose thought. And he was large, with each feature sharp and arresting. His hair was dark, like shining sable, and pulled back at the nape of his neck, which was broad with muscle and sinew. His eyes were brown, the color of rich tea. His nose was not straight or perfectly formed but bowed slightly outward in the center. His cheekbones were high, his mouth full. And at his hip he wore a sword now, a long, scroll-handled weapon that seemed almost a part of his very being.

He was not a pretty man. So why did her hands sweat when he was near? Why did her heart race like the skittering hoofbeats of deer at dawn? She was to be a nun. A nun! Pure. Unlike him—a man who would hold the object of a poor postulate to gain his own ends.

Despite the circumstances, however, she would return to the abbey with the little cross in its rightful place about her neck. She had made a vow, and she would keep it, regardless of Satan's temptations.

Oh, yes. He had been sent by Satan. She had no doubt, for no man had ever stirred her desires as he had. All day, she'd refused to allow her gaze to stray to him, for the sight of him was too disturbing. And yet many times during the journey she had admired him—sitting straight and tall on his white stallion, looking for all the world like a romantic statue carved of stone.

Now, in the darkness, she admitted that he did not look like stone, but like warm flesh. She watched him silently, feeling breathless. She'd always been a strong girl, and though small, she'd assisted her father in his work better than many a young man. But this Scot . . . Her eyes fell to his hand. It was sun-browned and strong, and his wrist, resting on his knee, was broad and flat. Her gaze slipped downward, over the thick, lean muscle of his lower leg, shown to perfection through his dark-colored hose.

"Like what ye see, wee nun?" he asked softly.

Rose gasped, both at his words and at the realization that she'd been staring at him quite boldly, and with more than chaste interest.

"What would cause ye to believe yerself destined to waste yer life in a convent?" he asked softly.

"You dare call the holy life a waste?"

"Na for some." He shrugged lazily. "But a woman like yerself needs sommat more."

"What do you know of my needs?" she asked raggedly, her breath coming hard now as a blush heated her cheeks.

"I know only what I saw at the lochan," he admitted finally.

Rose felt the blood drain from her face in a cold rush. God's toenails! He *had* been there. "What did you see?" she whispered weakly, nearly unable to voice the question, but surely unable to remain unknowing.

"I found sommat ye'd lost," he hedged softly. "And I asked meself, how did the wee nun's possession come to be here in this quiet place outside the walls of the nunnery."

Rose blinked once, a slim ray of hope finding its way into her being. It seemed he had not witnessed her shameful disrobing after all, for surely he would boast of seeing such an act. Hardly was he gentlemanly enough to keep such knowledge to himself. But did he have the cross?

"And what is it you found?" she asked, her voice unsteady as she remained on her knees, facing him.

He watched her in silence, his expression curious. "Ye dunna ken?" His tone was nonchalant.

He was toying with her! "No!" she snapped angrily, then steadied the tremble of her hands and smoothed her voice into something that very faintly resembled the Lady Abbess'. He was merely a temptation sent by Satan to test her, she reminded herself. "I do not know," she murmured, lowering her eyes.

"Then why, I ask meself, did ye come?" queried Leith.

"Because there was need," Rose answered stiffly, her mouth pursed again.

"And what *is* yer need, wee one?" he asked huskily.

"Not mine!" she countered irritably. Did this man know nothing of pious martyrdom? she wondered, then smoothed away her angry expression and clasped her hands more firmly together. "I have no need but to serve my Lord."

"Are ye certain?" Leith asked casually, canting his head a fraction of an inch so that the moonlight flickered across his dusky features.

For a moment Rose was transfixed by the look of him—his arrogance, his massiveness, the sheer force of his presence. When the Lord sent a temptation, He didn't do it in small measures. "Of course I'm certain," she said finally, pulling her eyes from him with a righteous effort.

He nodded, and, bending forward slightly, dipped his hand to his pocket. "Then . . ." he said with a shrug. "Ye dunna care to have . . ." His hand appeared, and from his fingertips dangled her humble wooden cross. " . . . this?"

It swayed on its coarse chain—held hostage by his fingers, and her gaze followed its arcing trail, mesmerized by its haunting presence.

She did not mean to grab at it. She had every intention of retaining *some* dignity, but just at that moment he grinned—that devilish expression of victory that drove her relentlessly past the point of caution.

Her lunge was ill-planned, yet she nearly had it—her fingertips just grazing the rough wood.

But he swung the cross in a simple arc toward his chest and Rose toppled forward, tipped off balance by her frantic movement and falling to all fours like a begging hound.

Leith stared at her in surprise, his wicked grin broadening "What is yer sin, wee nun, that ye would feel such a powerful need to hide it?"

Rose stared up at him from mere inches away, her eyes as wide as the moon, her composure torn asunder. Her mouth fell open. Her lips moved. God's toes! There was something about this man. Something intangible and dark, something so deep and tempting that she doubted her will to resist. But no! She would not fail the test.

Rose scrambled backward, her robes scrunching beneath her to fall straight finally as she jerked hurriedly to her feet. "I was hot," she said quickly, her hands grasping each other as he rose to his feet before her. "I but went to the lake to feel the cool breeze against my face. Is that such a dreadful sin?"

Leith watched her carefully. Her face was a flawless oval, her nose small and straight.

"I didna say it was," he answered, taking a fluid step nearer. "But I ask meself—is that yer only sin, wee nun? Discounting, of course, yer terrible temper."

"I do not have a temper!" she declared, her left eyebrow high, barely making a wrinkle above her amethyst eyes.

"Aye, lass," he breathed from close proximity. "Ye do."

"Well, hell!" she breathed, then grimaced at her horrid language and wrung her hands in abject mortification. "The likes of you would cause a saint to curse."

He chuckled, the sound coming from deep within his broad chest. "Aye. Mayhap I would, lassie," he admitted evenly. "But ye most assuredly are na a saint."

She drew her back to ramrod stiffness. Who was this heathen to find fault with her attempts at piety? To force her from her homeland with blackmail, then insult *her* faithfulness? "I would guess my solitary escape from the abbey is far less a sin that the ones you practice on a daily basis," she said tonelessly.

"Probably so, wee nun," he said as he advanced toward her yet again. "But I wonder now if that was yer worst transgression. Mayhap there was another. Mayhap ..." She was backed against the smooth bark of a rowan tree and he lifted his hand to touch her cheek with the broad backs of his fingers. "Mayhap ye met a lover there."

"How dare you!" She slapped his hand away. "I did no such thing!"

"Na?" He canted his head quizzically at her, as

if wanting to see inside her mind—to read her thoughts.

"No! My only sin was my need to escape the confines of the abbey for a short time."

He dropped his hand, his expression thoughtful, his brows momentarily raised. "Then ye dunna consider yer actions to a be a sin?" he asked quizzically.

Rose's body felt as if it were made of coldest granite. Her eyes locked on his. "What actions?"

He did not smile, did not move but for the slight lift of his massive shoulders. "Disrobing by moonlight, lass. Ye dunna consider it a sin?"

Breath gasped between Rose's parted lips as she pressed back against the slanted trunk behind her. "You saw!" she whispered.

"Aye, lass."

Her hand rose shakily to her throat. "I thought . . ." she breathed, her voice dropping even lower. "I thought I sinned only before God."

"I doubt na that He saw too," Leith murmured huskily. "But I dunna think He enjoyed it as much as I."

She hit him with all of her considerable strength, striking his cheek with the solid force of her doubled fist.

The impact knocked Leith back a step, though he outweighed her by nearly a hundred pounds. He stood in wordless surprise, listening to the smacking echo of her assault rumble through his senses.

"Leith!" Colin appeared in a fraction of a second, his claymore drawn, his face a solemn mask. His body was tense and slightly bent, his legs widespread. "Is all well? I heard a noise."

Rose could not help but notice the taut muscle that jerked in Leith's lean face, the anger that sparked in his deep, deadly eyes. And for a moment she wondered if it might be prudent to beg forgiveness—if not from God, at least from him.

They stood unspeaking, both watching the other in tense wariness before Leith eased his fists open.

"All is well, Colin," he said finally, his tone stiff.

Quiet pervaded the woods. Colin lowered his claymore and paced quickly forward to stand beside the two. Rose knew he was there, though she dared not draw her gaze from Leith's.

"Indeed," said Colin finally, sheathing his broad sword and placing his fists on his hips. "Ye were right, brother. The sight of her does not blister me face." His gaze rested on Rose for a tense moment. "Which makes me wonder," he said, turning to Leith in some bemusement, "what has caused the mark on *yer* face."

The angry muscle jumped in Leith's jaw again. "We were discussing sins," he said in a deadly even tone.

"Ah," exclaimed Colin, smiling outright. "And what sins specifically?" He turned his gaze from Leith to the girl's sparkling eyes. "Murder?"

"Fornication," Leith corrected dryly.

"One of me favorites!" Colin exclaimed happily. "And what decision did ye arrive at? Is the lass for or against?"

Leith did not remove his gaze from the lass' enraged face. "Her lips say against," he said wryly. "But her eyes say for."

"You are surely the spawn of the devil himself," declared Rose furiously.

Colin laughed. "Nay, lass. Auld Horney would na claim him. So the clan Forbes took him to its bosom."

Rose's gaze remained on Leith, her shoulders drawn sharply back and her mouth pursed. "You do not realize the sins you heap upon your soul by your hideous words to a woman of the holy order."

"And ye dunna admit yer own needs," countered Leith darkly.

"I have no needs but to serve my Lord!" breathed Rose.

Quiet filled the spot and Leith's brows rose skeptically. "We shall see," came his solemn prediction.

"My lord?" Devona Millet hurried through the undergrowth toward them. "Is all well?" She looked from Leith to Rose and back. "I feared for your well-being."

Colin watched as the woman hurried forward, one hand lifting her bright, full skirt. "Supper awaits," she reminded them when no answer was forthcoming. "My lord?" she repeated, looking worried and breathless. "Are you not hungry?"

Leith Forbes carefully extracted himself from the glittering depths of the young postulate's gaze. "Aye," he murmured finally, glancing distractedly at the dark woman beside him. "I dunna deny me own needs," he said, lifting his eyes to Rose's heated gaze once more. "Aye. I am indeed hungry."

Chapter 5

"**C**anna ye press yerself a wee bit closer to the Forbes, Widow Millet?" asked Colin.

Leith chuckled, as much at Colin's tone as from Devona's wit. He did not know what disagreement had transpired between the widow and Colin, but he could guess.

His little brother Colin was not known for his patience. Possessing the good looks and charm of their mother, he neither expected nor appreciated rejection. And the widow Devona, it would seem, felt the same about being propositioned.

Leith chuckled again, leaning low to whisper something in the buxom widow's ear.

Her laughter was husky and sensual, but her gaze slipped momentarily to Colin.

So he was right, Leith thought. Devona flirted with him only to cause Colin some discomfort, perhaps to prove she could attract even the somber laird of the clan while rejecting the advances of the younger brother.

Normally Leith was not one for playing games. And yet . . . For a moment he lifted his gaze to the firelight's edge. The wee nun still knelt there in prayer, her pale, narrow hands folded in silent reverence, her head bowed. But what of her thoughts? Not so pure as she would wish him to believe, he would wager. No. Not nearly so pure, for he had seen the amethyst light in her eyes as she had perused him.

She was an apprentice to the holy order, true. But she was a woman first. And a woman of fire.

What if he stoked that fire? What if he ignited her sensuality, nurtured her imagination, opened her eyes to the possibilities of a fuller life? Would she not then admit she had no calling to be a nun?

Again he remembered how she had studied him in the near-darkness only minutes before, how her eyes had lingered on his hosed leg. How much more she would see once he again donned the garments of his ancestors. But until then it would not hurt to flirt with the bonny Devona, for she was eager to do the same, and at the firelight's edge Rose Gunther heard their laughter. He was certain of it.

The widow was giggling again.

Rose clasped her hands until her knuckles went white, then cursed in silence. She then cursed herself for cursing and added another dozen Ave Marias to her penance.

Her knees ached, her head throbbed, and her stomach rumbled. But she would *not* leave her prayers. She would show that godless barbarian her true mettle. The rutting boar! So he thought he could tempt her with his blatant masculinity. Hah! She hadn't even noticed that he was built like a Herculean destrier. She hadn't noticed that his hands were broad and calloused and could handle the giant white stallion without conscious thought.

So he believed her lips said one thing and her eyes another! Hah again! Keeping herself from him was no hardship. Hardly that! Never had she been tempted by a man and he was far from the type to make her start now. It didn't bother her in the least that he sat by the fire with the fat-chested widow with the sultry eyes. Not in the least.

Leith's dark, deep-throated laughter rumbled forth and Rose just barely stopped the awful word that threatened to spill from her lips.

It was merely the thought of impending sin that bothered her, she reasoned sensibly, for it was obvious what course the two by the fire were following. It wasn't as though she cared if the Scottish pig laid with a dozen women at once. Why should she? But it was her Christian duty to care for the bastard's immortal soul.

Was "bastard" considered a curse? Rose winced. There were so many curse words. And her father had been rather free with his tongue. Still, she'd managed quite well to staunch her own colorful language—until she'd met the Scotsman.

She had slipped abominably. God's toenails, she'd hit the man! Not that he hadn't deserved it, but she'd never hit another living creature in her life. She hadn't been prepared for his devilish nature. Her temper had been stoked and the temptation to strike had been too difficult to resist. Circumstances were different now, however. She knew he was the devil's own spawn and from this point on she would refuse to allow him to rile her. She would simply hold her tongue, fast, and pray, and before long she would be safely back at the abbey.

Yes, this was her penance—God's means of teaching her discipline, and she would not fail. She would live staunchly by her new watchwords.

Hold! Fast! And pray!

The widow giggled again. Rose clenched her teeth. *Hold, fast, and pray*, she vowed to the darkness.

*   *   *

They must be nearing the border of Scotland,
Rose deduced. The countryside was splendid, with
hills draped in varied shades of lush green. Overhead, the sky was blue as a robin's egg, with just
a smattering of clouds to accent the broad expanse.

Off to the west Rose caught a quick flash of
tawny color. Silken. He still followed then. Memories of the wildcat made her wistful, bringing back
the warmth of days past. Exploration of the hills
with the wildcat cub at her side. The sound of her
mother's sweet voice singing. Long, wild rides beside her father on a fleet, spirited animal.

Beneath her the mousy-colored mare trotted at a
backbreaking gait. Ahead the Widow Millet rode
the fiery black beside Forbes' snowy-white stallion.

The woman rode like a sack of moldy grain,
thought Rose uncharitably. But despite the widow's lack of equestrian finesse, she managed to
keep herself ever so close to the Forbes.

It made Rose's teeth ache to watch.

Hold, fast, and pray. She closed her eyes. But the
movement without sight increased her dizziness.
How long could she go without food?

There was a quick-flowing stream near where
they camped. It bubbled over its bed of smooth
stones, murmuring quietly as it went.

Leith had picked this spot for many reasons.
There would be water for drinking and cooking.
Abundant game was scattered in the woods, and
here the wee nun could watch him bathe.

He almost smiled as he eyed her small, robed
back. She was praying again, or at least she was
kneeling. And, bless her temptestuous soul, she
was facing the water.

" 'Tis a bonny place, is it na, wee nun?" he asked now, stopping a short distance from her to gaze across the stream toward the north.

She did not answer. He was not surprised.

"A fine evening for a bath."

Utter silence enveloped the woman beside him, but when he turned his head, her eyes were wide open and her lips slightly parted.

"Dunna ye agree, wee one?"

She did not speak, but clasped her hands together until her knuckles shone white and her fingers bright-pink.

He chuckled low in his throat, amused by her expression of terror. "There is na need to look so dismayed, wee one, for surely even ye must bathe at times. Do ye na?"

Still no answer.

"Ah, but of course. Ye had planned to bathe in the lochan by the moonlight not many nights back. I do apologize for disturbing yer bath." He smiled, noting her pale features and round eyes. "But mayhap ye would care to test the waters here?"

Her lips moved, but no words came and he chuckled again. "Nay? Then suit yerself, wee Rose, but I will be putting the stream to good use." With that he reached for the buttons of his doublet. They fell quickly open, revealing the white of the voluminous shirt beneath. In a moment he had loosed the laces that held up his trunk hose, and then, pulling the jacket from his arms, he glanced once at the girl on her knees.

Her eyes, if possible, were even wider and he turned away, hiding his smile as he set his fingers to the buttons of the ruffled shirt. It was open in a moment, allowing him to feel the light breeze against his chest. It caressed his flesh like gentle fingertips, and he pulled the edges of his garment down his arms.

'Twas indeed a bonny spot. A dove called from the woods. The warm air kissed his bare chest, and the wee nun watched.

He could feel her gaze on his back as he drew the sleeves from his arms and tossed the shirt atop the doublet near his feet.

Perhaps, Leith mused, she had been right and he truly was the spawn of the devil. He squatted, flexing the stiffness from his back. But she was surely no saint herself, for there was nothing keeping her there, forcing her to watch him.

Scooping water into his hands, Leith grinned. He was not charming like his brothers, nor fair, he knew. But he was a man, broader than most, taller than all in his clan, battle-scarred, and tightly muscled. Splashing water over his arms and chest, he did not deny or belittle his allure for women. Always he had fascinated them, but rarely had he had the time to entertain their interest, for he was laird, with much to occupy his time.

Now, however, circumstances had changed. Now he must pique the interest of a woman, and not for his own pleasure, but for the well-being of his tribe. 'Twas an onerous task, he thought, remembering the moon-gilded fairy form by the lochan. But the job needed doing.

Still in a squatted position, Leith turned slightly. The muscles of his chest and abdomen were bunched above the laces of his trunk hose, which gaped casually away from his hard waist while gripping his lower regions in an intimate fashion.

"Ye dunna wish to bathe, wee nun?" he murmured. They were but a few paces apart. Water beaded on his chest and belly, slipping lower to be absorbed by his taut English garb. " 'Tis enough water for two."

"Hold. Fast." Her tone was stilted, her words nonsensical. "And pray," she finished, though her lips failed to close completely.

Leith watched her. "Shall I take that to mean ye do not wish to share me bath?"

"God save me."

"I am certain He will, wee lass," he said with a chuckle, and straightened, letting every hard muscle flex and shift as he stood. "For He has sent me to do the job." With that he bent, retrieved his discarded garments, and strode languidly back toward camp.

"We will reach the border tomorrow." Leith stood no nearer the wee nun than need be. A full night and day had passed since his bath in the stream, giving the girl plenty of time to ponder her fate. Surely it was enough time for her to realize her mistake, to admit she was not meant to be a nun. But still she had not eaten or spoken. Her face was drawn, her eyes as bright as rare jewels and larger than ever in her gaunt face.

Sweet Jesu, she was as stubborn as any Scotsman—and more beautiful than any Scotswoman. The thought caused anger to swell within him. "Ye need to eat," he said in rumbling disapproval.

She stood as straight as an unbowed oak, her chin slightly lifted, her face a study of serene obstinateness. "I will not."

He felt the muscle jump in his jaw. Perhaps washing in front of her had been a poor idea, for while it had ignited his own sexual imaginings, it seemed to have done little to further her interest in him. "Ye will," he countered. "We will be riding faster come morn. The border country is dangerous and ye will need yer strength."

"The Lord is my strength," Rose answered.

"Yer own damned stubbornness is yer strength," Leith growled in return. "And ye will eat."

"I will not!" She had each of her hands placed inside the sleeve of the other arm and gazed up at him with violet fire sparkling in her eyes.

Strangling her was not out of the question, Leith reasoned. She was intentionally baiting him. But to murder a woman of the holy order ... It would probably be frowned upon in heaven, though God would certainly agree there was provocation. He unclenched his fists with a conscious effort. "As ye wish then," he said, and, turning away, strode into the dark woods.

"Leith." Colin was there, not far into the trees, and stopped him with his voice. "All is well with the nun?"

Leith stiffened. "She willna eat," he answered through gritted teeth. "She is being difficult."

Colin shrugged. "She is a woman," he said, glancing toward camp and considering his own troubles with the female gender.

"Aye," Leith grumbled in return. "That she is."

There was definite emotion to Leith's response, Colin noted, and turned back toward his brother with some interest. "She is a bonny mite, though."

No answer was forthcoming from the laird of the Forbes, piquing Colin's interest even more.

"Eyes like Highland jewels," prodded the younger brother.

In the darkness Colin thought he saw Leith's fists clench. "She is a woman of God," Leith said, his tone flat.

"Aye," agreed Colin gently. "But she strikes a blow like the devil's own, does she na?"

"I dunna care to discuss her."

"Then why do ye drag her along?"

" 'Tis na yer concern," stated Leith. "Keep yer mind on yer watch. Ye have seen na signs of trouble?"

Nothing as obvious as Leith's strange temper and actions, Colin thought. Why did he wish to take the wee nun back to Scotland? "Na trouble," he said finally, then corrected himself with a frown, "There is a cat. He follows us by day. Beds down nearby at night."

Leith remained silent for a moment, then said, "I have noticed the cat."

"Shall I kill him? 'Twould make a fine hide for—"

"No!" Leith ordered quickly, then drew a breath and shook his head. "He does us na harm. We shall do him none."

Colin was quiet, watching his brother's face in the darkness. He had fought beside Leith, had buried loved ones with him, and would, perhaps, die with him. No one knew his liege better than he. "Ye ken sommat of the cat?" he questioned softly.

The brothers' eyes met, Leith's dark and solemn, Colin's bright and questioning.

" 'Tis na yer concern," Leith said again, but the younger man scowled.

"We take a young postulate from a holy abbey and ye say 'tis na me concern?" he asked, his ire rising for the first time.

"Do ye challenge me right to her?" asked Leith, his voice low.

"Right to her?" Colin countered narrow-eyed. "I didna ken we were speaking of a leg o'mutton."

Leith took a single step forward, looming large in the darkness. "She is me responsibility, brother," he warned. "Dunna interfere."

The scene by the fire that night was much the same as the night before. The Widow Millet was adhered to Leith's side while the little nun was propped on her knees at the firelight's edge.

Tonight, however, Colin watched with a more discerning eye. What were Leith's intentions? *"Dunna interfere,"* he'd said. But interfere with what?

Leith chuckled at the widow's comment, but his gaze, Colin noted, had slipped to the spot where the wee nun knelt.

What did he want from the lass? Why did he bring her along?

"More bread, my lord?" Devona leaned closer, the food held between her fingers.

"Na. I've had me fill."

"More venison, mayhap?" she asked softly, her wide brown eyes lifting to Leith's.

"Na." He failed to look into her appealing gaze and Colin chuckled aloud.

"Isna there sommat else ye might offer the Forbes?" he asked cynically from the far side of the fire. "Sommat more personal, mayhap?"

For a moment Devona glared at him. "I will take food to the postulate," she said, and rose stiffly to move toward the fire, but Colin caught her arm.

"He is laird of the Forbes," Colin said, "and not for the likes of ye."

"Indeed. But you cannot blame a girl for dreaming," she murmured, and, jerking her arm from his grasp, lifted a filled plate to stride toward Rose.

"Damn her stubborn hide," swore Colin.

"Aye," said Leith in low agreement, but his gaze had not shifted from the kneeling figure.

Chapter 6

In her mind's eye Rose could still see Leith's naked chest. It was bold and broad, beaded with water and indecently alluring. Dear God, she was a weak-kneed simpleton. Had she been thinking properly, she would have taken herself far into the woods to continue her prayers in private. Or she would have prayed aloud for his obviously irreverent immortal soul. Or . . . There were probably a hundred pious things she might have done. Staring, openmouthed, like a beached fish was not amongst them.

God had vowed not to tempt His children beyond their endurance. But Leith Forbes' very presence in her life made her question that vow. Not that she was tempted by his masculinity, of course. She was merely tempted by anger, incensed by his immodest behavior, outraged by his . . .

God's toenails, the buxom widow again had her mount pressed up close beside Leith's. One would think the man was the Lord's own blessed saint, come down to grace them all with His glowing presence. When in truth he was nothing but a . . .

She was *not* going to curse. He couldn't make her, even when he laughed in that gravelly way he had, making the sound rumble up from his massive chest to curl into the pit of her stomach. Her *empty* stomach.

God Almighty, she hated him. Despised him! He

interrupted her prayers. How could she concentrate on being pious while she was thinking up new and intriguing ways to kill him? A seductive image of herself slipping a noose about his neck nibbled at her consciousness. Of course she could simply filch the little cross and ride like hell for home, but that would not be nearly so much fun.

And too, they'd catch her without half-trying, for she rode a lumpheaded goat while the honored Lady Devona rode the fine black mare with the prancing step.

Rose's mood darkened, causing her to ignore the fact that she had refused to ride the spirited mare herself. Still, Forbes could have tried harder to convince her. But why should he? He was more than content to ride ahead with the widow.

She supposed the men thought Devona was kindly, after the woman's offer to give her food the previous night. But Rose knew better. It had almost been a pleasure to refuse, despite the hunger that tortured her, for she knew the plump-breasted little hussy only hoped to attract Leith's attention.

Her ploy was most definitely working! But it was no concern of Rose's, of course. For all she cared he could drown in her cleavage, never to be seen again—swallowed up like a small paper boat on a swelling wave—sinking, sinking...God Almighty, she was losing her grip on reality and needed to get a hold on herself. Watchwords! She must concentrate on her watchwords.

Hold. Fast. And pray.

The bonny widow—bless her soul—was forever at his side, Leith thought gratefully. And though he might believe she was attracted to him alone, he did not, for her gaze often went to Colin. Was she trying to make his brother jealous, just as he was trying to do with Rose?

Without looking back, Leith wondered if the wee nun still watched them as she had earlier—with that violet, gem-hard spark in her eyes. The first awakenings of sensual desire? He believed so. A flicker of jealousy? He hoped so. But were her emotions even more basic than those? Rage perhaps? He had, at times, seen her eyeing the pocket where he kept her wooden cross. Would she dare make a grab for it again? And if so, would she, the pious little holy woman, attempt to slip his own dirk between his ribs while doing her pilfering?

The idea seemed ridiculous, unthinkable, until one looked into the eerie, bottomless fathoms of her eyes. There were indiscernible thoughts there—unreadable emotions. Still, any emotion was preferable to her prayerful indifference, for he had an urgent mission and very little time.

Scotland lay ahead, soothing his soul somewhat. "The border to me homeland," he said quietly, pulling his thoughts from the lass who plagued him.

"Let us both find our hearts' desire there," said Devona quietly.

Leith could feel two pairs of eyes watching them as he lowered his gaze to the woman beside him. "What is yer desire, Devona Millet?"

Her eyes were dark and sincere, her expression solemn. "I would have a man to love me," she said honestly. "A man to care for."

Leith saw sadness on her face and having no wish to add more, admitted, "I am not that man."

"No." She shook her head in agreement. "You are not."

Leith nodded, knowing now that he truly understood her words and actions. "Jealousy can mayhap be harnessed."

"Mayhap," she agreed softly. "Tell me of your brother."

His eyes held hers. "He is a good man. And one to make a fine husband."

"I believed it from the first," she admitted. "Felt it in my heart, despite his aggravating belief that he could have me at will. And you?" She did not remove her gaze from his. "Why do you pursue Rose Gunther?"

For a moment Leith was surprised by her perceptiveness and considered not answering, but Devona was risking much to travel with them. "'Tis for a worthy cause, Widow Millet," he said evenly. "I will na harm her."

She watched him solemnly before nodding. "Then we are agreed."

"Aye." He too nodded. "We are," he said, and, leaning from his great steed, kissed her full on the mouth.

Colin watched the pair kiss, feeling an emotion that melded anger and jealousy. He'd deduced that Leith did not care for the widow. And the widow? She was not capable of caring or surely she'd see that she had the wrong broth—

A movement caught his eye and he turned in his saddle—just in time to see Rose's pale-robed body plop to the earth. His brows rose in astonishment. Now this was an interesting twist, he thought. Dropping the packhorse's rope, he slipped to the ground, to stride forward and scoop the girl's flaccid form into his arms.

Her lovely eyes were shut, her skin pale, but she still breathed. He touched his hand to her brow. No fever, but she was so very delicate, like a fine work of art. But stubborn to a fault—starving herself. And for what? For her religious beliefs? Suddenly he doubted it. Did she fast then simply to torment Leith? Colin touched her cheek, liking her more with each new thought. The lass had enough spunk to trouble Leith for a lifetime. He smiled. But the girl moaned now and so he subdued his cheerful expression with wise self-control and called, "Brother! We have a wee problem here. If ye can scrape yer eyeballs from the widow's bonny bosom, ye might come have a look."

Jerking away from the kiss, Leith snapped his gaze to the bundle in his brother's arms. *Sweet Jesu*, he swore in silence and in a moment was before them.

"What happened?" he questioned, his eyes pinned to the girl's pale face.

"Methinks she fainted," declared Colin.

"I know she fainted, God damn it!" snarled Leith in return, not taking his eyes off Rose's face.

"Then why did ye ask?" queried Colin, snuggling Rose a bit closer to his chest.

Leith's scowl darkened at his brother's actions. "Did ye na see her fall?"

"Aye, I did," Colin assured him blithely.

"And ye didna catch her?"

Colin's brows shot up as he watched his laird's face. It looked nearly as pale as the girl's, he noticed with avid interest. "Ye are right," he said, nodding gravely. "It be entirely me own fault. Thus I will care for her." He pulled Rose nearer yet and shifted to move away, but Leith's hand was on his arm.

"Think ye that I trust ye with a woman of God? Give her to me!"

"Think ye that I trust *ye*?" retorted Colin, intrigued by the intensity in his brother's face. "I will keep her."

"Ye willna!" Leith's tone was deadly flat, brooking no argument. "I will take her." Silence settled about them, punctuating each unspoken thought. "Now!"

Colin shrugged finally, fighting down a grin and extending his burden toward the other. "As ye wish."

Leith gathered Rose's limp body into his arms, keeping his expression impassive. But still Colin could read the worry there, stamped hard upon his rugged features.

"We will stop for the night," Leith commanded, his tone tight. "Make camp in the woods and see to the widow."

"Aye, me liege," answered Colin dutifully, and, catching the loose horses, strode merrily toward the trees, stopping only long enough to wink at Devona.

Her back stiffened as she stared down at him and snapped, "And why do you grin like a demented fool?"

"Na reason, dear lady," he said, then laughed aloud, throwing back his golden head and thinking her temper was a marvelous thing. "Na reason atall."

Leith held Rose gently, watching her lovely face in silence. He'd removed the woolen cloth from her head, baring the winterberry-auburn of her flowing hair.

"Awaken, lass," he ordered gently.

Rose heard the heavy burr of Leith's voice as if it came from a great distance.

"Open yer eyes, lassie," he whispered, so close

to her ear she could feel the vibrations of his voice. "Or I will kiss ye awake."

Her eyes snapped open.

The rogue was smiling.

"Ah," Leith breathed softly, caught in the glorious depths of her violet eyes. "So I now ken how to make ye obey." His smile deepened as he touched her cheek. "Threaten ye with kisses."

She blinked twice. He was so near he made her head spin, or was it the strange weakness that seemed to lay like a soaked coverlet upon her limbs? "What happened?" she whispered groggily.

"Ye are such a frail thing." He caressed her cheek with the pads of his fingers. "Ye swooned," he murmured. "And after only three days of starvation and many miles on yonder nag's jolting back."

There was humor in the warm depths of his eyes. She could see it and felt drawn irresistibly to it. "I . . ." She blinked again, realizing for the first time that he held her in his arms. "I fell?"

"Like a stone, lassie."

"Oh." Never in her life had she fainted. What would have caused her to do so now? Oh, yes.

It wasn't the hard days of riding or the gnawing hunger she remembered, but the kiss. He had kissed the dark-haired widow—damn his worthless hide.

"Let me up," she ordered now, struggling to rise, but he held her in place with no obvious effort.

"Ye will stay as ye are," he said casually.

"I will not." Anger streamed back to her senses. Not long before he'd been kissing the widow. Now he held her as if he had every right to do so. "I will get up!"

"Ye willna." Their gazes caught and kindled. "Ye are as weak as a newborn cub. Ye will eat before ye move."

"No!" she argued, incensed by his imperial manner.

"Then . . ." He leaned closer, the ends of his loose sable hair falling upon her robe. " . . . I will kiss ye."

Breath whistled down her throat as she leaned back into his arms, which were hard and broad, strong with sinew and muscle. "Ye wouldn't dare!" she said, but her denial was little more than a whisper.

"Aye, lass." His vow was a husky assurance. "I would."

"The Lord would surely strike you dead."

Leith stared at her in wonder before tilting up his lips slightly. Small wrinkles appeared beside that sensual mouth and beside the outer corners of his deep-hued eyes. "Ye must think well of yerself indeed, lass, to believe the Lord would take such offense to a simple kiss. When in truth . . ." He bent lower, until his lips were mere inches from hers. " . . . I spoke to Him regarding the matter. He said He had no objections."

Rose could find no words. Her heart thundered like a thousand stampeding horses, and her gaze was caught on his mouth, which was sensuously curved and dangerously near.

"He said," Leith whispered smokily, "that though ye are marvelously well-meaning, ye were na crafted to be a nun. Ye were made to be a woman—and kissed well and often."

"Blasphemy." She meant it as a denunciation, but the strange, breathless tone more closely resembled a plea. "You would not dare." She meant to turn her gaze from his—to search for some help, but her eyes would not leave the dark, alluring features before her. Still, she must try to fight.

"Your . . . your brother would stop you," she murmured weakly.

Leith raised his brows at her. It was an odd assessment of his relationship with Colin, he thought. Then again, perhaps not. Colin had indeed seemed earnestly concerned about the girl's well-being. And somewhat distrustful of Leith's intentions. "I am his laird," he explained simply, not quite losing his smile. "He would eat Beinn's saddle if I so commanded."

She let her mouth fall open, hoping to scathe him with some caustic remark, but nothing came.

"And too, lass," he murmured, "Colin is na here. He takes first watch at the top of the *droma* behind us."

"*Droma*?" she questioned weakly, struggling to straighten the facts in her mind.

His fingers brushed downward, caressing her cheek, then sliding lower, across the small promontory of her chin to the delicate pulse in her throat. "Ridge." Leith nodded, seeming no less distracted than she. "He is on the ridge with the widow."

Rose swallowed hard. "Oh," she whispered foolishly, then realized belatedly that his fingertips were touching the bare flesh of her neck. "Where . . . " She reached up shakily, pressing her own fingers beside his. "Where is my wimple?"

"Wimple?" He raised his brows, wondering at the term, then smiled. "Ye mean that awful bit of woolen that hid yer bonny neck?" His fingers trailed softly downward and she shivered. "We Scots also use the word," he said, his gaze following his hand. "But we have a different meaning."

Rose was mesmerized by his touch, breathless at the sight of him—so close. So achingly close. Silence shivered between them until she could bear the quiet no longer. "Oh?" she said, forgetting their conversation, her watchwords, and every single important fact she'd ever learned in her life.

"Aye." Leith lifted his gaze from her slim throat to her violet eyes for just a moment. She was as light and delicate as thistledown in his arms—as soft and firm as a wildcat cub. "It means . . . a crafty twist." The exploration of his fingertips was arrested at the top of her robes, causing his fingers to lie, warm and tingling, against her collarbone. "Yer swooning now . . ." His hand moved slowly outward, brushing against her hair, which she realized abruptly had been freed and spread across his knees in shameful abandon. "Might it na be called a 'wimple'?"

She had turned her gaze to watch his hand caress her hair. It was a strangely sensuous movement that caused her breath to come in short, hard gasps.

"Dunna ye agree, lass?"

"What?" Her question was barely audible.

"Dunna ye think yer swooning might be considered a crafty turn, seeing as how I was just kissing the widow?"

Rose swallowed hard and raised her eyes to his. "Were you?" she asked breathlessly. "I—I didn't notice."

Leith chuckled. "Aye, lass," he disagreed gently. "Ye did."

"I did not." She lied—but poorly.

"Ye are the most contrary woman I know, wee nun."

"And you are the most . . ." *Magnetic*, she thought hopelessly. " . . . brazen man."

He chuckled again. "Ye sorely disappoint me, lass." He sighed. "For I waited with baited breath for a compliment."

His fingers slipped into her hair, massaging gently, and her eyes fell closed of their own accord. "You shall get none from me," she promised.

Sweet Jesu, he could not resist her. "That I believe, wee lass," he said, and kissed her.

His lips felt like fire against hers. Like the first rapid touch of flame, before it is possible to discern whether it is hot or cold. She did not open her eyes but felt the caress of his mouth sear through her tingling being, felt his tongue gently touch her lips, felt her body jerk with the shock and excitement. Her own lips opened without her command, allowing his entrance, and his tongue slipped inside— caressing, arousing, until she found to her stunned disbelief that her arms had crept about him so that she hugged him to her.

Dear Lord, what was she doing? She must remember her watchwords!

Her eyes opened abruptly. Her arms drew away just as quickly. One hand pressed against his chest. "Please." The single word was breathless and wavering.

"Anything, me wee one," he responded, his voice no more certain.

"Let me go."

"Anything but that."

"I am meant to be a nun," she breathed.

"Ye are na, lass. Ye are meant to be loved." He stared at her in some awe now, for he had tried to say she was meant to be a woman, but the words had not come out right. "Loved by me," he murmured, failing to correct his statement.

"No." She shook her head faintly. "I have promised to keep myself apart from human weaknesses, to fast and—"

"The fast has been broken, wee one," he said huskily.

Confusion showed in her eyes, so that he lowered his mouth to hers again, touching her lips with a brief, searing flame. "Well broken, lass," he breathed. "And there will be more. Much more."

"No!" Her eyes looked as frightened as a fawn's. "Please."

"Please what?" he whispered.

"Please," she repeated, but could find no way to finish the plea.

"I will, lass," he promised huskily, listening to her inner voice, ignoring her words. "But first ye must eat."

Had she just begged for his favors?

Did he believe she had? Was she losing her mind? Or just her struggle for purity?

Hold, fast, pray. "No!" she rasped suddenly, and attempted to rise. "No! Let me up!" Her legs flailed and her arms pumped, but she went nowhere.

"I have said," Leith rumbled, his lips close to her ear, "the fast is broken."

"No!" She continued to struggle, though it seemed she was only falling more firmly into his grasp. "I must atone for my sins." And what sins! Cursing! Striking! And now this! Kissing! Good Lord, her sins were mounting about her ears like so many bushels of barley.

"What sins now, wee nun?" he asked, seeming nonplussed by the commotion she was making— like a beached codfish in his lap.

"Sins, sins!" she sputtered, still flailing wildly. "Hell, I have sins beyond number!"

He laughed, both at her poor attempt to escape and her poorer attempt at piety.

"Damn! I did it again," she wailed in feverish frustration. "Let me up before we're both struck dead by a bolt of righteous lightning. This is all your fault!"

"Me fault?" With one large hand Leith captured

her left arm, then pressed his body tightly up against her other, holding it firmly between them. Her struggles gradually decreased in violence, until only her eyes flailed him.

"Of course, your fault!" she snapped. "You are constantly tempting . . . I mean," she sputtered, feeling the heat rush to her face, "provoking! You are constantly provoking me!"

"To do what?" he asked innocently.

He had the most perverse grin, and she wondered suddenly if she shouldn't wish to slap it from his face. But she did not and that was probably just as well, for the good Lord was likely getting weary of her striking him—even though he fully deserved it. "Provoking me to anger!" she said finally.

"Ah." His brows rose. "I thought I provoked ye to do this . . . " His mouth lowered toward hers but she scrunched back against his arm like a cornered hare.

"Please don't," she whimpered.

"Na?" His lips were only a hairsbreadth away.

"No," she whispered. "Please no."

"Then ye will eat?" he questioned softly.

She remained silent for a moment, then, "Give me that damned saddle."

Leith's brows drew together in question, but in a moment he remembered his boast of his brother's obedience and he laughed, tilting his head back slightly as he did so. "Na saddle for ye, me wee, clever lass," he crooned finally. "But venison." He leaned across her to lift a piece from a nearby plate. "From me own fingers."

"No." She eyed the meat and drew back. "Please. I do not eat meat."

"Ye will eat this," he ordered gruffly.

She merely shook her head, however, making

not a bit of fuss, simply refusing. "I will not. I do not eat the flesh of animals."

"Why the hell na?" he asked, taken aback by her strange ways, but she only shrugged, feeling rather silly with his dark eyes so hard upon her.

"Daniel and Meshach were not eaten in the lion's den."

Leith stared at her. Was she suggesting that he was a lion or that she feared he might eat her—or both?

"And too," she said softly, afraid to meet his eyes, "I've known animals I like better than . . ." She lifted her gaze finally. "Some people."

He chuckled quietly. "Ye are the strangest lass alive," he said, remembering the tawny feline shadow that had watched him from beyond the firelight's reach just minutes before. "And ye must eat."

"I will!" She fairly spat the words in her haste to get them out, lest he kiss her into submission. "Fish. I eat fish. Or bread. Bread will do me fine."

Leith shook his head but could not resist the plea in her jewel-bright eyes. "As ye will then, lass," he agreed finally, and, leaning across her, crushed her breasts and abdomen against the hard planes of his chest. Heat spurred throughout Rose's already warm body.

But in a moment he straightened—cheese and bread in his hand, his face only inches from hers.

"Hungry?" he asked huskily.

Rose nodded numbly, finding she had no strength to hope her admittance would press him back, and realizing too that she was uncertain what she was most hungry for—food, or the taste of him.

The thought caused panic to spurt wildly through her. "If I eat," she whispered weakly, "will you let me be?"

His expression was somber finally, his nostrils slightly flared. "I fear ye have na the strength for what I ache to do," he confessed hoarsely.

They were held in silence, both tense and breathless, but he moved back eventually, drawing air deep into his lungs so that his chest expanded against her breast and arm. "Eat, me wee nun," he whispered, and she did.

The bread was stale, hard—and heavenly, the cheese sharp, and each bite taken from his fingers. There was a strange sensuality to the act, an undeniable intimacy as her lips touched his fingers, taking the final piece of cheese.

He drew his hand away, licking his fingertips as she watched, her eyes wide in her pale face.

Quiet fell again and she lay in his arms, feeling silly enough to have her ears boxed and searching raggedly for something to say.

No clever comments came to her mind, however, and he seemed to feel no need to talk, for he lifted her finally, bearing her easily to the spot where several blankets waited.

"Ye will sleep," he breathed, settling her gently atop the bedroll before covering her with a tartan woolen. "Beneath the plaid of the clan Forbes."

She touched the brown and green tartan. It was soft and warm and, strangely enough, reminded her of something. Something so far away that it tipped just past the edge of her consciousness, giving her that uncanny feeling that had so worried her mother. She scowled a little, trying to recall, but she was tired. So very weary, so very . . . Her eyes fell closed and Leith watched, touching her cheek with tenderness.

"Sleep, wee nun," he whispered. "Soon we will reach our home."

*   *   *

From the ridge above, Colin watched with a grin. So he'd been right all along. Not only was Leith interested in the lass, but he was interested enough to show patience and tenderness, two characteristics not generally associated with the great laird. Turning, Colin hurried back into the darkness.

Not far from his watch-place, the widow slept. He stepped closer, gazing down at her. She was not his type, of course. Too sharp-tongued and aloof. He liked women who swooned over him. Still, she was a bonny lass. Stepping a pace closer, he squatted, noting how her lips were slightly parted, her eyelids heavy with thick lashes. She was indeed a comely thing. He reached forward and ever so gently caressed her cheek.

She moaned and turned her face so that his fingers pressed more firmly against her flesh.

"Devona." He said her name softly, feeling her allure whip a hard response from his deprived masculinity. "Bonny Devona."

She twisted slightly, so that her blanket was pulled lower, exposing a half-bare shoulder.

"Mayhap, ye are na so aloof as ye seem," he whispered.

Her left leg bent and straightened, pulling the blanket lower still, revealing further charms.

"Mayhap," Colin breathed, "ye dream of me just as I dream of ye."

She moaned again and in that moment it seemed to Colin she revealed the truth of her need. She was not detached and cool, but lonely and vulnerable, keeping herself from him only by the harshest discipline. *Poor lass*, he thought, and, realizing he could no longer delay the kiss, he leaned eagerly forward.

"Leith," she whispered in her sleep.

Colin's head snapped back. Leith! He was on his

feet in a moment, glaring down at the first woman who had refused to be moved by his presence. Leith!

"Dream on then, widow," he declared, striding away to his post.

And in the darkness, Devona smiled.

Chapter 7

"Awake, lass."

Rose heard Leith's voice through the fog of her slumber, but her dreams were too rich and warm for her to be drawn immediately from sleep. He was there again. The tall, sable-haired man with the compelling eyes. He was there in her dreams, kissing her, his chest bare and . . .

"Mayhap I shall need to kiss ye again," Leith suggested.

Rose's eyes popped open.

God's teeth! He was there—in the flesh and . . .

"Where—where are your clothes?" she gasped, taking in his changed appearance with open-mouthed shock.

Leith placed his fists on his plaid-covered hips and laughed aloud. "I am a Scotsman, wee Rose," he reminded her. "Na one of yer coddled English lords."

"But . . . " She'd known he was a barbarian, but never had she seen his barbarism displayed with such breathtaking boldness.

His hair was dark, long, and loose but for the narrow braids—one nestled beside each ear. His shirt was made of brown wool, soft as hide and open at the neck to show his broad, dark throat. A length of plaid wool crossed his left shoulder, pinned by a pewter brooch, and wrapped around his chest and abdomen to meet the same tartan fab-

75

ric that was held to his waist with a broad leather belt. In the center, but just below the belt, was a leather bag, perhaps the width of both her fists side by side. It was covered with a flap of the same fine hide and kept closed with a narrow thong. Against his right hip his sword was strapped and across his thighs lay the pleated wool of his plaid.

But below that . . . God's ears! His lower thighs and knees were bare—broad and corded with muscle above the tall horsehide boots that covered his flesh from toe to upper calf.

"You . . . cannot mean to tell me you go about wearing tiny gowns?" she murmured in awe.

"Gowns!" began Leith with a scowl, but Colin's laughter cut him short.

"Leith wears a wee gown." He chuckled, striding forward to stand beside his brother, arms akimbo in the same manner. "But we true Scotsmen wear *plaids*."

Rose's eyes widened even further, for Colin too wore the indecent garment. "But your . . . " Her voice failed her for a moment. "Your knees are . . . naked!" she squeaked.

Leith's scowl deepened. "Need I remind ye, wee nun, that I've seen ye . . . "

Her eyes were huge gems of terrified amethyst as she stared at him in mute appeal, begging for his silence.

Leith's dark eyebrows lowered even further, but in a moment his expression softened. "That I've seen ye . . . sleep too long," he finished roughly. "Get yerself up, lass," he said. "Today ye see Scotland."

The countryside had changed little since they'd crossed the border, Rose thought. But everything else had. No longer did they travel at a moderate rate. And no longer did she ride in the rear.

Leith kept her at his side now, seeming ever-watchful and causing her to wonder whether he half-expected her to drop from the saddle again like an overripe plum.

The day turned gray and the wind rose, but they hurried on, keeping their mounts at a rapid trot.

Rose bounced along beside Leith's noble stallion. A trot, she knew, greatly increased their pace while saving their mounts' strength. But still . . . Her head snapped up and down, and her bottom burned like fire, making her regret her refusal to ride the smooth-gaited black.

It seemed her pride was causing her bottom to take a terrible beating, Rose reasoned, wincing with the thought. For the black moved like a feather on the wind, while her own humble gruella bumped along like a lumpy boulder down a mountainside.

She winced again. Of course it was all Forbes' fault. If he hadn't been trespassing by the lake, she wouldn't have lost her cross. And if she hadn't lost her cross, he wouldn't have been able to blackmail her into coming along. And if she hadn't come along, she wouldn't have hit him, or cursed him, or kissed him. And if she hadn't done any of those awful things, she wouldn't have to pay penance by refusing to ride Maise.

In short, Leith Forbes owed her bottom a grave apology, Rose reasoned, and was kept busy for quite some time with the image that thought conjured up.

"What think ye now, me haughty widow?" asked Colin, leaning toward Devona with a grin. Her presence beside Leith had tormented him over the past days, though he was unsure why. She was only a woman, after all, though a bonny one. And yet his dreams were filled with her, his thoughts torturous, for he could well imagine holding her in his arms. "It seems another has taken yer place beside the laird," he teased, but Devona only raised her nose in the air.

"Does my refusal of you still sting so that you must prick me with your tongue?" she asked smoothly. "Or is it the refusal of all the women in your past that bothers you?"

"All the women!" Colin snorted. " 'Tis true ye are the first to—"

"And the wisest, it would seem," Devona interrupted. Setting her heels to Maise's glossy sides, she kicked the mare into a gallop before he could respond.

Colin watched her flee, feeling anger and jealousy wrench his gut. 'Twould serve the haughty wench right to spend the rest of her days alone, he mused, but just then her black mare jostled Rose's mount from behind.

There was a squeal from the gruella, who lashed out with her hind feet. Maise reared, forefeet flailing and eyes wild as she jolted Devona off balance.

To Colin it seemed to happen in slow motion—like a half-remembered dream, played back in the minutes before dawn. One second the black was slicing the air with her trim, round hooves and the next she was falling, thrashing over sideways, with a pale-faced Devona clinging to her mane like a rag doll in the wind.

"Dear Jesu," Colin breathed, for Devona's leg was pinned beneath the black's great weight.

The mare thrashed again, trying to rise, but her rider's weight combined with her own ungainly position held her down.

"No, Maise," Rose pleaded, and, throwing herself from her mount, she raced through the prickly gorse to the downed pair.

Colin was on his feet now, fear constricting his throat as he ran to Devona, but already Rose squatted beside the panicked black, one palm placed gently on the mare's delicate face. "No, love. No," she breathed. Gradually the mare's flailing legs slowed. "Quiet now, my beauty. Be still."

Leith was there suddenly, freeing Devona's left foot from the stirrup as Colin cradled her unconscious form in his arms.

"Now, lass," commanded Leith quietly. "Let her up—gently."

Rose did just that, crooning the whole while, urging the mare slowly to her feet, her hooves well away from Devona's still body.

"There now. There," Rose soothed, her hands still on the black's velvet muzzle. "It is not your fault."

The wild eyes calmed. The head lowered.

"So that be yer gift?" Leith murmured close at hand. "Ye speak with the beasts!"

"I do no such thing. Well—leastways, they do not often answer back."

Leith snorted, shaking his head. "Am I to be grateful for that then?"

"I do not care—"

"Please," Colin interrupted, holding Devona carefully to his chest and seeming to feel her pain in his own being. "Let us care for the widow."

"Her leg is not broken," Rose said.

They'd covered Devona with several blankets. Her face was pale, her brow wrinkled with pain.

"This place is na safe." Leith glanced toward the north with a frown. "We must ride on."

"She cannot," stated Rose flatly. "There is a bruise to her head. If she is moved this day, it may cause her death."

"And if we are found by brigands, worse may befall her," countered Leith, his voice taut. "This border country is unsafe even for a full troop of well-armed warriors. How much more so for a frail, wee nun and a wounded widow!" He glanced at Devona's pale countenance. But when he looked back at Rose, her arms were akimbo and her expression angry.

"I am not frail," she stated coolly.

"And I am na a Scotsman," Leith retorted in his heavy burr, his own hands now on his hips.

"Then discard that silly skirt and don decent clothing," ordered Rose, eyeing his bare knees with disdain.

"Hear this, English," growled Leith, stepping closer, "I wear me plaid with pride and na woman will—"

"Canna ye two kill each other at a later time?" questioned Colin in a low, irritated tone. "The widow is in pain."

Rose crossed herself, speedily saying a prayer for forgiveness for her neglect, and hurried to the packhorse that carried her medicine jars.

In a moment she had collected her cures and was pouring two cups of water from a flask. After adding a smidgen of gray powder to one, Rose tasted the product and scowled thoughtfully. She added a bit more powder and stirred before she retrieved the other cup and carried both to the injured woman.

"Here." She squatted beside Devona's prone form. "Drink. It will dull the pain and help you sleep, but you must drink it all at once."

Devona did as she was told, gulping the liquid in one speedy quaff before screwing her face into an expression of horror and shivering from the awful bitterness. "Water," she croaked, and found the second cup thrust into her hands.

She drank deeply and came up breathing hard, shivering again. "What is that horrid brew?"

"It's . . ." Rose began but shook her head, thinking better of it. "You don't care to know," she assured her kindly, "but Uncle Peter called it . . . barn dew."

From a short distance away, the men saw Devona smile, saw the pain slip gradually from her features.

"Yer wee nun," began Colin in quiet wonder, "is more than ye bargained for?"

Leith was lost in thought. Who was this lady who wrapped herself in the homely robes of Christ, yet spoke in bawdy terms to lighten another's anguish? Her burnt-crimson hair was hidden beneath the awful wimple again, her body shielded by heavy layers of wool, yet it was as if he still viewed her full beauty as revealed to him near the enchanted lochan.

Her hands looked pale and delicate as they moved over Devona's forehead to check for heat. She seemed so frail in the soft light of gloaming. But beneath her lovely flesh Leith had found a core of tempered steel. He could not forget how her eyes flashed when she challenged him—how she'd raised her wee nose to glare up into his scowl. No lass had dared defy him—not since his fourteenth summer when he had stood on the sacred stone and become laird of the Forbes.

Who was this woman who dared provoke his anger? Who spoke to beasts and healed with mystical draughts? His gaze bore into her and from across the fire she stiffened and turned, as if called by his thoughts.

Their eyes caught and held, their expressions somber and tense. There was a strangeness between them at times—an eerie sensation they both felt, drawing their minds and their gazes as the camp was held in silence.

"Ye are scairt," Colin said simply.

"What?" Leith asked, forced from his reverie and lowering his brows over dark, deep-set eyes.

"I said—" Colin smiled disarmingly—"ye are skilled . . . at being laird."

Leith watched his brother in silence. The lad was deriving far too much enjoyment from his difficulty with the fiery lass. "I *am* laird," he agreed darkly. "As well ye might recall."

Colin chuckled. "Did I na just say so? Ye are laird, and must decide whether we continue on or stay." His face sobered as he glanced toward Devona. "As for me, I will care for the widow, no matter what the circumstances."

Leith watched Colin, reading the concern in his brother's eyes, and thinking Devona had set her cap for a good man. "She would suffer much from the journey to Glen Creag," he said darkly.

"She would."

"The journey ahead will be harsher than the journey behind," Leith added. "And I have na time to tarry. I need to reach the MacAulay, with the wee nun at me side, ere he breaths his last."

"So she is to pose as Fiona then. The auld bastard's daughter," Colin observed quietly.

Leith lifted his gaze to Rose, who squatted beside Devona.

"She has the fire of a Highlander."

"But will she agree to yer game?"

"She was na meant to be a nun. That I ken. And I will treat her well," Leith vowed.

Colin shook his head. "I wish ye luck, for I think mayhap ye have met yer match."

"And ye?" Leith asked, shifting his gaze back to his brother.

Colin only shrugged. "I will see the widow safely back to her kinsmen, for ye will surely reach Glen Creag before she is fit to travel there."

For a moment they were silent, knowing the import of his words.

"There will be danger." Leith spoke for them both, and though he referred to Colin's return to England, they knew his own travels north might prove far worse.

"I am a Highlander," said Colin soberly.

There was silence again, broken only by the soft, eerie whistle of wind through the new leaves on the branches overhead.

"Aye," Leith said finally, and, with a nod, clapped a firm hand to his brother's arm, feeling the rugged strength there. "Aye," he said again, his tone as grave as his expression. "Ye are indeed a Highlander. Let the brigands be warned."

Chapter 8

They made their camp less than half a mile from where Devona had fallen, at the top of a pleasant hillock, where gnarled pines grew in a dense clutter, diffusing the smoke of their fire.

Rose turned restively beneath the warmth of the soft plaid, feeling the strange disquiet that sometimes plagued her. Devona slept soundly and, although Colin watched for enemies, she could not rest. Close at hand Leith lay with his back toward her. She wondered if he too remained awake, watching the darkness.

Time slid by and no evil came. An owl cried his eloquent night song and Rose relaxed a bit, listening to the noises of the darkness—a time she had long cherished, when the world was filled with mystery, and she could dream of things that might be.

Half in sleep the noise came to her—a scraping of sound, a footstep. Or was it a noise at all?

Evil! The sensation spilled around her like curdled milk, filling her senses, and suddenly she was on her feet.

"Leith!" She screamed his name in unison with a wildcat's shriek. "Leith!" She was frozen to her spot, but the Forbes was already standing, sword in hand, his broad legs spread as two assailants flew through the darkness toward him.

84

"Dear God!" she whispered, scrambling backward, terror gripping her.

Colin was not far away, his back to her, his sword clashing with another's.

Behind her, Devona screamed. Colin's war cry wailed and his rival fell. Rose saw him run, sprinting past the sputtering fire to the widow's side.

But now there was no more time for thought. Three men surrounded Rose, their expressions hard and leering as they tore at her clothes. She shrieked in roiling anguish, but the sound was lost in her thrashing. Fabric tore. She screamed again, forgetting to pray—forgetting everything but the consuming terror.

A man shrieked in pain.

"No time!" hissed an assailant, his breath fetid against her face. "Take her along."

Rose shrieked again, but the sound was cut short as an arm encircled her throat, muffling her wail. "No!" Her cry was no more than a sob. The arm yanked at her and she was spun about, dragged into the darkness.

Dear Lord! There were more men! Panic held her in its icy clasp, stiffening her knees, and she fell. Shadowy forms circled her, one clutching her to him.

He smelled of sour sweat and horrid, indistinguishable things.

"Pretty wench," he crooned, grasping at her.

Sweet Jesus, save me! She managed a silent prayer and jerked spasmodically away, leaving her woolen wimple behind in his hand and trying to lunge for safety. But there was no escape. Other hands pawed at her, groping.

"Leave be!" roared a voice. "We have no time now. Did you get their horses?"

"All but the white beast," snarled another, cradling a wounded arm. "I will cut the devil's throat."

A shriek of agony sounded from camp. Rose's breath came in hard gasps of terror, her body stiff with fear.

"They fight like men possessed," growled a man. "Tie the bitch on a horse. We ride now. Kill any that follow."

She was bound and tossed roughly into Maise's saddle. Breath jolted from her lungs. She steadied herself against the mare's neck, striving for balance in a world gone mad. Then suddenly they were off, galloping behind another's racing mount.

Rose clamped her knees against the mare's black sides and prayed in earnest now. If she fell here, there would be no hope, for trees and rocks were on every side, blurred by the speed of their passing.

Behind her, two men followed. Three men against the brothers Forbes—if they survived the attack of the others.

Beinn stumbled only once going down the rocky slope. Leith felt the horse's huge body jerk and recover. The animal was wounded—sliced by a brigand's sword, but as yet unslowed by the injury. Leith gritted his jaw, setting a hand to the stallion's bare withers and praying for the destrier's strength and speed. He would need them now as never before.

Darkness sped past. Across Leith's back was slung a bow, in his hand lay his trusted claymore—Cothrom, The Bringer of Justice. His dirk, still wet from the blood of his last kill, emerged above the leather of his belt. But it was not his weapons, or the sticky blood upon his blades, that would have caused his enemies to shudder.

It was his expression.

In the darkness, Leith's face showed no emotion. His eyes were flat, his hands steady. Though blood streamed from a wound in his chest, his heart burned with a killing rage as his senses screamed for justice.

Just ahead, the earth leveled and the trees thinned.

Beinn snorted, warning Leith of enemies nearby, and suddenly they were upon him—two men, swords raised.

Cothrom arced smoothly, almost of its own accord, its path like white lightning as it whistled through the air to end its quest in a brigand's throat. The man gurgled in agony, his clawed fingers going stiff. But before his sword dropped, Leith had turned, swinging again.

Fury met fear. Steel met steel, sparking in the darkness. A sweep, a parry, a thrust, and Leith withdrew, seeing the blood on his blade, watching the man fall, dead before landing.

Beinn whirled and lunged, back on the trail. Leith leaned across the lashing mane, fire pumping in his veins.

The trail twisted and dropped. Waves of midnight rushed by on thundering hooves. Another turn and there—up ahead—two horses fleeing side by side. Leith tightened his grip on the deadly claymore.

Just ahead a devil held the wee nun. He would die slowly!

In the darkness, the distance between them was swallowed up with each of his stallion's mighty strides.

A cairn of rock appeared, hiding the fleeing figures.

Rose's life was most in danger now, Leith knew, for the cur was nearly run aground.

Beinn heaved around a turn, his great hooves throwing up turf and mud.

Ahead the villain had stopped. "Hold!" He shouted the word. In one hand he held the reins of both horses, while his other gripped a sword. It gleamed dully in the moonlight, the sharp edge pressed close against Rose's robed side. "I would as soon kill 'er as spit!" he cried.

Leith pulled his stallion to a shuddering halt. Air gasped through the beast's extended nostrils, sounding like the wind from a dragon's fiery throat.

"Let the lass go." Leith's voice was barely raised, yet drifted easily through the darkness. "Let her free and ye may yet live to see the light of dawn," he said, pressing his stallion a step closer.

"One more pace, warlord, and she dies now!" shouted the outlaw, his voice raspy.

Beinn Fionn stopped short at his master's command. The outlaw chuckled, the sound shallow and chilling. "That is wise, 'Ighlander," he crooned. "Now drop your sword."

Leith waited, his mind racing, his body weakening as blood soaked his dark shirt.

"Now!" shouted the villain and Leith lifted his arms, faintly hearing the clatter as his sword dropped to a rock below.

"That's right," chuckled the thief, drawing the black mare closer. "Now if you're good, I may let you watch as I take your lady friend." He reached out, dropping his own reins and reaching for Rose.

Leith heard her whimper of fear, felt her terror, and suddenly, as if on command, her black mare rose on its hind legs, its pawing hooves striking the reins free.

Jolted off balance, the villain struggled to right himself, to retake the reins, but in that second, Leith lifted his bow.

Snatching an arrow from its pouch, he set the shaft to the bow's sinew. The horses pranced. Darkness obscured Leith's view. His arm trembled with pain, hindering his aim. But there was no time to waste. He freed the missile with a shuddering prayer.

A shriek of agony split the night and the outlaw fell, the arrow buried a scant inch from his heart.

Leith slipped from Beinn's back. Retrieving his claymore, he flew to Rose's side.

Somehow she had remained astride. He looked up into her pale face, noticing the gaping rent at the front of her robe.

"They did na harm ye?" he asked, his tone hard.

"No." Her voice shook and Leith raised his arms to her. Like a trembling child, she slid against his body.

A shuddering sob scraped her throat.

"Ye are safe," he breathed, holding her close, feeling the horrific shivers that racked her. "Ye are safe, lass. Avenged."

A dozen strides away, the villain writhed in agony, a feathered wooden shaft protruding from his chest.

Rose shuddered again, her eyes wide in the darkness as she lifted her bound hands to her mouth.

They shook like the leaves of a willow before a strong wind and Leith took them in his, holding them gently to cut the bonds away with his blood-stained dirk.

Her hands fell apart, but she remained immobile, staring down in silence.

"All is well, lass. Come, sit on yon rock and recover," Leith said, but a rustling from behind drew her attention and she lifted her eyes to stare over his shoulder at the dying villain.

"W-w-we . . ." she stuttered, a shiver racking her again, her tone low and murky, "we cannot leave him . . . like that."

In her eyes Leith saw an emotion he could not read but felt he understood. Anger. Fear. The consuming shock of being forced to look upon the very face of death.

'Twas a frightful experience—even for a seasoned warrior scarred and ready for battle. How much more so for this wee lass?

"He will die, lass," Leith assured her, his tone even. "He will na bother ye again."

"But . . ." She shook her head and swallowed. "But we cannot . . . Let him . . ."

Drawing his claymore slowly from its scabbard, Leith rotated it in his hand, extending the scrolled handle toward her. "The blade Cothrom," he said solemnly. " 'Tis Viking-crafted and handed down to me from me father's father. The name means justice—but 'tis yers to mete out." He nodded once. "Take it now and see justice done. 'Tis yer right."

Rose stared at the double-edged sword. It was long and cruel and bloody. "My . . ." Her hand trembled at her throat. "No. I could not. I do not seek revenge." Her eyes lifted to Leith's in fresh, sweeping panic. "I but meant we must not let him suffer."

Leith's brows lowered as he absorbed her meaning. Who was this lass who could so easily forget the bitter taste of impending death? "He would have defiled ye, wee nun," Leith said, canting his head at her. "He would have taken yer pride and slit yer throat, yet ye wish to end his suffering?"

There was little she could say. No way to explain. "Please," she whispered with a shivering shrug, but just at that moment the outlaw rose, wavering to his knees, a knife gripped in his bloody hand.

A scream froze in Rose's throat, echoed by the savage shriek of a wildcat's cry.

From the darkness streaked a tawny mass of feline destruction. Leith whirled about, but already the cat had pounced—and the outlaw was dead.

Utter silence filled the glen. In the darkness the cat turned, forepaws on his victim's chest, fresh blood upon his jaws. Turning golden eyes, he found Rose with his eerie gaze.

"Silken." She said the name on a whisper, but the cat's ears flickered, forward and back, before he finally shifted his gaze to Leith with wary caution.

Forbes stood with legs apart, sword hefted and ready. No words. No motion, only watchful stillness before the cat turned and stalked back into the woods from whence it had come.

Weakness flooded into Leith like high tide at dusk, washing over him in warm waves that threatened to pull him under. "Yer . . . familiar?" he asked softly, struggling for strength, his gaze not leaving the spot where the cat had been.

"What?" Rose asked with a feeble shake of her head, not comprehending.

"The cat." Leith turned, his eyes finding the girl's in the darkness. "He does what ye command?"

"Silken?" she asked foggily, trying to laugh at his words but managing only a wobbling hiccup of sound. "No." She shook her head again, feeling faint. "Don't be silly."

"Silly." Leith nodded, drawing a deep breath, forcing the tension from his muscles. "Then every

Englishwoman has a wildcat to protect her person. Aye?"

She actually managed a laugh then, though the sound was gritty. "Do not speak such foolishness," she chided. "Silken is only a wildcat that I but cared for as a cub."

"And he does na follow ye to protect ye?" asked Leith, wondering if his weakness was caused as much by the cat's eerie presence as by his wounds.

"Of course not," scolded Rose. "You see mysteries where there are only shadows."

"And a fairy where a wee nun stands," said Leith. Then, "Aye," he agreed finally, wiping his claymore on the small portion of his shirt that remained unsullied by blood, then eased himself onto a large, nearby rock. "Only shadows."

"Certainly. And . . . Oh!" gasped Rose, sucking a cold breath of night air into her throat. "You did not tell me of the wound."

"Na," murmured Leith faintly. "That I didna, lass."

His eyes fell closed as he waited for her gentle touch, her concerned ministrations. Moments ticked away. But no words of praise were issued, no healing touch given, and he finally opened his eyes.

"Rose?" She was not to be seen and he shifted his gaze quickly, searching for her in sudden fear. "Rose!"

"There now, my brave warrior," she crooned, but her words were not for him. No. Beinn Fionn was the object of her concern.

She stood some small distance away, before the pearl-white stallion, arm outstretched, voice soft. "They have wounded you," she said, taking a step nearer. The animal tossed his head, causing his heavy forelock to spray out and then fall across his black eyes once again. "You ran like the wind to save us, did you not?" she asked, before her voice finally trailed off, leaving crooning compliments drifting on the night air.

Leith saw Beinn's ears flatten. "Get back, ye daft woman," he ordered angrily. "Before the beast takes yer hand from yer arm."

"He's been hurt," she countered, not moving from the spot. "I will see to him."

"Ye willna," argued Leith, his tone flat. "He is a horse of war. His strength comes from his heart." He grimaced at his own painful wounds. "He has na need for a woman's coddling."

"There now."

He heard her crooning again and gritted his teeth. "Take care!" he snapped, but saw now that Beinn's head had dropped and was resting against the woman's plain robes.

"It is not so bad," she murmured. "Just a scratch for a brave warrior such as you. In a day's time you will hardly remember the pain. It will not even shorten your great stride and yonder mare will swoon at the sight of your power. You—"

"Sweet Jesu!" Leith swore aloud, his voice low and peeved. Damn it to unholy hell, he had been sorely wounded in his ride to save her, and yet there she was—singing praises to his horse. "Come here, Rose."

"I am talking to Beinn," she said.

"Come here, woman!" he ordered gruffly, but she remained as she was.

"You would likely be dead long ago, were it not for his strength," she said, sounding rather peeved herself at Leith's lack of appreciation. "It was he who carried you to safety."

"Safety, my ass," growled Leith irritably. " 'Twould na be a great surprise if I bled to death here at this place."

"And yet he makes no complaint," she continued. "You might consider whether you are worthy of such loyalty, Scotsman."

"Woman," he warned, feeling his patience ebb, "I am telling you—"

"You are telling me you care little for the sacrifices of others," she said, stroking the smooth strength of the stallion's thick neck. "I suppose you would take the credit for your victory, and not give the animal a bit of praise?"

No answer came.

"Is that the way of it?" she asked tartly.

Still no answer.

"Forbes?" She finally turned. He was nowhere in sight. She scowled. The man would do anything for attention, but she supposed he too deserved a bit of credit for her rescue. She found him with his back propped against the boulder, his head lolled to the side.

"Leith?" She blinked down at him, surprised by his lax position. Had he swooned from sheer nerves—the aftershock of trauma? She'd seen it happen before. "Leith?" She reached out slowly, touching the great expanse of his chest.

It was sticky with blood.

"Well, hell" she breathed in sharp surprise.

At the sound of her voice he opened his eyes and lifted his head from the rock. "Ye swear like a warrior," he accused weakly.

"Why didn't you tell me you were wounded?"

"Well, lass . . . " He raised one hand palm up, but, realizing he received more attention when he acted as if he were near death, let it fall back to his side. "Ye were busy making love to me horse."

She put her hands on her hips and glared at him. "I should take my cross and leave you to contemplate your sins."

"I would return as a ghost and haunt ye, wee nun." He grinned, finding a strange comfort in her anger. "I fear we are destined to be together."

"Destined . . ." Rose dropped her hands and leaned closer. "You speak like a madman. I am destined to serve my Lord. To be a martyr for His—"

"What better way to martyr yerself than to be me wife?" he asked with an unbridled grin.

"Wife?"

When he realized his mistake, he dragged his eyes to watch hers. They were wide and angry.

"Listen, lass," he whispered, "mayhap ye could kill me later. After we reach camp. I fear for me brother and the widow—and I canna feel my left arm."

"Oh." She crossed herself speedily, her face showing that familiar look of guilt. "I beg your forgiveness." She touched his chest tentatively, feeling the blood that had already congealed on his shirt. "You have been badly hurt."

"It is good of ye to notice, wee nun." He sighed, and did not add the word "finally."

"It pains you greatly?" she whispered.

"Aye, lass." He lifted his right arm, gently touching her cheek. "That it does."

She shivered beneath his touch "I . . ." She was stunned by his will, that he could speak so casually while bearing such a wound. "I will make a fire and fetch my herbs."

"Nay." He held her arm in a gentle grip. "We dare na risk a fire here. We will return to the camp on the hill."

"You cannot ride," she argued gently, her hand still touching his chest.

"Then ye shall ride with me, wee nun," he said. "To hold me astride."

Chapter 9

The situation truly made no sense, Rose realized, somewhat bemused. For though she rode the stallion with Leith, she did not ride in back but rather in front, allowing her little opportunity to hold him astride as he had suggested.

The black mare followed behind, seeming besotted by Beinn. The riders sat in silence, finding their way easily up the slope by moonlight.

Leith kept his right arm about Rose's waist, holding her tightly to him as she held the reins. His breath was warm against her cheek and his thighs felt as hard as oaken boughs against the backs of hers.

Their position made her breathing speed and her body grow warm—responses that had little to do with the plaid he'd placed about her shoulders.

She tightened her grip upon his tartan, hiding the torn front of her robes and trying to think of something other than his large, hard body behind her.

"I . . ." she began weakly, tracing a wrinkle in the plaid and clearing her throat. "I suppose the Lord will forgive my proximity to you . . . considering the unusual circumstances."

He said nothing. The high portion of his chest ached, but in truth it was her nearness that occupied his thoughts. She was warm and soft, and as he'd settled his plaid about her shoulders he'd seen the dramatic rise of her breasts above the edge of her linen undergarment. That memory caused the heat in his loins and the tightness of his grip about her tiny waist.

Her hair, set free by the thieves' harsh hands, was like firelight only inches from his face, each strand gleaming in moonstruck tones of burnt reds.

"After . . . after all," she continued, made nervous by his nearness and silence, "He would hardly wish me to allow you to fall from your steed."

Leith shifted his gaze downward. She'd twisted about slightly, turning her face so that he could see the curve of her cheek, the sweet swelling of her parted lips.

He could kiss her without undue difficulty, he thought. But he'd seen her swoon from a horse before and did not wish to be the cause of her faint. Still, the possibility of making her light-headed did much to improve his mood. "Ye think, then, that the good Lord cares even for barbarians such as meself?" he asked, remembering her derogatory words in the old abbess' parlor.

Rose swallowed once, then sucked in her lower lip and shifted nervously. "It has occurred to me that perhaps I owe you an . . . ah . . . apology," she said gracelessly.

A falcon, scared from its resting place on a bare nearby branch, took flight, its splendid wings noiseless in the still night air.

"And . . . perhaps an expression of appreciation for . . . " Rose paused, sucking in her lip again and remembering his kiss from the night before. *Hold your tongue, fast, and pray,* she reminded herself raggedly. But he sat so damned close that talk seemed amongst the safest of her options. His presence made her hungry. And damned if she could, at the moment, remember a single prayer. "For . . . " she began again, but just then his grip tightened a bit, causing her to feel the hard length of his manhood pressed against her back.

Hot blood suffused her face. Damn the hold, fast, and pray idea! She should scratch, kick, and run. The problem was—she didn't want to.

"Do ye mean to thank me?" asked Leith smoothly. "For saving yer life?" His lips were very near her ear. "Na to mention yer honor?"

Rose swallowed hard. "Yes," she squeaked, and nodded shallowly. "For that."

"Ye wish to thank me?" he asked again, as if the idea was a bit difficult to believe.

Rose bit her lip hard and felt scared enough to faint dead away, but should she faint she would have to drag her gaze from his lips and she found she could not do that. They were full lips, seductive, lifted slightly with humor—and waiting.

"I—I—" she stuttered. "I just did—thank you."

"Na, lass," he breathed, forgetting his wound as he pressed nearer. "Ye did na."

He was about to kiss her. She knew it and her entire being waited, held in trembling anticipation.

His lips neared. She closed her eyes. Her body shivered.

Nothing happened.

"Lass," he whispered.

"Mmm?" She shouldn't allow him to kiss her, of course, but he was so much larger than she. The Lord could not expect her to hold such a giant of a man at bay.

"We're here, lass," he murmured.

Her eyes snapped open. There, not fifteen feet away, stood Colin.

"Good Lord!" she breathed, not failing to notice the young man's obvious amusement.

"So . . ." Colin said, making no effort to control his grin. "Ye are safe."

"Aye, lad," answered Leith, and in outraged dismay Rose realized he too was grinning.

Well, hell!

"I trust the thieves didna die too soon," added Colin, sobering a bit.

"They wouldna have," said Leith, "if it were na for the wee nun's bloodthirsty nature. It seems she could na wait and decided to hurry the death of the last of them."

Rose's jaw fell and she muttered a few incoherent words that well might set any saintly ears to burning, if there had been any saintly ears about.

"Truly?" Colin raised his brows, setting his arms akimbo and canting his head.

"Aye." Leith nodded. "Beneath her homely robes she hides a verra passionate nature."

"And ye are determined to stoke that passion?" quipped Colin.

"Aye," Leith agreed. "That I—"

Rose's elbow caught him just below his lowest rib. It was not a tentative love tap, nor a teasing admonishment, but a full-scale effort to wound.

Leith drew a startled breath and attempted to tighten his grip on her, but her temper was at full tilt, and she scrambled from the stallion, arms and legs flailing in all directions.

Her bulky robes, however, snagged beneath his heavy thighs, so that she dangled in midair like a misbegotten puppet.

Hot embarrassment colored her cheeks and she squirmed more violently, legs bare to the thighs, where her robes swept across her bottom to hold her aloft.

From the stallion's back, Leith chuckled at her

predicament. "Need help, wee lass?" he asked, amused that he could hold her captive without raising a hand.

"Let me go, you black-hearted heathen," she demanded, damning his devil's soul with scalding rage.

"Ye want to go?" Leith questioned innocently, leaning toward her slightly. "All ye need do is ask nicely."

"I hope you die with your guts strewn from here to the Holy Land," she hissed, slapping auburn hair from her face and thumping poor Beinn with her knees.

Leith's smile broadened. "Na exactly what I wished to hear, wee nun," he said finally, "but surely such a creative curse deserves some reward. Ye may go," he said, and, lifting his heavy thigh, released his hold on her robes.

She slipped, and clutched frantically at his arm to keep from falling.

Wincing at the pain in his chest, Leith nevertheless grasped her arm to keep her safe from Beinn's prancing hooves.

For a moment their eyes met. Heat sparked between them, igniting some tinder-dry place in their hearts, stopping their breath in their throats.

"Wee lass," Leith murmured, feeling the hot pull of her on his senses, "some women might be flattered by me interest in them."

"Oh!" Rose gasped, shocked by his arrogant gall, and found the unearthly spell he had on her was well broken. With rage fully restored in her breast, she gathered all her strength, wedged her knees up against Beinn's solid side, and yanked—jerking Leith along with her.

She hit the ground only a moment before Leith

did, but while *she* was afoot in a moment, he remained in a prone position with one clawed hand holding his wound.

Rose skittered away like a frightened hare, then stood at a safe distance to watch him.

His face was ashen, his eyes closed, his teeth gritted.

Pain! It was stamped across his features.

Rose bit her lower lip. Of course he deserved it. But . . .

Contrition seeping rather slowly into her being, she clasped her hands finally and took a step nearer. After all, he *had* saved her life. Of course she wouldn't have needed saving if it hadn't been for him. Then again . . .

A single moan escaped his lips. In a moment she was on her knees beside him.

"Are . . . you all right?" she asked, bent like a twisted root to peer into his face.

He did not answer, his tight-sinewed fingers shifting slightly over his wound.

Dear God, what if she caused his death?

"Colin," she called, her tone strained, "fetch hot water and my medicine jars. I am sorry," she whispered, never turning her attention from Leith and placing her hands gently to his steel-muscled arm. "Mayhap I do have a bit of a temper."

Leith slowly opened his eyes to squint at her. "Mayhap," he groaned in return.

"But you deserve it," she added speedily, already drawing back. "You're a—"

"Nay." He shook his head as if even that simple movement pained him greatly. "Dunna spear me with yer tongue just now, wee nun," he admonished. "I canna bear to lose more blood."

Rose's face went dead-white as guilt settled

heavily upon her. "I am sorry," she whispered, tears filling her eyes.

Though distracted by his irritating pain, Leith saw those tears—those fat diamond drops that displayed her misery. She was truly sorry, he thought in some amazement, and that knowledge made him wish to quiet her fears, to take her in his arms and tell her all was well. It was only a flesh wound, after all, and would heal quickly enough if he were allowed a bit of rest.

And yet . . . He must not forget that his bargaining power was considerably increased when she felt guilty. Mayhap she could be made to see things in a different light. Mayhap this was his best chance to save his clan from their own senseless annihilation.

"Forgive a foolish Scotsman," he said huskily, letting his eyes fall wearily closed. "Ye canna blame me for wanting a glimpse of heaven afore I die."

"Die?" Rose gripped his shirt with frantic fingers. It was stiff with blood now—both his and others'. "You'll do no such thing."

Leith nobly stifled a gasp of make-believe pain. "I fear tis na yer decision," he rasped.

"Leith!" She leaned close, tears flowing readily down her face now, her eyes round with panic. "Do not die."

Sweet Jesu! Either she truly did care or she was a far better actress than Leith had deduced. He felt a good portion of guilt for his own act as he tried to discern her emotions. "I thought ye wished me guts to be strewn from here to—"

"Shush," she ordered, her eyes wild above tear-streaked cheeks. "Do not say such things."

"Then do ye care for me a wee bit, lass?" Leith

asked, forgetting his ploy for a moment as he reached out to touch her wet cheek.

She stared at him in numb silence and he shook his head weakly, realizing this fortress would not be so easily taken. "I admit that I thought I might care for *ye*, lass," he whispered, not knowing now whether he acted or spoke the truth. " 'Twas a sin, I suppose, to become enamored of a postulate of the Lord who wanted na part of me." Grimacing again, he let his hand tremble over his wound. " 'Twould hate to beg entrance to heaven with that sin fresh upon my soul."

" 'Tis not true," she whispered, harshly gripping the woolen fabric of his shirt. "I did want . . . a part of you."

Leith could not help but wonder exactly what part she referred to, for she was indeed a passionate woman, and certainly not so pious as she wished him to believe.

"Lass," he gasped, gripping her arm. "It is going dark."

"No! Leith! You must not leave me. You must not!"

"One kiss?" He opened his eyes abruptly, noting the utter whiteness of her face. "Before I . . . die."

God's toenails! He was about to die and it was all her fault. How many Ave Marias were required to clear one's soul of murder?

"Please," he whispered.

There was naught she could do but agree, for he was so wracked with pain.

Leaning forward, she touched her lips to his.

Fire sparked between them, and for one painful second Rose realized what she would miss with his passing. Passion? Yes! And perhaps more. Perhaps much more.

"Yer herbs and water," said Colin, watching the

entire exchange and realizing that Leith, that
deadly warrior, his honest brother, his solemn
laird, was faking impending death to urge a kiss
from a wee nun-in-training. It was despicable—
without honor. Brilliant! "Is he bad hurt?" he asked
with what he hoped sounded like genuine concern.
But it would take a full score of large warriors with
battle-axes and bad attitudes to lay Leith low, Colin
thought, finding it hard to keep a straight face.

The pair on the ground failed to respond—failed
to hear, in fact.

"I said, is he bad hurt," Colin repeated.

"Oh!" Rose drew away with a start. "Yes," she
said finally. "I fear he is."

"Who . . . is here?" asked Leith, his voice barely
audible.

"It is your brother," she said gently. "Colin."

A dark scowl settled over Leith's face as he
shook his head. "Colin?" he questioned. "What has
happened? I canna recall."

"You fell from Beinn," Rose explained, her
knuckles white as she gripped his shirt.

"Beinn?" Leith shook his head again, letting
worry settle onto his features. "Rose! Dunna let me
go. Kiss me." He pulled her quickly to him, meeting her lips as he waved an imperial dismissal behind her back at his brother.

Colin contained his chuckle as best he could.
"Well, lass, I see ye have things well in hand here.
I will make certain the widow yet sleeps." He
turned, shaking his head, then paused to turn back.
"And Leith, me honored liege," he added in solemn Gaelic, "I would beg that ye dunna play this
game too long and anger the lass, for I have
dragged enough dead bodies from camp already
this night."

With that, Colin's footsteps could be heard pacing away. Leith let his right hand slip lower, over the fine curve of Rose's buttocks. She stiffened against him, drawing her mouth away, and he scowled.

"Rose," he breathed. "Me wife. What troubles ye? Dunna stop me now. For I need ye as never before. I need ye as a man needs his woman, a final reminder of heaven on earth."

Rose was caught in his eyes, in his heated embrace, in his husky tone. He cared for her. He cherished her. He thought she was his *wife*, for God's sake! She could not deny him. She kissed him again, feeling a delicious, heady desire pour through her. But as her hand slipped from his neck, she felt his blood-soaked shirt and drew away, employing all her strength.

"Leith," she said softly. He opened his eyes. They were as deep as the sea, soft as warm honey. "I must tend to your wound—first."

"First?" he murmured.

God, he was beautiful, his face well-sculpted and rugged, his body as broad and muscular as yon war-horse's. "First," Rose promised breathlessly. "Here." She pressed carefully away from him, letting her fingers open his shirt. It was crusted to the gash, but came away after a moment.

The wound was a frightening sight. It stretched the full length of her hand, she determined quickly, but its depth was uncertain for the flesh had swelled and purpled, and the light was poor.

"Leith," she said weakly, finding her squeamish reaction surprising after all the injuries she had mended in the past. Still, it seemed different with him, for he was her . . . Her what? Her breath stopped at the thought. What was he to her? To her utter surprise she realized she had no answer and yet, when her gaze lifted to his, that familiar shock remained, that spark of fire that proclaimed him to be somehow very important.

Rose drew a deep breath, calming her nerves and stilling her hands. "It is indeed a wicked-looking wound, my lord."

She was so lovely. Leith could not take his eyes from her. Her face was a small perfect oval, her eyes like sparkling amethysts. Her mouth was a tiny pink bow, puckered with worry and waiting to be kissed. And her hair ... He reached up to gently caress the gleaming mass of fire-bright tresses. Surely it was a sin to trap such beautiful hair beneath the weight of that awful woolen sheath she called a wimple.

Perhaps he owed the thieves a word of thanks, for not only had they lost the lass' wimple, they had torn her robes as well, making the garment no longer usable.

His gaze fell to the spot where the high tops of her breasts were just visible above her chemise. He smiled.

Rose watched his face and scowled. He'd lost his mind. She'd seen it happen before. Great pain could cause a person to lose his grip on sanity.

"Leith?" she said tentatively. "I fear you are badly wounded." She swallowed, unable to bear the thought of his pain. "The treatment will hurt, my lord."

He smiled again, lifting his gaze from her breasts to her eyes and letting his hand drift to her cheek. "I like the way ye say 'my lord,' " he admitted quietly. "It sounds verra lovely on yer lips."

"Leith." She closed her eyes, setting a trembling hand to his and turning the palm upward to kiss it. How difficult it was to see his vast strength lost, to know the pain he suffered was so great that he was out of his head. "Do not die," she whispered, finding her own strength insufficient.

"Sweet Rose," he said, genuinely touched by her emotion, "I trust that if anyone can save me, ye can."

She stared at him in silence. God's teeth! Had she fallen in love with this man? "Yes." She nodded quickly. "Yes, Leith. You must believe. The Lord and I can save you."

It took only a moment for Rose to tear a wide strip of fabric from her own robes, then, immersing the material in hot water, she opened a cloth bag to rummage through its contents.

She drew out a leather pouch and dumped its herbs into the steaming water. After swirling the rag about, Rose dunked it several times.

A tangy aroma drifted to Leith's nostrils. He breathed deeply, enjoying the fresh scent.

Her gaze rose to his, her face tense. "This will hurt," she warned, but he only nodded.

Perhaps it was best that he was out of his head, she thought. Perhaps then he would not feel the pain. She stared at him in silence, wishing she could spare him.

"Dunna worry so, sweet Rose," he sighed. "Methinks I can withstand whatever punishment ye mete out."

He was so brave. So brawny and fair and alluring. She felt lost in his gaze, pulled under by his magnetism. But there was not time to lose. She'd delayed too long already.

Drawing her eyes from his, she wrung the excess water from the rag, then, with only one quick prayer, she set it to his wound.

He did not so much as flinch beneath her touch. His eyes did not leave her face.

"Ye are verra beautiful, me wee lass," he breathed.

Rose's hands stilled their movements, her eyes round. "I am?" she asked, shocked by his words.

Leith chuckled, the sound coming from deep in his throat. "Aye, lass," he said. "Ye are."

She blinked in wonder, then lowered her gaze and scowled. The fall must have injured his brain more than she'd realized. No one called her beautiful, except Uncle Peter once. Though Rose had assumed he was teasing her, her mother had shushed him, seeming overly distraught by his words. But then, her mother had been very plain and Rose had assumed she was too.

She moved the cloth gently over his wound, washing away the crusted blood.

"Ye dunna believe me?" he questioned softly.

"Oh!" She raised her eyes to his, not wishing to hurt his feelings, nor worry him with the sad revelation that he'd lost his mind. "Yes. Of course. If you say it's so."

He laughed again, seeing her doubt. "I do, lass."

Her eyes caught his. He looked quite sane, but . . .

Rose pulled her gaze away, dipping the rag once again in the water. The wound did not now look so bad as she had feared, hence it must have been the fall from Beinn that had addled his brain.

Her ministrations were somehow soothing, Leith thought dreamily. Perhaps they should hurt, but the girl's gentle touch and clever herbs seemed to cause no pain, only a slight tingle in his chest and shoulder.

She moved away after the cleaning was complete, and rummaged once again in her bag. In a moment she drew out a small jar filled with dried grayish-green leaves.

Rose squatted beside him. "I will return shortly." She touched his hand. "Do not fear," she added, and was gone.

Leith did *not* fear. Above him the branches obscured his view of the sky. He could see several stars nevertheless. Lucky stars, he thought vaguely, for things were going very well indeed. Much better than he could have hoped.

He smiled in anticipation. Tonight he would introduce the wee nun to the joys of sheer, ungodly lust.

Chapter 10

White bandages crisscrossed Leith's chest, keeping the healing herbs packed against his wound and making him appear even more untamed and barbarous than usual.

Naked to the waist but for the bandages, his chest was dark, marred by innumerable battle scars, and rippling with strength. His belly was lean and hard, undulating with hillocks and valleys of pure muscle.

Dear God, thought Rose, leaning back to observe her handiwork. Even without his array of weapons the man looked to be the consummate warlord. Dressed in nothing more than his plaid and knee-high horsehide boots, he seemed not the least bit embarrassed. Nor did the wound seem to pain him now as he lay back upon a spread tartan.

"How are you faring, my lord?" she asked, noting with some misgiving that her voice was husky and low from the sight of him thus.

"Come here, lass," he said simply, and though she knew she should not, she did so nevertheless, for she could not resist him.

Their kiss was like magic, soothing and giving, yet frightening too, scattering a bevy of sparks through Rose's tingling body.

"Are ye a witch?" breathed Leith, his mouth moving seductively from hers to blaze a trail down her throat. "Or are ye an angel?"

"I . . . " She could not think when he kissed her so. "I fear I am neither." His kisses slowed, lingering on the delicate hollow where her pulse thrummed a quick rhythm. "I am only human. Nothing but flesh and . . . " She drew a sharp breath between her teeth, shivering when his tongue lightly touched the wee valley between her collarbones.

"Ah, me Rose," he whispered. "But such glorious flesh ye are. So soft and full and sweet. Well worth the fall from Beinn Fionn."

It took a moment for his words to sink into Rose's brain, but she stiffened finally, then pulled to the limits of his grip. "I thought you did not remember Beinn," she said softly.

Leith grimaced mentally. He was no good at lies or even shading the facts. He was a man who described things as they were and bore the consequences of those truths.

Sweet Jesu, why had he pretended to be mortally wounded? he asked himself. But when he looked into her eyes he knew the answer. She was not a woman to come easily into his arms, and he would lie again to feel her thus.

"I thought you did not remember," she repeated, a bit louder now, though she prayed she was wrong—that he had not lied to gain his own ends. But there was raw honesty in his dark eyes now. An honesty that made her heartsick.

"Leith," she said weakly, perhaps hoping he would lie again, to let her believe for a moment longer that he had not played her for a fool—made her pity him so that she would touch him—and be touched by him.

"I . . . " Leith paused, he too wishing to delay the pain, to prolong the pleasure and push reality aside. And though he knew it was not possible, he shrugged stiffly and tried a feeble excuse. "Me head has cleared?"

For a moment there was absolute silence as Rose tried to pretend she hadn't heard his pathetic words. But it was no use. "You lied to me," she said evenly, her face expressionless as she pulled from his arms. "Somehow I did not think you would lie."

"Rose," Leith said, moving to stand, his arms outstretched, wanting to draw her back into his embrace before it was too late.

But it was already too late.

"You lied to me!" she accused more harshly, fists like small mallets at her side as she backed away.

"Rose," he said again. "I didna—"

"Didn't what? Didn't really forget your fall, your horse, your—brother?" she shrilled, raising her fists slightly as her teeth gritted. "God, you must think me a fool!"

"Nay." He paced after her. "Nay, lass, but I didna ken how else—"

"Don't come near me!"

"Lass." He stopped, his expression losing some of the tension, for her anger seemed an easier thing to deal with than her pain. "I said things I should na have. But . . ." He shrugged again, hoping time would cool her temper. "I was wounded—and on yer behalf. 'Twas na thinking clear." He touched his brow with his fingertips and tried another step toward her. "But me head has cleared now and I—"

"Your head has cleared?" Rose backed away another step as she snarled the words.

He took an additional stride.

She stumbled backward, over a branch, and, glancing down, saw the stout limb as a certain gift from God. Stooping quickly, she grasped the branch in both hands and raised it to shoulder level—drawn back and readied. "I'll give you something to clear your head!"

Leith caught the branch only inches from his skull. "Hold, woman!" he ordered, his voice low, his patience ebbing. "I freely admit I said things I should na." He scowled at her, still holding the far end of the branch, and looking as if she should expect no more from him. "What ails ye now?"

She gasped at his cocky attitude, and, snatching her makeshift weapon from his grip, circled at a half-crouch. "You ail me!" she snarled, and swung a second time.

Leith snatched the branch again, but this time his left hand instinctively responded, catching the branch in a tight grip. Pain raced along his arm and shoulder and he winced. He drew a ragged breath between his teeth and glared. "Put down the stick, lass."

"I shall not," she declared stubbornly, but suddenly he yanked the limb and she was propelled forward. She fell with a thud against his naked chest.

They hit the earth together. Leith was on the bottom, his face pale from the trauma to his wound.

"Oh!" Rose gasped, seeing his expression.

Her eyes were wild and bright, her hair a fiery mass of glory about her lively face as she tried to pull away, but already his right arm had found its way about her back.

"Rose, sweet," he murmured, ignoring his discomfort and hoping they could find some sanity now. But he'd misread her mood.

"Don't!" she warned furiously, pushing away with all her strength.

It was simple luck that caused her knee to strike his groin.

The air left his lungs in a hissing whoosh of anguish. One muscle in his face twitched with pain and his hands curled to fists. He dropped the branch.

"Don't you touch me, you depraved, warty-faced hog," she hissed, scrambling to her feet. "I'm going home. You can lie there and die for all I care."

She turned rapidly, searching for the black mare, but Leith had already gained some control and his fingers curled about her ankle in an iron grip.

"Ye willna turn back," he vowed. "Ye will come to Glen Creag!"

"Not till bluebells grow in *hell*!" she spat, bracing herself to give her ankle a wild jerk.

"I've been to England, lass," he growled, "and bluebells *do* grow there."

"How dare you . . ." She fell to her rear with a plop, gasping for breath. " . . . besmirch my country, you barbarian snake!"

"I do as I please," he snarled, drawing her nearer—hand over hand by the bare expanse of her leg.

Rose barely noticed Colin's arrival beside them, for she had just reached her beating stick. Taking a wild swing, she clobbered Leith, who only flinched slightly under her blows as he continued to reel her in.

"Ye are in my care, lass," he said. "And I'll—"

"Care!" She smacked him a particularly sound thrashing across his back and laughed, tossing wild tendrils from her face. "You call this care? I am mauled and—"

"Ye blame the action of brigands on me?" snapped Leith, his face only inches from hers.

"I speak not of the brigands, you braying ass. I speak of *your* maulings." She swung the branch again, but was too close to do any real harm.

"Maulings!" he snorted. "Ye play the prancing mare in heat. Only hiding behind yer robes when ye have na the nerve to admit yer needs!"

"Mare in . . ." She gasped in outrage. "Mare in . . ."

"Save yer sputtering pride for another," Leith warned, nostrils flared, eyes hard. "I know ye for what ye are."

"Mare in . . ." she gasped again and just when he reached for her arm, she kicked.

The sandals she wore were simple and soft-soled, yet the thud of her heel against his fresh wound made him suck in breath through his clenched teeth.

Even Rose's face blanched at the suffering she'd caused, but when his gaze lifted to her, she did not wait to inquire about his health.

Raw, erupting rage shone in his face. She scrambled backward, finding her feet in a rush and fleeing with all the strength in her legs.

She made it a good fifty feet before he tackled her. They hit the ground hard with Leith taking most of the impact on his right hip and side.

Still the fall crushed the breath from Rose's lungs and she lay motionless and stunned just long enough for Leith to turn her over and struggle on top of her.

Fresh blood had seeped through his bandages but his hands were like steel bonds as he pinned her wrists to the ground above her head. She fought like a badger in a trap, writhing wildly against his heavy weight.

"Hold still, ye little she-devil," he grunted as her knees pummeled his backside, "or I'll forget meself and teach ye a lesson ye shan't soon forget."

"Teach me . . . " She bucked violently, nearly spilling him from his perch. "You couldn't teach a skunk to stink."

Leith's brows rose slightly as he considered her words. "Ye mean to insult me?" he asked with casual interest.

"You're damned right I mean to insult you, you lying son of—"

"I would help," called Colin from a safe distance, "but I canna decide who needs me assistance the more. And too"—he grinned—"I . . . "

His words stopped, his hand dropping cautiously to the dirk in his belt. "I think we have company."

All eyes turned to the tawny shadow at the edge of the woods.

Silken had returned, his sleek, powerful body pressed to the earth, his ears flattened as he waited.

It took a moment for Rose to realize the circumstances and even then the situation seemed incredible. Could it be that the wildcat had indeed followed her trail to protect her?

Her eyes turned to Leith's. "You may enjoy browbeating a poor postulate of the Lord," she said, her tone low and smug. "But would you care to try your luck with Silken?"

It was the biggest cat Leith had ever seen. Beneath the tawny coat each sinewy muscle was taut and ready. The golden eyes did not blink but watched him with breath-stopping intensity.

Leith remained as he was. He'd been wounded and battered and pummeled. He could not battle the cat. But neither could he allow Rose to leave, for her *own* safety as well as the safety of his clan. Many lives were at stake. Many precious lives.

"I may die, lass," he said softly, his eyes not leaving those of the golden beast's. "Or the cat may die. But I willna let ye free until ye've fulfilled yer promise."

Rose's breath came hard, for he was sitting on her abdomen and he was not a small man. But it was his eyes that held her attention. They were hard, flat, and deadly sober. He would die, torn to shreds by the razor-sharp claws of Silken before he would turn her loose.

"If ye care for the animal," he continued softly, "send him away."

"Get off me." Her tone held the same matter-of-fact flatness as his, and Leith loosened his grip on her wrists, slipping from her body without a glance at her face.

Rose drew a single deep breath and bent to a sitting position. "Silken." She said the name softly, holding the cat's gaze with her own. "Go play. Go," she wheedled gently, her tone much different now.

The cat remained flattened only a moment, then rose, his eerie eyes skimming to Leith and Colin before returning to Rose's face.

"Go," she urged again, and he left, slipping like a silent shadow into the darkness.

Colin drew a deep breath, his hand dropping from his dirk.

Against her thigh Rose could feel Leith's tense muscles relax slightly.

"Now," said Colin, settling back with a grin. "Ye two can continue where ye left off."

Every inch of Leith's body ached with an individual pain, with the whole of his form throbbing in synchronized agony. His eyes caught Rose's. They were wide and bright. Her face was pale and smeared with his blood. And her expression—pitifully guilty.

"Me," he said quietly, resisting the urge to touch her, "I would rather fight the cat."

Rose felt as if she'd been punched in the gut. Was it her imagination or had she just been beating the man with a tree limb? And the blood that seeped from his bandage and was smudged along his heavy forearm—had she caused that?

She crossed herself without thinking, then lowered her gaze to shakily draw up the fabric the brigands had torn at the front of her robes.

Though the humor of the situation was not lost on Leith, he did not smile, for he doubted if he could withstand more of the lass' temper without kissing her again. And truly, it would not look good for the laird of the Forbes to be killed by a mere girl for the sake of a kiss.

He cleared his throat and tried to do the same with his thoughts. "We will need to find ye a new garment, lass," he said softly.

Rose blinked before raising her eyes to his. "Got any sackcloth?"

He chuckled quietly, unable to resist her clever wit, though her expression was painfully woebegone.

"Colin," he called, not taking his gaze from her sweet, pale face, "fetch the woman's garments from me pack."

Colin rose with a frown, but paused before leaving. "Ye willna start battling again afore I return?"

"Colin," Leith warned darkly, and the younger man laughed.

"Garments it is, me liege," he acquiesced meekly, and strode off toward his brother's pack.

Silence settled over the camp, but despite herself, Rose found she could not raise her eyes to Leith's.

"I fear I have behaved . . . " She curled her fingers, scrunching the torn wool of her humble gown and clearing her throat. " . . . in a rather . . . unholy manner."

She looked like a forsaken puppy, aching to be held. But beneath that soft flesh lay the body of an enchanted fairy and the spirit of a wildcat, Leith knew. "Ye think ye acted in less than a saintly manner?" he asked with careful sobriety.

Rose scowled, seeming distrustful of his somber words. "Well, it's your fault!" she declared.

Despite everything, Leith threw back his head and laughed. Never in all his life had he met such an entertaining woman. Contrite one moment. Enraged the next.

Bringing his amusement under control, he eyed the girl's angry expression and found she watched him as if wondering where to punch him to obtain the most beneficial results.

"What has happened since I left?" questioned Colin, hurrying back to the scene.

"The lass apologized," Leith said, choking on the chuckle he confined in his throat.

Rose's left brow rose with her ire and Leith lifted his hands in panicked appeal.

"Please," he said, doing his pitiful best to stop the laughter. "Forgive me, wee Rose. It is just that ye have such a . . . " He shook his head helplessly. "Such a . . . winning way about ye."

"That she does," agreed Colin. "But I like her best when she's flailing ye with a tree limb. Have ye plans to do so again this night, lass?"

Rose shifted her eyes downward in abject guilt and Colin sighed.

"It seems na," he deduced with some disappointment. "So I will see to the widow, who sleeps like the dead." He turned, then paused to add, "Have a care what she mixes in yer drink, brother, or ye may sleep till the Christ's next coming." From

the darkness his laughter drifted back to them as
he strode away.

Rose cleared her throat, then sucked in her lip.
Her scowl was solemn. She cleared her throat
again. "You might be surprised to know that
I . . . " She paused, still holding her poor mistreated
robe together at its top. "I used to be quite a nice
person."

Leith didn't dare challenge her words.

"It's true." She nodded, as if he must surely be
doubting her. "There were people who actually
liked me. My father called me his sweet, gentle
babe."

"Sweet, gentle babe?"

"Don't you laugh," she warned, her expression
as dark as a storm. "Or I shall do something I'll
regret."

"And I shall regret more, no doubt," Leith
added, keeping his expression sober as he covered
his wounded chest with a hand.

She lifted her eyes to his, then dropped them mo-
rosely. "I'm a horrid failure," she whispered
hoarsely.

"At being a nun?" he asked, watching her small
face.

She nodded, her bottom lip trembling, and
against his will, Leith reached for her.

To his utter astonishment she did not resist, but
drooped against him—like a parched flower too
long in the sun.

God! The touch of her fine, young body against
his bare flesh torched Leith's senses, but he closed
his eyes above her head and steeled his will. "There
now, lass," he soothed gently. "Ye take this too
much to heart."

She said nothing, but sniffled again and he

shifted his hand to the bright mass of her glorious auburn tresses.

"What made ye think to become a nun, lass?" he questioned absently. "Surely there is nothing in this world ye fear, that ye would lock yerself behind those sacred walls."

Still she did not speak and he raised his brows and continued. "Was it a man, then? Someone already wed, mayhap, who hungered for ye, causing ye to choose such a course?" He glanced at her face. A pair of fat tears had squeezed from her eyes, wetting her downy lashes. "Or . . . "

" 'Twas my mother," she said quietly.

"Yer mother?" he asked in surprise, then nodded and sighed. "Ah, I ken. The good woman always wished for ye to become a nun—in atonement for her own sins."

"No." Rose shook her head. His chest felt firm and lovely against her cheek. "She never mentioned such a course until . . . "

"Until," he prompted.

"Until her illness," Rose finished brokenly. "She took the fever, shortly after Father died. She said . . . " Rose scowled at his chest, trying to stem the tears as she smoothed a wrinkle from the bandage where it crossed near his nipple.

The shock of her fingers brushing his flesh sent excitement rippling through Leith's body, but he hardened his jaw and remained still. "Go on, lass."

"She said that it was Father's wish too." Rose raised her eyes to his.

Leith didn't breathe. Her eyes were as deep and mysterious as the loch near Inverness. A man could become lost in those eyes—never to return. Never to wish to.

"But why?" she asked softly.

Why? Leith had completely lost her line of

thought and he exhaled, longing with every inch of his being to lay her down and stoke her desire. But common sense held him still. Let the lass speak, he thought, for her soul ached.

"Why would they wish for me to be a nun?" she questioned. "They were not the religious sort. Oh . . . " she hurried to explain, her wide eyes on his face, "they were good people. So good, so kind." She smiled. "But they were . . . " She shrugged. "They were not afraid to laugh."

He stroked her hair and kept himself from touching her lips where they curved up at the memory of her parents.

"Ye miss the laughter, wee lass?" he whispered gently.

"Yes. I mean, no!" Her body became immediately stiff as she tried to pull from his arms. "I am to be a nun. And a nun is what I shall be," she assured him quickly.

He loosened his grip only slightly. "Whether God wills it or na?"

She nodded, then scowled and shook her head violently, realizing her mistake. "Let me up."

"We were discussing yer parents," Leith reminded her, trying to soothe her with his tone. "They gave na reason for their request?"

She settled back against his chest with a sigh, realizing somewhere in the hidden recesses of her mind that there was nowhere she'd rather be. "Mother said—just before she passed on, that I was too . . . odd to trust . . . " Rose sucked in her lip and wondered for the hundredth time at her mother's words.

"To trust with what?" Leith scowled and Rose's eyes fell shut.

"To trust to this world," she finished hollowly.

Leith urged her head gently against his chest.

"Me sweet, gentle babe," he murmured. "And ye thought her words a rebuke?"

Rose could hear the strong beat of his heart and above that thrum was the endearment her father had used. "*Gentle babe*," he had said, but the words sounded different from Leith's lips, like a forbidden fruit, sweet and dangerous.

"What else but a rebuke?" she asked, raising her gaze.

He shook his head. "Ye dunna see yer gifts, wee lass, for it seems ye have long denied them. And ye are too young to know the punishment for being special."

She scowled at him.

"The English still hang witches, lass," he said quietly, seeing her confusion.

"Do you call me a witch?" she breathed. Did he believe the very thing she feared herself? Did he believe her to be evil? The devil's tool? Could it be so? Or was there some other explanation for the shadowy images that appeared with more and more frequency in her mind?

"There is a great difference betwixt what ye *be* and what people *deem* ye to be, wee Rose," Leith murmured gently.

A hundred thoughts scrambled through Rose's mind, but she lifted a hand to cover her eyes and shook her head. "I do not know what I am, but this I know—I have promised myself to the abbey. And I shall keep my word."

"Rose—"

"No." She uncovered her eyes, placing both hands against his hard form. "I cannot deny that you move me," she whispered hoarsely. "But I must do what I must do."

Their gazes held, and neither one breathed.

But Leith spoke finally, his voice so low Rose had

to lean slightly closer to hear him. "Did ye know I had a sister once, lass?" he asked.

Rose frowned, wanting to ignore his words, to be alone with her thoughts, but the image of a feminine version of Leith suddenly seared across her mind.

"She was beautiful," Rose said softly, suddenly knowing that it was true.

Her words hung like a cloud in the air, quiet and eerie.

Leith pulled himself from the pools of her eyes, only vaguely understanding the impact of her words as he nodded.

"Aye. That she was. Lovely as a spring flower."

Suddenly Rose could see her. She was a dark-haired girl, with a ready smile and a small dimple in her chin that deepened when she laughed. A bonny, friendly imp of a girl who could wrench one's heart with her laughter—who could—

Dear God! Rose panicked, feverishly swiping the image from her mind. Where had such a vivid mental portrait come from? Perhaps she *was* a witch. Perhaps Leith's words were true, she reasoned, but he was now deep in thought, not realizing her terror.

"She was dark like our mother," he murmured. "With black hair and dimples when she smiled. Sweet as an angel. Gentle as a wee lamb."

"Yes, well..." Rose began, groping for some way to banish the eerie feelings that crowded in on her, smothering her senses. "Heritage is a strange thing."

Leith scowled questioningly at her words.

"Gentleness," she answered quickly, her face tense. "It is strange how Eleanor inherited gentleness, while you . . . " She nodded toward his broad, bandaged chest.

"Ye imply I am not gentle?" Leith grinned, leaning close to prove otherwise, but suddenly his expression changed to stark intensity. "How do ye know her name, lass?"

Raw terror tore through Rose as she stared, horror-struck, at his face.

"Eleanor," he whispered hoarsely. "How did ye know?"

"I don't know," she breathed, her face ashen.

Leith reached for her, but she'd already sprung to her feet and was fleeing toward the horses. He followed more slowly, wanting to allow her time to think, yet worried for her safety.

When he reached her, she was struggling to tighten the girth about Maise's glossy barrel.

"Rose." He stood some feet behind her.

"No!" She refused to face him, but hurried all the more at her task, though her fingers felt stiff and uncertain. "Do not speak. I must return home. I must." Her voice was weak.

"Eleanor died on MacAulay land," Leith said quietly.

"No." Rose closed her eyes, saying the word like a prayer. "I don't wish to hear."

"Because ye already know," he guessed.

"No!" She turned quickly, her hands curled to fists, her words panicked and quick. "I don't know. How could I? I was not there. How—"

"Shh." He reached her in a moment, enfolding her in his arms, and she clung to him.

"How could I know?" she whimpered fearfully.

Leith remained silent, closing his eyes above her head and stroking her hair.

Midnight noises surrounded them. Her arms were tight about his hard waist.

"Ye have the gift, lass," he said in a ghostly soft tone. " 'Tis naught to fear."

"No." She breathed the denial against his bared chest. "I am a simple postulate. I am to become a nun." She pulled quickly from his arms. "I must return home."

A thousand reasons for her to stay crowded Leith's mind, but his gaze fell to the white stallion that stood not far away. Dried blood made a dark stain on his massive shoulder. "Ye must do what ye must," he said quietly. "But first I ask that ye would see to Beinn Fionn. He has need of yer gentle healing."

"Beinn?" Rose drew a shaky breath. Her eyes shifted to the stallion and she nodded. "Yes." She sounded relieved to put her hands to something she understood. "I will need hot water—and your assistance," she said softly, and Leith nodded.

"I am here for ye, lass," he assured her quietly. "I am here."

Her hands were like magic, Leith thought, watching her quick, careful movements.

Beinn Fionn did not move so much as one heavy forelimb as Rose cleaned the blood and debris from his wound.

Leith watched in silence. Many of his warriors had refused to touch the stallion. In fact, it was a joke amongst his clan that should any man shirk his duties, that same man would be put in charge of the white destrier's care. 'Twas a threat capable of striking fear into the most stout of hearts. And yet here was this lass cleansing the beast's wound as if he was no more fearsome than an orphaned fawn.

Leith shifted slightly so as to watch Rose's fluid movements. She'd pulled a long black hair from Maise's tail and now threaded the coarse, pliant strand through a needle.

"Ye will stitch his wound closed?" Leith asked.

Rose pressed the flat of her palm to Beinn's heavy neck and spoke softly. "He is such a handsome beast. The stitches will hide the wound. It would be a shame to have his fine coat marred."

Leith raised his brows as he eyed the many battle scars that marked the stallion's gigantic body. "As ye say, wee lass."

Beinn's hide twitched once as the needle pierced it, but he did not move. Leith tightened his grip on the rope nevertheless and set his mind to his mission.

"Eleanor rode a white steed," he said softly. "Beinn's dam, in fact—came home with an empty saddle one autumn day."

Leith could see Rose's face but could discern none of the girl's emotions.

"We followed her hoofprints and found me sister's body at the bottom of a gorge on MacAulay land."

Silence echoed around them, broken finally by a soft question wrenched from Rose's heart. "How did she die?"

Leith shook his head, thinking perhaps it would make more sense to ask *her* that question. "I once believed Owen MacAulay, the laird's son, had strangled her before throwing her body to the bottom of the gorge."

"And now?" Rose placed the last stitch and raised her eyes to Leith's, not wanting to hear his response, but unable to avoid asking.

He was silent for a moment, watching her.

"Now," he said, his voice low and gravelly, "I ken that Owen was na the murderer."

"Then who?"

He shook his head. "I dunna ken, but this I know—enough blood has been spilled." He clenched his fists, and on his right cheek the jagged line of a scar showed clearly against his dark skin. "Young Myles lost the use of an arm during a raid on MacAulay's cattle. And bonny Rachel ... " He leaned his head back slightly, blaming himself for the pain endured in the few years since the feud caused by Eleanor's death. "Rachel died bearing a child forced upon her by a MacAulay. The bairn lived for two days before following his mother into eternal sleep. How many more need die?"

She said nothing.

"I would have me people see peace."

"But they cannot forget Eleanor's death," Rose murmured.

"There is much for us to forget," Leith said. "And much for the MacAulays also, for they surely mourn young Owen's death just as we do Eleanor's."

"Owen is dead?" Rose whispered, seeing a handsome man's face mirrored in her mind.

"Aye. He is dead. Killed and thrown into the same gorge where Eleanor was found."

Rose remained still as a thousand thoughts pressed forth for consideration.

"There is much to forget," Leith repeated, shaking his head. "Much that will *na* be forgotten if the MacAulay dies. For though he is a wily bastard and a thieving hound, he does na want bloodshed."

"And what if I go with you? What if I do all I can, but the Lord takes the MacAulay to his final resting place—despite my efforts?" Rose asked softly. "What then?"

"Then Dugald will be chieftain," Leith said. "Dugald, whose wife was Owen's sister. Dugald, who has sworn to avenge the death of his brother by law." He nodded slowly, his expression solemn. "There will be blood."

Chapter 11

Rose had given Devona another soothing draught and wrapped her ankle in strips of cloth to protect it from jarring. Though her leg must have hurt a great deal, she seemed in good spirits—considerably better than her own, Rose thought.

"You will be safe," said the widow suddenly.

Rose scowled up into the woman's brown eyes.

"The Forbes is a great warrior," explained Devona. "He will keep you from harm."

"And who will keep me safe from the Forbes?" Rose asked, surprising even herself with her honesty.

Devona laughed. "And why would you want to be safe from him, Rose Gunther?" she asked. "I myself would have set my sights on the elder brother if I did not have a weakness for fair-haired charmers. But no." She lifted her gaze momentarily to watch the two men not far away. "I am an excellent judge of people. And this is as it should be."

Rose's scowl deepened with her perplexity, but before she could question Devona's words, the widow turned the gruella's head toward the south with no explanation.

"I will miss yer claymore at my right side," Leith said, resting one hand on the bridle of his brother's horse as he looked up at Colin. "But 'tis our duty

to see the widow safely back to her people, for she
canna now travel at the pace we will set for the
Highlands."

"I will make certain no evil befalls her," Colin
assured him. "And see ye soon in the hall of our
father."

Leith nodded. "Take care, brother."

"That I will. And ye care for yerself. There are
many who would be glad to take the life of the
laird of the Forbes."

"That willna happen," Leith said, releasing the
bridle to stroke the bay stallion's slick neck. "Remember, I have the wrath of the wee nun to protect
me."

"Farewell then, my liege," Colin said with a grin.
"Farewell, Rose Gunther. God be with ye," he
called, then set his heels to the stallion's sides to
hurry after Devona's retreating form.

The days passed, mile by rugged mile.

Leith spoke little, but seemed ever alert, rarely
sleeping, always watchful, now and then pointing
out a distant view as the land rose more and more
steeply about them.

There was an inexplicable allure to this craggy
country. A wild, almost eerie beauty that left Rose
stunned and silent.

At times she would see a flash of Silken's golden
form as he paralleled their course, but even that
sight could not keep her long from thoughts of her
future.

How had life changed so for her? Even her
clothes. She glanced down, noticing the fine embroidered skirt and mantle she now wore. There
seemed to be nothing left of Rose Gunther, postulate of Saint Mary's. And yet, it was difficult to

mourn the English girl's passing, for here in the Highlands a new person grew, a free-spirited lass whose hair blew behind her, grazing the black hide of the beautiful mare she rode.

Thunder rumbled through the sky as Rose crested a rocky knoll. The country spread out below in shades of green, broken by jagged ridges of rock and sparse copses of trees. A maverick gust of wind brushed her face with unusual force and she lifted her chin, filling her nostrils with the sweet scents of heather and rain.

Leith felt his heart swell as he watched her. No matter her heritage or place of birth, in her soul she was a Scot. He could see it in her face, in the way her hands held the black mare's reins, in the way her violet eyes swept the land—as if it were hers, handed down to her through countless generations.

He had no reason to feel guilty. What did it matter that she thought he had brought her along to heal the MacAulay? In her heart she had no wish to return to England. She would be happy as his wife. And he . . .

Leith felt his manhood harden as he thought of her in his bed. Aye. She was meant to be his, meant to be the instrument that brought peace to his clan. And in years to come she would thank him.

"It will rain soon, lass," he said softly from some paces to her left. "We need to find cover."

It took Rose a moment to pull her eyes from the surrounding country. It was a magical place, windswept and crisp, with a chattering stream rolling beside them. A wondrous place—sacred maybe—making her heart ache with its rugged beauty. What it was about this country that touched her, she did not know, and yet she felt its effects like a

strong tonic. "I do not mind a little rain, Scotsman," she said finally, her tone almost reverent.

It was the answer Leith had wanted. She was the
very embodiment of Scotland, and would make old
MacAulay a better daughter than the child he had
lost.

Leith watched Rose's face as she reined her
mount down the hill. He had been patient, giving
her time to think, to accept the changes. But he
could wait no longer. Her nearness made him ache.
Of course that was not why he would teach her the
meaning of desire tonight. Hardly that. Tonight he
would stoke her passion to prove the rightness of
their union.

Aye. Leith smiled as Beinn followed the girl's
mare. Tonight she would agree that she belonged
to him forever.

The rain drove hard into their faces, and though
it was warm, Rose shivered violently, her heavy,
saturated clothes no barrier against the sharp wind.

"Here," Leith called from somewhere ahead and
Rose squinted through the dense sheet of rain,
pressing Maise carefully down a water-slick de-
cline.

Beinn appeared only a few feet ahead of her,
Leith a dark shape atop his back. "Come, lass," he
called, gesturing toward her. "I have found us a
wee bit of comfort."

A copse of trees stood blown and dark before
them. Rose dismounted stiffly, finding her legs
cramped and her fingers aching, nearly unable to
hold the water-softened leather reins.

"This way," he called, and she stepped into the
woods, slipping in a puddle and feeling the mud
splash cold and gritty against her face.

In the trees the rain was not so dense but fell in hard, fat drops that coursed down her neck to chill her to her bones.

Ahead Rose could see the white stallion, his back already bare. She hurried forward, anxious to be out of the rain. But in her haste she failed to see the smooth rock, and skidded momentarily on its broad expanse before landing with a squishy thump atop its ungiving surface.

A few of her father's choice words slipped with devilish verve from her lips.

"There now." Leith appeared from nowhere, a chuckle issuing from deep within his throat as he bent to lift her. "This be na place to rest, lass," he chided.

"I fell," she grumbled irritably, and he chuckled again, pressing her soaked form closer to his chest and saying nothing.

Only a short distance farther on, the trees ended at a rough-hewn cliff of rock. The stone there rose sharply, bending toward them and creating below a miniature cave—a sheltered haven, hidden from the rain and driving wind.

Leith carried her there, several feet into the hollowed rock to a fat log that had been placed beside a black circle of ashes.

"It seems the MacGowans have left us a place by their camp," Leith said, eyeing the half-consumed, charred logs.

"The MacGowans?" Rose echoed shivering.

" 'Tis their land," explained Leith. "But mayhap it was the Lamonts that used this place, for they often raid the MacGowans' herds. Either way, it is good this place is na occupied for neither clan is friendly with the Forbes."

"Why?" she questioned, trembling as she looked up at him.

He shrugged. "Feuds in the Highlands go far back and are honored long after the memory of the original cause."

"So you fight for no reason," she said with some perplexity.

"Na," he objected briskly, still holding her against his soaked chest.

"Then why?"

"'Tis because . . ." He scowled. "Because . . ."

"They have no cause," she repeated with a fresh shudder. "And so it is silly to fight."

He watched her in silence, wanting to disagree, but wasn't it the feuds that tore the Highland people apart generation after generation? Wasn't it peace that he wished for above all else?

For a moment more he held her—until he could no longer find an excuse to do so. Stepping forward one more stride, he bent and set her on the aged log before drawing back, allowing her to regain her balance.

"How is it that you found this place?" she asked, talking to hide how conscious she was of his touch.

"'Twas naught but luck, lass," he admitted. "Methinks ye bring a good portion with ye."

Through the open neck of his saffron shirt Rose could see the clinging gray bandage she had used to cover his chest wound. His hair was soaked and dripped in dark, heavy waves past his shoulders. His brow, broad and dark-skinned, bore a small, purplish circle where she feared she had kicked him in her frantic effort to escape his grasp.

Indeed, she thought with sarcastic misery, she had certainly brought him good luck.

"Get ye from those wet clothes. I will search for wood to make a fire," Leith said.

"I . . ." Her teeth chattered a bit, making it difficult to talk and reminding her of her brave words about not resenting a little rain. "I have no other clothes to w-wear."

"Aye." Leith placed his fists to his hips and nodded. "But I could only guess at yer size when ye wore the humble rags of the abbey, hence ye canna expect me to have purchased more than a few garments from the village. Indeed,'tis a pity, but ye will have to do without," he said, and left.

Rose stared after him, watching the spot where he had disappeared. He had not sounded overly sorry for her plight, she thought ruefully, making his comment somewhat suspect.

It was not the first time she had realized how dependent she was on this man, but it felt different now. In the two nights past, the only nights they had spent alone, he had seemed distant, never touching her and barely speaking. But now his mood seemed to have changed.

She shivered again, hugging her chest with shaking arms and thinking this was a poor way to die.

"Canna ye obey a simple order?" Leith was back already, his thick arms miraculously full of dry firewood and his expression rather amused.

Damn him for not shivering as she did.

"I told you," she said grumpily, "I have no other clothes."

Leith dropped the firewood with a muffled clatter, causing her to jump as he placed his hands on his hips again. "And I said it be a pity. Now get yerself naked afore ye catch yer death."

Rose's lips were numb. "I have nothing to wear," she insisted.

"The good Lord did give ye skin, did he na?"

"I must quit kicking you in the head," Rose said irritably. "I fear it has addled your thinking. Of course He gave me skin."

"Then it shall dry quickly and keep ye warmer than what ye now wear."

"You," she declared, "are a raving lunatic."

He spread his legs, looking large and formidable with his arms akimbo and his expression dark. "I have traveled far from home and hearth to find ye, lass, and would be sorely disappointed if ye died on me now."

"As would I," she assured him. "C-cannot you built the f-fire before I am frozen in this position for all eternity?"

"Ye must disrobe."

"No." She shook her head emphatically, giving his statement not a moment's consideration. "I must not."

His gaze caught hers which was lifted stubbornly to his face, and he shrugged. "As ye wish then."

To her surprise he turned away without another word. In a moment he had the firewood arranged to his satisfaction. It took him a bit longer to strike a blaze with his flint and steel, but finally the tinder caught a spark and was blown into a flame.

Rose stretched her hands toward the minute yellow fire, waiting breathlessly for the heat it would create.

"I would share me dry plaid with ye," Leith said from across the fire, "but it would do little good over yer soaked gown."

His tone sounded ever so casual, thought Rose, all her concentration directed toward the first faint flicker of yellow heat. One would think he were discussing the time of day rather than her continued survival—which was most uncertain if she did not warm soon.

"Do . . ." she began, but when she raised her gaze, her jaw dropped. "Wh-what the devil are you doing?"

Leith grinned before pulling the simple, voluminous shirt over his head. "I am a practical man,
Rose," he said, still grinning as his head emerged,
his wet hair slightly ruffled while his manner was
not. "*I* am disrobing."

"God's toenails!" she gasped, jerking to her feet
to scramble backward over the log on which she'd
been sitting. "Not—not completely."

His grin broadened. "But I am completely wet,
lass."

To her horror she realized he'd already removed
his boots. Her gaze skimmed to the soggy mass of
horsehide buskin, then hurried back to his bare
feet.

They were broad and powerful, with taut sinews
extending from instep to toes. His ankles were as
wide as her upper arms, but it was his calves that
arrested her attention. They were thick with
bunched, rock-hard muscle that blended upward to
his exposed knees and the lower regions of heavy
thighs beneath his tartan.

She stared openly, not noticing his actions until
the plaid shifted and dipped, dropping over one
knee. Her gaze shot up to where his hands were
just now tugging his wide leather belt free.

She stood transfixed, watching the wet, woolen
slide with ridiculous slowness from his rippled abdomen to . . .

She jerked about at the last moment, covering
her eyes as she faced the stone wall. "Good God,"
she gasped. "Have you no shame?"

His chuckle seemed to come from somewhere
deep within his broad-muscled chest. "Nay, lass, I
am na ashamed of what God has given me."

"W-well . . . " She was breathing hard and the
hand before her eyes shook visibly. "You are indeed a barbarian. A . . . " Her free hand circled

rather wildly as she searched for words. "A . . . "

"A man, sweet lass?" he whispered, his breath suddenly brushing her ear.

She all but screamed, jumping from his startling nearness. "God's t-t-toenails," she rasped, rattled to the core of her being. "Are you n-n-naked?"

"Nay, lass." He chuckled again, the sound so close to her quivering ear that she felt the shivering effects of it course its way through her entire body. "Turn and see."

Her knees quaked as he prodded her stiff body toward him. She moved woodenly, feeling suddenly warmer and rather faint. He grinned as she looked at him, and she found she could not move, could not speak, and certainly could not force her gaze from his irritatingly mesmerizing face.

"Ye tremble, lass," he said softly.

She did not respond, for suddenly she was lost in the midnight-dark depths of his eyes.

"And I ask meself . . . do ye tremble from the cold . . . or some other cause?" he murmured.

She was vaguely aware of the soft plaid that hung from his shoulders, for he gripped her upper arms, allowing her fingers to brush the soft, dry wool as it swept downward.

"It is not decent that you stand before me like . . . " Her words, abruptly freed from her stiff lips, tumbled to an abbreviated halt as she flicked her eyes downward for the briefest of seconds. The quick, furtive gaze confirmed her worst suspicions. Beneath the gaping blanket he was naked. She was sure of it, though she had not spared enough time to actually *see* anything that might cause her to faint dead away. "Like . . . that!" she croaked breathlessly.

His mouth quirked. "How is it that ye are ashamed of God's handiwork?" he asked softly.

"God's . . ."

"Ye think that He wasna the One to craft our bodies?" Leith murmured. "Ye think He is shocked by the sight of me thus?"

Her eyes were as wide as the amethyst brooch the abbess had given him. And she looked for all the world as if she might drop to the earth in a dead faint.

"Mayhap Englishmen are different than we Scots," he continued, gripping her arms a bit harder lest she plummet like a rock from sheer shock. "Mayhap English bairns are born fully dressed, with tiny broadswords strapped to their wee hips. Aye?" he asked, dark brows raised.

Her expression had not changed in the least, Leith noticed, and he devilishly considered all the things he might do to shock her further still.

The thought broadened his grin, and accelerated the already rapid beat of his heart.

"You're insane," she murmured, and he chuckled aloud.

"Nay, lass," he said with a slight shake of his head. "Me mind is quite sound, as is me body. I only ask ye to think and answer. What sin is there in being as our Maker crafted us?"

"You think it best that we all run about bare-naked?"

Their eyes were caught in an unbreakable hold—violet on brown.

"Only when there is a likely purpose, lass," he breathed, leaning closer. "And now is as likely a time as ever there be."

His lips met hers with such shocking heat that the touch of them stunned her senses, sending sparkling bits of reality scrambling into the nether regions of her mind. His right arm reached about

her body, igniting flames where he touched her
and making her senses reel.

Leith felt the slight dip of her body against his
fingertips and knew that the hardships of the journey had been too much for her. Or was it his kiss?
He grinned at the thought and bent to lift her into
his arms.

"Come, lass." He cradled her against his chest.
"I will see thee warmed."

Rose could not fight him, for . . . she didn't want
to. He was too marvelously muscled, too magnet-
ically formed, both in body and spirit.

He laid her down next to the fire. His plaid fell
away, exposing the dark, muscled expanse of his
chest, crossed by the gray, saturated bandages.

"I must get ye from these wet clothes, lass," he
whispered gently. "For I have waited too long to
lose ye now."

"Waited?" she breathed, her eyes not leaving his
face.

"Aye, lass. I have waited." His fingers reached
to the laces below her arm, tugging the wet fabric
free. "As the laird of the Forbes, many have
thought it me duty to wed, but I have not." He
loosed the laces under her other arm. "Though I
knew na what I waited for."

Her chest felt tight with the breath she held and
the flesh along her limbs stood in aching bumps
that bristled as her sleeves were pulled away.

"But now, sweet, gentle babe," he breathed, pulling the gown down, over her hips and away, "before me lies the cause for me delay. Ye are the
reason," he said.

Suddenly she was dressed in nothing but a linen
chemise, and although it began low on her chest
and fell to her ankles, she felt as if there was nothing between her flesh and his. She shivered,

shocked as much by his words as his nearness.

He had waited—for her. This mesmerizing man, this bold, masculine warrior had waited for her. Never in her life had Rose felt such excitement, such exhilaration and breathlessness.

He tugged the chemise away. She was naked now, and even lovelier than he had remembered. Her breasts were proud, high, and full, capped with puckered pink nipples. Below, each rib was visible, slanting down toward the flat, smooth expanse of her belly.

Leith's nostrils flared as his gaze fell lower, over the tiny valley of her navel to where crisp, dark curls were caught in the apex between her slim, flawless legs.

"Sweet lass," he breathed, for a moment too dazzled to do more, "ye are surely God's finest creation."

" 'Tis not right." Rose's words came like a whimper as she drew herself into a self-conscious ball, pulling her legs to her chest. "You must not see me thus," she said, knowing with sudden, aching realization that in some secret, unspeakable way she wanted him to. Wanted to be seen and to see.

Leith did not mistake her fear or her desire. "Sweet Rose," he murmured, but did not reach to touch her. Instead he took the plaid from his shoulders, tugging it from his own body to wrap it gently about hers. "Me God is a practical God," he whispered, close to her ear. "He would na create such a marvelous form such as yers if He did not wish it to be seen—and appreciated." He drew her into his arms now, noticing how the high swell of her breasts was still visible above his woolen plaid. It was that sight that made him ache, that caused his hands to tremble slightly as he reached to pull her wet hair above the warmth of the tartan.

She felt the tremble and found his eyes with hers. He was a big man, a warrior. Wounded and scarred and unafraid. And yet when he touched her, he trembled. The thought stunned her and her lips parted as she searched for a question.

Leith watched her in silence. Her winterberry hair streamed across the plaid. Her high breasts peeked above the top, and her wide-eyed violet gaze was caught on his. Sweetly parted, luscious lips seemed to call to him and he could wait no longer.

The kiss was not unexpected. In fact, if the truth be known, Rose had been waiting for it, and yet the heat of it seemed to torch her senses. She felt his tongue tickle her lips, felt the tight bands of his arms press her against the rugged wall of his chest.

Hold, fast, and pray, a voice said from her conscience, but it seemed distant now, and rather non-sensical.

She opened her mouth and her arms to him. The plaid parted to encompass him. Flesh met flesh, titillating and warm and sensual. He moved closer, until the hard shaft of his desire was pressed against her.

She gasped against his mouth and pulled away, shocked by the sheer maleness of him.

"I m-must n-not," she stuttered, but his hands had slipped behind her, kneading her aching back.

"Dunna be scairt, sweet Rose," he breathed. "I willna hurt ye."

Hurt? It was the last thought on her mind. Rose's eyes fell closed as his large hand slipped lower, sweeping gently over her right buttock.

His touch felt like heaven. She'd been riding for days on end. Every muscle ached.

He heard her moan of pleasure and though he

ached for a different reason he was not fool enough to take her before the time was right.

"Sweet lass," he murmured, shifting her slightly so that she straddled him. The brown and green plaid fell lower and he slid onto it while pulling some of its great length high about her shoulders again. They were completely enveloped in the tartan now, warmed by it, the fire, and each other. "I have pushed ye too hard," he continued, letting his fingers massage where they would—her back, her buttocks, the firm, smooth muscles of her thighs. "Ye have ridden rough country at a hard pace." He leaned closer, letting the throbbing length of his manhood press against the moistness of her. His own eyes fell closed as he gritted his teeth against the painful desire to enter her. "Were things different, I would have ye take a more pleasurable ride now."

"Leith." She could not open her eyes, for she knew what she would see. Sin! But if she remained blind she could only feel the wonder of his hands, which worked together now, pressing gently up her back in tandem waves of pleasure, smoothing the ache from it and making her arch nearer the fire of his form.

"What, lass?" He barely managed the question, for the peaks of her breasts were now pressed against the partially bandaged mass of his chest.

"Leith . . ."

Somehow they had begun a slight rhythm, rocking gently against each other.

"What, love?" he rasped, his hands still moving as he leaned forward, kissing her lovely ivory throat.

Her head fell back. She arched nearer, breathing hard. "I think . . . I like this."

"It is right, lass," he breathed. "Ye are a woman, meant for loving."

"It is . . . " She pushed harder against him so that her mouth fell open slightly as the pleasure mounted with the heat of his shaft. "It is not right."

"Aye, love." His kisses dropped lower, nearing the crest of her breast. "It is."

Her desire was so intense now that it felt like pain, like a fire about to devour her.

His tongue touched her nipple and she gasped, her body jerking involuntarily.

He suckled her! Dear God! He suckled her!

Hold, fast—and pray, her conscience screamed, and so she clutched the blanket about his shoulders, holding him fast to her . . . and praying, "Please Leith . . . "

"What, me love?"

"I—I need . . . "

"Aye?"

"I need something."

"Aye," he growled and, pushing back her crimson hair, kissed her neck. "Ye need to be loved. By me."

"But . . . " She gasped as his kisses swept lower again, grazing the crest of one breast before slipping down to blaze a scorching trail across her abdomen. "I am to be a nun."

"Nay," he murmured against the flaming warmth of her flesh. "Ye are meant to be mine. Destined to spend yer life by me side." His lips skimmed upward again, through the valley between her breasts to kiss her tingling ear. "Promised to me. Already promised," he murmured, more to himself than to her. "So surely there is na need to wait. Who will know?" His eyes were dark and intense as they found hers. "Who will know if we share ourselves now?"

By the firelight's glow Rose watched him. Every instinct demanded that she pull him to her, that she fill the void inside and ease the ache. But his words made no sense.

"Promised?" she asked breathlessly.

His gaze held hers. "The MacAulay did vow to give me Fiona as me wife should I bring her back to Scotland."

Silence held the place.

"Fiona is dead," Rose breathed softly. "Resting in the abbey's gravesite."

Leith nodded. "And hence God brought ye to me. To forge peace between the clans," he breathed. "I have waited so long for a means. Ye will be Fiona, for the auld man will na know ye are na his daughter."

Fiona? Rose struggled to find some sanity in his words. What was he talking about? He had waited for a means to forge peace? He had used her? "What?" she asked weakly, pressing away.

"The MacAulay shall believe ye are his own," said Leith, touching the flaming glory of her hair, sure that she must ache for him just as he did for her, and sure that that flaming desire would win his cause. "He will accept ye, for ye are the very spirit of the Scots. Bold. Bonny," he murmured. "Ye will be Fiona and ye will be mine."

"Yours?" she breathed.

"Aye, lass." His fingertips brushed a damp curl from her face. "And I shall pleasure ye for ye are the very tool I have long awaited."

"Tool?" She still straddled him but had pressed far back now. "I am but a tool?"

"Nay! Na *but* a tool," he corrected, mesmerized by her beauty and thinking of the pride he would find in calling her his wife. "Ye are to be me Fiona."

"Fiona!" She gasped the word at him as she jerked to her feet, straddling him like a warrior ready for the killing blow. "Fiona! You bastard. You lied to me. Said I was needed for a godly mission, to tend to the old lord. While all along you planned to use me, to cause me to break my vows, to defile me!"

"Defile ye?" he questioned softly. She was a magnificent sight, a naked angel, haloed by a glorious mass of hair that flowed in drying rivers of auburn fire, caressing her breasts, brushing her hips, leaving only her nether parts utterly naked to his gaze.

"I would never defile ye, lass," he promised, his bold gaze caught on the apex between her spread legs. "I would . . . give ye great pleasure."

"Pleasure!" she gasped, jerking from above him to stand, legs together, at his side. "You would force me to . . . to lie with you."

His grin was devilish, his chuckle deep and suggestive. "I willna need to force ye, wee one, for ye are as eager for the joining as I. Ye will come willingly to me bed."

"Never!"

"Ye shall be me bride," he said, rising slowly to his feet, his expression solemn now.

She did not back away but watched his face with sudden arrogance. "You dream . . ." she began, then gasped, widening her eyes and pointing frantically past his shoulder.

He wheeled like a trained destrier, knees bent, muscles bulging and ready as he raised his claymore to protect her.

But there was nothing to cause alarm. He shifted

his gaze, searching the darkness outside for danger. "What did ye see?" he demanded, his tone low and deadly. But his only answer was the rapid patter of bare, retreating feet.

Chapter 12

"Lass! Come back!" Leith roared, but it was no use, for nothing but black silence answered him.

Damn it to unholy hell! This was not a safe place for a warrior fully armed, much less a slip of a girl with no clothes and very little wits. Leave it to her to stumble into the river in her haste to escape him.

What had set her off? One moment she lay warm and soft in his arms and the next she was fleeing like a hare from a wolf! Women! They were a plague upon mankind.

But there was no time to waste now. Folding his plaid into quick pleats, he lay down on the thing, rising a moment later to belt it rapidly about his waist. His shirt was gone, he learned with a scowl. So the lass was not bare-ass naked after all.

Thrusting his claymore and dirk into his belt, Leith ran barefoot from the shelter. He'd tied the horses only a short distance from the small cave but only the stallion remained, fretting against his tether as he tossed his thick mane and pranced in place, lifting heavily feathered legs in rhythmic displeasure.

The knot of the saturated rope was hard and stubborn, resisting Leith's hurried attempts until he finally wrestled it free. In a moment he was astride and they were off, racing through the thick underbrush after the midnight mare.

Wet branches slapped at Leith's face and legs. Mud slipped beneath the stallion's churning hooves. To their left a stream tumbled southward, swelled and turbulent from the recent rains.

A sturdy tree limb thumped Leith's wounded shoulder, stunning him with pain and nearly knocking him to the ground, but he gritted his teeth and grappled for Beinn's mane, holding on by sheer tenacity.

The stallion slipped, heading downhill. Through tattered clouds the moon skittered overhead. Ghostly mist rose from the glen below. A pale, motionless figure could be seen, seeming strangely disembodied. "Rose," Leith whispered, realizing now that the pale fairy was the lass, encased in his saffron shirt and riding the black mare that was nearly invisible in the darkness.

She was safe. All was well, he thought, but a man's scream jerked him to reality. Leith twisted about, not seeing Rose slip to the ground.

Danger! Where? Leith searched for it, his gaze skimming the darkness until he saw his shirt flitting through the night.

Dear God, what was she doing? For a moment Leith remained frozen, stunned by her foolishness, until he saw the warrior, his weapon raised. And another form that stood before him.

The warrior raised his axe again.

"No!" It was Rose who screamed the word, diverting the attacker's attention and causing his blow to go slightly awry, only skimming the other man's head.

Nevertheless, his victim fell backward, tumbling into the rolling burn behind.

The warrior turned, weapon raised, and in a heartbeat Beinn was running, thundering down on the man, hungry strides eating the distance between them.

Every detail was sharply etched in Leith's mind. Rose was running along the burn toward the south—the warrior following. Sweet Jesu! He carried a battle-axe! But who was he? Only a few horses' lengths lay between Forbes and his quarry and at the last moment Leith turned his claymore, holding the blade in his bare hand as he swung for the warrior's head. There was the sound of metal against bone and the man crumpled.

Beinn turned with the lithe speed of a giant cat. Leith's eyes searched the riverbank, but she was gone. God's wrath! Where? Had she fallen? Had the other man . . .

There! He caught sight of his shirt again, close to the earth now.

"Sweet Jesu!" he rasped. She'd been felled, but how?

"Catch my hand!" Her voice was loud and strong, jerking Leith from immobility.

"My hand!"

What now? Leith urged the stallion on until they skidded to a halt only inches from the girl's squatting form.

"Here!" she yelled to someone in the water, one hand gripping a branch as she strained farther over the rushing burn. "My hand!"

Above the boiling river a head bobbed and an arm reached, grasping her small hand in a slippery grip.

"Hold now! Hold!" she commanded, but her own small body was sliding, pulled along by the ferocious power of the swollen water. "Oh!" She shrieked as her body hit the stream, and with a vehement curse Leith followed.

The water was cold as hell and shocked his senses with the efficiency of a blow from a soldier's club, but he caught her about the waist and held on, fighting for footing in the sliding sand.

The man's head bobbed above the waterline again, and in that moment Leith realized the truth. Rose had caught the injured man's hand and now held on as desperately as he did to her.

"Let him go!" Leith roared, hauling back with all his might, but she would not and in the end he battled his way ashore, dragging the two along behind him until all three lay gasping and panting on the rough, soggy slope beside the river.

"Ye could have . . ." Leith panted, gritting his teeth against the pain in his chest as he gripped Rose's arms in rough hands. "Ye could have been kilt."

"And so could have . . . he," she managed, nodding toward the dark form that coughed and sputtered near her bare leg.

"Have ye no sense at all?" Leith rasped, shaking her slightly. "Ye dunna even know this man. He may be a thief! And a murderer!"

"And so might you," she snapped in return, feeling the cold bite her so that she trembled against the wind, though she refused to turn her eyes from his.

"Lass," he growled, feeling such a heavy relief for her safety that it made his arms go weak, "if ye ever do such a foolish thing again I shall—"

The half-drowned man moaned beside them and Rose jerked her arms from Leith's grasp. "Perhaps, my lord," she said stiffly, her tone chilly, "you might threaten me later. After we see to the murderer and thief." She bent toward the downed man and Leith watched, noting how his saffron shirt drooped away from her bosom.

"Lie still." She touched the man's forehead, testing the scrape there. "You are safe now."

The man's eyes opened, focused, and widened. He was dressed in a dark plaid and shirt, his left hand bound in a gray bandage.

Quiet held the place, broken only by the sound of water—the rush of the burn behind, the drip of fat drops from nearby leaves.

"*Bean-sith*?" he whispered into her moon-gilded face.

Leith scowled.

Rose shook her head, not understanding his Gaelic.

Silence again, then, "Be ye a fairy?" he asked, changing his words to heavily burred English.

"No." She shook her head again, brushing dark hair from the man's slight wound. "I am only mortal."

In truth the wounded fellow was little more than a lad, Leith realized, noticing his wide, round eyes, his narrow build.

"Nay." The young man shook his head weakly. "I dunna believe any lass so bonny and slight could have saved me from old Bertram's blow and pulled me from yon burn—unless she be of the magical folk."

"Just rest," said Rose, swiftly pulling open his shirt to check for further wounds. "Do not talk."

The lad stared at her as if he had glimpsed an angel. "It matters na what ye be," he said finally, reaching up to grasp Rose's hand in his own. "I would have ye whether ye be mortal or na."

"Dunna talk!" growled Leith, and, curling his hand into a fist, thumped the lad on the head.

The boy looked only momentarily stunned, then slid without a word into unconsciousness.

"What—" gasped Rose.

"Ye said ye didna want him to speak." Leith grunted darkly. "I only aided yer cause," he explained, and, rising stiffly to his feet, strode quickly away.

The man he had hit with the hilt of Cothrom was gone. Leith studied the place where he had fallen, then rose to follow the faint, erratic trail that headed north into the darkness. Whoever the warrior had been he would nurse a headache for a time. That realization lightened Leith's mood a bit, but brought his thoughts back to the lad by the stream. Too bad he could not thump that one with the same force he'd hit the seasoned warrior. But Rose would likely take exception after going to the trouble of fishing the lad from the burn.

God's wrath, he had no time for such things. At this moment the MacAulay might be breathing his last. There was no time to waste, and yet the lass was being . . . rather difficult to persuade about the rightness of their joining.

First things first, however, and just now he had the bedazzled lad by the stream to be rid of. Turning, Leith strode quickly back to the pair.

Rose was still bent over the boy as if he were her long-lost friend, her bosom only inches from his hand as she patted his fingers.

"Wake up. Wake up, I say."

"Anything to please ye," murmured the lad, gripping her hand in his.

"We must get you dry," said Rose soberly. "Can you gain your feet?"

"I dunna know," said the lad. "Mayhap I will need yer help."

She did not hesitate a moment, Leith noticed, but wrapped her arm about the other's back as if he were an innocent babe.

"There now, lean on me. That's it," she encouraged as the lad stumbled weakly to his feet, draped cozily against her side. She staggered a bit against his weight and the boy grinned, slipping his arm about her waist as if to gain support.

"Ye liked the water, lad?" Leith asked, close enough to grip the other's arm.

"Nay," he responded, turning toward Leith with a cautious expression.

"Then I suggest ye walk alone," Leith rumbled.

His meaning was not lost on the boy, despite his woozy mind. His arm fell away from Rose and he struggled to stand alone. His legs were not quite ready for independence, however, and his knees buckled, spilling him toward the ground.

Leith caught him by the collar just before his face hit the dirt.

"For the sake of Jesu!" Leith cursed, his teeth gritted and gleaming dully in the light of the besieged moon. "Get yer mare, *wee nun*, and if ye dunna want the lad to swim again, bind up yer garment."

He strode off then, dragging the lad along as if he were a sack of grain.

She could leave them both, Rose thought with a scowl. But she supposed it was her duty to see to the boy. And too, she was shaking uncontrollably again, and the thought of the fire was too much for her to resist.

Back under the ledge, the blaze was still strong and warm. Leith dropped the boy beside the flames, making no effort to cushion his fall.

"I will secure the horses," he said, stepping toward the darkness, then stopping before retreating beyond the ledge. "But if ye remove so much as a thread of cloth from his body, wee Rose, I will tack his carcass to a tree as a feast for the crows."

Rose scowled at Leith's back. He was an arrogant lout, and she hated him with all her strength.

"Ye are wed to him?" asked the boy.

Rose lowered her gaze to him. His eyes were pale-blue, his hair lighter than it had seemed earlier. "I would prefer to be boiled in pitch," she said evenly.

The boy smiled. He had a good face. Not at all like Leith's, but young and merry, with a straight nose and ready smile. "It is glad I am to hear it." He nodded once, watching her as she studied his head wound more carefully. "I am Gregor, the son of the laird of the MacGowans. I—"

"Then I would think ye would have more pride than to be fussed over by a lass," said Leith from the edge of the firelight.

Rose raised her eyes to glare at him. The man moved as quietly as a cat. And what had happened to the idea of securing the horses? she wondered.

But the lad was not concerned with such matters. "It seems *ye* were na too proud to suffer her ministrations," he said, pointing to Leith's crossed bandages with a good deal of foolhardy arrogance.

"The lass is me—" began Leith darkly, taking a warning step nearer.

"I only journey with Leith Forbes to—"

"*Laird* Forbes?" Gregor asked, turning his wide gaze quickly to the tall Scot.

Rose scowled, resenting the respect that shone momentarily in the younger man's eyes. "As I was saying," she continued. "I only journey with Laird Forbes to tend an ailing old man. I am a postulate of St. Mary's and will return henceforth to England to renew my vows to my Lord."

"A nun?" The lad's eyes widened even more but

as his gaze shifted slowly from Rose's face, down over the well-molded fabric of the oversized shirt to her bare legs, he smiled. "I think na, sweet lass."

Rose frowned. Damn these Scotsmen for their contrary ways. "I think it wise not to argue with a woman of the Lord," she suggested, jerking free the filthy bandage that bound one of his hands.

The boy grimaced with pain and Rose sucked in her breath.

"How old is this wound?"

"I received it from a Lamont blade a fortnight ago," he said, his tone proud.

"And here you are fighting again?" Rose shook her head disapprovingly. "'Twould seem you Scotsmen are slow to learn. Who has been seeing to this injury?"

The lad shrugged, his pallor decreasing a bit. "We have none skilled in healing. But 'tis nothing."

Rose settled back on her heels, only taking a moment to push the tail of her borrowed shirt more closely to a half-bare thigh. "'Tis nothing if you care naught for your hand," she chastised. "But it is deadly serious if you wish to keep it."

The boy paled again. "Is there sommat ye can do?"

"There is much." She rose swiftly and the lad watched, sighing aloud as the shirt fell back past her knees. "The first of which would be to warn you to cease your foolish battles."

The lad actually laughed. "Cease raiding and warring against the Lamonts? I think na, lass. Especially now that I owe auld Bertram a swim in the burn."

"You enjoy it, don't you?" Rose asked.

Gregor grinned. "A man needs his diversions."

"Diversions!" Rose gasped, but Gregor still grinned and Leith stood silently by, seeming to be in agreement. Men! She shook her head in irritated bemusement. They were a stupid lot, she deemed, and turned, hurrying into the darkness in search of black mud with which to pack the wound.

It was just past the midnight hour when Gregor MacGowan rose from the fire to reach for Rose's hand. His own was freshly bound and his complexion already looked healthier.

"I willna forget yer kindness, lass," said Gregor, raising Rose's fingers to his lips. "Nor yer beauty."

His kiss was gentle and his pale-blue gaze was warm as it touched her face. "Be warned, lady of St. Mary's—I dunna think our Maker would waste such as ye, for ye would look magnificent with a MacGowan bairn at yer breast."

From across the fire, Leith ran a thumb along Cothrom's razor-sharp edge, and wondered if it would be seemly to decapitate the lad for tarrying too long over Rose's hand. He'd wrapped his own plaid about her shoulders, hoping to hide the most luscious of her personal parts from the lad's prying eyes, but MacGowan's interest seemed little deterred.

With a slight scowl Rose pulled her fingers from Gregor's grasp. "I will be returning to England," she said firmly. "Make no mistake."

"Lad," said Leith, making his tone low and dark as he held Cothrom in both hands before him, "I suggest ye leave now, for me own aim is bound to be more deadly than a Lamont's."

Gregor grinned, nodding briefly at Rose before turning. "We will meet again, Laird Forbes," he said smoothly. "Rest assured."

Chapter 13

66"**W**hy did ye encourage MacGowan?" Leith asked, his face illumined by the flickering of the nearby flame.

Rose was genuinely taken aback. "Encourage him?"

"Ye didna have to tarry so long over his wounds," said Leith. "Indeed, ye didna have to see to him atall."

"You brainless son of an ass," said Rose in a deadly even tone. "How dare you accuse me of a dalliance when I only wished to mend your own countryman."

"Methinks ye concerned yerself over much with him," countered Leith darkly.

"Well, methinks you're a fool. An insulting, overbearing bas—"

He was around the fire before the words were finished.

"Dunna call me bastard, lass," he warned grimly, "for what I am, yer babe shall surely be also."

She stared at him in open-mouthed, dumbfounded bemusement. "Babe? How like you to think yourself capable of fathering a child without even . . . " She waved her hand vaguely, feeling heat suffuse her cheeks.

"Without what, lass?"

She stared at him.

He grinned, lifting his brows in question.

"You know damned well of what I speak."

"Methinks ye regret the fact that we didn't complete the act."

"You conceited—"

"Na bastard," he warned, lifting a finger. "For ye'll wish yer bairn to have a name."

"I will never bear your child, Scotsman," she said. "If I know nothing else, I know that."

"Then you know yerself to be barren?"

"I know myself to be sane," she explained, raising a brow. "Too sane to commit such a sin with the likes of you."

" 'Twill na be a sin," he countered. "For we shall be wed."

"Not while I have breath in my body."

"Aye, lass. We shall be wed and ye shall bear me child."

"Never!"

"Because ye canna resist me," he said, and suddenly she was in his arms. "Because ye were made to be properly loved," he whispered against her ear.

"No." Her denial was no more than a whimper.

"Ye know 'tis true, lass. Ye want me just as I want ye. And 'twould be a poor nun who moans for me in her sleep each night," he murmured, kissing the scroll of her ear.

"I will not . . . " She drew a sharp breath in through her teeth. " . . . moan."

"Aye, ye will, lass. Ye will yearn for me touch." His fingers had reached beneath her hair, and skimmed along the sensitive length of her neck now. "Ye will crave me kisses," he predicted, and in that moment found her lips with his own.

She was trapped by his magnetism, by the feel

of his hard body against hers, the heat of his searing kiss.

"Marry me, lass," he whispered seductively, but
she shook her head, her eyes still closed.

"I cannot. I am promised to the Lord."

"The Lord?" Leith growled, shaking her slightly.
"How can ye be so blind? Do ye na see what we
could have?"

She shook her head, denying her own desire, for
he had lied to her, time and again, and only hoped
to use her now to gain his own ends. "And what
could I have?" she asked. "The pain of bearing
your children? The hardships of this country?" She
raised her hand to indicate the harsh, rainswept
land about them, not admitting the exhilaration it
made her feel.

She could have *him*, Leith thought grimly. She
could fill that void in his life. That void that he had
never known existed. His clan and their needs had
been his only concern—until now.

Such weakness! It shocked him, for he was laird
of the Forbes, promised to protect the clan. To forget his own needs, abandon his own desires to care
for his people.

And yet—was that not what he wished to do?
To bring peace to his people through this girl? That
was it then. It was not any longing for the lass that
prompted his actions, but his need to bring her
back as Ian's daughter.

"Ye need na love me to marry me," he said
grimly, not acknowledging the ache that reverberated near his heart. "For in truth, little nun, I dunna
care for ye."

She drew herself from his grip, her back straight.
"And I do not care for you," she lied.

He did not reach for her, though somewhere in-

side he ached to do so. "Then there is na reason
why each of us canna profit from the other."

"Profit?" she asked blankly, lifting her chin a
notch.

"If ye will but marry me and do as I command,
I will see that ye are rewarded."

God's teeth! She should kill him and be done
with it, she thought grimly, but there were no
likely means of death close to hand, so she gripped
him by his crossed bandages and growled low into
his face. "Get this, Scotsman . . . you cannot buy
me, not with a thousand gems. Not with the whole
of the wealth of your country."

He looked down at her small face. "I dunna
mean to buy ye." He scowled, feeling her fists
tremble against his chest with the strength of her
anger. "I only mean to make a favorable match for
us both."

"Favorable!" She tried to shake him but found
his weight was far too great, so that it was *her* body
that swayed back and forth with her wrath. "Favorable? You think any marriage to you could be
favorable?"

For a moment a small muscle twitched in his
cheek but he relaxed his jaw and narrowed his
eyes. "Then would ye consider handfasting?"

Rose loosened her grip slightly, seeing her temper was having little of the desired effect on him.
"Handfasting?" she asked, canting her head
slightly, eyes narrowed cautiously.

" 'Tis a common and time-honored custom,"
Leith explained evenly, "for the daughter of a chief
to live with the laird of another clan for a year and
a day. If a child is created, then they are considered
wed. If na . . . " He shrugged. "They are free to find
other, more suitable partners."

There was only a moment's delay before she swung for his cheek with all her might. He caught her wrist with his right hand, bearing her arm firmly down between them.

"I thought that might be yer answer, lass," he stated with a sigh and a scowl.

"How can you think that I would live with you in sin when I will not marry you?" she asked, fuming.

"Is it na a greater sin to live together with na commitment between us?" he asked stiffly.

His left hand had caught her other wrist, leaving her little to do but glare at him. "This I promise you," she vowed. "I will never live with thee."

"And this I promise ye, lass," he answered back. "I willna let ye go until ye have satisfied the need I have for ye."

Need? What need?

They silently asked the question in unison, for even Leith did not know of which need he spoke.

Heated silence waged between them.

Rose felt the strength of his hold on her, not just his hands on her arms, but also that terrifying grip he had on her heart. "Why?" she whispered weakly, realizing she must return home before it was too late, before she could resist him no longer.

There were a thousand answers, he thought, looking into her wide, violet eyes. "Because me clan has need of ye," he said grimly, ignoring the other answers that crowded his mind.

"What need now?" she rasped. "Need of a healer? But no. That was a lie, was it not?"

"'Tis a long tale. Come by the fire," Leith suggested gently, "that I may tell ye the truth."

She watched him in silence for a moment, but finally followed him to the bright blaze.

"I suspect ye willna let me take that wet shirt from ye," he said with dim hope.

"Not if you wish to live till morn," she said, her expression grim enough to make him see some humor in the situation.

"Then remove it yerself, lass," he ordered, "and wrap up in me plaid. I've na desire to carry a corpse back to the auld abbess."

She considered telling him to go to Hades, but—firstly, she was freezing, and secondly, he was probably headed toward hell anyway and would need no orders from her to find himself damned to eternal agony. The thought made her feel shamefully more lighthearted. "Turn your back," she demanded but he raised his brows and shook his head.

"Nay."

"You're despicable!"

"Aye, lass, that I am," he agreed. "But remember this—the last time I turned me back ye flew out into the darkness with yer ass naked beneath me shirt." He shook his head again, arms folded over his bare chest. "Disrobe, lass, for I am unafraid to force the issue should ye refuse to see to yer own health."

In the end she could only turn her back and hope he did not see too much between the exit of the shirt and the donning of the plaid.

But behind her Leith saw far too much for his own peace of mind. Her back was smooth and graceful, her hips gently flared and softly molded, and he felt the hard nudge of desire rage even before she whisked the earth-toned plaid over her nakedness.

Rose felt the heat of his gaze and knew she blushed as much at her own rampant thoughts as from his attention. She closed her eyes, and, remaining with her back to him, tried to smooth the tangles from her hair. There was no hope for it, however, and finally she gave up, letting her fingers fall away before she paced slowly to the fire.

He had seated himself near the blaze. Rose glanced at him quickly. His expression was solemn, his gaze caught on the lively flame. She bit her lip, and, pulling the woolen more closely around her, stepped nervously to the log nearest her.

Between them the fire crackled and warmed.

Neither spoke.

"The MacAulays were na always our enemy. Me mother used to assemble lively festivals with them, for they were her distant kin. And though she died of the ague while the twins were yet in swaddling, we remained on good terms with them." Leith's tone was low, seeming to match the shadows around them. "In truth," he said softly, "the auld laird was much as a father to me for a time after the passing of mine own." He paused, drawing in a deep breath to study the blaze with narrowed eyes as he nodded. "He taught me much, did the auld man." He seemed far away—in a different time. "Aye. We were friends—the Forbes and the MacAulays."

He paused, his jaw going hard, the small muscle in his cheek jumping. "What I didna know was that me sister, Eleanor, also befriended someone."

Rose sat in silence, feeling that same eerie sensation she had noticed before with the mention of his sister.

Leith rose abruptly now and paced, not looking to Rose. "As I have said, we found her dead at the bottom of a gorge on MacAulay land. I wished to believe that she had accidentally fallen to her death. But there were bruises on her throat." He closed his eyes for a moment. "As if she had been strangled," he added. "I could na bear the thought. 'Twas bad enough seeing her dead, but knowing a MacAulay had kilt her..." He shook his head. " 'Twas too much to bear. I wished to make all MacAulays pay then. But Dermid, the sheepherder, came forth, saying that he had seen her lying in the heather with Owen, Dugald's brother by marriage.

"I was incensed and declared it to be a lie, banishing auld Dermid to the outer regions of our land. For Eleanor, I thought, could na be capable of such a sin, and must have been lured onto MacAulay land and kilt there."

Leith closed his eyes, feeling the anger again. His voice was weak when he next spoke. "There was much battling then, for I wasna the only one to think Eleanor above reproach. All our folk loved her and believed she could do na wrong." He tightened his fists again, his expression pained. "I wanted to tear the heart from the man who was said to be her lover. But..." He opened his eyes. They were deep set and dark with harsh memories. "But when I had me hands on his throat..." He curled his fingers, simulating the motion, and shaking his head. "Owen would na fight me." His hands went lax. His eyes were haunted. "He wouldna defend himself. And then I knew..." Leith turned his gaze to the girl across the fire, finding no strength to hide his emotions. "I knew it was true," he whispered. "He had loved her."

Rose felt his pain like a knife to her gut and when she spoke, her words were no louder than his. "And you could not harm him."

"I wished to," Leith murmured, closing his eyes, but only for a moment. "I wished to wring the pain from me heart," he said, emotion choking the words as he shook his head again. "But he didna

care if he died. In truth, he asked for that escape."
His hands lifted, entreating. "What would make
young Owen wish to die, unless he felt unable to
live without her?

"I thought to defend her honor with his death,
or at least erase her sin if she had sinned." He
paced before Rose, and she looked up into his face.
"But is it a sin, lass? Is there sin in looking to find
and give pleasure?" He shook his head and sighed
deeply. "I am na so young as I once was, and I
have learned much. Cattle have been stolen and
stolen back. Innocent lasses have been raped. Men
have been maimed, leaving them unable to care for
their families. But has any of this sorrow helped
ease the pain of Eleanor's passing? Nay. Even Ow-
en's death did na. She is gone, and there be na way
of calling her back from the grave. MacAulay pain
will na quell me own. It will only sharpen it and
fuel the feud so that it might go on forever. I would
have peace for me kinsmen—all me kinsmen, for
in truth the MacAulays share our blood. They are
a strong and fierce people."

Leith paced back to the log, clenching his fists
and staring at the fire in deep reflection for a moment. "When auld Ian MacAulay sent for me, I
knew his words would be of import. But I didna
think he would ask me to find his daughter." Leith
lifted his eyes to Rose's, which were a cool, soft
shade of violet. "He told me of his English-born
wife, whom I had met but once. Told me of her
beauty, of how the bards yet sing of her." Leith
turned back toward the fire, seeing a face there—a
face with deep-hued eyes and sweeping auburn
tresses. "She was a rare beauty," he said softly,
"but she didna love the ways of the Scots, and
when Ian was gone hunting she left with their wee
daughter—Fiona."

Leith fell silent and Rose watched him. Never had she wanted to hold him as she did now. Never had she yearned to touch him simply to ease the pain that lingered on his brow. He had always seemed so strong. Indestructible, mayhap. But now, with his defenses peeled away and the truth bared, he appeared like a large boy, with a soul of hurt and a heart that yearned to do good.

"Auld Ian searched long for her. But she hid herself well." Leith drew a long breath and leaned his head back slightly. "He married again finally. But there were na heirs. Nor other daughters. He is an auld man now and longs to see grandsons, or at the least, the daughter of his loins. So much that he called for me and offered his daughter as me own bride should I be able to find her."

"So if you found her you would wed—thus joining the clans," Rose said softly. "And when you learned Fiona was dead, you thought you might take me instead, pretending that I was she."

Leith nodded solemnly, his expression weary and filled with deep sadness. "Ye think as a Scot, wee Rose," he said. "And ye have such a face that the auld MacAulay might believe was the produce of his first wife's loins, for ye are as beautiful as she was, with the same bonny hair and unearthly eyes."

"So that is why you . . . kissed me?" she whispered. "Why you made me . . . " She paused and scowled. "Why you tried to make me desire you—to convince me to play out your scheme?"

In the firelight's glow, Leith thought she was surely the most beautiful woman alive. Draped in his native plaid, she looked as natural as the earth, as delicate as a spring blossom—so fair and fine that it made his heart ache to look upon her.

"There are many reasons why a man might wish

to seduce ye, wee Rose," he murmured. "But I deny na me plans. I would do much to preserve me tribe."

He did not care for her, she concluded painfully. Was only using her to mend the lives of his clansmen. And what would happen when he no longer needed her? Would he send her back to England after she had borne his children—after she had fallen in love with him? Dear God, she could not let that happen. "I will never marry you, Leith Forbes," she said quietly. "I will return to the abbey as I have said. You cannot condemn me to a life away from my homeland."

"And yet ye would condemn me people to destruction by their own hands?" he asked, his voice just as quiet. "Would ye have them murder each other for na cause? For they surely will do so with na bonds to bind them. They will feud and war and lay their young men low before they reach full manhood. But ye could prevent it. Ye wouldna have to devote yer life. But only . . . a year. Na more. In that time new bairns would be conceived. MacAulays would foster Forbes babes and the other way around. Strong bonds of caring and kinship could be renewed." He entwined his fingers together. "Sealing me people with theirs."

She stared at him in silence, her eyes large and dark now, so that Leith felt he could read her thoughts, could sense her uncertainty.

"Save them as surely as ye saved Gregor MacGowan, Rose," Leith pleaded softly. "For he would have lost his life had it na been for thee. Could ye na care as much for me people?"

"It is not my responsibility," she countered, closing her eyes to the faint, eerie images that haunted her thoughts. Images of a dark-haired young woman, laughing in the heather with a handsome lad. Images of a babe with red-gold hair and deep-blue eyes. "It is not," she repeated, more to the images than to Leith.

"Neither was MacGowan yer responsibility," reminded Leith. "Yet ye risked yer life for his."

"Do not do this to me!" she pleaded, angry at life for demanding things she did not want to give, at him for caring so deeply for his clan, but not for her. "I cannot pretend to be what I am not. 'Twould be a sin."

"A far greater sin to let me kinsmen die," he argued. "For surely the Lord curses death more loudly than lies. Surely He would frown on—"

"Would you swear not to touch me?" she asked suddenly.

Leith's brows quirked in question.

"If I lied," she said. "If I proclaimed myself to be Fiona MacAulay, would you keep yourself from me and return me to England when I had done what I could?"

He shook his head once, knowing his own weaknesses well. "I am but a man, wee Rose."

"Damn your Scotsman's blood!" she stormed, rounding the fire suddenly to grip his bandages again. "You think I do not know you are only a man? In truth you are barely that!" She jerked one hand free to sweep it upward and down to indicate his near-nudity, his barbaric, well-honed form. "You beg me to help your people when you yourself are not willing to keep one simple vow?"

He shook his head slowly, staring into her beautiful face.

No. The truth was he could not keep a vow not to touch her, for it would be beyond his ability. "'Twould seem ye are much stronger than I, wee nun," he murmured.

She drew herself away slightly, letting her gaze

skim down the mounded muscles of his chest to the hard width of his rugged legs. "And don't you forget it," she said. "I am the stronger and therefore I will set the rules."

Leith's heart beat a faster pace as he held his breath and waited.

"I will not marry you," she vowed. "But I will say that I am Fiona MacAulay. I will play the part for one year."

"Na!" He drew her hands from his chest, his face as hard as his grip. "Ye will marry me in truth."

"I say no!" she argued, her expression resolute. "And you cannot change my course. I will not marry you, Laird Leith Forbes, so you had best be grateful for what I offer. And what I offer is this. I will declare myself to be Fiona MacAulay. We will say I am indeed the daughter of the old lord but that my mother would not allow my return to Scotland."

"And how will ye answer the questions Ian will ask about the dame?"

Rose paused, scowling in thought. "I will say she died when I was but a babe. I remember naught of her, for the sisters raised me from my youth."

"How is it then that ye have learned to handle a horse so well?" questioned Leith. "That ye swear like a warrior and—"

"I do not swear."

He did not laugh but shook his head once. "Me people are na fools, lass. They would find ye out."

"Then what do *you* suggest?" she asked roughly.

"That ye believed the Gunthers were yer parents. That they nurtured ye until their deaths, when ye went to the abbey to mourn their loss and promise yerself to our Creator."

"Who would believe such a story?" Rose asked.

"Who would na?" he countered.

"I forget that they are Scots and therefore—"

"Dunna say it, wee lass," he threatened softly. "For I hold me heritage very dear."

She raised her chin. "I will agree to the story," she said finally, "if you will agree not to try to bed me again."

"I willna promise that," he said with flat finality.

"You hypocrite. You beg for my understanding and say that my lies are well worth the gain, but when you must bend the least from your set course, you refuse." She stood slowly, pulling the plaid about her like a royal mantle. "Remember this then, when your people fall by their own stupidity. You could have prevented it." She turned, but already he clasped her arm to pull her back.

"The lies abound, wee Rose. At the least we could make the marriage good and true."

For one aching second she was lost in his eyes. There was something in their depths, some hidden need that could not be satisfied by the great strength of his hands. Her chest ached with the thought, but her soul hurt with the knowledge that he only used her. And though it seemed he meant to use her for the good of others—still the thought was bitter.

She drew away slowly, employing all her strength. "You have heard my offer, Scotsman. I will play the part for one full year—but only if you promise not to . . . " She swallowed hard, trying to find a word for what she longed to do with him. "If you will not . . . defile me."

She looked like some earthy goddess from centuries past, wrapped as she was in his simple plaid, her blazing hair a halo to attest to her glory. There was a pride in her that nothing could shake, he thought, and suddenly he realized he wanted her like none before.

"Defile ye," he whispered gently, touching a curling tress where it rested on the plaid upon her breast. " 'Tis a strange word for what we could share."

She did not draw back, though she felt her breath cram in her chest. "Will you agree?"

He shook his head once, not dropping his gaze as he looked down into her bottomless eyes. "Though auld MacAulay promised peace if I but produce his daughter, he is a wily bastard to be sure, and I canna trust him. Therefore, we shall need to be handfasted at the least, and Ian himself proclaim us to be duly bonded in order to convince both tribes of our good faith."

Rose opened her mouth to speak but he raised his hand, pressing one finger gently to her lips. " 'Twill only add a wee bit to the lie, lass. And though I am but a man, this I promise. Should ye agree to the farce, I will never force ye. Never will I insist that ye be mine in truth. Only if ye beg will I give ye the pleasure I long to give."

Her lips parted numbly. He had only to touch her and she already felt the weakness. What would cause her to think she could resist him? She drew a breath, preparing to shake her head, but he grinned goadingly.

"It shouldna be such a hard task, lass. For as ye said, ye are the one with the strength of character. Surely ye willna be over-tempted by such a barbarian as meself."

She drew herself up, already angered by his roguish grin. "You are right." She gritted her teeth and pursed her lips, her watchwords once again set firmly in her head.

Hold her tongue, fast, and pray.

True, they had failed miserably in the past but she had only to remain strong for twelve months.

Just twelve and then, when no child was born to them, she would be returned to her homeland.

"It is a bargain then, Scotsman," she said stiffly.

"Aye." He gripped her hand in a hard clasp to seal their vows. "A bargain," he agreed solemnly, but in his eyes was the spark of a smile—the hope of things to come.

Chapter 14

⌒⟨◯◯⟩⌒

The loch was as dark as night, and still at this early hour, its midnight-blue waters smooth and glassy.

Rose stared at the silent lake, pulling the red-toned tartan of the MacAulays more closely about her shoulders, though it was not cold. "What do you call this place?" she asked.

"It is called the Great Glen," Leith answered, watching her carefully.

"The lake," she corrected, seeming mesmerized by the eerie feelings here. "What do you call the lake?"

His careful perusal of her went unseen for she had eyes only for the wide, still expanse of fresh water. "It is called Loch Ness, wee lass. Why do ye ask?"

Rose shook her head. "No reason," she said faintly, and after a moment more, turned to urge the black mare away. But a movement caught her eye and for the flash of an instant she sensed a great, looming presence in the lake. "God's teeth!" she gasped, twisting abruptly about.

There was a flutter of water, causing ripple upon ripple that reached in wider and wider circles toward the shore—but little else, save perhaps a splotch of dark at the very center of the wavering ripples. Nothing but that and the spine-tingling sense of something's eerie passing.

Small hairs raised along Rose's arms in shivering response. "What was it?" she whispered, her gaze still fixed on that spot where the dark shadow had been. But Leith only shook his head.

"I dunna ken, lass. Some say 'tis the monster of the loch." He shrugged. "The waters of Loch Ness are deep and chill and could hide many mysteries. Though . . . " He canted his head slightly, his eyes dark in the early-morning light. "Ye would ken the answer better than I, wee Rose, for 'tis said that the creature of the loch most oft appears to those gifted with the sight."

"The sight?" Again her words were whispered, but she turned her gaze now, no less frightened and wide, to his face.

"Aye, lass," he said softly. "But ye've na need to fear, for we in the Highlands have naught but respect for those so gifted." He turned the white stallion northward, calling over his shoulder, "Yer sight will make our tale all the more believable, for many MacAulays are blessed with it. Owen's sister is said to see much that others canna, and even the auld MacAulay sometimes knows that which canna be explained."

Rose watched him go, and then, feeling one last shiver, turned to gaze momentarily into the dark, bottomless waters. Ripples again, but nothing else. "God's knees," she whispered, and, turning the mare, hurried after the Scotsman.

"We will spend the night here," Leith said, drawing Beinn to a halt in the shade of a gnarled pine.

Rose sighed and stretched, weary from the endless hours in the saddle and grateful for the reprieve, though the sun was farther up than it usually was when they stopped for the night.

It had been a rare day, of azure skies and unusual warmth. The land was rugged all around, graced with endless, windswept slopes, bodies of crystal water, and sheltered, timbered glens.

It was in just such a glen that they now dismounted. Rose placed her knuckles to the small of her back and arched again, trying to draw the ache out. "How far till we reach your home?" she asked, fretting over what was to come, yet eager to have the journey behind her.

"*Our* home," he corrected, taking Maise's reins from her hand to lead both horses toward a small, nearby lochan. "And we are there."

"What?" She all but spat the word. "We are on Forbes' land?"

"Aye." He led their mounts to the water's edge, letting them drop their muzzles to the clear blue waters.

"We are there and you did not tell me?" she persisted.

"Ye didna ask," he replied, nonplussed as he patted his stallion's pearly neck.

Rose pursed her lips, placing her hands to her hips. "You, Scotsman, are a—"

"Now, lass," he chided, leaning casually against Beinn's saddle. "Remember, ye too are Scots now."

"I am n—"

"Aye. Ye are," he argued, raising a palm to halt her denial. "For ye agreed to play the game and the game begins now. We Scots are na a trusting lot, and me kinsmen may be scouting verra near. We wouldna want them to hear ye deny yer heritage, now, would we, lass?"

As he said the words, one corner of his fine mouth lifted, as if her predicament gave him great pleasure, and for a brief moment Rose wondered if she might manage to push him into the water if she rushed him.

From near the horses, Leith watched her watch him. She might not have been Scots in fact, but in spirit ... He nearly chuckled aloud, reading her thoughts clearly—seeing her imagine his fall into the water, then watching her turn away as she decided she herself was not ready for the drenching she would probably take with him.

Ah, yes. In spirit she was Scots.

Supper had been eaten and the remainder of the food packed away when Leith rose to stretch the kinks from his legs.

"Best to find sleep early this night, lass," he said, looking to the north. "Tomorrow may well be a hard day."

"Hard?" Rose asked, looking up from her spot near the fire. "We could not possibly ride faster than we did today."

"Nay." He shifted his gaze to he her. "The ride will na be hard. 'Tis the meeting with the Mac-Aulay that ye may find difficult."

"You mean ... " Rose jerked to her feet, her eyes wide and stunned, her fists clenched. "My father?" she breathed. "We'll meet with my father ... to-morrow?"

Leith raised his brows at her. She played the part of the old laird's lost daughter very well when the mood suited her. "Aye." He nodded. "Yer father."

"W-well ... hell!" she sputtered. "Why didn't you tell me? Let's get to your holdings that I might make myself presentable."

Leith was truly taken aback and struggled for a moment to keep the surprise from his face. After all, she had entered into this bargain unwillingly. What now made her so eager for this encounter?

"That is to say," she said, wringing her hands, "if I am to play this game, I will play it well. 'Twould be unseemly for me to meet my lord as I am."

His eyes did not leave her. "We willna go to Glen Creag first," he said pensively, "for I dare na wait longer. Though we are on Forbes land, we are verra close to the MacAulay border. 'Twill save time to go straight there."

"But . . ." Rose pressed her palms to the gown he had given her some days since. It was a fine garment, and far better than anything Rose had worn in the past, but it had seen hard wear and much rain and hardly looked its best. "I do not mean to be petty, Leith," she said softly, "but if I am to meet the laird of the clan MacAulay as his daughter, would it not be wise for me to look the part?"

Look the part? Leith repeated in his mind. He remained silent, still watching her. Her hair was loose again, her small oval face deadly serious and her unearthly violet eyes blazed.

Never in all his life had he imagined a woman who would look the part of a Scottish laird's daughter more completely than she, and for one moment he was sorely tempted to take her into his arms and tell her so.

He clenched his fists, silently cursing himself for his vow of self-control, and finally turned to rummage in the large saddlebags that held their possessions.

Drawing out a parcel, he carried the bundle to her. His gaze met hers in a momentary spark of brown against violet.

The campsite was quiet and still as their

thoughts and desires whispered together in un-
heard tones.

From a nearby oak an owl hallooed, its lonesome
call breaking the spell.

Rose drew a deep breath, sucking in her lower
lip before shifting her gaze to her feet.

The small muscle jumped in Leith's cheek, but
he relaxed with a conscious effort and finally
spoke. "I have planned hard for this meeting," he
admitted softly. "And in the hopes of finding the
auld laird's daughter alive and with much the
same build as her mother before her, I brought this
as a gift." With a sharp, single nod he set the pack-
age into her hands. "It is yers now."

Again their gazes met—hard, needy. And then
without another word he turned and strode to the
water's edge.

Rose blinked once, then, bending, placed the
bundle on the ground. It was wrapped in lightly
oiled skin and leather bindings which she drew
quickly away. Inside was a linen cloth, and inside
that, carefully protected from the elements of hard
travel, lay a gown.

She took it out like a precious jewel, for in truth
she had never seen anything so fine. It was forest-
green velvet. The skirt and sleeves were slashed
and in the folds of those cuts the fabric was finest
yellow silk.

She drew the dress reverently to her cheek, feeling the rich softness of its nap before she lifted her
face.

Leith had turned and was watching her, his expression solemn and shadowed.

"It is . . . " she breathed softly, then hunched her
shoulders and shook her head, suddenly remembering who she was. "It is too rich a garment for
me," she said. "For I am sworn to—"

"Ye are sworn to be Fiona MacAulay," Leith interrupted, his tone rich and low. "So ye must dress as such."

"But . . ." she began, then stopped, for though her wants might have been evil, his desire to save his clan was not. "Then I thank you, Laird Forbes," she said. "It is truly beautiful." She bit her lip again and pressed the bundle self-consciously against her chest. "But 'tis a far richer gift than I should accept."

Again their eyes met in breathless anticipation. Air jammed in Leith's throat and his palms felt strangely moist. But her eyes were shining with some great emotion and he could not stop his smile.

"Then mayhap such a rich gift can still my guilt somewhat," he said, lifting one hand to his chest and hauling up the chain that lay beneath his simple shirt.

Upon his calloused fingers lay her wooden cross, bound with brass wire and seeming strangely at home as it hung from its humble chain about his broad neck. "Mayhap I could keep this now," he said softly, not looking at the cross but rather at her wide-eyed face. "Until the year is complete."

For the life of her, Rose could think of nothing to say. Words clogged in her mind, tumbling over each other in helpless frenzy.

There was something about the thought of her simple cross lying hidden and inexplicably secure against the deep strength of his chest that made her feel warm from head to toe.

She bit her lip, nervously swiping one hand against her skirt and failing miserably to answer.

"There is a shallow place in the lochan," Leith said as he tried to draw himself from her gaze. "If ye wish to bathe, the water will be warmer there, and I will watch to make sure ye are safe."

Rose nodded abruptly, then halted the movement with a start. "You cannot watch."

Leith tucked the cross back beneath his shirt and allowed his mouth to lift at one corner. "Ye are to be me bride, Fiona," he reminded her blithely. " 'Tis me right and duty."

"It most certainly is not," she said breathlessly, her eyes wide, but he was already before her, his hands gentle on her arms.

"Ye will need to play the game much better, lass, if ye are to fool the most simple-witted, but I will cede this once, so that ye dunna raise the heavens with ye arguments. Should ye have need of me, however, I will be near enough. Ye have only to call."

For one aching moment she longed to draw him near.

His gaze held her and his brows rose. "Or do ye have need now?" he asked softly.

"No!" Her face flamed and she stepped back, still holding the precious gown to her chest.

He reached for her again, but in a moment drew his hand away, fighting again for control and finally shrugging. "Remember, ye have only to call," he said, his voice low and suggestive. "It can be the verra devil trying to scrub one's own back."

The water was not exactly tepid, but neither was it icy-cold and it felt warmer than the moon-frosted night air. Rose enjoyed the bath greatly, staying to the shallows and letting the soothing waters ease her aches. She was a fair swimmer, for her father had not had a son and had, on occasion, played with her in the small stream near their home.

Those memories flooded back to her now—her

mother's contagious laughter and, her father's
large hands and swarthy complexion.

What would they think to see her here now—
denying her simple heritage and pretending she
was someone she was not?

Rose floated for a time, letting her hair stream
behind her like windswept fire. The water felt
smooth and gentle against her flesh, like a soft caress. She blushed at the thought, for there was no
use pretending she did not think of Leith, of his
touch, of the narrow grooves in his cheeks when
he smiled, of how the hard planes of his body felt
against her breasts.

Clutching her fists, Rose drew her knees to her
chest before pressing her toes into the soft mud at
the lochan's bottom. Damn it all, she could not
think of him this way. She had agreed to a fool's
bargain, but she would not be a fool herself. She
had no use for him, or for the life he offered.

She would remain aloof henceforth. Would keep
to herself and return to her former life as soon as
possible. Surely God would forgive her sins. Surely
He understood—considering the circumstances.

With that logic firmly set in her mind, Rose hurried to the shore to retrieve the hard bar of lye and
tallow soap before slipping her chilled body back
into the water. She washed her hair quickly, for her
thoughts had made her ill at ease, and in a moment
she was bending her head back, letting the gentle
waves lap the soap from her tresses as she did her
best to smooth the tangles from the thick strands
of hair.

That job done, she kicked gently toward shore,
feeling the soft swish of her hair as it swirled about
her back and flicked lightly against her buttocks.
The air was cold against her skin as she emerged

from the lochan, and she scowled, turning her head quickly to peer behind her.

Had she sensed a movement? Had Leith been watching after all? The possibility started a tingling blush through her body, but in a moment her gasp filled the still air.

A man stepped smoothly between her and the water, his face shadowed and sinister.

"Sweet Jesus," she whispered, sweeping her arms up to cover her bosom as a noise came from the bushes behind. She swung wildly about and confronted another stranger. He was dressed in a tartan, she could see, but there was little more to be discerned in the still darkness, though he stood not three full paces from her.

He lifted his hand, holding something in his grasp and speaking incomprehensibly in the Gaelic she'd heard Leith use with Colin.

Rose shook her head spasmodically, trying to sidle out from between the men, and in that moment realizing it was her garment he held.

There was a rustling behind her, and the startling grasp of hard fingers about her arm.

She shrieked in alarm, but the sound was cut short as her captor covered her mouth.

He whispered something close to her ear, but a moment later his own shriek echoed through the night as he was plucked from her like a ripe fruit.

Rose had only a moment to watch him fly weightlessly along before he dropped like a stone to the shore. There was a bellow of rage, and suddenly the second man was piled atop the first.

Leith stood with his feet braced and his gaze steady on the pair. "Cover yerself," he said quietly, and handed her the garment he had snatched from her assailant's hand.

Taking her chemise, she turned shakily to do his

bidding, but in that moment a third body hurtled from the bushes, flying at Leith's back like a stone from a catapult.

Silken's scream sounded. But Leith needed no warning, for already he was bending. There was a twist and a thrust, a momentary shuffle, and suddenly the third man was soaring, winging his way through the air to land with a muffled thud upon his companions, his buttocks high above his head and his legs pumping.

Rose watched for only a moment before skittering to the bushes to pull the chemise over her wet skin and wrap the red plaid about her shoulders. Peering from the safety of the bushes, she watched wide-eyed as Leith stalked toward the tangled trio.

There were curses and jolts before the three finally became disentangled and scrambled groggily to their feet. But even before Rose could wish for a weapon to assist Leith, the young men were lined abreast like so many soldiers, with every jaw agape and every eye trained dead-center on Leith's furious face.

"Laird . . . " choked the first lad, the whites of his eyes very clear in the darkness. "Me . . . laird."

The other two remained speechless, the horror of their actions seeming to come home to their addled brains with a vengeance. In that moment Rose realized they were no more than boys really, none probably having passed his eighteenth birthday.

"I would hear an explanation," growled Leith, his voice as deep and treacherous as the bottomless sea. "Before I tear the three of ye limb from limb."

Three mouths opened to emit three noiseless stutters and Leith's scowl darkened. "How dare ye molest an innocent lass on the land of the Forbes?" he bellowed.

Garbled explanations sputtered forth, with none

discernible in the frenzied rush of words.

From the safety of the foliage Rose could imagine the muscle jumping in Leith's jaw as he raised his hand for silence. "I will hear the words from Hector," he declared. "And in English, so that the lady might understand."

"Judging by her plaid we thought her to be a MacAulay, me laird," gasped the tallest of the lads, his face a sickly green in the moonlight.

"And so ye thought ye might torment her!" raged Leith, stepping forward.

The three quailed, seeming to shudder under his wrath, but he drew himself up a pace from them and swung an arm wide. "Take yer worthless hides home to yer mothers," he ordered. "And tell me household to prepare a feast for the morrow's eve. Until then, think hard on yer sins, for I surely will do the same."

They looked now to be no bigger than shivering whelps, Rose thought, and could actually feel some pity for them.

Leith, however, was not of a similar mind, and roared for their retreat when they seemed rooted to the ground.

Shaken from their spots, the three scurried into the darkness like routed rats.

Feeling the soft brush of fur against her hand, Rose glanced down to see Silken beside her, his golden eyes lifted to her face. For a moment she stroked him, letting his presence ease her nervousness and giving him her silent thanks for his nearness. A rumble of contentment sounded from his throat, but in a moment his ears twitched and he moved away, losing himself easily in the brush.

In an instant Leith stood before her.

"It seems you have saved me yet again, my laird," Rose said softly.

It took Leith a moment to draw himself from his dark thoughts. " 'Tis a foolish and dangerous game we play at, Rose Gunther," he said softly, but she shook her head and set a hand to his sleeve.

"No, my laird," she said quietly. "My name is Fiona. And we do not play, but labor for peace." She looked up at him, her expression solemn. "Peace for the Forbes, the MacAulays . . . and for Eleanor."

Mist rolled like the magical smoke of ancient dragons in the glen below. Through the predawn fog Rose could see little of MacAulay Hold. And yet she felt as if she had seen it all before, the gray timber of the wall, the weathered, rough-hewn stone of the tower.

It was an eerie feeling, but a feeling that was no longer unfamiliar. Perhaps, she thought, this was indeed her calling, for each step she took seemed to bring her deeper and deeper into that strange, almost visible world of her mind. That world where she could sense things without seeing them, could feel emotions almost like tangible objects.

Downward they rode, with Leith leading the way until they halted their horses before the wall that surrounded the MacAulay castle.

"Who comes to our gate at this early hour?" shouted a man from above the uneven wall.

Leith waited only a moment, not letting his eyes fall to the girl, for her image was clear in his mind. She rode like a princess, clothed in velvet green, with her head and shoulders covered by the red MacAulay plaid.

"I am the Forbes, of the Forbes," he called, his voice strong in the stillness, and even from this distance Rose could hear a sharp intake of breath from behind the wall.

"Ye are na welcome here, Forbes," shouted the man in return. "As ye well ken."

Leith straightened slightly, his expression somber, and his tone deepening a bit. "We have come at yer laird's request. Let us enter or be assured ye will feel the auld man's wrath."

There was stillness behind the wall and Leith scowled. His dreams had been evil and frightful on the previous night, and he had insisted they come early, lest all should be lost.

"Have the MacAulays become so weak that they canna dare a single Forbes into their midst?" he asked, his voice rising in vehement insult.

There was a shuffling above and then stillness, but finally the gate swung open to allow the guard through. Behind him the portal closed with a rusty rumble. The guard raised his lance in arrogant challenge, but beneath his flattish, woolen cap, Rose noticed his pale, strained face.

What did they know of this laird of the Forbes that made them fear him so?

"Ye will drop yer weapons," ordered the guard, but his voice shook slightly.

"And ye will guarantee us safe passage through yer hold?" asked Leith, his back ramrod-straight, his expression hard.

"Aye . . . laird." He gave the title grudgingly, but he gave it nonetheless, offering some respect with that single word. "That I will, if ye promise ye will make na trouble."

Leith pulled his sword from its scabbard, his dirk from his belt, and, turning the blades, handed them to the man on the ground. "We come in peace," he said simply, and with a nod the guard lowered his lance and took the weapons.

Leith willingly forfeited his trusty bow and arrows as well, which were kept feathers-up in a leather pouch against Beinn's pearly flank.

The gate swung open again, but for a moment Rose was tempted to turn and run, for the shadowy images of past lives suddenly flooded her senses, momentarily granting her a vision of people she had never met and yet knew in her heart. It terrified and immobilized her, for though she had often felt a twinge of eeire sensations, never had she felt the sight so strongly as now, nor allowed herself to believe in the gift.

From atop his great stallion, Leith paused, sensing Rose's uncertainty, though he could not see her face, hidden by the plaid she wore as a head shawl.

The guard had retreated behind the wall again and Leith spoke for her ears only. "I give ye this one last chance to turn back, lass. For after this venture, destiny will decide our course."

The place drew her, and in some shadowed recess in her mind Rose wondered if she would find her death there. "Nay, my laird," she said softly. "Henceforth for a year, I *am* Fiona MacAulay."

Chapter 15

The grounds were nearly empty of people, but those who were about stopped their business to follow the pair. The laird of the Forbes was tall and dark, riding on a white stallion, his back as straight as a lance, his pleated plaid concealing only part of his muscular legs.

Beside him on a mare as black as ebon rode a woman. Although her face was shadowed and hidden, her form and stature spoke of royalty. People stopped, frowning. Upon her head and shoulders was the plaid of their own clan.

Rose barely noticed the tower as it passed to their left, for before them now was the great wooden structure of the hall that adjoined it. Behind them the guard fidgeted, uncertain of his actions, but Leith dismounted smoothly, as though there was nothing unusual about coming thus to the hall of his old mentor. Opening a bag behind his saddle, he drew forth a small tartan which he tucked securely beneath his arm.

Handing his reins to a nearby lad, Leith left Beinn and raised his hands to the lass called Fiona MacAulay. She was soft and light as she slid down before him, yet she felt stiff and uncertain and Leith allowed his hands to remain on her waist, squeezing lightly in an attempt to assure her.

"All is well, lass," he said softly. "Together we will see this through."

For a fleeting instant their eyes held. "Aye," she said softly. "We will see it through."

Inside the massive doors, the hall lay before them—wide and deep. Rushes covered the floor. Deerhounds, tied to rings in the stone wall, set up a chatter, yipping at each other and the newcomers.

From nearby an old man descended the stairs toward them.

Rose's heart tripped rapidly in her chest. Was this to be her father? Her breath came hard and for a moment she wondered frantically why she had come. She did not know these people and owed them nothing.

"They have come to see our laird," announced the guard. He had left behind his lance and now held a sword in a grasp so tight it whitened his knuckles.

The old man faltered momentarily and for just an instant Rose thought she saw the spark of something deep inside his ancient eyes.

"So ye are come, Laird Forbes," he said, reaching the floor and pacing across it with stiff but sure movements.

His gaze caught with Leith's. A cautious smile lighted his face.

"I have come, Torquil," Leith said.

The guard fidgeted again and the old man shifted his gaze, speaking in fluid Gaelic.

Without understanding the words, Rose could feel the guard's relief. In a moment the door creaked and a light draft lifted from behind, heralding his exit.

"I would see the MacAulay," Leith said formally. "For I have brought that which he requested."

The old eyes turned slowly to Rose, and though her face was mostly hidden, he drew himself taller, as if he was looking upon something that inspired the return of his youth.

Silence filled the hall.

"We will see him," Leith repeated, drawing Torquil's gaze.

"The MacAulay is verra ill," Torquil said softly. "Na one can see him."

"So Dugald is laird?" Leith asked stiffly.

"Nay," said Torquil, "but he rules until that time when me laird can once again take the reins of leadership."

Quick footsteps pattered down the steps. A small boy dressed in a long, pale shirt and naught else appeared. A wooden sword was clutched in one hand and his eyes were round with awe as they settled on Leith. For a moment he stared in open wonder, before skimming his gaze to Rose.

He was a handsome lad with bare, knobby knees, and she smiled.

He lifted the sword and said something she could not comprehend.

"In English," Leith prompted and the boy tried again, this time a bit more slowly. "Arthur gave me this," he announced, his brogue charming as he looked up at her. " 'Tis a grand sword, 'tis it na?"

"Yes. It looks to be quite . . . deadly," she said.

The boy could not control a wide, dimpled smile. "Aye." He puffed his narrow chest. "I go to show me granddda."

"David," said Torquil sharply. "Go to yer mother."

"But, Torie," said the lad, his smile drooping sadly, "I have na seen him in ever so long."

"We must let him rest."

"But—"

"Go," ordered Torquil in a tone that seemed to belie the caring Rose sensed in him.

The boy turned forlornly, his bare feet noiseless, his wooden implement bumping along behind him.

"I will see him, Torquil," Leith said tersely, "for I have come a long hard way to bring him his fondest wish."

Again the old man's gaze settled on Rose. "This is she?" he asked in a near-whisper.

"It is."

"Come," Torquil said. "Before it is too late."

The MacAulay's room was near the base of the stairs. Rose knew it with some inner sense she could not name, and she walked beside Leith feeling as if she were in a dream, wandering through rooms she had never seen and yet remembered.

The door opened and the trio stepped inside, then closed the portal behind them.

The old man lay asleep, his face ashen, surrounded by the immense green drapery of his bed.

"Father," Rose breathed, stepping forward to touch one of his ancient hands.

There was a moment of stillness. But only a moment, and then his eyes opened. They were deep-blue. His lips parted but he did not speak, and one side of his face seemed strangely immobile.

"Me laird," Torquil said, his voice choked with emotion, "'tis Leith Forbes, returned from his quest."

Ian MacAuley's gaze held fast on Rose's face as he lifted one unsteady hand to push the shawl from her head.

Morning light streamed through the window, turning Rose's hair into a thousand glistening rubies.

"'Tis yer daughter," Leith said, his voice low. "Fiona—found in England."

Still the old man said nothing, but only stared, as if mesmerized by the vision before him.

"And here," Leith continued, taking the tiny tartan from under his arm and unfolding it before Ian's eyes. "Here is the wee plaid the lass was wrapped in as a bairn. And the brooch . . ." He paused, lifting the jeweled clasp from its woolen bed. "The brooch ye gave to yer wife."

Silence gripped the room.

"Say sommat, auld man," growled Leith finally, but Rose lifted a hand.

"He cannot," she said softly. "Can he, Torquil?"

"Nay. He has na spoken since his fall some days ago. I had hoped yer arrival would . . ." Torquil's voice broke.

"He cannot speak?" Leith asked in disbelief. "After I have traveled all this way, nearly losing the lass to brigands, leaving my brother behind in an unfriendly land?" He scowled. "Ye will speak, auld man," he vowed, "for ye owe me that much. Ye owe me yer daughter—handfasted to me for a year and a day at the least."

Ian said nothing, but remained as he was, staring numbly up into Rose's lowered face.

"Father," she said again, but so softly now that Leith could barely hear, " 'tis my wish."

His nod was almost imperceptible, and then he pinched together his index finger and thumb and moved his hand erratically up and down.

Leith shook his head in bewilderment, but Torquil smiled. "A quill," he said, and produced the necessary implements.

Again Ian's gaze held Rose's.

She nodded once, slowly, and he took her hand, but in a moment he placed it atop Leith's, pressing her palm to his knuckles.

"It is done then?" asked Torquil solemnly. "They are handfasted?"

The old man nodded once toward the quill.

Torquil penned the necessary words, before turning the parchment so that Ian might read it. Striking a flame, Torquil melted a bit of red wax, letting it drip to the document before handing the official seal to the MacAulay.

Ian's hand shook as he stamped the wax, but when he lifted his gaze there was the shadow of a smile upon his wan face.

"It is done then," said Leith. "She is—"

"Forbes!" The portal swung open with such force that it rebounded against the wall. In the doorway a man stood with drawn sword, and behind him a half dozen warriors guarded his back.

"Dugald," Leith greeted him. Though his tone was casual, he stepped forward, easily shielding Rose behind his great form.

"Ye will explain yer presence here," snarled Dugald, sword lifted, "before ye die."

"I came at yer laird's request."

"Ye lie!" accused Dugald, but at that moment Rose stepped from behind Leith's back, her head high and her expression somber.

"How dare you threaten bloodshed in my father's bedchamber?" she demanded haughtily.

"Elizabeth?" a warrior murmured from behind Dugald. Silence settled for a moment, and then the name was whispered by others who craned their necks for a better view of Rose.

"Nay." It was Leith who spoke. "She is the auld laird's daughter—Fiona MacAulay."

"Lies!" a woman's voice shrieked, and suddenly she thrust herself forward, her face a mask of hatred as she stood beside Dugald. "More lies from the Forbes!"

"Nay, Murial." Leith's words were soft, though

his eyes were narrowed, his expression cautious. "She is indeed his daughter, and now duly handfasted to me for a year and a day so that there might be peace between yer family and mine."

"Peace!" She screamed the word, taking a bold step forward with her hands squeezed into fists. "Ye kill my brother and think to have peace between us? Never!"

Leith straightened slightly. "I didna kill Owen. In truth he took his own life to—"

"Nay!" Murial cried, and, reaching out, she pulled a sword from a nearby soldier's sheath, grasping it in both hands. "Ye shall na defile his name again," she warned, advancing slowly, blade held tight. "Owen would na have shamed me family so with his death. Ye kilt him as surely as ye lie now—bringing this bitch to me home, proclaiming her kin. But she will die this day!" she shrieked, and flew across the room, sword lifted.

In one deft movement Leith swept Rose behind him, but before Murial reached them, Ian was out of bed and standing, still and solemn, facing down the enraged woman.

"Me laird." She stumbled to a halt, her face going ashen as she let the sword droop toward the floor. "She is na yer daughter," she whispered.

The old man lifted an unsteady hand to take the blade from her.

"The lass has our laird's blessing," said Torquil, stepping forward. "And Leith Forbes holds the document saying they are properly handfasted."

"Nay," moaned Murial.

"Aye. They are bound with the MacAulay's blessing," countered Torquil.

"There *will* be peace," assured Leith. "For I have na wish to fight the MacAulays."

"Get out!" raged Murial, stepping forward again, fists clenched. Dugald caught her, gripping her arm to hold her at bay.

"Quiet, wife," he ordered, but Murial was beyond reason.

"He spews lies about me brother. Lies about the bitch. She is na a MacAulay!"

Ian's knees buckled.

"Laird," Leith murmured, and, slipping forward, caught the old man before he reached the floor. The MacAulay was not a small man, but Leith lifted him easily to the bed, settling his head gently upon the pillow.

"Ye shall leave now," ordered Dugald grimly.

"No. Please," Rose pleaded, "let me stay with him. I can help."

"Ye shall na touch him!" growled Dugald, his grip hard on the handle of his claymore. "Take her away, Forbes, or there will yet be bloodshed."

Leith straightened, his eyes clashing with Dugald's, but finally he nodded. "Come, lass, there is naught ye can do now."

For just a moment Rose's gaze caught Ian's, and in the depths of his soul she saw him smile.

"Aye, my lord," she said softly, and, turning, strode from the room, Leith at her side, down the corridor lined with wordless warriors.

Outside the air was still, as if the entire world waited, and for a few frantic moments she wondered if she would die with a sword in her back. But they gained their horses with no further incident and in a short time they were through the gate, then over the narrow bridge that led toward Glen Creag.

She knew the moment they were spotted, for a high-pitched cry filled the air. A moment later it was echoed farther away, and then farther yet.

"We are home." Leith sounded weary, yet relieved, as if he had long yearned to ride upon his own lands again.

From seemingly nowhere men appeared, dressed in the brown woven tartan of the Forbes and barely visible until they stepped out of the surrounding trees and lifted their fists skyward in a salute of welcome.

With the passing of that last mile Rose could easily discern the emotions of the soldiers that lined their path. They had gathered to greet a man they respected—a man they honored.

The stares Rose received were not so simple to read. They were curious, true, but there was more. Animosity? Or merely uncertainty? How much had these people known of Leith's mission? It had been simple enough to deduce that the MacAulay clan had known nothing of Leith's quest to find her—except old Torquil, who seemed to know everything.

She wished now that she had questioned Leith more about his people. Rose turned her gaze slightly, noting the solemn warriors that followed them with their eyes. They were a rugged collection of men, broadly built, some barefoot, while others were shod in shoes of hide and wore varied colored tartan hose that rose to just below their knees. Their plaids were all of the same hue and weave, and though some were bare-chested, most wore loose-fitting, saffron-toned shirts, much the same as Leith usually wore. Even the brooches pinned at their shoulders were little different from the pewter one that held Leith's plaid in place.

Another cry went up and many voices answered.

Rose's heart beat heavily in her chest. She'd been raised a simple crofter's daughter. How the devil had she ended up here, and what awaited her in this foreign land?

They were climbing now, up a rugged, tree-cropped hill, with the speedy white waters of Burn Creag burbling beside them and a hundred barbaric warriors lining their course. A short distance ahead Leith rode on, his back straight, his head rarely turning except to nod in acknowledgment of some spoken word.

Maise skittered, made nervous by the watchful men, and snorting indignantly at her temporary position behind the huge stallion. In a moment Beinn was halted and Maise lifted her delicate muzzle to pull at the bit.

Rose gave her a little rein, wishing for one frantic moment to be gone from here, away from the sharp eyes that watched them. But there was no stopping them now.

Maise tossed her head again and pranced up beside Beinn.

"Glen Creag," Leith said. Below her lay a mystical kingdom.

Her lips parted slightly and in that moment she forgot the cluster of men about them. She forgot who she was and who she pretended to be.

It was not the fact that the entire castle was built of stone that affected her so, for in truth, she was too naive to realize the cost and energy needed to build such a fortress. Neither was it the sheer size of the place that stunned her.

It was the setting.

Before them, the land fell away in a rush. At the bottom was a river, lined with banks of jagged rock that led down like the huge, rough-hewn steps of a giant.

And at the very top of the steps was the giant's

castle, built of brown native stone that seemed to reach for the very sky.

"Your home?" she whispered, and found to her surprise that he was not looking at the castle, but at her.

"*Our* home," he corrected softly, and she swallowed, half-terrified of her own future.

Leith pressed his mount onward and the mare hurried along behind.

The bridge they crossed had been hidden from their vantage point on the hill. Wide enough to allow a wagon to pass with room to spare, it creaked under the weight of their horses.

Ropes the width of a man's wrist were attached to the far end of the bridge. Rose laid a hand on Maise's neck, trying to calm the mare while absorbing every strange detail.

But there was too much. Too many faces, too many voices raised in greeting. She slipped from Maise's back into Leith's arms and was escorted through heavy timber doors into a huge hall.

The bustle there was frenetic. Women and men hurried in every direction, carrying tables, raking aside crushed rushes, and scurrying past them in their haste, directed, it seemed, by a small, plump woman with jittery hands and a round face.

It was that woman who noticed them first.

"Leith!" Her jaw dropped as her hands flew to her mouth, which formed a pink oval of astonishment. "Leith!" she said again, and suddenly she was catapulting toward him and flinging her arms about his waist. "Me lad," she crooned, though the top of her head barely reached the middle of his chest. "Me lad." She patted his back as if he were no more than a child, and he cleared his throat, seeming ill at ease as he turned his gaze to Rose.

She watched with fascination and a slight smile.

Never had she seen another embrace the formidable laird and she wondered about the woman's relationship to Leith. How little she knew of this man, she thought suddenly. How much there was to learn.

"Ye have returned," the woman said, finally pulling herself from Leith's chest with an expression of slight embarrassment. With one hand she tried to right the square of linen that covered her hair but somehow it gave the effect of being forever askew. "There now, I've na need to act so silly," she chided herself. "Of course ye've returned." She took her two fluttery hands in a firm grip as if to admonish herself for such an unseemly display of emotion. But she could not quite stop the smile as her wide, round eyes shifted shyly to Rose. They were brown eyes and not unlike Leith's. "And ye've brought..." She actually giggled. "Yer bride-to-be?"

For just a moment Rose thought she felt Leith tense beside her. Though she did not know who this woman was, it was clear he did not like the thought of lying to her.

"We are handfasted." He settled his arm at the waist of Rose's green velvet gown again. "So mayhap in time—"

"Na mayhap," said the plump woman with a shake of her head. "She shall be yer bride." She smiled, looking pleased enough to perish from it.

"Aye." Leith nodded stiffly. "Me bride."

That was it. All he said was "me bride"—like she was so much grain just brought in from the field. Rose considered giving him a good sharp elbow to the ribs to goad an introduction, but the plump woman seemed to need no prompting.

"Well, lad, does she have a name?"

Leith's brows lowered slightly, and he shifted his

weight, as if made uncomfortable by the question. "Aye, Aunt Mabel, that she does," he said softly. Most of the laborers had ceased their duties by now and were staring at them in open curiosity. "But we have ridden long and hard, and I would have the lass sup and rest before any introductions are made."

"Oh!" Mabel's hands fluttered again. Her fingers came to a brief rest on Rose's arm. "Ye must think me a heartless ninny. Of course." In a moment she was clapping her hands. "Hannah. Judith. The laird has returned," she declared, as if everyone present had not taken full note of that fact. "With his young bride-to-be." She said the words with a half-suppressed sigh and a delighted smile. But she straightened suddenly in a businesslike manner, clapping again. "Fetch food up to the laird's chambers. And ye others," she said, "ready the hall." She waved. "Ready the hall. There will be a feast this night."

The laird's chamber was large, its walls covered with bright tapestries, and its window slits tall and generous, but it was the bed that drew Rose's attention. A sudden weariness had overtaken her.

She'd slept little the night before, for she'd worried and fretted over her meeting with Laird MacAulay. And now that that meeting was behind her, all the events of the past weeks seemed to weigh down upon her, pressing an ache to every part of her body so that the bed drew her like a fly to honey.

"Are ye tired?" Leith stood a pace behind her, his back to the door, noticing how her shoulders sagged. She'd handled herself like a battle-seasoned warrior, had survived more in a few short days than most women endured in a lifetime. Aye, she had done much to prove she was indeed a woman of few needs.

His own needs, however, were neither so few nor so simple, and the sight of his own bed made him ache. But not with fatigue.

"Rest," he urged, realizing his tone was a bit tight from the pressure of his surging desires. "Ye are tired."

"No," she lied, not pulling her gaze from the bed. "I'm not tired."

Leith shook his head as he stepped behind her. "Surely ye are the most stubborn lass in all Christendom," he said in husky tones. "Ye *are* tired." He placed his hands on her arms and felt her stiffen. Was it the fact that it was *his* bed that made her refuse to admit her own fatigue? Or was she still insisting she had no physical needs? Whatever the reason, he found he respected her fortitude while simultaneously resenting her reasons. It was strange indeed how she forever seemed to put his emotions at odds.

"Sleep, lass," he urged softly, pressing the warring thoughts from his mind as he turned her gently. "It shall be a long night."

Seeing the slight flush of her cheek, Leith realized the full implication of his words. And yet he could not regret his lack of tact. She was so lovely, so tempting, that the thought of bedding her seemed to be forever on his mind.

"I didna mean that quite as it sounded, lass," he murmured softly. "But that doesna rule out the possibility, if ye are so inclined."

Rose stared into his eyes, saying nothing, and he waited with bated breath. But just as it seemed she might speak, there was a knock at the heavy portal.

Leith mentally ground his teeth. Damn him to unholy hell if he hadn't seen a spark of desire in

her eyes. Holy Jesu, now was not the time for an
interruption.

"We bring yer meal, laird," called a timid voice.

"Aye." Though he feared his own tone sounded
only slightly warmer than a wolf's growl, the
thought of Rose willing and soft in his arms made
him want to shut out the world, leaving him to
explore the desire he had momentarily sensed.

But she stepped from his hands like a bird frightened to flight. Leith watched her, noting again the
lovely flush of her cheeks, the delicate structure of
her face.

With a silent sigh he turned to the door.

A servant carried in a large trencher covered
with meat, cheeses, and bread. Leith lifted his eyes
to Rose where she had seated herself beside the bed
on the room's only chair.

"Mutton?" he asked.

Rose squeezed her hands and shook her head.

"Ye shall waste away to little more than a wisp
of hair and bone, lass," he said, but took a portion
of bread and cheese and ordered the second serving girl to bring in bowls of soup.

A small, sturdy table was pulled before Rose's
chair. On it were placed two bowls of soup, red-
streaked cheese, bread, and a huge tankard of
home-brewed beer.

"Eat," Leith ordered, fists on hips. "And sleep."

"But what of you?" Rose asked.

For a moment Leith's heart threatened a violent
escape from his chest. Never had he considered
that taking her far from her homeland and flinging
her into a strange culture might make her long for
the relative security of his presence. God bless Scotland and its foreign ways!

"I will eat below," he said, sternly subduing his
suddenly buoyant mood. He was laird here. He

had no time for romance, and yet, just seeing her in his chambers seemed to lighten his heart. "I have much to discuss with me people," he explained brusquely.

"Oh." She looked lost and helpless and for a moment he was tempted to order the serving girls from the room and take the auburn-haired lass to bed. Never had he wanted a woman so much. "Will you . . . be gone long?" she asked hesitantly, her small face pale.

Her brow wrinkled slightly when she was worried, and she sucked her lip seductively between her small, even teeth. "Na so long, lass," he said, wanting to stroke her hair, to scoop his hand behind her velvet-soft neck and pull her into his arms. "Though . . . " He dropped his voice, allowing no one else to hear his words. " . . . it will seem so."

He left a moment later. Rose eyed the huge amount of food and wondered whether Glen Creag had a small army that might be in need of her meal.

After a moment and a few questions spoken in a language Rose failed to understand, the women left too. With the closing of the door, Rose felt the raw ambush of loneliness, and the heavy need for sleep.

Regardless of her fatigue, however, she was determined to take a few bites.

The bread was made of coarsely ground wheat and freshly baked. The cheese was sharp and tangy, and the soup a wonderful blend of broth, barley, and onions that soon sated her hunger.

With a full stomach, she saw no reason to deny her fatigue, and so she pushed the table aside and rose to her feet.

A knock sounded at the door again, a quick, woodpecker rap before Mabel's voice chirped through the portal. "Might I come in, lass?"

A moment later the plump woman stood in the middle of the large chamber, clasping her hands and smothering a nervous giggle.

"Ye see, the situation is this," began Mabel in a rather apologetic tone, her hands already fluttering about. "Leith has never been wed before. And we are ever so glad to have ye here."

"But . . ." Rose found her voice with some difficulty. "We are only handfasted. And as the tradition was explained to me, Leith and I shall part ways if there is no child—"

"Hush. Hush now," said Mabel. "Of course there shall be a bairn. What with Leith being such a strong laird and ye so lovely." She giggled, then covered her mouth with her hands. "I have wished for children in the hall for so long. And so . . ." Her hands found each other again. "When young Harlow gave us the news that Leith had returned with ye, well . . ." She lost the grip on her fingers and they sped apart. "I fear I took the liberty of ordering some gowns begun." She waved to a woman who apparently waited in the hall and suddenly the entire room was filled with a troop of milling seamstresses. "Ye see," she explained, her voice still apologetic, "I bought a wee bit of fabric through the years, but I have na great need for rich gowns and thus . . ." She motioned to the bed where a dozen half-finished garments were already being laid out.

Rose's jaw dropped. "For . . . for me?" she asked breathlessly.

"Aye." Mabel bobbed her head, setting her chins to jiggling. "I do hope ye don't mind. This will na take long. Only a few hours to try them and make adjustments, and then ye can sleep."

Chapter 16

Images of years past drifted gently through Rose's sleep-fogged mind. Sunlit days. Laughter. Pleasant jaunts with Silken by her side. The low nickers of the draft horses as they waited for their barley.

These were the things of her childhood—the simple experiences that had made life worth living.

Memories of the abbey slipped in. Prayer. Cold feet. The unrelenting but unspoken questioning of her purpose there. Her mother's final words.

Loneliness. Rose felt it like a draft of cold air.

Then the images changed, shifting mistily till finally a deep, gravelly voice came, low and husky. Dark hair with narrow braids beside a strong jaw. Long fingers, calloused but gentle, playing softly against her skin. A reluctant smile that lifted only one corner of a seductive mouth. And then the fingers again, warm and languid, brushing her skin like golden shards of sunlight.

She moaned in her sleep, arching slightly toward those imaginary fingers. Life had been so cold and lonely, with no promise of warmth or friendship. But now, deep within the comfort of this dream, she found heat forged with an intense interest in life. Here she felt alive and needed. If only she could sleep forever.

The fingers slipped like silk over her lips, then curved downward, cresting her chin and falling

water-soft down her throat. She shivered as they
caressed the tops of her breasts. But it was the press
of a warm kiss to the base of her neck that urged
her arms to move heavily, as if searching for her
misty dream-lover.

Instead of feeling air, however, her sensitive fingers touched warm flesh. Rose's senses reeled,
fighting to find the safe folds of sleep again. But
now the scent of him filled her head. That masculine scent of horse and leather. That scent of . . .

Her eyes opened.

"Leith!" she whispered breathlessly, and found
she was staring directly into the warm, honeyed
depths of his eyes.

"Aye, lass," he murmured, raising his brows at
her surprise. "Did ye think there might be another
dallying here?"

He wore no shirt, she realized with bedazzled
wonder, and noted too that her humble little cross
lay with shameless carelessness against his left nipple.

That fact bombarded Rose's already trembling
senses like a broadside to a sea-tossed ship. She let
her lips part slightly as she frantically sought something intelligent to say.

"Ye didna answer me, lass," Leith murmured,
his fingers taking up their momentarily abandoned
course along her collarbone. "Who were ye expecting?"

Who indeed? she wondered dizzily. For all she
knew, there might not be another man in the
world, for she had never met one who made her
body ache for release and her palms sweat.

"Where am I?" she asked.

"Methinks ye are avoiding me question,"
scolded Leith, his fingers blazing a new trail down
a naked . . .

Naked!

The truth of her nudity hit Rose like cold water in the face, causing her hands to fumble for a sheet to cover herself.

"A . . . oh . . . please!" She pushed his hand aside with an elbow. "Where are my clothes?" That last, and singularly coherent sentence was delivered with narrow-eyed suspicion, but met with nothing more than Leith's devastating grin.

" 'Twas wondering the same, lassie," admitted Leith lazily. "Has some scoundrel been here afore me?"

Her jaw dropped, her brows rose, and her pert pink mouth formed a silly oval of amazement. "No." She shook her head so that each strand of firelight hair tossed with the movement. "You're the only one."

He could only assume she meant he was a scoundrel, but took some solace in the fact that he was, at least, the only scoundrel in her bedchamber. "It seems ye survived the day well enough without me," he observed. His fingertips trailed smoothly down her arm again, which was bent now to pull the sheet tightly to her chin.

She shivered when he reached the sharp bend in her arm, and he canted his head, wondering at her reaction.

"Day . . . without you?" she said witlessly, gripping the sheet even harder and trying to do the same with her scattered senses.

"Aye," he said, but his attention was diverted now as he grasped her wrist in a gentle attempt to pry her hand from the sheet.

She held on like a terrier to a rat.

"Truly, lass," he cajoled, his tone deep with amusement, "ye are so tense. Ye need to relax."

"I'm not tense." She said the words through gritted teeth, and he laughed aloud, finally succeeding in wrenching her hand from the linen.

"There now." He held her arm in one hand while massaging it gently with the other. "Tell me of yer day, and I will ease the ache from yer muscles."

"My muscles do not ache," she said stubbornly, but winced slightly as his clever fingers found a particularly sore spot.

"They dunna?"

"No," she lied, but he was working his way gently up her forearm, causing her entire body to begin to relax, and forcing her eyes to fall momentarily closed. "I've never felt better."

"Truly?" he asked, noticing how her other hand's grip on the sheet had already slackened a wee bit. "Ye are indeed the strong one, lass, for in truth . . . " He leaned closer, letting his kneading fingers slide sensuously up her arm. "I ache."

Some area of Rose's numbed brain noticed that he did not mention what part of his anatomy was aching, and against her will her gaze fell lower.

She saw that he wore, blessedly, his usual tartan to cover his abject nakedness, but his chuckle made her realize rather belatedly that her relief did little to prevent him from relishing her line of thought.

Immediately her face flamed with embarrassment. She did her honest best to wrestle her arm from his grasp, but he held on with gentle strength until she ceased her struggles.

"Nay, lass," he crooned softly, and, bending, placed light kisses on her wrist. "Dunna be ashamed of yer curiosity. For in truth I find it to be quite . . . uplifting."

Again she did her level best to jerk away before her face burned to ashes, but he would not let go.

"Tell me about yer day, lass," he urged again. "Try to distract me." He stared at her in silence before adding with a grin, " 'Twould be the godly thing to do."

This time he kissed her midway between wrist and elbow. Rose jerked at the spark of pleasure.

"My day," she said quickly, trying to ignore the thrilling shiver his touch sent through her. "It was fine." His kisses were continuing, as was his heavenly massage of her arm.

"Your aunt . . . " She tried to conduct a normal conversation, but now his lips touched the crease of her elbow and she jerked involuntarily.

"Ye have the most sensitive arm, lass," he murmured, remaining bent over that trembling limb. "I wonder how receptive the rest of yer bonny person might be."

"Please!" She could not bear such sweet torture. "Please . . . "

"Ye were telling me of yer day," he reminded her.

"*Oh!*" She wasn't sure what prompted the strange sound that came from her throat. But perhaps it was the fact that both his hands and his mouth had moved to her fingers. Who would have thought the simple massage of them would feel so luscious?

"Yer day," he reminded her again, glancing up at her wide violet eyes as he turned her palm upward. "Ye can remember, can ye na?"

"Of course I can," she said, and though she had intended to snap the words at him, she found the sentence came out on a breathy moan of pleasure, for he was now rotating his thumb in the center of her palm. He made her feel like melting ice, like a frozen pond in the midst of a spring thaw. Her

head tilted back as she opened her eyes just in time
to see him touch his tongue to that same tender
spot on her palm.

There was no use trying to pull away now,
though Rose supposed it would be good to try.

But she had never been very good at being good.

"Mayhap ye could begin by telling me who took
yer clothes," urged Leith as he nibbled his way
down her quivering pinky and gently sucked the
tip.

She sighed, forgetting to feel guilty.

"Clothes," he reminded her, moving on to her
next finger.

"Clothes . . . yes," she echoed. "Pray tell, what
has happened . . . " She gasped as he sucked her
middle finger into his mouth, but failed yet again
to try to pull away. "What has happened to *your*
clothes?"

He drew her hand nearer so that her palm finally
rested against the tight slope of his bare chest, just
beside the dangling cross. His bandage was gone
now, exposing the reddened, healing wound near
his shoulder. " 'Tis good of ye to notice that I am
na fully dressed."

Oh, God, yes. She had noticed. Beneath her hand
he felt as taut and rugged as an animal of prey,
and when she raised her eyes to his, she found they
reflected that same predatory sharpness.

He nudged her wrist slightly so that her hand
brushed across his smooth nipple. They moaned in
unison.

"Me sweet lass," he crooned, drawing nearer so
that her hand slipped along the slant of his lean
ribs to his back. "I could remove me plaid also that
I wouldna have ye at a disadvantage."

Disadvantage? The truth was, she was hopelessly

disadvantaged, for she ached to feel him stretched against her skin, naked and hot and hard. But she was supposed to be the strong one, to hold him at bay, to fast and to pray.

While in truth—they'd all be lucky if she didn't eat him alive.

His lips found hers and suddenly she was pressed up against him like butter on bread. Through the sheet and his plaid she could feel the hot length of his manhood, and knew that if she but slipped her hand lower she could reach beneath his simple garment and grasp the length of his throbbing need.

The thought should have shocked her, she was certain. In fact, she tried to be shocked, but all she could manage was breathless anticipation. It seemed she was beyond embarrassment now and all she knew was her own ravishing desire.

Too long had she been untouched.

Somehow the sheet fell away and his arms encircled her. She felt the hard press of his chest against her bosom and arched, pressing herself more firmly to him.

"Sweet lass," he rasped again, feeling such an aching need that he found it hard to speak. "Let me be rid of these—"

A quick knock sounded upon the door. "Yer bath, me laird."

On the bed the two froze together like ragged miscreants caught in a crime. Leith's heated body screamed for justice, for some ease from the fever in his loins. All he need do was send the woman away, his reason declared, but one glance at the violet eyes below him said otherwise.

Cold, hard, good sense had flooded back to Rose's expression, and in her eyes he saw she realized what they had almost done.

"Get up!" she ordered.

"Lass, I—" he began.

"I'll scream," she warned. "I swear I will."

His first thought was *Scream away, lass*. After all, who was there to stop him? He was laird here, for Jesu's sake. But common decency and an inherent sense of fairness prevailed, making him release her with gritted teeth.

When he stood, Rose could not help but notice that his plaid stuck out at a strange angle near his hip. His eyes followed hers before he turned his back with a scowl.

"Come in," he called, and in a moment the door cracked open.

"Me laird?" questioned Hannah timidly, making Leith realize he had barked the words. "Shall I return later?"

Later? Leith scowled. Later would be no better. The girl could wait with his bathwater till hell froze over, but Rose Gunther would not see it in her heart to be less difficult. "Nay." He did his best to temper his tone. "Bring it now."

Two young men carried the wooden vat that served as a bathing tub, and it was with renewed embarrassment that Rose recognized one of them as the lad who had seized her clothes during her bath by the river.

His eyes flicked over her and though it was but a momentary glance, it was enough to send rage flaring through Leith's overheated body.

"Harlow!" he bellowed. Every person in the room jerked at the sound.

The lad halted mid-stride, his posture tense. "Aye, me laird?"

"I will see ye and yer two cohorts by the north wall."

"Aye." The lad's back was as straight as a lance, though his face was pale.

"Now!" growled Leith and the lad flinched before hurrying from the room.

Leith's gaze shifted to Rose's lowered face. "Ye may bathe first," he said, forgetting to smooth his gruff tone before he exited behind the boy.

Striding down the hall, Leith felt the lingering effects of his rampant desire. He'd created himself a hell on earth.

The lass was his. Yet she was not truly his.

She shared his bed. Yet she did not share his bed.

She was Fiona MacAulay. Yet she was not.

His hands curled, and he wished, with the logic of pure frustration, that he could hit something hard and solid. She tempted him with her every move. Sweet Jesu, she tempted with her very presence. It took no more than the sight of her face in slumber to stoke his desire to raging proportions. And as if that were not enough, now it seemed he needed to deal with the desires of every half-grown whelp with the first growth of moss fuzz upon his jaw.

He should have left her in England. He should have taken one look at her innocent doe eyes and run like hell.

Or he should have ravaged her, then married her in earnest. For God's sake, she wanted him! She ached for him. He knew it. He could feel the hot excitement in her each time he touched her velvet skin, her silken hair. And yet she would not admit it. She had not admitted to a weakness of any kind.

She was making him insane, constantly occupying his thoughts, causing him to forgot all the things he had kept sacred his entire life—all the things he had sworn to protect when he took his vows as laird of the Forbes.

When he'd entered his chamber he'd had no thought of ravishing her. In fact, his body had ached with fatigue and he'd thought only of a warm bath and some rest.

But there she'd been, naked but for a single linen sheet, and his primal instincts had taken control. They'd been so close to consummating their relationship. And he'd never even gotten past her arm. Holy Jesu! What if he got a chance to actually touch her knee? What if he was able to lay a hand on the steep curve of her waist or feel her heart beat like a running steed's beneath his cheek?

Dear God. He must find his wits, he thought, striding through the bustling hall and outside.

Passing under the rowan trees that grew in the courtyard, Leith bent down and grasped a branch that fit nicely into his sweating palm. There were few options now, he realized. He'd set his course, and he would follow it to the end. Peace needed to be wrought between his clan and the MacAulays. Further bloodshed must be prevented. He had brought Rose Gunther with him for that purpose and for that purpose alone.

He had a year. And since that might not be enough, he would woo and caress her. He would pull down her defenses one by one until she could do naught but admit her desire. Nay . . . her *love*.

Yes. He filled his lungs with fresh air—like a stallion testing the scent of his range. She would love him. He swung the branch again.

And he . . . He would care for her as he cared for his clan. But she would not touch his heart. A Scottish laird had no place for softness.

Leith lifted his gaze, noticing the trio of lads that waited near the north wall. They winced slightly each time he swung the stick, he noticed, but he found no pity for their obvious fear, for they surely deserved to be punished.

Thinking of the incident by the lochan, Leith swung the tree limb into his other hand. Bracing his legs like a warrior awaiting a battle, he stared at the three from less than a full stride away.

"So . . ." His voice was a gravelly growl. "The three of ye are interested in me woman."

"Nay," the three lads stuttered at once. "Nay, laird. Nay!" they echoed.

"It seemed otherwise last eventide," he said, and the three backed away a step, bumping into each other and against the stone wall behind them, but finding no escape.

"Why?" he asked, his voice like midnight.

Two lads mouthed noiseless responses while the third stood unmoving and silent.

"I'll have an answer," Leith stepped forward, and suddenly his ears were assaulted by a cacophony of rushed and garbled apologies.

Leith listened for less than two heartbeats before he raised his hand and lowered his brows in anger. "Cease yer prattle," he demanded, noticing that Harlow had not entered into the frenzied explanation. "I but ask ye this. Whose idea was it to accost the lass by the river?"

There was utter silence. Each young man watched him in breathless horror, none wanting to condemn himself or a friend. But in a moment Harlow stepped forward. His back was straight, his face pale, and in that moment Leith realized the boy's courage.

In truth, he thought, the lad had become a man in that last, short year.

"It was me idea, laird," he said stiffly, his clenched jaw held high.

Leith studied him. Harlow had been orphaned at

an early age and raised by Nicol Fordyce—a good crofter but a harsh man, with little patience or softness. There had been trouble between the elder man and Harlow, he knew, for the Highlands of Scotland was a small place where everyone knew the business of all. It was also known that young Harlow had been the source of petty troubles for a number of years—from the theft of old Evander MacCain's apples to numerous fights with other Highlander lads.

"Why?" Leith asked again, the question heavy on the air.

"What, me laird?" asked Harlow, gripping his hands into fists and standing his ground with stubborn pride.

"I asked why," Leith rumbled and now the two behind Harlow stuttered into jumbled explanations.

Leith gritted his teeth and counted backward from two. He had never been a patient man. "Harlow!" he raged, his voice low. "I want to hear it from *Harlow*."

"Me laird," said the lad, drawing his back even straighter, "we were but hunting when we saw the lass by the lochan. We ... " He swallowed. "We watched for a time, sir, and saw that she wore the plaid of the MacAulays. We thought she was one of them—on Forbes' land."

"And so ye thought to rape the girl?" thundered Leith, anger searing through his senses at the thought of his Rose being so mauled.

"Nay!" Harlow denied, shock stamped across his rugged features. "I swear we considered na such thing. We planned but to scare her. To teach her to stay on her own land."

Mayhap it was true. Leith loosened his grip on the tree branch he held and tried to breathe more easily. Mayhap the lads had meant no real harm, and yet who could say how circumstances might have proceeded had he not been close to hand?

Eyeing the three, he could well remember his own steaming desires in his adolescence. Hell, his desires had not cooled yet, he thought, remembering the auburn-haired lass who graced his bed.

What if Harlow's desires had gotten the best of him? What if Rose had been an innocent MacAulay lass whom they had taken against her will? Why should such injustice be allowed to exist just because of the difference in their surnames?

"Hear me. And hear me well," Leith said, his tone low and deadly earnest. "For the sake of me lady I willna punish ye. For to do so would but draw attention to yer deeds and cause her greater shame. But I tell ye this . . . " He stepped forward, the branch held again in both hands. "Should I find any of ye accosting another maid, be she MacAulay or otherwise, I will take the strap to yer backs with me own hand. And I willna care if ye draw yer last breaths on the whipping post."

The lads stood silent, their eyes round with fear.

"As for me lady," continued Leith, his tone more gentle now. " 'Tis said that it does na hurt to look, is it na?" he asked.

The boys nodded eagerly, their faces losing some of their strain.

"Well 'tis na true!" roared Leith. "It will indeed hurt to look. And it will hurt bad. So keep yer eyes to yerself. She is mine and mine alone, and ye shall surely feel me wrath if I find ye near her again until ye have regained me trust. Do ye ken me meaning?"

The nods were quick again and Leith drew a deep breath. "That is well, for I willna tolerate yer pressing yer randy attentions on an innocent lass, be she mine or some other's."

"Aye. Aye, me laird," they said, shuffling their feet in relieved anticipation to be off.

"Ye lads may go now," Leith said, nodding to the other two. "I will have a word alone with Harlow."

They could not have exited faster had they had wings, and now Harlow stood alone, silent and pale and seemingly aware of his vulnerability.

"How is it that ye are gone from auld Nicol's home?" Leith asked finally, his gaze hard on the boy.

"He na longer wanted me there, me laird."

Leith only raised his brows and waited.

"He said I ate more than I was worth and sent me on me way."

Leith curled his fist tighter around the tree limb and cursed himself for his own short sightedness. He should not have placed the lad with Nicol, for they were too much alike—too stubborn, too . . . Scottish. At the least he should have corrected the situation before now—at the first sign of trouble— at that first stolen apple. 'Twas his fault.

"I have need of more soldiers," he said abruptly, stamping the end of the staff into the ground before him. "Could it be ye have the makings of a warrior?"

Surprise shone on the lad's face. "Me?"

"Aye," Leith said, hoping he was not wrong in believing the lad could be forged into a worthy soldier. "Do ye think yerself up to the challenge, lad?"

"Aye." It did not seem possible that the boy could draw his back any straighter. "Aye, me laird."

"It is good," Leith said simply, nodding. "Then

ye shall report to Alpin, captain of the guard, on the morrow."

"Aye." The boy did not smile, but held himself very still. "Is that all, me laird?"

Leith watched him for a short time. "Dunna forget what I have said." His voice was low again. "For ye shall dearly pay for yer next mistake."

Chapter 17

Rose's hands felt damp as several women straightened and smoothed her yellow satin gown.

Tonight her presence would be announced to the Forbes clan. Tonight she would stand before them all, claiming to be the daughter of Laird Ian and the handfasted maid of Laird Leith.

Dear God! Rose closed her eyes. Lies. Her entire life was now based on lies, so that she stood arrayed in the finest garments imaginable, pretending to be that which she was not. Pretending to be bound to a man she barely knew.

But in truth, was she not bound to him?

She well remembered Leith's eyes as he had stared into hers only a few hours before. He'd awakened her from dreams of him, had touched her skin. Had he also touched her soul?

Why did her thoughts constantly turn to him? She had vowed to be a nun. And yet that idea seemed so distant now—like another life, while Leith Forbes seemed so real, so warm and close, and magnetic.

For just a moment she tried to imagine life without him, and suddenly she could not.

"Ye look lovely," said Hannah. "Our laird will be more smitten than ever."

Smitten? Rose turned her gaze to the pretty servant, trying to make sense of her words. Leith was not smitten with her, and never had been. In fact, he had brought her here under false pretenses. He had lied to her. Blackmailed her. Very nearly seduced her. And yet, she now stood ready to pretend to be that which she was not, in order to fulfill his wishes. Why? The question echoed in her mind. In order to get back her lost cross and return to England? Or because she loved him?

The thought left her breathless. She did not love Leith Forbes. Could not afford to love him. For surely he did not love her. He only used her and she must not forget that. She did not belong here. It was not her home, and in a year and one day, she would leave.

Leith straightened his doublet, staring for a moment from a window slit of the room two doors down from where the women fussed over the wee nun's gown. The time of reckoning had come. Tonight his people would meet Fiona Rose MacAulay. Worry assailed him. Perhaps he had been a fool to set these events into motion. Perhaps Dugald MacAulay would learn that the girl was not who she claimed to be and the feud would escalate. Perhaps even the Forbes clan would not accept her. There were a hundred worries, and yet . . . The one that concerned him most was none of these. It was the thought of her leaving that tore at his mind.

Rose did not wish to be there. Indeed, she had promised herself to the Church, and he had all but forced her from that sanctuary to this foreign land. She would not forgive him for that, and she would not stay once her commitment had been honored.

Sudden, aching loneliness flooded him. How had she so quickly become the center of his life? Why did she remain at the core of his thoughts even when he told himself his clan's well-being must come first.

Leith scowled at the grounds below where people milled and laughed, waiting for the festivities to begin. They were his tribe, blood of his blood, and had always been his first concern. Now would be no different. He would convince Rose to stay—for the good of his people.

With that thought firm in his mind, Leith stepped from the room.

She was there!

Breath caught in his throat as he stared at her. Holy Jesu! Gone was the poor postulate. Gone was the fiery-haired sea fairy.

In their place was a princess.

He drew her in with his eyes, soaking up every detail, every movement, every scent. She was as lovely as springtime. Her uncovered auburn hair was braided into a heavy rope that was pinned around her head like a glistening halo. Her neck was bare, that lovely, graceful neck that made his mouth water. Her gown was made of yellow satin and just capped her shoulders. It covered the sweet curves of her breasts and was bound close underneath with a dark-blue damask girdle that fell down one hip to end in intricately worked metal ends. The sleeves were fitted snugly against her slim arms, and her hands, pale and delicate, were clasped tightly together.

"Your aunt had the gown sewn for me," she said shakily, looking young and painfully beautiful.

Leith did not respond, for indeed, he felt as if he could not. Gone were all his good intentions. Before him stood an ethereal vision. An angel dressed in yellow.

"She . . ." Rose began, but suddenly she could not remember what she had planned to say, for she had fallen into his eyes. They were deep and warm and as unflinching as Silken's. He wore a midnight-blue doublet that accentuated the width of his shoulders. Beneath the doublet he wore a snow-white shirt with a single ruffle at each wide wrist. Gone was his simple sporran, and in its place was one of a more intricate design, displaying supple leather tassels and a large, single jewel at its center. Beneath the handsome sporran was a tartan of bright reds and blues.

"My ceremonial plaid," he explained, then raised his brows. "Are ye satisfied with me appearance?"

Rose lifted her gaze to Leith's. "I'm sorry." She could feel a blush suffuse her face. "I did not mean to stare."

"Ye did na?" he asked, one corner of his mouth lifting. "Then I can only assume ye could na help yerself."

"Please." Rose dropped her gaze to her clasped hands, feeling as if she would die of embarrassment, and remembering the bevy of women she had left in the room behind her. "Do not tease me now."

"Tease ye?" He took a step forward, his gaze not leaving her face. "I was na teasing. I but wondered if ye found me lacking."

For a moment she closed her eyes. Tension made it difficult to swallow, while the heat of his nearness made it impossible to think.

"Answer me, lass. Do ye find me lacking?"

Lacking? The word was so far from Rose's opinion of him that her lips twitched in amusement. But she could barely breathe, much less laugh.

"No, my lord," she said softly, refusing to raise her gaze. "You look quite fit."

"Fit?" he repeated, and though she refused to meet his eyes she could tell he was smiling. "Ye are na overly generous with yer praise, wee one. But I fear I canna be so distant as ye, for ye are far too lovely."

Against her will, Rose again raised her eyes to his.

Heat flooded between them, making her feel weak.

"Ye are as bright as a midnight star, wee Fiona," he whispered. "'Tis proud I will be to show ye to me people."

"I'm frightened." The words slipped unbidden from her lips, and though she knew her greatest fear should be the clan's reaction, she was not certain that was so. For the sight of him so near and handsome made her tremble.

"All will be well, lass," he said softly. "For we labor to do what is right."

His hand reached for hers, warm and strong against her cool palm.

"Let there be peace between us, lass," Leith murmured close to her ear. "For we shall surely need it if we are to see our course through to its end."

Rose nodded, saying nothing. Below, a hundred voices swelled to a crescendo before fading back to a loud rumble. She felt herself pale.

"Remember, lass," Leith whispered soothingly, "ye are MacAulay. And ye are Forbes."

In his eyes Rose saw pride. Pride in himself and in his people. But perhaps there was also pride in her. She straightened her back, believing suddenly that she could change the world, and so they walked together, side by side to the top of the stairs where they paused.

The hall was filled to overflowing, crowded with

trestle tables and people milling and shouting and laughing.

Gradually the faces glanced up toward them. The noise subsided. Fingers tugged at others' sleeves and urged silence.

"Me people," Leith called, his voice strong and resonant.

"Laird," they boomed back, lifting mugs of ale that had already been filled and refilled.

"I've called ye here to meet . . . " He lifted Rose's hand and drew her forward a scant step. " . . . me lady."

"Lady!" The hall reverberated with their greetings. Flagons clashed in salute.

"Her name. Tell us her name, laird," called a single voice above the others.

Leith drew himself even straighter, looking down at the mob of his kindred. They were a rough and brave lot. Good people and strong. But set in their ways. He had hoped this day would be different. He had hoped to stand before them with Ian MacAulay by his side, for though he was their enemy, he was respected by all. Words of peace from the old laird's mouth would surely have added strength to Leith's own statements. But such was not to be.

His gaze shifted over the crowd, noting the uplifted, expectant faces. These people depended on him. Trusted him. But did they trust him enough?

"Her name?" another prompted, drawing him back to the present.

He raised his hand, stilling the mob and feeling the dull ache of uncertainty deep within his chest. "Her name," he repeated, his tone bold and strong again, "her name is Fiona."

There was a pause before the throng's next roar,

but Leith's hand remained up, his palm facing them.

"Fiona Rose MacAulay, Laird Ian MacAulay's only progeny!" From his sporran, Leith pulled the rolled parchment stamped with the old laird's seal. "Fiona Rose MacAulay, handfasted to me by the auld laird himself."

Dead silence fell on the place. Men, poised to cheer, lost their voices at the news.

" 'Tis a new age for the Forbes," Leith called, shaking the hall with the force of his feeling and lifting the parchment high. "There is a new king in Scotland. A king for the Highlander. A king who speaks the Gaelic!" Leith shouted. "King James wants peace for his people. And with this union . . . " He lifted Rose's hand again, his voice booming. "With this union between yer laird and Ian's daughter, we will put the past to rest and forge a new and wondrous future for ourselves and for our children. With this union," he roared, "there shall be peace and prosperity for all the people of Glen Creag."

Rose stood frozen in silence, not understanding the words spoken in a language that was strange to her, not understanding the unprecedented twist of fate that had brought her to this foreign place. Not understanding her own muddled emotions.

Her gaze skimmed the hall, noting the lifted faces below her.

Utter silence held the place.

"Ye will accept her," ordered Leith, exercising his authority. "Just as ye accept me."

Someone raised a mug to her, and a few called her name, but most remained silent.

"Ye *will* accept her!" roared Leith, and now a few

more voices were raised in greeting. But still the tension remained.

Beside her, Leith lowered and squeezed Rose's hand, transmitting his feelings to her as surely as if she had seen into his soul.

She turned, catching his gaze with her own, seeing his emotions like visible entities.

Where was his confidence? His arrogance? Uncertainty and concern replaced his assurance, she realized suddenly.

These were Leith's people.

That weighty truth settled upon Rose for the first time. These were not merely his servants or his countrymen, but his family. His blood kin. And he loved them.

No—more than loved. Cherished.

Her heart did a strange little trip in her chest.

Leith Forbes, laird of the Forbes, cherished these people enough to search all of England to find the means to protect them.

And Rose Gunther? She was only the means. Nothing more. She was not his family. In fact—she was no one's family.

Loneliness as empty as death besieged her. Not loneliness for her homeland, but loneliness for someone who was hers. Someone who would care. Someone like . . .

For a moment his soul was in his eyes, and for a moment she was lost there, wandering aimlessly, aching to hold him.

Five hours later Rose sat alone in the center of Leith's velvet-draped bed.

Pulling up her knees, she rested her chin on the plaid blankets that covered them. Her hair had been uncoiled and brushed until it glistened about her shoulders and breasts, and lay finally in a crimson pool on the bedcovers.

She wore a voluminous white linen gown, cuffed at her wrists and laced at her throat, and waited now like a bride for her groom.

Only she was not a bride and Leith was not a groom. It was all a hoax. A ploy. A sin!

She closed her eyes and wondered how long it had been since she had belonged, for surely she did not belong here. And the people knew. Only Leith's aunt Mabel, and perhaps young Hannah McCain, made her feel more welcome than a fox in a chicken house. Oh, they had tolerated her. Some had even managed a smile or two. But none, save the children, had accepted her.

The door swung open. The single, nearby candle flickered in the billowing draft, then straightened to shine its misty light on the towering form of Leith Forbes.

Rose watched as he closed the door behind him. He paused, his gaze going to her, noting the burnt-red glory of her hair, the flawless oval of her delicate face.

"So ye are here," he breathed.

Her expression was absolutely solemn. "Where else would I be, my laird?"

He shrugged, feeling strangely self-conscious under her deep-violet gaze. She looked small and forlorn and so beautifully innocent that it stung his heart.

"Mayhap I feared ye would fly back to England," he said softly, stepping toward her.

She lifted her jewel-bright gaze to his as he reached the bed.

"I am sorry, lass."

It was the last thing she had expected to hear from him.

"I fear it will take me people some time to become accustomed to the idea of a MacAulay in their midst."

So he had noticed the coolness with which they had greeted her. Rose tried a smile and failed miserably.

The corner of her mouth lifted, Leith noticed. But the expression looked more like a grimace of pain than of humor and that knowledge ripped at his heart, for it was his fault she was there, his fault she was a stranger in a strange land.

"Why am I here?" she whispered desperately.

Sweet Jesu! If he could but hold her. If he would but be allowed that one favor. He settled himself slowly on the edge of the draped bed, drawn there irresistibly. "Because ye are good, lass," he murmured low. "So good. That is why."

"Good?" She seemed to choke on the word. "Good, my laird? So good that I would break my vows to the Lord? So good that I would lie to your people? So good that I would pretend to be that which I am not, to save myself from the humiliation of admitting the truth. That I had escaped the walls of the abbey and lost my cross by the shore of the lake. That I had broken my vows and become a failure in the sight of all."

"Nay." He watched her face, knowing her pain. "Na in the sight of all, lass," he murmured, and with gentle care smoothed a few bright strands of hair behind her small, shell-like ear.

He knew his mistake immediately. Had he not learned the hard way that he could not touch her without losing his head?

The kiss was inevitable. He leaned forward, touching his lips to hers.

She was warm and soft beneath his caress.

Leith's heart sped along at a faster rate, his senses aroused to painful awareness.

She sat silent and unmoving, and then with just the slightest bend of her neck she was kissing him back, cautiously, shyly.

She was kissing him back. Sitting on his bed like a lost, enchanted wood sprite and kissing him back!

His hand trembled slightly as it scooped about the back of her slim neck, pulling her nearer.

Sweet Jesu, she was soft. His breathing raced along at a breakneck course now, followed close behind by the rapid thrum of his heart.

Gilded cinnamon hair caressed his arm and he shifted closer, letting his hand drift down her back, drawing her soft breasts against his chest.

Ice-hot desire hit him.

Beneath the sheet his arm curled about her waist, tiny and taut and moving gently with the rapid pace of her breathing.

She wanted him, he realized with heated elation. Wanted him as badly as he wanted her, perhaps. Sweet Jesu! She was ready. She was hot. She was . . .

Lonely. The single word slipped unwanted into his mind. But he knew the truth. She was horribly, achingly lonely, and only looked to him now because of that loneliness.

The movement of his hand was arrested, but his loins screamed a protest. He could cure her loneliness. He could, he promised himself.

But how? By increasing her guilt for the desire he could make her feel? Make her hate herself for her own weakness?

"Lass." He leaned away slightly. "I . . . fear I have little control where ye are concerned. Me . . . apologies."

Apologies? Vaguely Rose wondered what that meant, but she had no strength to consider it, for she

ached. Ached, down deep in the pit of her stomach.
Ached in her heart. In her soul. Ached . . . for him.

"I canna trust meself with ye, lass," he continued. "Me servant, Ranald, has made his bed outside our door. I will take his usual spot on the floor
beside this bed tonight." It took more willpower to
turn away than he thought he possessed, but when
he did he found her small hands caught on the
lapels of his doublet.

"Please . . ."

His heart and other parts of his burning anatomy
jumped at her plea. He could not be responsible for
his actions when she pleaded.

"Please don't leave me, Leith. Not tonight." Her
eyes searched his. "I will trust you not to . . . defile
me if you but promise." Her eyes were as wide and
dark as the loch at Inverness and Leith felt weakness creep into his soul. "Please," she whispered
again, her breath warm against his skin. "The bed
is soft and . . . large enough for two."

A muscle beside his mouth twitched. His loins
ached. Holy Jesu! Everything ached. She trusted
him!

But how could she trust him? Trusting him was
foolhardy. She must not trust him. He was a barbarian. She'd said so herself. He'd lied to her.
Repeatedly. He'd blackmailed her. Sweet Jesu!
He'd . . .

"Please," she whispered again, and he made the
fatal mistake of looking into her eyes.

"Aye." The word sounded like the parched tone
of a tortured man. "Aye, lass," he agreed, and, not
removing a single article of clothing, he stretched
out stiffly atop the blankets beside her.

Chapter 18

The hall was filled with people who had come to voice complaints to their newly returned laird. Rose watched him from the corner, her mood morose.

He had not touched her on the previous night, which, of course, did not explain her dejection. It was merely that she felt lonely and out of place. In truth, she should not have asked him to stay in his bed with her, but the thought of being utterly alone had terrified her. She was weak. And Leith? He was not. For he'd been true to his word.

Rose scowled, still watching him.

He sat on a great chair of carved rowan which was placed on a slightly raised dais near the center of the huge room. Suspended behind the chair was an elaborate tapestry, embroidered with a large, dark rock over which a yellow, striped wildcat stood on its hind feet, claws extended, white teeth bared.

As her gaze swept the length of the hall, she saw the same design on several shields that graced the stone wall above the massive fireplace.

At the far side of the hall a harpist plied gentle notes from his instrument. Was it an intentional attempt to soothe the people as Leith considered their grievances? Rose's gaze moved to him again. His chin rested on a hard fist, his elbow was propped upon the arm of the great chair as he listened to a dispute between two of his kinsmen.

His expression was solemn, his dark brows drawn together. He looked at home there—at the head of his clan, firmly in command. So natural, so self-assured.

Her heart lurched in her chest as the truth came to her again. She did not belong. Not in an abbey. Not in all of England. And certainly not here.

Hannah had helped her dress, choosing one of the many gowns Mabel had ordered sewn for her. Compared to the garment Rose had worn to last night's celebration, today's gown was simple. Still, it was far richer than any Rose had owned in England.

It was the color of Highland heather, a lovely pink-lavender garment that hugged her breasts and waist before falling in soft pleats to her feet. Her hair had been stroked back from her face by Hannah's ministrations with a boar-bristled wood brush, and now flowed over her back and shoulders, unadorned and unfettered.

"Yer bannocks, me lady," Hannah said, slipping the oatmeal flatbread and a bowl of honey before her and frowning as she struggled for the proper English words—a language not unknown but not often used here in the wild Highlands. "Milk?" she asked, but Rose's mind was focused exclusively on the laird of the castle.

He was the most alluring man she had ever seen, but something else drew her to him. Something far deeper. His confidence. His composure. His command of every situation. Or perhaps it was something more intangible still. Mayhap . . .

"Me lady?" Hannah questioned a bit louder, causing Rose to start in surprise.

With a quiet gasp Rose guiltily yanked her gaze

away. But another visage caught her attention.

Harlow! The young man who had accosted her by the river. His expression was solemn and unreadable, his gaze bearing steadily in her direction. Frightened and skittish, Rose looked up at Hannah once again.

"I beg your pardon," she murmured, her face red with embarrassment, her already shaky composure further upset.

"Milk, me lady?" Hannah repeated. "Or ale?"

Rose drew her thoughts together, trying to concentrate on the young maid's words.

"Ale—for breakfast?" she asked dubiously, the thought making her nose wrinkle in distaste and her already temperamental stomach churn.

" 'Tis often drunk," Hannah assured her. "Even to break the fast."

"Oh." Rose did not grimace this time for fear of insulting the girl. "I am not much accustomed to the drinking of spirits. Mayhap I had best have the milk."

"Aye, me lady," said Hannah as she turned, then, glancing nervously toward Harlow, hurried to do Rose's bidding.

Rose glanced at the bannocks. It seemed she was the only one who had not yet eaten. The thought made her self-conscious, as if she were being watched.

Harlow was gone. She drew a deep breath, knowing she should feel relieved, but still experiencing that tightness in her chest, as if someone were contemplating her presence there.

Feeling her breath come hard, Rose shifted her gaze, searching for the cause of her discomfort.

Her eyes caught Leith's like the clash of steel against steel. Breath caught in her throat so that she felt as if she'd been struck on the chest with something broad and hard.

From across the hall she could feel the force of his emotion, and yet she could not discern what that emotion was. His body was tense and unmoving, his gaze unwavering and deep.

God's teeth! How was it that he could affect her so powerfully with just a glance? she wondered, her heart thumping wildly.

A richly dressed merchant raised his voice, drawing Leith's attention back to his complaints.

Feeling shaken, Rose dropped her gaze to her breakfast. Dear God, she had to get a grip on herself, had to learn to be as unmoved by Leith's presence as he was by hers.

But how would she ever become accustomed to his presence when she could not even breathe when he was near?

Several days later, the hall was once again filled, but now most of the occupants were the soldiers of Glen Creag, many of whom she recognized from other meals, although those who lived and served in the castle ate there also.

There was a camaraderie in the hall, an easy feeling of belonging that Rose did not share.

To her left, Leith chuckled at a companion's jest, intensifying her sense of isolation.

Each night he came late to their velvet-draped bed, but he neither undressed nor spoke, seeming instead to wish to avoid her.

For a moment she glanced at his profile. He was a handsome man. Also a good man, for he was fair, wise, and absolutely loyal to his clansmen. In the few days since their arrival he had solved all manner of problems—from petty theft to the humiliation of a broken betrothal.

The people liked him. What was more, they respected him. He was set above them, and yet he was one of them—an admirable position for a laird, Rose supposed, but a position that left her alone, for he had many duties to occupy his time.

She didn't long for his company, she told herself, but if only there was someone to talk to, someone who trusted her.

It wasn't as if the people hated her. Indeed, they were polite enough. But they did not like her, and Leith's command that they accept her could not force them to care for her. It was as clear as the color of their plaids. They did not want her in their midst.

Sitting quietly, Rose pushed her cooked lobster about with a knife, realizing she was not hungry. She was feeling sorry for herself and she knew it. But the lies were already beginning to wear on her nerves, even though she'd had to answer very few questions regarding her past.

Beside her, Leith leaned forward, spearing a bit of venison with the tip of his knife. His thigh pressed against hers.

Their breaths caught in unison, and before either of them could glance at the other, he jerked his leg away.

Damn. Leith forced himself not to grit his teeth and ate fast. *Don't touch! Don't think! And no matter what, don't look*, he ordered himself, for he knew every detail of her. She was dressed in a blue gown that accentuated her beauty—the depth of her eyes, the softness of her figure. And her hair ⁄ . . It was down again. Full and bright, and so long it caressed her buttocks. There should be a law against her wearing her hair loose, because . . . well . . . it caressed her buttocks.

Sweet Jesu! Her buttocks . . . He had felt them,

had cupped his hands over them, had cradled them in his palms to pull her warm . . .

Good God! She was doing it again. She was making him insane. Every day he struggled to go about his business. Every night he tried to sleep. But damn it to unholy hell. How could he sleep when she was right there beside him? When she trusted him? Who had ever asked her to trust him? Certainly not he. He knew he wasn't trustworthy where she was concerned.

And that was another thing. She didn't seem concerned. Not in the least. Didn't she know that his palms sweated every time she was near? That he longed to take her into his arms, to kiss her until her eyes shone with that violet passion that was so distinctively hers? Didn't she know how close to the edge of control he was? That he lay awake with his back to her and stared at the wall until exhaustion finally afforded him a few hours of tortured sleep? Didn't she know he was made of flesh and blood, for God's sake?

Didn't she *feel* anything?

He had promised himself he would woo her. But how could he woo her when he could not allow himself to talk to her? In order to talk to her he had to look at her. And if he looked at her . . . Well, all would be lost, for she was, without a doubt, the most sexually alluring woman on the face of God's earth.

Every man knew it. *They* all looked. But they could afford to look, for they thought she was the laird's woman, and therefore were not tempted to take her. Or were they? Suspicion and jealousy nagged at him. And when he spied a man glancing her way, it was all he could do not to shake him till his brains rattled.

Yes. He was losing his mind. Leith gritted his teeth and clasped his knees tightly together to keep his legs from accidentally touching hers. Touching was even worse than looking. Touching was purgatory.

Behind him the door swung open and Leith turned, eager for any diversion.

"Ho."

Rose turned too, her attention drawn to the familiar voice from the doorway.

Colin? Or—

"Roderic," a soldier shouted. "Returned from wenching and wining."

The young man, tall, fair-haired, and the spitting image of Leith's other brother, stood with fists on his hips and a smile on his devilishly handsome face. "Returned from hard labor and a wearisome journey," he corrected dramatically. "Where's me meal?"

There was laughter and clever rejoinders as Roderic's gaze flitted over familiar faces and landed with a jolt on Rose's.

"Jesu!" He said the word with flat finality but quiet fell over the hall as he lowered his fists and strode toward her.

Rose could not take her eyes from his face, for it was as if she looked into the double of the young man they had left in England.

He stood before her, his square face lowered slightly, his sky-blue eyes fixed on hers.

"Mother of God," he whispered.

Beside Rose, Leith drew his brows into a dark scowl. Sweet Jesu! All he needed was Roderic's return to the castle. As if his life wasn't difficult enough without his woman-charming brother to confuse matters.

"Roderic," he greeted, low-voiced. "Welcome."

Roderic failed to answer, for his attention was riveted on Rose's upturned face.

"Be ye a *bean-sith*?" he murmured in husky Gaelic.

Leith gritted his teeth, counted backward from two, and swore he would not kill him—unless he touched her.

Rose shook her head with a shrug, painfully embarrassed by the man's attention. "I don't speak—"

"Of course." Roderic dropped smoothly to one knee, gripping her hand suddenly as he changed his words to English. "The princess of the fairy people would na speak as we."

He was touching her, Leith noted, fists clenched and waiting. "Brother." His voice was admirably steady as he contemplated the other's imminent death. "Meet me lady—to whom I am handfasted," he said bluntly.

Roderic drew back as if slapped, but in a moment he leaned forward again, pulling her hand closer to his chest. "Tell me 'tis na true," he entreated boldly. "Ye would na bind yerself to another without giving me a chance to win yer heart."

Rose's mouth opened soundlessly. Never had she been the object of such blatant flirtation and she was ill-prepared to handle it now.

"Tell me, lass," he continued, ignoring his brother, who steamed in rigid jealousy beside her. " 'Tis na true."

"Brother," Leith repeated, "she is indeed bound to me and well bedded, and if ye dunna take yer hand from her, I shall be forced to wrest it from yer arm."

Roderic drew his gaze upward as if from a

trance. "Me liege," he said solemnly, "I didna see ye there."

There were enough chuckles to dissuade Leith from committing any crimes he might regret for an eternity.

"I am returned, lad," he grumbled low. "With me lady. Fiona Rose MacAulay."

"Fiona?" Roderic breathed the name and leaned forward as if to study her beauty. "But, aye. Of course. The lady Elizabeth's renowned comeliness, born again in the lass. Where did he find ye, Fiona?"

"I . . . I . . ." Rose stuttered, feeling caught between Leith's granite glare and Roderic's hard charm, "I was not aware of my heritage until your . . . brother found me," she said, trying to subdue her breathing while chanting her memorized lines.

"Ah, lass, but ye couldna have committed yerself to him so soon," he argued. "For surely—"

"She did!" growled Leith, barely keeping himself from catapulting the boy from the nearest window. "And *she is mine*. Now find yerself a seat and shove some food in yer mouth."

Roderic raised his brows before drawing Rose's hand close to his chest again and laughing aloud. "Me regrets, lady, but I must leave before I am short one arm." He stood, still watching her face. "But if ye have need of me, I will be just yonder." Lifting her hand, he kissed the back and stood. "Dreaming of yer beauty."

Rose watched him stride away and wondered foggily if fathers regularly locked up their daughters when he rode past.

Beside her, Leith dared lean a wee bit closer and whispered, "Shut yer mouth, lass, or I will kiss ye here and now."

Rose's teeth met with a snap.

In a moment Roderic was seated and was soon surrounded by an avid crowd of listeners, for he was well-known for his story-telling.

Rose sat in silence beside a scowling Leith.

Anger emanated from him. But why? She had not denied that they were bound by a mutual agreement. She had not denied anything. Of course, she had hardly spoken at all, but Roderic was the kind of man who was apt to rob a woman of her tongue. Even now he was surrounded by women. Did Leith dislike his younger brother or was it Rose's presence he could not tolerate?

Perhaps he now regretted bringing her there. Perhaps Roderic's words had made Leith realize that she would always be the butt of jokes, that she would never fit in.

Depression settled over Rose like a heavy cloud. She sat unmoving, her hands crossed upon her lap and her shoulders slightly hunched as she watched the camaraderie of those around her.

Roderic's tale must be warming up. Though she could not understand his Gaelic words, she could see the rapt interest on the faces of his listeners. Her attention wandered.

The hall was brimming with Scots. Rose's gaze skimmed the faces, some young and fair, some old and scarred. At the end of a bench sat a young man, his eyes round as he listened to Roderic's tale, which came to an abrupt and apparently hilarious ending.

The hall burst into roars and peals of laughter as each man present seemed to talk at once, giving his own accounting of the tale, praising Roderic for his skill at weaving a story, slapping companions on sturdy backs.

All but the man with the round eyes, who sat nearly immobile, his hand raised to his throat. Beside him . . .

Hand to his throat?

Rose's attention drew back to Round Eyes. Something was wrong, though he was ignored by the others, momentarily forgotten by his boisterous friends.

She could hear no noise from him, could not discern the problem, and for a short time he was hidden behind a trio of men. She craned her neck, trying to see, and in a moment he stumbled into her view, clutching his throat, his face a strange tinge of . . . blue!

God's whiskers! He was choking! She was penned in on all sides by burly bodies but there was no time to waste. Sheer instinct took over.

Like a loosed goat she scrambled onto the table and ran down its length. Ale splashed upon her shoes. A trencher of venison clattered to the floor but her eyes were fixed on the choking man.

He hit the floor with a groping crash. Heads turned. Silence descended.

Rose launched herself over the last trestle and flew to his side. No respiration! He was blue as a harebell. Sweet Jesus! He was dying! Something must be lodged in his throat. She struggled to raise him to a sitting position, but he was far too heavy.

"Forbes!" Her voice fairly shook the hall. "Forbes!" she screamed. "Come here!"

Jaws dropped. People gasped. Eyes grew round in surprise as Leith, the great, intimidating laird of the Forbes, charged through the throng to her side.

"Sit him up. Sit him up!" she snapped, and he did so, pulling the soldier up by his arms. "There. Hold him steady," Rose ordered, and, drawing her arm back, she smacked the downed man sharply between the shoulder blades. Nothing happened. "Damn it to *hell!*" she raged, and, drawing back again, thumped him twice more.

The wad of venison flew out like a loosed arrow, barely missing Leith's face. But still the victim failed to breathe.

"Lay him back down," she cried, and, after sucking in her lip for one uncertain moment, she leaned over, placed her mouth to the soldier's—and breathed.

The hall was silent as a tomb. Every eye was trained on her in incredulous awe.

It seemed like an eternity before he breathed on his own, and even longer before he opened his eyes.

His skin was mottled now, his eyes wide and blue as they stared into hers. "Be ye a fairy?" he croaked.

Rose pushed her hair back with a trembling hand and shook her head.

"Na a fairy?" he asked incredulously, and promptly turned over to spew the contents of his stomach into the rushes.

Chapter 19

The following morning, Roderic was the first to pretend to choke. He grasped his throat with dramatic flair, stumbled about like a drunken lout, and collapsed dead away onto the heather-strewn rushes.

For one panicked moment Rose tried to go to him, but Leith held her wrist in a firm clasp until one burly soldier knelt beside the downed fellow and threatened to practice the revival technique Rose had employed the night before.

Roderic arose with a start and a curse, backing away from the gap-toothed soldier and muttering a threat of his own.

Roars of laughter shook the hall, Leith joining in, until Rose could not help but smile as well.

Later that day two more men choked, three were wounded, and one creative fellow insisted he was possessed by a demon.

Fiona Rose saw them all, bandaged a few, soothed one, and laughed outright at others, who accepted her amusement with grins of their own, and went on their way with glad hearts. For hers was the kind of beauty that made men happy simply to be near.

Leith watched the proceedings with a mix of joy and jealousy, for while it was true that the Forbes men were beginning to accept her as one of their own, it was also true that they were getting a bit too close for his peace of mind. But . . . Looking at Rose's expression, he realized the truth.

She was happy. He could see it in her unusual eyes. Could hear it in her laughter. She knew most of the men were unhurt, but also recognized a few potentially serious problems, and mended those men to the best of her considerable ability.

The land was suddenly abuzz with talk of Fiona's miraculous feats. She had snatched poor Malcolm from the jaws of death. She was not the snooty, better-than-thou beauty they had thought—but a healer. And a bold-talking healer at that, they said. For with each passing hour the story of how she had snapped orders at Laird Leith was told and retold.

Leith heard the stories and didn't know whether to laugh or scowl, for to hear the tale one would think the lass was not only a miracle-worker, but also a harridan who dragged him around by a ring in his nose.

She stood now, checking the bump on poor Malcolm's head as Roderic watched. Her fingers were quick and clever as she moved closer to her patient, her breasts mere inches from his head.

From where he stood Leith saw Roderic's brows rise.

"I'm feeling a wee bit of pain in me head too," he stated blithely.

"And ye'll be feeling more should ye get any closer," warned Leith, moving up beside them.

"Ah, me liege," said Roderic with a grin. "I didna see ye there. Strange, but ye seem to be forever close to hand these days."

"Aye." Leith nodded. "That I do, lad, and best ye dunna forget it."

* * *

The breeze was crisp and clean against Rose's face. She lifted her chin slightly, filling her lungs with the fresh air and feeling Leith's presence beside her like a strong tonic. From the top of the ridge where she sat astride her black mare, she could see Burn Creag rush along its rocky course. Trees towered above the white-capped water, dark-green and majestic. Closer, and just below their vantage point, a sheltered valley lay in soft, grass-covered peacefulness.

Rose breathed deeply, holding Maise steady with the slightest of pressure to the reins. "It is a beautiful land, this Scotland of yours."

"Aye," Leith agreed, nudging his stallion closer. Sweet Jesu, she was the picture of youthful beauty. She did not ride perched sidesaddle as he'd seen Englishwomen do, but rode astride, her long, slim legs gripping the black mare with easy strength. Without the slightest difficulty he could envision those limbs gripping him, could imagine the euphoric feel of her womanhood closing . . .

Woo and charm, Leith reminded himself angrily. He was here to woo and charm her, not to pounce on her like an oversexed hound. Sweet Jesu, he could not trust himself even to get near her, but he would accomplish this task if it killed him—which it might, he decided, glancing at her lovely face.

Woo and charm, his mind chanted, and he gritted his teeth and set his mind to his job.

" 'Tis indeed a bonny place," Leith said, tearing his eyes from her and hoping to appear casual. " 'Tis na easy for a Highlander to leave his homeland. In truth . . . " He looked to the north, remembering old Ian's stories of long ago. "I have heard of warriors who would fill their boots with the soil of Scotland before they journeyed, so that their feet might never truly leave the land."

"And did you stuff your boots so?" she asked, smiling a little.

"Nay." He shook his head and found he could not draw his gaze from her face. "I dunna care for dirty feet. But . . . " He watched her laugh and practically had to slap himself to remember his line of thought. "But 'twas na easy for me to be gone from this place. Though . . . finding ye made it well worth the hardships."

He meant it was worth it because of the good she could do his clan, Rose thought logically, but looking into his eyes, she thought he seemed to mean something more.

"How is it that you were able to find St. Mary's?" she asked, keeping her tone steady as she pulled her gaze from his with great force of will. But what she really wondered was how he could act so casual in her presence when she could barely breathe in his. Did he feel some of the same hair-raising exhilaration when they touched? And what would he do if she asked him to accompany her to the cool shelter of yonder oak?

" 'Twas a long and difficult course," said Leith, as he too looked away. But not so difficult as keeping his hands from her. Not so difficult as seeing her breasts rise and fall and preventing himself from carrying her to that shaded spot beneath the oak to take the clothes from her body and seek the comfort of her core.

Their gazes slipped, caught, melded. And for one trembling instant, their thoughts mingled and their breathing stopped abruptly in their aching chests.

The shady spot beneath the oak beckoned.

"Rose." He said her name in a hoarse tone, his face tense. Hers was no more casual.

"Yes?" she breathed.

Woo! Charm! Damn!

He drew a great breath and tried to relax. "We should be getting back. Ye must be tired."

"Yes." She shifted her gaze regretfully to that seductive, shady spot beneath the tree. Yes, she *was* tired—of aching for his touch, she thought raggedly, then drew her gaze to where her knuckles formed a bumpy ridge over her clenched, sweaty palms. "We'd best return."

It was dark. The room was silent. On the far side of the door Leith's servant, Ranald, slept. On this side of the door, two bodies lay on a velvet-draped bed as far apart as was humanly possible.

Tonight Leith had dared remove his shirt, for the night was warm. He stared at the wall and considered his options.

He could lie here night after night, so close he could smell her sweet heather scent, could hear every breath she took as she slept, could imagine every rise and fall of her luscious breasts—and still not touch her. In short, he could lie here and go insane.

Or he could get roaring drunk.

Or he could ravage her before she awoke.

Going insane had its obvious drawbacks.

Large quantities of intoxicants held little appeal.

But ravishing her . . . Leith gritted his teeth, giving that option more consideration. It was a time-honored tradition. To the victor goes the spoils and all that.

He was the victor. She the spoils. And she was hot for him. So why not?

Because he was supposed to woo her! Because he was supposed to make her love him, to agree with his plans, to stay forever, pretending to be

Fiona. Because he was doing all of this for his clan! Remember?

No. He would not take her. He was strong. He was Scots. He was laird.

He was dressed.

He was . . .

She rolled to her back, her eyes closed, breathing softly.

He was horny! Damn it to unholy hell, he was so ungodly randy he could not bear it.

His hand touched her hair. It was soft and inviting.

Beneath her white nightrail her breasts rose and fell. Rose and fell.

Sweet Jesu, how was he supposed to keep himself from her when she kept breathing like that?

He could no longer resist.

He kissed her on the neck where her hair caressed her ivory skin. It was not a hard, passionate kiss, but a gentle kiss that made his rock-hard body tremble and spoke of all the badgering demons that possessed him.

He was kissing her neck, Rose thought in swirling wonder. What the devil should she do now? And . . . would it be too outrageous if she ripped his clothes off?

She moaned as his kisses trailed upward along her jaw. His tongue touched the curved ridge of her ear, slid down it. She was breathing hard.

His teeth nibbled at her, and then without warning he pulled the soft lobe into his mouth and sucked.

God's toes! She jerked spasmodically, her eyes flying open.

"Ye awake, lass?" he murmured, so near her ear that she shivered.

"L-Leith!" It was not difficult for Rose to make

her voice sound surprised, as if she'd just been awakened, for in truth it was always a surprise to realize how desperately she desired him.

"Were ye expecting another, lass?"

"Nay."

One corner of his mouth lifted as he slid closer. "Ye know, love," he whispered, one hand moving to caress her neck, "ye are beginning . . ." He kissed that delicate spot just behind her ear, making her shudder with sheer, raging desire. " . . . to talk like a Scot."

"No," she said, her breath catching as his fingers dipped to the satin ties that held her nightrail fastened.

"Aye," he said. "And ye look like a Scot."

The tie had come loose in his hand and she swallowed hard. "N-no," she repeated intelligently.

"Aye," he countered, moving on to the next tie. "Yer hair is the red of the holly berries in winter. Yer eyes are the hue of Scottish jewels. And yer skin . . ."

"Leith!" Her hands caught his arm, to prevent it from moving, for the last tie had already fallen victim to his fingers. She had to stop him before it was too late. *Too late*, her mind echoed. Then, "Leith . . ." she whispered breathlessly. "What about my skin?"

He kissed her mouth then, full force and trembling with urgency. "It's soft and smooth as drifting snow," he murmured. "Blessed as white heather."

"Leith," she breathed again, every nerve vibrating with excitement. "I need to . . ." She breathed hard and fast. What did she need? Hold, fast, and what? "I need to . . ."

"Aye, love." And he kissed her again.

Her legs bent of their own accord. The nightrail

slipped toward her waist, and her hands, eager and hot and trembling, moved down his muscular body, over the lean, rippled length of his torso and downward.

His leather belt was wide, his plaid was soft. She tugged the wool slowly upward. Against her breasts the hard, naked expanse of his chest pressed more firmly as he kissed her throat.

She could feel her own pulse there, thrumming wildly against his lips, urging her on. With a brazenness that surely should have shocked her, Rose slipped her hands lower still, feeling the hard, bunched muscles of his massive thighs, and the throbbing length of his turgid manhood.

"Leith," she whispered, pressing her head back into the pillow as his kisses raged on, "I fear I'm not . . . the strong one."

He did not respond for a moment, but hurried his kisses toward her shoulder, pressing her nightrail aside as his hot caresses burned her flesh.

"Then we are indeed in trouble, lass," he finally whispered. "For neither am I. Kiss me."

She did just that, finding his lips with hers and branding them both with her shocking passion.

Against her thigh she could feel his manhood throb with insistent need. Her hand slipped of its own accord around it.

"Holy Jesu!" he groaned against her mouth. "Sweet lass, what are ye doing?"

She arched toward him. "I know not what I'm doing," she said, still holding him tightly. "But it feels right."

"Lass . . . I . . . " He was breathing hard and had to stop talking as he arched his head back, fighting to maintain control. "Ye are an . . . innocent."

Her fingers moved in a slow, firm rhythm along his shaft.

"Innocent," he repeated raggedly. "And I would . . ."

Her lips parted slightly, and her eyes closed. He could see the pink tip of her tongue and hear the coarse rasp of her breath as she rocked her hips against his.

"I would . . . take this . . . slowly," he continued.

"Slowly?" she asked, not opening her eyes.

"Aye."

"Why?"

" 'Tis supposed to be better."

"Better than what?" she asked, still pressing rhythmically against him.

"Please, lass, I dunna wish to hurt ye."

"Hurt me? Leith. I hurt now."

"Ye do?"

"Aye."

"Then I have the cure," he murmured, and, guiding her hand away, he moved over her and with one thrust buried himself to the hilt.

There was a spark of pain, and then rampaging desire.

They were joined, throbbing and feverish, and rode now, the pace hard and fast.

Rose's feet left the bed and in a moment her ankles were locked behind his back.

"Holy Jesu!" A demon possessed him. He bucked against her again and again, knowing he should slow to await her pleasure. But, if he waited he would surely be left behind, for the little vixen was determined to reach the crest in record time.

"Leith!" She called his name just as ecstasy took her, and though he longed to watch her face, his own need was too fierce. He bucked instead, pulsing out his seed in deep, urgent spurts.

Every fiber of his being went limp. His heart

pounded against hers. Their frenzied breathing mingled, and finally slowed.

"Fiona Rose." He murmured the name as he nuzzled her cheek in rapt appreciation.

It was wet with tears!

He drew back with a scowl. "Rose, what . . . "

"Please get off me," she whispered.

"Rose," he soothed. "Don't cry. I'll . . . "

"No." She shoved at his chest, her eyes closed. "Don't say it. Please, just get off."

Leith slipped onto his hip, watching her face, but her eyes did not open as she turned her back to him.

"Please, lass," he pleaded, touching her shoulder as he heard a sniffle, but she jerked from his hand and rose abruptly to her feet.

"Don't. Please." Her eyes were wild now and her breathing labored as she faced him in the darkness. " 'Twas wrong of me. And I am sorry."

"Lass, come back to bed."

"No!" she cried, and, spinning about, raced across the room. She jerked the door wide and disappeared into the hallway.

Chapter 20

"Fiona!" he rasped, but she was already gone, slamming the door behind her and stumbling over poor Ranald, who grumbled and sat up groggily. "Fiona!" Leith yelled again, nearly jerking the door from its leather hinges before he also half-fell over Ranald in his haste.

Fumbling with her nightrail's loosened ties, Rose scurried down the steps.

She must leave! Go back to England where she would be safe from her own desires.

A few candles still burned in the hall. Roderic sat beside the cool hearth with his friend Alpin, their hands gripped as they wrestled to determine which was the strongest.

Their gazes lifted as she flew past, her voluminous gown billowing behind her. Their brows rose.

"Fiona," they greeted with studied casualness just as Leith rushed down the steps, his feet bare, his plaid askew.

"Leith," they greeted.

"Fiona!" Leith called again, ignoring them completely and striding across the stone floor. He caught her by the arm just before the door. "Where are ye going?"

There were tears on her cheeks as she faced him. "Back to England."

Their gazes caught, violet on sable.

"Nay, lass. Ye canna."

"Why?"

"Because . . . " He could not live without her. "The clans need ye, lass."

She shook her head. "I cannot stay," she whispered, feeling lost to her own rampant need for him. "Please do not ask me to."

"Come back to bed, lass, where we can talk."

"Nay." She shook her head again, terrified by the emotions that raged within her. "I cannot."

"Why?" The single word was no more than a whisper.

" 'Tis a sin."

"Nay."

"Yes, it is," she said, letting her eyes fall closed.

"Come back, lass."

She could not open her eyes, could not look at him, for surely she would be lost forever.

"Fiona."

She remained as she was, saying nothing, and in a moment he bent, placing an arm behind her knees and lifting her into his arms.

She could not help but let her head fall against his shoulder, nor could she stop the painful thrill that went through her at his closeness.

From near the hearth Alpin and Roderic nodded their good nights, their hands still locked in immobility.

Leith took the stairs two at a time.

Ranald remained groggily before the door, but Leith stepped quickly over the cot bearing Rose into their chamber and closing the door with a foot.

He did not speak as he settled them onto the bed. She was nestled comfortably on his lap. Her hair was soft against his bare shoulder, her tears warm on his chest.

"Lass," he said gently, reaching up to press a

bright thistledown tress from her face, "have ye considered that mayhap this is what the Lord wishes for ye?"

She remained silent, her face still turned into his shoulder, and he sighed.

"'Twas a blow when I first found the tombstones in the auld abbey, for I thought surely all chance of peace was lost. But something led me to the lochan, and there, beside those quiet waters, I saw a fairy." He stroked her hair back again, letting his knuckles skim her cheek. "She had hair as bright as a Scottish morn, skin as soft as heather, and beside her . . . " He paused, looking into her bonny face. "Beside her was the very symbol of the Forbes people. A wildcat—but na wild. Na." Leith shook his head before sighing again, lost for a moment in the memory. The cat had been tamed, and purred beside the fairy like a wee, harmless kitten. "Aye," he whispered, "she had tamed the beast, just as I fear she has tamed me."

Rose lifted her gaze to his and again he touched her face, but so softly it was like the brush of a butterfly's wing.

"Rest, sweet, gentle babe," Leith murmured. "And think on what I have said." Lifting her from his lap, he set her gently to the mattress. "I will sleep elsewhere this night and give thee time to consider me words." He smiled, feeling the firm press of her thigh against his. "For I fear I am na better armed against yer charms than I was earlier." He stood slowly, not lifting his gaze from hers and feeling lost in its deep-hued depths. "Sleep well, lass."

Rose's head hurt as she descended the stairs the next morning. Her thighs ached, and that secret place between them felt raw and strangely swollen. Reaching the floor, she glanced quickly about, hoping to catch a glimpse of Leith, for, true to his word, he had slept elsewhere for the rest of the night.

Despite her hopes, however, Roderic was the only man in the hall, reminding her again of her shameful attempt at a midnight exodus. Surely he must think her insane, after her frenzied flight across the hall.

She sighed. A part of her still wished to flee, while a larger part of her wanted to be held again in Leith's strong arms, to hear him croon words of comfort.

Where was he? Rose swept the hall with her gaze, feeling that dreadful emptiness in her chest again.

In an effort to soothe her own thoughts and busy her hands she had repaired her old nun's habit. Rose smoothed a hand down the coarse fabric, realizing she had done a poor job of mending it, and wondering why she had forgotten how the thing itched.

Even after such a short time, it felt strange to don that humble garment again, and she scowled. Was it a sin, she wondered, to wear the robes of the Lord after the night just past? Or would God understand her need to don the garment as she tried to sort out her thoughts?

Upon her head she'd tied a plain linen kerchief, which held her hair from her face and freed her movements for the chores with which she hoped to occupy her time.

Hannah approached from behind and set a deep, wooden bowl of hot sowens before Rose, who lifted a spoon and tried to conjure up some appetite for the oat-bran porridge.

"Me lady?" Hannah spoke softly, her bright-green eyes wide in her oval face. "A favor I would ask of ye."

"A favor?" The scowl dropped from Rose's face. Vaguely she noticed that Harlow had entered the hall. But in an instant he turned, departing quickly. "What is it, Hannah?"

The girl's face flushed, and with some interest Rose noticed that she did not turn to see who might have come and gone so abruptly. "Me sister," said Hannah. "She is heavy with a bairn."

"'Tis a blessing of God," Rose said.

"Aye. But, ye see . . . " Hannah wrung her hands nervously. "She has lost two bairns already. Dead at birth, and after a terrible laying-in. I would na ask," she hurried to add, "if I didna fear so for her safety—and for the safety of the bairn. But she is me only sister, ye ken, and I am scairt of what will happen to Eve if she should lose this wee babe too."

"You want me to help with the birth?" Rose asked.

"'Tis a great deal I ask, I ken, me lady, but her time draws near." Hannah lowered herself quickly to the bench beside Rose. "And ye have proved yerself to be so kindly that I—"

"Hannah," Rose chided gently, "I am honored that you would ask." She took the girl's hand and watched as Hannah's eyes filled with tears. "Now don't cry," she said stiffly, for already she felt moisture clouding her own vision. "Please," she entreated, but it was too late.

"I love her so, and I do thank ye," sniffled Hannah.

Rose lost the battle with her tears.

From a short distance away, Roderic watched, making Rose feel foolish.

"Don't cry now," she said sniffing, "or we'll flood the entire keep. I will see to your sister when her time comes. Just make certain she remains as quiet as possible. No unnecessary work. In fact, no work at all. If she truly wants this child, she will remain abed until her time arrives."

"Abed?"

"Aye." Rose nodded, wiping away her tears with the back of her hand. "Tell her not to move unless it is absolutely necessary."

"Aye, me lady." Hannah nodded thankfully. "I will tell her."

"And see that she follows my advice, or—"

The hall door burst open, and a small lad staggered in, his arms filled with a long-haired sheephound that was nearly as large as himself. His breath rattled in deep gasps from his hurry, and his voice was a speedy jumble of Gaelic.

Rose stood quickly, noticing the dog's blood-coated fur, its limp neck. "What has happened here?" she asked, but now someone else stormed through the door.

He was a big man with oily, shoulder-length hair, a scowl on his face, and a stout stick held in a meaty hand. He spoke harsh words and, stepping forward, whipped the branch across the boy's back.

The lad barely grimaced, though his grip on the hound tightened protectively. "Dora—" he began, but the man snarled in return and raised the switch again.

In a single heartbeat Rose placed herself solidly between them.

Her feet were spread apart and her fists planted firmly on her hips.

"Touch the lad again," she said, her eyes narrowed to dangerous slits, "and I'll serve your head for supper."

The switch drooped for a moment as the man stared at her in shock. Then he snorted in derision.

"Out o' me way, slut!" he growled in English. "Or ye'll feel the switch yerself. The lad has shirked his duty once too often and will learn better by me hand."

Rose did not turn or flinch but stared him straight in the eye, her body stiff with rage. "It looks to me as though the boy has brought his dog to be healed. A task you would not be wise enough to do yerself."

It took a moment for the insult to seep through to the big man's brain, but when it did he raised his hand again to strike.

The switch never fell, however, for suddenly his wrist was caught in Roderic's steely grasp.

"Before ye hit her, know this," he warned, his tone low and raspy. "Me laird and brother has asked that I protect the lass while he hunts." He paused, letting his words settle for a moment. "Methinks he would be somewhat put out to see welts on his *lady's* face. Especially if they were put there by wolf bait like thee, Dermid."

Dermid's face paled three shades and his arm went limp so that Roderic finally relinquished his hold. "Nay! She is na the laird's lady!" denied Dermid.

"Aye." Roderic smiled grimly into the other's unshaven face. "She is. And if ye'd left yer hovel long enough to attend the feast, ye would have known as much."

" 'Twas busy," growled the man, lowering his switch but holding the timber hard.

"Busy starving the lad, looks like," said Roderic with a sneer. "What think ye, Fiona? Shall I take

the stick and give him a taste of his own broth?"
he asked, raising his voice slightly. But she was
already gone, directing the lad to carry his precious
bundle to a pile of rushes near the corner. "It seems
our lady has already forgotten ye, Dermid," he
said, and, placing his fists on his hips, widened his
stance and added, "A good thing horse dung is so
simple a thing to forget."

The man jerked. "Here now, the lad is me own
since me sister's death. He'll come home with me
now."

"He'll na," corrected Roderic, "unless ye wish to
leave yer head for the feast the lady described."

Dermid shook the mentioned head, and Roderic's smile brightened.

"Then I suggest ye let the boy rest the night here
and return on the morrow."

Blood rushed back to Dermid's face, but saying
naught, he turned with a snarl and left.

In the far corner the lad gently laid his hound on
the rushes. Below his threadbare plaid, Rose noticed that his scuffed, knobby knees shook with exhaustion.

"What happened, lad?" she asked, feeling the
dog's blood-soaked throat for the fragile pulse that
still beat there.

It took the boy a moment to speak. He swallowed hard, his green eyes round with unspoken
emotion. "Me and Dora . . . " he began finally, leaning forward on his knees between the dog's outstretched legs. "We took the sheep to Gorm Glen."
His hand wavered unsteadily as he wiped a filthy
hand across his nose. "I didna see the wolf. They
dunna attack in the summer, ye ken. I fell asleep."
He admitted his weakness with unbending stout-
ness. Not crying, not whimpering, merely saying

the words like a small soldier in shock. "I didna see him come. But Dora . . . " he said, stroking the long, tawny fur, "Dora . . . " His grubby hand shook again and his lips quivered.

"You are a brave lad," Rose whispered, feeling the painful lump of misery in her throat.

"Nay." A single denial wobbled from his gap-toothed mouth, though no tears fell. "I am na. I am worthless just as Dermid says." His voice trailed off and his lips quivered again, but he drew his back straighter, though his fingers were still tangled in the dog's fur. " 'Tis me fault."

Rose could barely make out his words and leaned closer, letting her own tears fall forgotten on the dog's matted fur.

He drew back slightly, as if he feared her nearness, but his voice came again, quieter still. "Me da gave her to me before he died."

Rose's throat ached with her sorrow. "Yer father must have loved ye dearly, for she is a fine dog."

"Aye." he nodded once, then wiped his nose again. "Aye. She was that. She was a verra fine lassie."

God's breath! Rose smeared her own tears across her cheek and let her nose run wild. "What do you mean 'was'?" she asked in feigned anger, though her voice trembled with a terrible sadness. "Did you not hear that I am a great healer?"

The boy nodded dismally, his mouth pursed, his cautious eyes showing the fragility of his belief in her. "Dermid doesna allow me to talk to others. But Douglas . . . " He swallowed again. "Douglas told me of yer miracles."

"And do you not believe I can mend your dog?" she asked, endeavoring to keep a haughty tone, though her heart felt like it might break within her chest.

He did not answer. He did not nod. Nor did he dare to ask even so much as a hopeful question, and in that moment Rose prayed as she had never prayed before, for if ever there was a child who needed her Lord's help, he sat before her now.

The divine answer seemed very clear to her and Rose smiled, ready to address the task before her. God forgive her for taking credit for the life she would now try to save. But the boy's sorrow wrenched her heart, and she could think of no other way to give him hope.

She could advise that he trust in God, but . . . Her eyes fell to a blistered welt that stretched across the back of his small hand. Mayhap he already believed in God, and had received little but pain for his faith. Let him believe in her for a short time and soon she would joyously give his faith over to the Lord.

"I shall need your help, young . . . "

"Roman." He said the name with some pride and drew himself rapidly to his feet, though his poor little knees shook with exhaustion. "I am Roman, me lady."

And God's most beautiful child, she thought. "Then, Roman, I will need you to sit right here," she said solemnly, unable to bear to make him stand a moment longer. Who knew how far he had carried the dog which weighed nearly as much as he? "You must talk to Dora," she commanded sternly. "Remind her of your love for her, and I am sure, if the Lord allows it, she will stay with you."

Roman sank slowly back down, and with a nod, placed a trembling hand on Dora's long, elegant nose.

From behind, Roderic cleared his throat. "Is

there naught I can do, me lady?" he asked, his
voice husky.

"Aye," she said, not taking her eyes from the
dog. "Get some hairs from a horse's tail ... and
pray."

Chapter 21

The flames of a five-prong pewter candelabra flickered in the momentary draft of the opened door, then straightened its slim lights to illuminate the shadowed hall.

"Welcome, brother," greeted Roderic, who stood and stretched. His tawny hair was tousled and on his handsome face was an expression Leith had learned to dread.

God save him from the amusement of identical twins.

"What is it?" Leith asked, his tone suspicious.

He'd left the hall early on the pretense of hunting, but instead had spent the day chasing his own scrambled thoughts and trying to make sense of the wee nun's confusing behavior. First she was cool, then she was hot—then she was crying, when he knew all along that she wanted him.

His own weakness irritated him and he scowled darkly. "What has she done now?"

Roderic laughed outright, entirely unimpressed by his brother's grim mood as he waved toward the far corner of the hall. "See for yerself."

Leith's dark gaze swept to the dimly lit spot indicated by Roderic's wave.

"For the sake of Jesu!" he exclaimed moodily before striding off toward the dim corner. "What is this?" he asked, not trusting himself to judge the situation correctly.

Roderic stopped beside him, gripping the handle to a mug of ale in each hand. "It's a dog, me liege, a lad, and . . . yer lady."

A muscle jumped in Leith's cheek. He allowed himself to speak the most impressive obscenity he could muster, but it did little to improve his mood.

Fiona Rose Gunther MacAulay Forbes lay upon the crumpled reeds like a felled fairy, her fiery hair billowing in every direction, her rose-petal lips parted with each gentle breath and her glorious body clothed in those awful rags in which he had first seen her.

"I know it's me lady," Leith said, "but what the devil is she doing here?"

Roderic lifted his brows and canted his head as he gazed down at her. "I dunna wish to assume too much, me laird," he ventured finally, "but it looks to me like she's . . . sleeping."

"Damn it to hell, lad," Leith growled. "I should have drowned ye like a runt pup when ye were first birthed. Either tell me what happened or get the hell out of me way so I may ask her."

Roderic laughed again, but softly now, for the lass had stirred and he had no wish to wake her. "Nay, brother. Let the lady sleep," Roderic managed finally, though he did not quite subdue his grin. Leith was a great laird, a fierce fighter, and a fine man, but he had no sense of humor, a fact that had always caused the twins great enjoyment. "She has had a long and wearisome day."

"Tell me."

"Have a drink," urged Roderic as he lifted a cup toward his brother. "Ye may need it."

Leith accepted the proffered mug, took a small, obligatory sip, and waited.

"The lad's name is Roman," Roderic said flatly and paused.

Leith's scowl deepened. "Roman?" he asked, then leaned closer to peer into the gaunt, filthy face. "Lachlan's lad?"

"Aye," answered Roderic grimly. "Dermid has been . . . caring for him since his mother's passing."

"Caring for?" Leith snorted, noting the bruises on the boy's thin, bare legs. "Like hell."

"Aptly put," acknowledged Roderic. "The lad was grazing Dermid's sheep in Gorm Glen. It seems he fell asleep. The dog was attacked by a wolf." Roderic paused, taking another sip. " 'Twould appear even young Roman had heard of the lady's great healing powers, and carried the cur here for help."

"Nay."

One grubby hand lay on the hound's bandaged shoulder, while the other was tangled in the dog's tawny fur.

"Nay." Leith repeated, shaking his head. " 'Tis three miles to Gorm Glen."

"Aye," agreed Roderic

"He could na have borne the cur all that distance."

Roderic shrugged. "He was given the dog by his father."

Leith swore again, his guilt an awful burden to bear. Before his eyes lay another child he had neglected to place in proper care.

"The lad's legs were shaking like the branches of a willow when he arrived," said Roderic. "But of course Dermid was chasing him with a switch. I suspect that would make any lad hasten."

"Chasing him?"

"Intending to beat him for leaving the sheep."

"Ye didna allow it?" Leith asked finally, his tone such a low rumble of anger that it was barely audible.

" 'Twas Fiona." Roderic nodded toward the sleeping girl. "*She* didna allow it."

Leith's brows shot up.

"Aye. 'Tis true," Roderic said, his own gaze steady on the lass. " 'Twould seem she had plans to serve Dermid's head for supper if he touched the lad again, and was na scairt to tell him as much."

"Nay!" exclaimed Leith, but his nostrils flared and his chest hurt with pride. "And what did Dermid say?"

"He lifted his hand to strike her."

"Nay!" This time the denial was a growl. "I'll reserve his eyeballs for mine own dessert."

"Dunna fear, brother. I prevented the wee lass from killing him so that ye may have the honor yerself."

Leith nodded. "Ye have me thanks." His gaze shifted from Rose's peaceful face to the hound. One leg was braced with flat wooden slats and bound with strips of cloth. Much of the tawny fur had been clipped away, revealing tidy rows of horsehair stitches, and near the base of the hound's neck was a fearsome wound that had been only partly sewn. Under the flesh and sutures ran a narrow piece of linen that stretched from one open end of the wound to the other.

"Holy Jesu!" said Leith, eyeing Rose's handiwork.

Roderic shrugged, easily admitting his perplexity. "The lass has her own way of doing things. 'Twould seem she thinks the poison will drain if she leaves the linen in."

Leith shook his head. He'd thought *he'd* had a hard day. But she'd been left to deal with a crazed Scotsman, a grieving lad, and his brother's tiring sense of humor. He should have stayed with her.

"She sleeps like the dead," he said, revealing none of his tender feelings.

"She sleeps like an angel," Roderic corrected.

Leith sighed, pulling his eyes from the lass. "Ye too, Rod?" he asked wearily, but Roderic only laughed with self-deprecating ease.

"Ye didna think ye could bring a fairy goddess to Glen Creag and expect us na to notice, did ye, brother?" he asked, then slapped Leith's arm in casual camaraderie. "The lass has had herself a long day. Let her sleep, me liege."

"Down here for every randy soldier to view at will?" Leith asked soberly. "Na," he answered himself, and, stepping forward, lifted Rose carefully from the reeds.

She was as light as thistledown in his arms. He breathed in her scent and bore her up the steps two at a time. She did not open her eyes till he set her on his own mattress.

"Roman?" She pulled herself upright, looking disoriented. "I must see to him. So much lost already."

"The lad is fine."

She shook her head with a scowl. "I must . . . "

"Lie down, lass," he urged gently. "I will bring him up."

Trotting down the stairs, Leith cursed himself for a thousand fools. He should have more pride than to let his supposed lady of the hall mess with stinking hounds. But then his chest again filled with pride at the thought of her and he bent, lifting young Roman into his arms.

"Please!" The lad's eyes opened wide in terror as he leaned sharply away from his laird. "I couldna leave her," he whimpered, covering his face with a hand and showing the evil welt across the backside. "Dunna let her die. I'll do better. Work harder."

"Sweet Jesu." Leith gritted his teeth and wished to hell Dermid was there to receive the brunt of his anger. "Nay, lad, dunna fret," he said, trying to soften his tone. "For ye are safe here with the Lady Fiona."

Roman relaxed marginally, though his emerald eyes did not narrow and he yet leaned away from Leith's chest. "And . . ." he began, swallowing hard. "Dora?"

"She yet lives, lad," said Leith, unable to meet the boy's frightened stare. "Roderic," he called gruffly, knowing he would be the laughingstock of the Highlands if others knew his softness. "Bring the dog to me bed."

Rose awoke with a start.

Where was Leith?

What time was it?

Had the old bastard Dermid returned?

God's whiskers! She must find Leith. Explain the situation. Plead for his understanding. She scrambled from the bed and her eyes widened.

Roman! And the dog Dora? On Leith's bed? But how?

Memories drenched in fatigue and uncertainty rose mistily to her still-fuzzy brain. Leith had returned, and carried her upstairs. He had held her in his arms. She could still feel the warmth and strength of him, and even now yearned for . . .

No. She would not think about it. Roman needed her. Old Dermid, damn him to hell, would return for the boy, but first she must convince Leith to protect the lad. She must, no matter how angry he was at her for interfering.

Her hands were sweating, she realized, and, chastising herself for her own horrid weakness, she hurried from the room.

She heard Leith's voice even before she reached the top of the stairs.

"I said nay!" he roared, nearly shaking the hall with his answer, before dropping his voice to a deep-throated growl. "Ye will na take the lad to-day, nor ever. Ye have given up all rights of blood, and I have claimed the lad for mine own."

"Ye canna . . ." sputtered a voice from below, but the sentence was never finished.

"I can do as I please!" snarled Leith. "And just now it would please me to see yer head on a pike!" He paused for a moment. "I suggest ye leave me hall before I see me pleasure fulfilled."

There was the sound of footsteps stumbling backward, and then a scrambling noise as Dermid spun about and fled the hall.

Rose saw him pass Harlow, who was on his way in, and was vaguely aware of the snarled curses the old man heaped upon the laird's head. Stopping midway down the stairs, Rose bit her lip, losing herself in thought, before she turned and hurried back up to Roman and his hound.

It had been a long day, spent mostly tending to Dora and Roman. At last, Rose lay alone, stretched beneath a plaid in her modest nightrail, waiting.

Time passed slowly, her thoughts drifted, but finally she heard steps in the hallway. He was coming, she thought frantically, and though she had carefully planned her words, she closed her eyes and feigned sleep.

Leith came quietly into the chamber, then closed the door behind him, shutting out the dim light from the hall.

In a moment he was across the floor and seated on the bed beside her. He removed his horsehide boots and sat for a moment, seeming deep in thought.

Behind his broad back, Rose opened her eyes and bit her lip. This was the moment she had prepared for, and yet she felt uncertain.

"My laird," she said softly.

He turned, looking formidable as he faced her.

"Fiona," he murmured. "I expected ye to be fast asleep."

She drew a steadying breath and propped herself up on one elbow, though she could not quite meet his eyes.

"I wished to . . . thank you, while we had some time alone," she said.

"Thank me?"

"Aye. For your kindness to Roman."

Leith drew a deep breath, letting his gaze skim her full lips. "Roman is me kinsman," he said quietly. " 'Tis I who should thank ye."

Her gaze rose to his face, which hid his feelings well. "I know what it is to be without parents," she reminded him softly. "He is lucky to have a laird who is so caring."

"Nay," Leith said soberly. "I should have seen to his welfare long before. I fear I have done the lad a grave disservice with me lack of attention to his needs."

"Do not worry for Roman," Rose said softly. "He will be a great man someday."

"And how do ye ken that, sweet lass?"

She drew a deep breath, fully acknowledging her gift for the first time. "I see it in my head. He will grow to be a strong, compassionate man. And who is to say, mayhap the years of hardship have made it possible for him to fulfill his destiny."

"Glad I am to hear that ye have accepted the sight," Leith said quietly. "But the fact remains that I have failed the lad."

"Nay, my laird," she said, finally daring to place a hand on his, where it rested on the bed beside his powerful thigh. "Ye expect too much of yourself. You are only one man."

He was silent for a moment. "Nay," he corrected, "I am laird."

She smiled just a little, amused. "But are ye not still a man?"

"Aye," he answered. "I am indeed a man."

"Aye," she agreed, nodding, her chest feeling tightly bound as she touched him. "Aye, a man," she whispered. "And a good one."

Sweet Jesu. Leith stared into her violet eyes. He loved her. His chest ached with that hopeless knowledge. But in a moment he straightened his thoughts. She would love him. She must. For the sake of his clan, he thought. But past the edge of conscious thought a voice whispered that he lied. She must love him for the sake of his heart.

"Lass," he said, lost in the depths of her eyes, "I would ask ye a question this night."

"Yes." Rose said the word quickly, looking frightened.

"What?" He canted his head at her, holding his breath.

"The answer," she whispered, seeming to read his mind. "It's yes."

Painful expectation gripped Leith, and a joy so great that it seemed to rip his heart, but he dared not misinterpret her words. "Ye shall be me bride?" he asked carefully, and Rose swallowed.

"I will lie with you as your bride," she corrected. "I will agree to the document signed by Ian

MacAulay. I will put this matter into our Lord's hands."

Leith felt breathless and tense. "And at the year's end?"

"If I conceive a child, I will consider it a sign from God that I should stay. And if I do not—"

"Nay." He lifted one finger, pressing it firmly to her parted lips. "Dunna say it, lass." He smiled, sure his heart would burst with the force of his hope. "For there will be a child."

"How do you know?"

Her voice was breathy, her eyes wide, and when his lips touched hers, he thought surely they would both burst into flame.

"Because it is meant to be, lass. 'Tis all meant to be," he murmured, and ever so gently touched her throat with his fingertips.

Her eyes fell closed and she trembled.

"Do I frighten ye, lass?" he whispered, and she shook her head.

"You do not." She opened her eyes to look deep into his. "But the wait worries me a great deal."

"The wait?" he asked, skimming his fingers down the graceful curve of her throat.

"Waiting." She shivered. "For ecstasy."

"Ah," he breathed, and, leaning across her, he smiled into her eyes. "Then ye shall wait na longer, lass, for I am yers."

"All of you?" she murmured huskily.

"Every thought." Taking her hand gently in his, Leith pulled it to his brow, where the dark hair was swept back. "Every beat of me heart." He drew her hand lower, letting it slide sensuously down his throat to rest under his voluminous saffron shirt. "Every touch." His kiss was butterfly-soft against her ear. "Every inch," he rasped, and bore her fingers gently down to where his manhood surged hard and eager against his flat abdomen.

She felt it through the soft wool of his plaid and her body grew hot and impatient. "You're an evil influence, my laird," she breathed, but her husky tone made the accusation a lie.

"Aye, that I am."

"And . . . hard."

"Aye," he agreed, letting his fingers find the edge of her nightrail and the soft, firm flesh of her thigh.

"And very . . . very large." Her hand enclosed his stiff rod.

He chuckled against her ear, sending shivers down her spine. "Aye, lass. That I am."

"And horribly conceited."

" 'Tis true." He sighed, and, leaning forward, kissed the delicate hollow of her throat. His kisses trailed sideways, widening the laced gap at the top of her gown, so that her shoulder was soon bared for his caresses.

"You know I am not a patient person," Rose whispered.

The gap widened further still, so that soon, with the help of one hand, he was able to press the entire garment downward.

He pulled back slightly, eyeing her lovely breasts with undisguised hunger. "A wise woman once told me that patience is sadly overrated."

"How very true." She nodded, holding her breath.

"I'm giving you to the count of five to remove your clothes," she whispered.

"And then?"

"I will not be responsible for my actions."

"Holy Jesu!"

"Save your prayers," she advised. "One. Two."

His clothes were gone before the count of four. In a moment she was pressed against his body, hard and strong above her.

His kisses were like midnight magic. His touch was like heaven. And when he entered her, she felt as if she would die from pleasure.

"Ye will be glad of yer decision to stay, lass," he murmured, establishing a slow, erotic rhythm against her.

"I already am."

"And it shall get better still."

"It can't."

"Ah, lass," he whispered raggedly, "never question the skill and endurance of a Scotsman."

"Why?" she rasped, closing her eyes to the crescendo of sensation.

"Because then I will be compelled to prove me mettle."

"God forbid," she groaned.

"Dunna groan," he pleaded.

"I . . ." She was breathing hard and fast, matching him stroke for stroke. " . . . can't help it," she moaned, tilting her head back slightly.

"Dunna do that either," he begged, trying to wait, to prolong the ecstasy.

"Leith!" she cried raggedly. "I need you . . . now!"

With a shudder he brought them both to the summit of pleasure, then tumbled with her over the far side.

Finally she curled against him, warm and soft and sleepy.

Leith sighed, kissing her forehead.

"Next time," he promised wearily. "Next time I will prove me mettle."

Chapter 22

The days hurried by for Rose, filled with the gathering of herbs and the bandaging of wounds.

On the second day Dora licked Rose's hand. On the third she raised her head to drink a bit of beef broth. Roman stayed by his dog's side like a tick; only his eyes followed Rose as she moved about the hall. It was filled with soldiers who jostled each other along the wooden benches and waited for the evening meal.

Servers hurried down the rows, filling bowls with hearty stew and sliding trenchers of brown bread onto tables.

There was the usual boisterous atmosphere, with voices raised and laughter booming. But all was different for Rose now, for though she was not fully accepted, she was certainly becoming so, and she smiled, feeling whole and alive for the first time in a long while.

Sensing Roman's gaze on her, she turned to smile at him. His charm had been diminished by a bath and a clean set of clothes.

"She is doing well?" Rose called across the din.

"Aye, me lady," answered Roman in Gaelic, for it had become his self-appointed task to teach her the language of the Highlands. A wayward thatch of carrot- bright hair fell over his eyes. He pushed it aside with a quick hand. "She is doing fine."

Behind Rose the door swung open and she turned, seeing a gray-haired man enter. He did not wear the plaid of the Forbes and she puzzled over his identity. But only for a moment.

"Ho, Bernard," shouted a soldier, and the call was taken up around the hall.

"Bernard, auld man, sing us a song," someone called.

"Aye." The bard grinned, his face lighting with a smile. "If it pleases yer laird."

"Aye," said Leith, already seated in his massive chair at the end of a trestle table. "But ye are welcome to eat first."

"Nay," countered the storyteller, and for a moment Rose wondered if she saw a spark of mischief in his eyes, "I would sing first, me laird, so that ye might decide if me tune is worthy of yer meal."

Leith's brows rose slightly, but he lifted his big shoulders and inclined his head. "As ye wish."

The bard nodded and went to pull a seat before the harp. Tilting the big instrument into his lap, he set his fingers to the sinewy strings. Music drifted upward like clouds on a clear summer's day, conjuring images with its sparkling notes.

Voices fell silent and finally Bernard's song lifted from his lips, the sound fair and enchanting. Old battles were remembered, lost loves, childhood dreams, all drawn forth by the beauty of his words, the magic of his melodies. Finally he paused, pushing the harp away to speak.

"I would sing to ye a special song now—at the request of the son of the laird of the clan MacGowan."

Murmurs rose from the crowd.

"Seems he battled with a fierce foe," Bernard continued. "And just when he thought all was lost, a fairy appeared. A fairy so wondrously bonny he could but stare in awe." Bernard's sparkling eyes settled on Rose, who watched him in surprise and some embarrassment as she remembered the night of the young man's rescue. The old bard shifted his gaze and smiled. "I will sing ye this song that ye may decide if she be a fairy or a lass of flesh and blood. And mayhap," he added, "ye may yet believe ye yerselves have been blessed with a visit from that very same *bean-sith*."

All eyes were trained on the mesmerizing old bard, for the meal was nearly finished and his words were indeed provocative.

His voice floated over the hall like liquid velvet, soft and lush, then rough and crisp. He sang of the miraculous appearance of a fairy queen who ascended from the bowels of night to save young Gregor from a watery death. Her hair, he said, was like living flame, her eyes like amethyst jewels, and at her lovely fingertips was the gift of life.

Large bodies shifted as man after man turned to grin at Rose, who squirmed nervously in her padded chair, avoiding their gazes. These Scots certainly knew how to embarrass a lass.

"But fairy or flesh," sang old Bernard in softly burred English, "young Gregor MacGowan will come to the lass and marry her yet. He'll come to the lass and marry her yet."

Silence filled the room for a split second before the hall erupted in noise.

"Nay!" shouted Alpin, captain of the guard. "The young swain is too late, for the laird of the Forbes has already claimed the fairy's hand."

"Indeed," agreed Roderic, standing to raise his mug. "He has claimed her for the clan Forbes."

"For the Forbes!" yelled the Scotsmen.

"Hail Laird Leith!" chanted the assemblage, and

then in a cheer that fairly shook the rafters, "Hail Lady Fiona!"

God's whiskers, thought Rose as tears filled her eyes. Who would have thought she would become so mired in Leith's devilish ploy? And who would have thought she would grow to love these people so well?

In her bedchamber that night, Rose allowed Hannah to wash her hair with fragrant soap. She had balked at the idea at first, for she had not yet grown accustomed to being waited on. But, sighing now, Rose found she did not regret her decision, for though her own nudity in front of another made her uncomfortable, the girl's gentle hands and thoughtful ministrations felt wonderful. Having applied a chamomile and herb mixture to her hair, Hannah gently tugged at Rose's snarls until they came free.

Finally the dark-cinnamon tresses were carefully rinsed with water still warm from the fire. Rose tilted her head back. Leith had said he would be late to bed, for he had a message to send to the MacGowans.

"One more bucket, me lady, and then Judith will bring yer warm milk," said Hannah, and carefully splashed water across her mistress' head and ears.

So it was that Rose failed to hear the door open.

Leith stopped as his gaze became riveted on the woman in his bath. Her eyes were closed, her head tilted back. With lush, taut breasts pressed toward the ceiling, Fiona Rose looked like the sea fairies Alpin had described to him as a wee lad.

That fanciful image had stayed with Leith through his adolescence, keeping him awake and fretful more nights than he cared to remember, until manhood came with the death of his father and he was forced to give up his vivid fantasies of luscious water nymphs and the earthy games one might play with them.

Now, however, there was one of the enchanted folk in his own chamber. In his own bath.

Hannah's eyes were wide with surprise, and though she did not stop the slow ebb of water over her mistress' face and hair, her cheeks were pink with embarrassment.

Leith managed some sympathy for her, for she was only a maid, but he'd be damned before he would leave the sea nymph's side.

The old bard's song had disturbed him no small whit, reminding him that the lass was not rightfully his and would flee at the year's end if a child was not conceived. Seeing her thus, however, drove away all thoughts but one. Desire. And so he trod carefully across the woolen rug toward the wooden vat.

Taking the bucket from the maid's hands, he continued the rinse while nodding for her to leave.

She did so in a silent rush, closing the door behind her.

He and the sea fairy were alone. With rapt appreciation Leith let his gaze slip across the delicate ridges of her nose and chin. Her neck was smooth, pale, and slightly arched, her shoulders neat hillocks of ivory. But it was her breasts that made his nostrils flare and his breath come hard.

Sweet Jesu, she had beautiful breasts. Firm, full mounds capped with rosebud tips that blushed with the promise of full bloom.

"All done, Hannah?" she asked, eyes still closed in anticipation of more water.

Leith's chest felt constricted. With some surprise he realized he was shirking his job, for the flow of water had stopped, though the bucket was not yet empty. Gently tipping the wooden pail again, he let the last of the rinse water fall over her hair before settling to his knees beside the tub.

Her lips parted slightly as she lifted a hand to smooth water from the crown of her head. "Done?" she asked again.

"Nay, lass. We have na yet begun."

Her eyes flew open. He was near enough for her to smell the warm, male scent of him.

"Where is Hannah?" she asked weakly, feeling her nipples tighten in the air that seemed suddenly charged with tension.

"She had other duties," Leith said. "And I thought meself capable of . . . this task."

Gently he lifted a ribbon of hair from her breast, not mentioning what other tasks he could think to do. Wet and smooth, the hair slipped with liquid softness over her skin, looking sable-dark and slick with water.

"In truth," he added, carefully placing the tress against the otter-sleek mass of her hair, "I wouldna have another do . . . this task."

"My laird," she whispered, still caught in that same pose that had caused Leith's nether parts to spring to life beneath his plaid, "my bath is complete." Regardless of her decision to fully act the part of a handfasted maid, Rose felt painfully embarrassed about her own nudity and Leith's nearness. "You . . . you may have the tub."

"Is that an invitation, lass?" he murmured, his lips so close to her ear that his words seemed to reverberate down her spine, sending frenzied sparks of excitement through her.

"My laird," she whispered breathlessly, "you must think me a brazen hussy indeed. When in fact . . . " she began, but just then his lips found hers and played with sensual purpose across them.

"Sweet, gentle lass," he murmured, cupping her delicate neck. "How could ye know just when I would arrive?"

She tried to deny his suggestion, but he'd already tired of words and now slipped his tongue sensuously across her lips. It caused her to tremble to the core of her being, but he had only just begun. His fingertips slid from beneath her hair and blazed a trail across one shoulder and between her breasts.

"Fiona," he whispered. " 'Tis a just name. Fair one. Daughter of the king of the seals."

She tried to respond, but his hand had dipped beneath the water to lightly skim the dark triangle of hair between her thighs.

A gasp was all the response she could manage.

"Fiona," he said again, kissing the corner of her mouth. "Perched upon a rock in her watery world, awaiting some mere mortal man to corrupt."

"As if any could corrupt you," Rose murmured, but now the flat of his fingers eased over the swollen folds of her womanhood, and this time her gasp was more of a moan, coming from deep in her throat as she pressed against his hand.

"Leith, we mustn't. Truly, 'tis not a good time."

"Aye, love," he crooned throatily, pressing his bare chest closer still. " 'Tis," he insisted, and she arched slightly upward, turning her face so that her cheek was against his hard, smooth chest.

His hand had taken up a rhythmic movement and her body followed of its own accord. Her lips were parted, showing the pearly rows of her teeth, and her eyes were closed, so that the dark forest of her lashes lay softly against her ivory skin.

He kissed her again. Not gently now, but deep and hard, and she answered back, forgetting everything and gripping his plaid where it crossed near his wounded shoulder.

Sweet Jesu, she was as hot as a glowing coal in his hand, as desperate as he for fulfillment. He could wait no longer. He could not. No man should be expected to do so.

Letting his hand continue to ride her, Leith drew his mouth away. She groaned and sought to drag him closer, but he was busy trying to loosen his belt single-handedly. She moaned in frustration. His chest was near and she kissed it, feeling him jerk at the touch of her lips. His obvious excitement only stoked her own and she pulled him closer with considerable force and found his nipple with her mouth.

"Sweet Jesu!" he rasped, jerking his hand from his belt. "Lass, do na—"

But she did!

He could feel her teeth and tongue as she suckled him.

"Please! Fiona!" He groaned and tried again to undo his belt.

She arched upward. Her breasts, wet and smooth, coursed against his belly.

Breath hissed between his teeth. "Jesu!" he gritted in agony and in that moment pulled the belt free. His plaid fell away and he rose quickly, dragging her with him.

She was hot and slippery and he pressed her to his chest with a groan.

Between them his engorged manhood throbbed with urgency. Her hand caught his hair and she pulled him closer, finding his mouth with her own.

"Sweet . . . " He caught her round buttocks in his spread hands, pulling her from the water, and she bent her legs to wrap them about his waist. "Lass!" he groaned, pressing hard against her.

They were so close—within a heartbeat of ecstasy, but footsteps sounded in the hall.

For one instant he was pressing toward his most earnest desire with desperate urgency, and the next he was grappling to hold her still.

There was a breathy shriek against his ear, a slither of luscious flesh against his, and then she was gone, flying across the room to yank a sheet about her.

"Me lady," Judith called, and in that instant, Leith swiped up a towel to cover his aching private parts.

"Yer milk, me lady." The door swung open and Judith stepped inside.

Her jaw sank like a rock.

Before her stood the laird of the Forbes, seeming to have just exited his bath, and caught in wordless immobility.

"Bless me!" Judith said, shaking so badly the warm milk sloshed over her fingers.

"Don't ye knock, woman?" Leith questioned, his voice low.

"I . . . Oh!" The elderly woman inched backward, bumping into the half-open door. "I . . . Forgive me!" she squeaked, and fled the room in panic, slamming the door behind her.

Leith turned with deliberate slowness, his manhood still high and aching behind the towel. "Come here, lass" he ordered.

Rose shook her head, backing away and trying not to laugh as she shook her finger at him. "I told you 'twas not a good time."

"Lass," he warned, "come here."

"Nay." She tripped on the tail of her sheet, only to bump into the bed behind her and finally stumble onto it. "'Tis very late. And I am . . . " She faked a yawn and hurried carefully backward across the feather tick. " . . . so very tired. Could you please ask Judith to bring my milk that I might . . . "

"I have brought ye sommat better," Leith growled, and, lunging forward, snatched her sheet away.

She fell to the bed with a squeal and a giggle, but both sounds were lost beneath his kiss and the sweet, hot press of his body.

The morning was wind-tickled and ruffled with clouds.

Rose stretched toward the turquoise sky and smiled, remembering the night just past.

Leith had left their bed early. So she had risen too, and stood now, holding Maise's reins and gazing out upon the beauty of Leith's domain. She'd left the castle with the promise of not venturing too far, and though she had earnestly set out in search of medicinal herbs, she'd been too intrigued by the awe-inspiring land around her to remember her promise to remain close to the castle.

As it was, she had gone farther than she'd planned and stood now beside Creag Burn. It was a noisy river that flowed with white-water quickness over the brown boulders it was named for. The chuckling sound of the river seemed to speak to Rose, and she bent to pick a few flowers and meander along the water's serpentine course.

To her left a tawny shadow followed her and she smiled. It had been long indeed since she'd been afforded the freedom to ride with the wild feline at her side. Silken had been seen bedding down in the loft above the stables, and she knew Leith was to be thanked for the animal's protection. Perhaps the Forbes felt a special kinship with wildcats, since their crest boasted that beautiful animal. Or, Rose thought, biting her lip, perhaps it was her own high regard for the cat that caused Leith to protect it.

That thought seemed to make Rose's heart beat heavily in her chest. Could it be that he cared for her just a little?

He was a laird to respect. A man to look up to. An enemy to fear. And a lover to make a woman's blood race.

Of course he did not love her, he only desired the magic they found together in his bed. But wasn't it possible that she might someday win his love? If she was kind and gentle? If she was soft-spoken and . . .

But she was not. She cursed like a warlord—by his own admission. She rode like a man. And once she had beat him with a felled branch.

Soft-spoken? Hah! She was lucky to avoid being dangerous when he was near.

From the bushes beside her, Rose heard Silken issue a strange sound from his throat. Turning, she saw him standing in the shade of a bent elder, his pointed ears pitched forward as he peered up the rocky slope from whence the water tumbled.

"What . . . Oh!" Rose drew a sharp breath.

Had she seen something move? Or was it simply a feeling so intense that a visible image had burned itself across her mind? Fair hair. Plaid.

"Silken?" She whispered the cat's name, though she knew not why. Dropping the flowers, she walked slowly toward the bottom of the slope.

Ahead, smooth brown rocks led upward in step-like ascent. Purple heather grew in clumps amidst prickly gorse and coarse grasses.

There! At the top. A movement!

Or not?

Rose shook her head, trying to deny the shivery feelings that skimmed up her arms. She should return to Glen Creag immediately. But . . .

A shadow flitted across her mind and she halted, waiting, breath held, heart thumping.

Nothing. No sound. But something called to her, something she could neither define nor resist.

She climbed despite the branches that grabbed at her skirt and the rocks that slipped beneath her soft-shod feet.

Her breath came hard and fast. Something drew her. Her eyes were trained on the top of the ridge and her heart pounded like a thousand hoofbeats in her chest.

Emotions of varying hues washed over her. She was nearly there. Only a few more steps and . . .

A flash of tartan!

"No!" she screamed, feeling the evil intent like a blow to her chest. "No!" She stumbled back. Terror gripped her heart, and then she was running, scrambling down the slope. Rocks slid and bounced away. From somewhere above Silken snarled, but Rose did not stop. Death! Death was near!

Panic rose like bile, stiffening her legs, and suddenly she was falling.

Her shoulder hit a rock, and then her hip. Plants flashed past. Her arms flailed wildly, searching for a grip, but suddenly the world stilled its careening movement.

Her breath came in painful gasps and she moaned, cradling an elbow in her opposite hand.

There was the sound of boots on rocks. Fresh panic nabbed her and she abandoned her elbow to cover her face with the back of her arm.

"Please," she whimpered, raising her eyes.

Harlow stood not three strides away. His expression was taut and unreadable. Over his shoulder hung a bow.

Her body trembled as chaotic emotions clashed within her. Fear? Relief? Terror?

Her hand slipped lower, her skinned knuckles pressing against her quivering lips.

"Harlow?" she whispered, premonition and logic merging and drowning.

Hoofbeats thundered toward them, and suddenly, like a flash of heat lightning, Leith was there, mounted on the pearly back of his great stallion.

"Leith." She said his name like a prayer.

He slid from Beinn's back even before the giant hooves were still, and in a moment he was gathering her into his arms, smoothing back her hair. "What happened?" he asked, his voice terse with emotion, his arms tight around her.

She tried to speak, but she could not. There was nothing to explain, for she understood none of what had transpired. Tightening her grip on his shirt, she viewed the evil again in her mind, though it was more misty now and already fading.

He felt her fear nevertheless, and his own body remained like a shield against hers. "Harlow?" he growled, his face a mask of horrible anger. "Did he—"

"Nay!" It took Rose a moment to understand his question, but she raised her eyes quickly. "Nay, Leith," she whispered, consciously relaxing her grip as she viewed his flint-hard expression. "He did not hurt me."

Leith's gaze remained on Rose's face, but his jaw was clenched and in his eyes Rose saw hot rage.

"Leith." She said his name softly, and, reaching up, touched the scar on his right cheek. "He did not hurt me. I was merely foolish and in my haste, I fell."

Uncertainty tortured Leith. Was she lying to save another? Certainly he could not rule out such a possibility, for she'd already proven her willingness to protect others despite great risk to herself.

Harlow was one of his own. He could not accuse the man without just cause. Did the incident by the river where Rose had bathed justify Leith's mistrust of the lad? Harlow had, at the least, planned some mischief there, even if he had not actually hurt the lass.

Rose looked up at him with those entreating violet eyes, mentally pleading with him to hold his temper. He could feel her thoughts.

Holy Jesu, how had they come to this point, where she was the protector of his people? *His* people, for whom he would give his life. But how much more would he give for her?

"Come, lass," he said quietly, though his tone was steely. "I will take ye home."

Her arms slipped about his neck, and as she settled her head against his chest, her gaze slid to Harlow.

He stood immobile, his hands clenched into fists, his eyes filled with hopelessness.

Chapter 23

Numerous pairs of eyes followed them as Leith carried Rose through the hall to the stairs, but it was Roman who drew her attention, for he stood at the foot of the steps, one small hand clutching Dora's fur, his green eyes wide.

"Me lady?" he said softly, and Rose noticed with heart-wrenching pain that his face was as pale as his hound's bandages. "Ye are hurt?" he asked.

"No," Rose said, peeping over the barrier of Leith's shoulder. "I am fine." She smiled, hoping to soothe his worry. " 'Tis just that our Laird Leith likes to display his manly strength by carrying me."

"Yer na hurt?" The lad's eyes were as large as goose eggs, but he followed behind them, his steps slow, his expression solemn.

"No."

"She is hurt," Leith amended, taking the steps in twos. "She's just too daft to know it."

Rose smiled at Roman again before glowering at Leith, who returned her fierce expression, though he now found he could not bear to worry the boy with theories of which he himself was uncertain. Especially after seeing Roman in the stable with Harlow just that morning—talking seriously with that young man as if they shared some history. And perhaps they did, Leith thought. The history of abuse and neglect. Sweet Jesu! A muscle jumped in his cheek, but Rose's continued scowl reminded him of the lad's worry and he brightened his tone to say, " 'Twould seem our lady thought she was a fine spring doe, and came scampering down the hillock. Only, she had but two legs and fell head over arse."

"Leith!" Rose scolded, hurrying her gaze to Roman again. "You mustn't use such language around the lad."

"Roman is a Scot," Leith said, finally reaching the bed to settle her gingerly upon it "With a brawny body and a sharp mind. He knows an arse when he sees one. Do ye na, Roman?"

"Aye." Roman came to a halt by the door and nodded solemnly. "That I do, me laird," he agreed, but his voice was faint and uncertain, as though he feared his words might cause anger.

Leith turned slowly, feeling dull rage fill his chest again at the thought of the lad's mistreatment. How could any man be filled with such hate that he would abuse a child so, battering his body as well as his mind? Leith placed his fists on his hips and leveled a stare at the boy.

"Our lady has been scraped and bruised because of her own foolishness," he said soberly. "It seems she will need someone to keep her put while I do a few tasks. Are ye up to the job, lad?"

Moving his gaze from Leith to Rose, Roman tightened his grip on Dora's fur and nodded earnestly. "Aye, me laird. I shall guard her with mine life."

A gentle warmth lit Leith's eyes and in that moment Rose was sorely tempted to kiss him, for no man alive could care more for this orphaned boy, she was sure.

" 'Tis a fine thing that ye came to us at Glen Creag," Leith said solemnly. "For it seems I need help protecting a lady as foolish as our Fiona."

For a moment Roman did not blink or breathe, but stood like one in fear of great pain. Nevertheless, he spoke finally, his small chin firm and slightly lifted as he dared gainsay the huge laird who would determine his future. "I dunna think her foolish," he said, his voice faint, his fingers firmly wound into Dora's fur. "Only high-spirited."

Leith's expression was somber. "Loyalty. 'Tis a rare and precious thing, young Roman," he said huskily. "The lady is blessed to have gained yers."

Leith was gone for nearly an hour, and in that time Rose discovered several things. Firstly, he had been devious in his means of keeping her still, for surely she would not injure Roman's tender feelings by trying to leave.

Secondly, Roman's charm had not been diminished by Dermid's cruel hand, though the lad seemed ever afraid of human contact and sat on the far side of the bed as he told stories he must have weaved for himself and Dora while guarding sheep.

And thirdly, Dora the dog stank to high heaven.

It was the third issue she was attempting to tactfully address when Leith returned.

He stopped in the doorway as she broached the subject of a canine bath.

Roman's voice chimed in. Rose answered, and Leith realized with some amazement that he was listening attentively to their words. Holy Jesu, even her simplest conversation held him breathless, while the sight of her upon his bed made his chest ache. But it was her with a child that made his heart hurt. If ever a woman was meant to nurture young ones, it was she.

But that was not his first concern now. What had happened by the river's falls? Had Harlow tried to harm her or had she merely fallen as she'd said?

His conversation with the younger man had revealed little, for Harlow had seemed tense and defensive, which had done nothing to lessen Leith's suspicions. But was Harlow at fault here? Had he meant to harm Fiona Rose or had he but seen her climb the hill and gone to make certain she was safe, as he had said? Leith did not know the answer but he could not forget the night by the lochan when the three lads had accosted Rose.

Mayhap he was being unfair. Perhaps young Harlow was utterly innocent of any wrongdoing this day, and after a lifetime of loneliness and rejection, only needed to be accepted and trusted.

Leith ground his teeth and grimaced. The fact was, there was little he could do but keep Harlow from the castle and watch Rose's every move.

"But is it safe to dunk poor Dora into the water?" young Roman was asking, his green eyes wide, his small fingers immersed in a patch of tawny fur that remained free of bandages. "If her smell bothers me lady," he said timidly, "I could sleep with her in the stable."

"No. No. It's simply—" began Rose quickly, seeing the hurt on the lad's thin face.

"Smell!" Leith scowled as he sniffed the potent air. The place reeked of sheep and worse. The blankets would need to be soaked for a month. "What is this talk of odor? I smell only the fragrance of the Highlands." He sniffed again—though not so deeply. "Lasses, though," he began, shaking his head solemnly, "they be fragile things who dunna always appreciate the sweet smell of livestock."

Rose gave him a peeved look over the lad's

shoulder but he only raised his brows, challenging her to say differently.

"And since she be our lady," Leith continued after a momentary pause, "methinks we should humor her sensitivities, and honor her wishes."

"And . . . it will na harm Dora?" Roman asked again, his concern for the dog so obvious Rose was prepared to abandon the entire idea.

"Na if our lady says it be so."

Roman turned quickly to her and she smiled. " 'Twould be good for her to have her wounds cleansed," she assured him gently.

The lad was silent for a moment. Finally he nodded, his face solemn, his bright hair falling over one eye again. "If me lady says it be best, then we shall brave the bath."

Leith could only assume the lad meant to bathe with his dog but found it beyond his will to dissuade him. "Then tell Judith to fetch water, lad. Fiona will wash first. Dora second."

Roman was gone in a moment, seeming more comfortable with his lady's ridiculous idea now that his laird agreed.

"I suppose I should feel honored that you did not suggest that *I* bathe with the dog, since you are so fond of the scent of livestock," said Rose glibly.

"Aye." Leith settled himself onto the edge of the bed. "That ye should, lass."

Looking up into the honeyed warmth of his eyes, Rose felt a familiar sense of anticipation. "Ye are indeed a generous lord," she offered breathlessly.

His gaze skimmed her face. It was uninjured, unlike her hands, and likely other parts of her body, which were decently covered by her gown. "Indeed I am, lass. Generous to a fault. But 'tis a common trait among us Highlanders."

"Truly?" Rose bit her lower lip as she stared at

him. "And what other attributes are common to your rare and noble breed?"

He leaned his torso over her legs, resting his weight on one palm to look directly into her eyes. "We are a handsome lot," he assured her earnestly.

She raised her brows and tried not to smile. "Aye?"

"Aye. And we are strong."

"Indeed?"

" 'Tis true. There is na another people in all Christendom or beyond that can best a Highlander in a scrap."

"Oh?" She widened her eyes innocently, remembering the sight of him on his white charger, his sword drawn, his face a mask of stark purpose as he avenged her assault by the thieves of the borderland. In all honesty, she could not deny the truth of his words, for surely, there had never been a more powerful—or gentle—man.

"But do ye know our most noticeable characteristic?" he asked, leaning closer still.

"Modesty?" she ventured weakly, visibly shaken by his proximity.

He shook his head, setting his braids to swaying slightly. "Nay," he answered honestly, his breath soft against her cheek, "we are"—he touched her lips with his fingertips, making her shiver—"randy as bucks in rut."

His lips were firm yet tender against hers, and where his hip leaned against her thigh, she felt the contact as if she were branded by his touch. Without warning his left hand slipped beneath her hair, cupping her neck and pressing her toward him.

She shivered in need—in anticipation. She was being drawn into the undercurrent of his embrace like a person drowning in desire.

His kiss stopped time and thought. Only he mattered, only his touch, his presence, and when he drew away she felt bereft.

"Judith." He spoke without raising his eyes from Rose. "Fill the tub, then take Roman and his dog to the kitchen for a bite to eat."

Judith was present, Rose thought dimly, opening her eyes like one in a trance and finding she was unable to remove her gaze from Leith's sharply hewn face.

"Ye willna be needing me and Dora?" asked Roman softly from the doorway.

Roman was also there, thought Rose numbly and wondered if the entire Forbes clan might be nearby to watch them kiss. And if so, did it matter?

"Nay, lad," answered Leith as he shifted his gaze to the boy's solemn face. "I shall have great need of ye soon. But just now ye must eat to replenish yer strength so that ye might protect our lady always." He slipped his attention back to Rose, his eyes still warm with emotion. "Just now though, lad, I will care for our Fiona meself."

God forgive her, thought Rose mistily, but she wanted to be cared for. She wanted to be touched and caressed, and . . . whatever else he could think to do to her.

It seemed that memories of her last experience in this bedchamber made poor Judith fairly fly through her duties, for soon the wooden tub was filled with steaming water, Roman was motioned from the room, and the door was quietly but firmly closed behind them.

"Yer bath awaits, me lady," Leith said softly. "It will soak away some of the pain of yer bruises."

Pain? She felt no pain. Except perhaps that luscious ache in the secret place between her thighs.

"I am but yer servant, Fiona," he murmured.

Servant. Imagine the things she could order him to do, she thought dizzily, forgetting to blush.

"Lass?"

"Yes?" Her voice was as dusky as nightfall.

"I am waiting."

"But . . . " She bit her lip. "Surely we cannot do it again so soon," she whispered, then raised her brows. "Can we?"

"Aye," he breathed. "We can."

"Oh." Her response was barely above a whisper, and when his hand reached for the laces that bound her gown, there was nothing she could do but hold her breath and hope he would hurry.

He did not.

Leith's fingers were warm and titillating, burning a fiery course downward as he drew her garments away.

Her elbows were skinned. One hip was bruised, and though her knees were badly scraped, she failed to care.

"Lass." He murmured the word like a supplication, his tone as hot and breathless as Rose's body. "Ye are a work of finest art. A masterpiece made for me."

She could not speak and did not try, but only stared in wide-eyed silence, waiting.

"I feel, me love, that I could better serve ye if I too were disrobed." He raised her hand to the wooden buttons of his simple shirt, but her fingers were hopelessly bumbling and he finally pulled the small discs through the holes himself, allowing her to watch as he removed his jeweled brooch and slipped the tartan from his shoulder.

His hands dropped now, pulling his long, saffron shirt from beneath his plaid. Masses of glorious, rippling muscle were bared, showing his belly, where the narrow band of dark hair ran downward—his ribs, where the rows of bones were fleshed in undulated waves of luscious brawn. His chest . . . Sweet Savior! His chest!

Rose's nostrils flared. God's knees, he was a glorious creature, all masculine excitement and rock-hard strength.

Grasping his shirt, Leith pulled it off, his arms flexing as his sleeves were drawn away.

Dear God, would it be a sin to beg him to hurry? Rose wondered. But yes, it probably would. Patience was a virtue.

She would, at least, wait until he was completely naked this time, she decided, but suddenly found that her hands were gripping his plaid with immovable strength.

"Lass, let go."

"Leith?"

"Aye?"

"Bar the door."

His jaw clenched and he swallowed, his eyes as dark and dangerous as a storm. "Ye are wise beyond yer years, sweet babe," he declared.

"I am randy beyond your wildest dreams," she corrected.

"Jesu!" he exclaimed, and, pulling her fingers from his plaid, rose to his feet.

"Nay." She caught his hand as he turned away, her eyes as hungry as a hunting cat's. "Disrobe first."

Chapter 24

"Sweet Jesu!" Leith moaned. He stood by the bed like a stud in the throes of lust and loosened his belt with one quick movement.

His plaid slid downward. His throbbing manhood sprang free and proud and turgid.

Rose's lungs were full to bursting. God's teeth, he was the very image of masculine perfection.

She exhaled slowly, trying to relax and letting her gaze dwell where it would. But the familiar heat of arousal had seared a ragged course through her impatient form.

"Lass," Leith growled, his jaw clenched, "dunna look at me like that. Na if ye wish to take some time at this."

Her gaze flicked downward like a living flame. "Patience—is sadly overrated," she said, her voice a husky whisper.

"Lass," he breathed, stepping forward, but she lifted a hand and sucked in a long breath.

"Bar the door," she insisted again.

His fists clenched and he turned.

Good Lord, he was as massive as a stallion, lean and hard and rippling with muscle front and back. And there, between his legs, she caught a glimpse of his manly parts as he walked away.

He hurried to lift the timber and settle it in place against the door, then turned, his face a taut expression of anticipation.

"Your boots," she murmured. "Take them off."

God's truth, she was as bold as an Edinburgh whore. Leith lifted his gaze to her face. It was flushed pink. An innocent whore, he corrected silently, and his. The thought inflamed him further and he strode back to the bed, then dropped his bare buttocks to the mattress to discard his footgear.

He made an intriguing sight as his muscular thighs bent and lifted, prodding his manhood higher, exposing the flesh below. In a moment his task was finished and he twisted about, his eyes as intoxicating as old whiskey.

She was propped on her knees, a triangle of curly hair between her legs, her stomach flat and firm, her breasts curving like soft hillocks above her ribs. Framing it all in tousled auburn waves was her hair, glorious, soft and enticing.

Leith settled his fingers in the thick of it, then pushed his hands beneath. Her skin felt like satin, her hair like velvet, and as he leaned close, her breasts caressed his chest, sending trembles through them both.

His lips caught hers. His manhood prodded her belly in an impatient demand. Her mouth opened as she panted for breath and his kisses slanted downward, over her jaw to her neck.

She shuddered against the delicious feelings, clutching him to her, but the blazing trail of kisses did not stop. Lower it went. Over her shoulder, down her arm. She shivered again.

He pulled her hand from him and, straightening her arm, nibbled his way to the crease in her elbow.

"Leith!" She rasped his name, trying to jerk free.

"Strange," he murmured, his breath a caress against her goose-bumped flesh. "Ye have the most sensitive arms. Look." He leaned closer, lightly touching his tongue to her inner elbow and she jumped again. Leith raised his gaze to her face, his brows high. "Is it na a marvel? Does it na make ye wonder what ye would do if I touched other parts so?"

"Leith!"

"Yer nipple, mayhap?" He drew close with breathless slowness and touched his tongue to her right nipple.

Her entire body jerked spasmodically.

"Intriguing," he observed huskily. "And what of yer other?" He touched that rosebud pebble next. She released a high-pitched gasp, quivering like a willow leaf in the wind.

He clamped his jaw shut as he channeled all his control into patience. Patience to explore this marvelous vessel that trembled with anticipation.

"And what of lower?" he asked, pressing her gently backward with an open palm.

Her legs unfolded slowly, revealing the core of her being to him, but he ignored that sweet source of pleasure as best he could, concentrating instead on mysteries higher up.

His tongue skimmed along the downward slope of one lovely breast. Her eyes were squeezed shut, but her lips were parted.

"Leith!" she cried again, but he shushed her like a patient schoolmaster just discovering a strange new phenomenon.

"Ah, love," he breathed, his gaze falling on the soft indentation of her navel. "What have we here?"

"Don't!" she pleaded, but his tongue had already dipped to that valley.

Every muscle in her body jumped, her hips actually leaving the bed as her fingers found his hair.

"Leith!" she panted. "I mean it! I'm trying to . . . to act demure."

He chuckled as his tongue dipped again. "And yer doing a hell of a job at it, lass."

"Leith." She wet her lips as her fingers tightened in his hair. "I fear you're a very bad influence on me."

"Indeed?" He slid upward, dragging his kisses along the midline of her body.

Heat spread from every point of contact, his lips, his nipples, his manhood as it was drawn slowly along her thigh.

"Indeed," she rasped in breathless agony, but he smiled into her eyes finally, his engorged shaft pressed firmly to the flaming mass of curls between her legs. "It used to be that I hardly ever ravaged anyone."

"*Hardly* ever?" he asked, raising one brow.

"Well—never," she admitted, letting her eyes fall closed as his fingertips caressed her neck into shivers. "And now I cannot wait to ravage you again."

"But ye have to, lass," he crooned. "For just now I am ravaging ye."

"I cannot wait."

"Ye must." His lips caught hers for a momentary kiss. "For ye have kept me waiting in the past. Tormenting me." He kissed her again, moving his hips. "Torturing me."

"Please, Leith."

"Please what, lass?"

"Please," she panted, pressing her head back as he kissed her neck. "Please take . . . "

He sucked on her earlobe, sending frenzied excitement to her breasts and loins.

"Please take . . . ?" he mused with a devious scowl. "Please take . . . it slow?" he guessed, sliding

a hand down her side to cup her buttock and tilt
her hips upward. "Please take . . . a moment . . . to
talk?"

Her face was a picture of rapt concentration,
with her sweet lower lip sucked between her teeth,
her eyes squeezed shut as she writhed her hips
against him.

"That's na it," he guessed, and slid his fingers so
that the tips just bumped the moist, swollen flesh
of her womanhood. "Lass," he admonished gently,
"ye must tell me what ye want."

She planned to do just that but his finger slipped
inside and she gasped.

"What is it ye want?" he asked, moving his finger slowly.

"Take me," she moaned, arching nearer.

"Ye are so demure, lass." Leith chuckled, fully
appreciating her husky demands, and stepped
from the bed to lift her into his arms.

His manhood throbbed against her buttocks, be-
lying his casual attitude. His lips caught hers in a
kiss so hungry it seemed to sear on contact. In another moment they were parted as he settled her
into the warmth of her waiting bath.

Her hair floated on the water's surface, her
breasts peeked above the waves, and though he
wished to stand back and gaze at her beauty he
found there was no hope, for he ached for her with
a need so deep it shook his soul.

He joined her there. The water rose as he settled
himself between her bent knees.

"Remember our last encounter at this tub?" he
asked, moving forward to press his broad manhood to her belly. "Remember how ye fled at the
last moment?" He nuzzled her breast, flicking his
tongue over its puckered peak.

She drew in a ragged breath.

"I have ached for ye ever since, lass." He suckled her gently. Her fingers caught his hair again, her hips strained upward, as she felt the rounded tip of what she desired slip between her thighs.

" 'Twas only last night," she said reasonably, but knew her own impatience was hardly logical.

"Nay," he breathed, " 'twas a lifetime since I last loved ye."

"Aye," she sighed. "A lifetime."

"Then let us end the wait," Leith said, and in one movement buried himself to the hilt.

They closed their eyes in unison, and then the rhythm began, slowly at first, and finally quicker.

Water splashed over the vat's wooden sides, but the lovers failed to notice, for they were drowning in sweetest euphoria.

The tempo increased. Their breath rasped together in harsh tones.

"Leith," she cried, teetering on the edge of ecstasy.

"Sweet . . ." He emptied himself in shuddering spurts and she pushed hard against his rod, peaking in flaming splendor. "Jesu!" he cried, dropping his head to her shoulder and hearing the frantic beat of her heart against his ear.

"Please," she whispered, her breath rapid against his hair.

Leith drew his head away with weary heaviness, bracing himself with one bulging arm against the tub's bottom.

"Nay, lass," he said in disbelief, the words coming between harsh intakes of air. "Dunna tell me ye want it again."

Rose grinned devilishly. "Nay, my laird," she crooned, glancing up through thick lashes. "I but wish for you to ease off me before I drown."

"Thank Jesu," he panted in mock relief, doing as she requested.

"I will give you several minutes," she said, putting her hand on his smooth, naked chest, "before I plead again."

"Ah, sweet babe." He sighed, kissing her gently. "Ye were made to be loved."

"Do you think so?" she asked softly, and in her eyes Leith saw the earnestness of her question.

So she was still at battle with her own purpose in life.

"Aye," he said firmly. "Our God wouldna have created ye with such fire had He na wanted ye to set something aflame." Drawing a wet line down her upper arm, he grinned mischievously. "And ye, wee lass, could ignite this verra water . . . if I were the kindling."

Rose raised her brows at him, feeling acutely responsive to his teasing. "And how is it that you know, my laird, that you alone could be the kindling? After all, I've spent all my adultlife in an abbey, with no chance to test your theory. Mayhap any man could—"

Her words were interrupted as Leith gripped her arms in a firm clasp. His face was only inches from hers as he pressed closer to her slick body. "Because ye are what ye are, lass," he said, his voice low.

She stared at him, her breath stopped in her throat. "And what am I?" she whispered raggedly.

"Mine."

Chapter 25

Dermid moved silently through the Mac-Aulay's woods. He had been this way before. Aye, many times. In fact, it had not been far from here that he'd first seen Eleanor Forbes and Owen MacAulay lying together in the heather.

He grinned, thinking of that time. Those had been good days. The couple had paid well for his silence, for Eleanor had been betrothed to another and well realized the scandal that would erupt should her sin become known.

Too bad she had refused to keep paying.

Dermid tightened his fists, remembering her threat to tell Leith the entire story—including Dermid's part in it. But she had never spoken.

He chuckled into the darkness, waiting, remembering how she had fought him, remembering how soft her throat had felt beneath his hands. She'd died quickly, and afterward he'd wished he had taken his time with her, had heard her whimper for mercy. As it was, he had been unable to keep her dead body close to hand as he had wished to do, for if his deed was found out, Leith would surely kill him.

It had been sheer inspiration to take her to the MacAulay's ridge and push her over the edge, watching as her body thudded to the jagged rocks below.

Owen's death had been neither so pleasant nor so simple.

"Dermid." Murial MacAulay's voice came clearly through the darkness.

"Aye." He stepped forward, squinting through the fog that lay heavy and thick in the valley.

"So ye have come again," she said, emerging from the mist, her slim body draped in a woolen tartan.

"Aye, me lady," he said with feigned respect. She could die as easily as Eleanor, he thought, despite her haughty ways, but for now she paid him well to spy on the Forbes. "I have come on this miserable night at yer request."

Murial remained silent, watching him, and he drew back a pace, hating the eerie way she stared at him. 'Twas said she could read a man's mind, and though he'd never believed such nonsense, she sometimes made his skin crawl.

"Did ye have need of me, me lady?" Dermid asked, eager to be paid and be off.

"Aye." She finally drew her gaze away and strode past him. "Have ye met the lass?"

So he was right. Murial had indeed called him there to discuss the laird's woman. "What lass might that be, me lady?" he asked, wanting to make her wait.

"The Forbes' lady," explained Murial irritably, coming to a quick halt. "The lass who claims to be the MacAulay's daughter."

"Ah, that lass." Dermid nodded, feeling some satisfaction at having riled her temper. "Aye, me lady, I have."

"As have I." Murial nodded. Her head was covered by the same plaid she had wrapped about her body. It shadowed her face, making it impossible for him to guess her thoughts. "But Dugald will na cross the auld laird, and already half-believes the witch is his daughter in truth," she whispered. "It must be done soon. Verra soon. Before all of MacAulay Hold believes in her. But I canna do the deed meself."

Dermid leaned closer, intrigued by her words. "What is that ye say?"

Murial abruptly drew her back into a straight line, as if he had disrupted her thoughts.

The night was silent, muffled by the fog.

"I want ye to kill her," Murial said.

Dermid drew back, forcing an expression of feigned shock to his face. "Kill the laird's lady? But surely ye must be—"

"Dunna pretend such shock with me, Dermid, for I know yer soul is black, though I dunna see what darkens it the most."

"Nay, me lady, I am—"

"Ye will kill her," Murial said quietly. "Just as Forbes kilt me brother."

Dermid remained silent. 'Twas a funny thing that he should now be paid to vindicate a death he himself had caused. "Aye," he said softly. "Owen's death must be avenged, but I canna do the deed, for I am a simple sheepherder who—"

"Yer refusal willna raise the price, Dermid. Ye hate the Forbes just as I do. 'Twill cause ye na loss of sleep to do him ill."

"Aye. Ye are right," admitted Dermid, raising his hands palms up, before him. "But to kill his bride-to-be . . . " He shook his head, already anticipating the murder. "It will cost ye a great deal."

"Me brother's life was worth a great deal," whispered Murial.

"Me laird," said Alpin, standing before Leith's carved chair, "the lone wolf has attacked again."

Leith did his best to put aside the worries that besieged him. For two days he had struggled to learn the truth of Rose's accident by the brook. Had Harlow attempted to harm her, or had she simply imagined some evil, as she had said? And if she had truly imagined the danger, could it not be that the sight was forewarning her?

He'd searched the hillock for some clue that might help him sort out the puzzle, but had found no evidence.

"Did ye hear me, me laird?" questioned Alpin.

"Nay," said Leith, clearing his mind to face his captain of the guard. "What's that ye say?"

"I said the wolf has attacked again."

"The beast that ravaged Roman's hound?"

"Aye. 'Tis thought to be the same. A great black beast that shows no fear. Rory of Sengal Glen bears the proof of his boldness."

"He attacked Rory?" queried Leith, his grip tightening on the chair's arms.

"Aye, me laird," said Alpin. "He left the calves to challenge a man fully grown."

"Nay."

"Aye," countered the soldier, his feet braced far apart and his brow furrowed. "Some say he is more than a mere wolf."

Leith's expression hardened. "More?"

"Some say he is Owen MacAulay, come back from the dead to seek his revenge," he said, nodding slowly.

"Owen is dead," Leith reminded him darkly. "But not by me hand."

"Then mayhap it is his spirit wandering in darkness," suggested Alpin. "For it is said he took his own life."

Leith's knuckles were white from his grip on the chair. "Nay, Alpin," he murmured. "For he loved

Eleanor. He would na punish her people."

The elder man paused a moment but nodded finally, his stance relaxing a bit. "It is sorry I am, me laird, to draw blood from an auld wound. But I thought ye'd wish to know what is being said."

Leith drew a hard breath. He had vowed to guard Rose carefully, but she was not one to stay safely inside the castle walls, and so he would see to the wolf himself, lest his failure to do so cause her death. "Ye were right to tell me, Alpin," he said, "for I need to know the thoughts of me people. I also need to prove them wrong.

"Ready me horse," he commanded. "We shall bring home the hide of a black wolf this day."

"Me lady." Roderic strode across the hall and seated himself before Rose. "Leith has ridden on a hunt and did na wish to waken ye. He has asked me to see to yer needs in his absence."

"See to my needs?" she asked, grinning a little. She'd found herself as adept at teasing as these Scotsmen were. Who would have thought it? "What horrid crime did you commit that you have been kept from the hunt and shackled to my side like some poor lady's maid?"

Roderic sighed, reminding her vividly of his twin's roguish charm and somewhat of Leith's more overwhelming masculinity. " 'Tis true," he admitted. "Would that I could risk me hide, riding all day with a bunch of sweating men, rather than entertain the most bonny lass in all of Scotland. Indeed." He sighed again. "Life is na fair."

Rose laughed at his melodramatic performance, for it had taken her no time at all to realize the young rogue's silver tongue. "How is it, Roderic," she asked, "that some bright maid has not bound you to her long ago?"

"Had I found one like ye, sweet Lady Fiona, I would have—"

"Me lady!" Hannah fairly flew through the door of the hall, her hands caught in tight fists. " 'Tis Eve. Her bairn comes early."

Rose stood quickly, all amusement gone from her face. "Did she na stay abed as I ordered?"

"Aye, she did, me lady. But when she went to empty her bowels this morn, the cramping began. Her husband, John, came here straightaway."

"How early is she?"

"Many weeks," breathed Hannah. "And I fear what will become of her if she loses this bairn too."

"Roderic," Rose said.

"I go to ready the horses, me lady," he said simply. "Ye gather what ye need."

They were riding before the sun topped the highest tree. Maise's stride was long and smooth beneath Rose. Roderic rode ahead, a claymore at his side and his bow across his back. Behind him came Hannah, her riding skills not great, but her concern for her sister urging her along at their swift pace.

The cottage was a low, simple building made of stone and pebbles and held together with mud. The roof was thatched with heather. No windows interrupted the rough walls of rock and mortar. A horse, borrowed from Glen Creag's stables, grazed beside the hut, testimony that the woman's husband John had arrived before them.

"Me lady." He turned quickly from his wife's bed as Rose entered the humble hut. "I fear it is much as it was before."

His face was drawn and pinched and his hands, Rose noticed, were not altogether steady.

"How long did the birthings take in the past?"

"Hardly na time," blurted John, his face turned

from his young wife's pale features. "Some say the bairns were lost because she didna suffer long enough during the birthings."

"Some would believe our Maker is a cruel God," rejoined Rose brusquely. "I prefer to believe He is a God of kindness." She stepped quickly forward, taking the woman's hand in her own. "A God who does not glory in our pain. How fare you, Eve?" she asked, lowering her eyes to the expectant mother's.

"I fear for the babe," gasped Eve, her lips parched, yet her brow damp. "I canna bear to bury another wee..." Her voice broke and Rose touched her cool palm to the woman's brow.

"Do not think of it," she crooned softly. "Think of..." In her mind she heard a child's laughter, high-pitched and filled with glee. "A son," she said distantly. "With your husband's dark hair and your father's name." She lowered her gaze to Eve's, her own wide from the clarity of her vision. "Somerled," she whispered. "'Tis a fine name for a strong lad."

Eve's face paled even more. "I've told no one of the name," she whispered hoarsely.

Rose's eyes held Eve's gaze. "The Lord can do many things. I believe He can grant you a healthy babe."

"Aye." Eve nodded, her lips lifting in a tremulous smile of painful hope. "Aye." She gripped Rose's hand firmly. "I also believe."

The hours passed slowly, for in truth there was little to be done but pray and wait. Rose had given her patient a tea brewed from valerian and birch leaves. It had done much to help her relax and slow her contractions, and while Rose worried now that it might delay the birthing too much, she brewed another pot and gave a mug to John and Roderic.

Men, she observed, were never good at waiting during the birthing process, and so she laced their tea with mild sedatives and tried to keep them busy gathering supplies that might be needed—extra blankets, a knife, wood for the fire, and as many other things as she could think of.

Meanwhile, Hannah sat at her sister's side, gripping her hand and crooning soft words of encouragement.

It was midafternoon when the pains began in earnest. Rose redoubled her prayers, ordered a fire built, and with all the knowledge and practical sense in her keeping, eased the new life into the world.

It was a lad, wizened and red with a mop of slick black hair and miniscule fists clutched to his bony chest. Rose, however, took only a fleeting second to notice these things, for the babe was so small and fragile that it could barely squeeze out a raspy whimper in protest to its rough welcome into such a harsh world.

Cradling it against her bosom, she hurried the tiny life to his mother's bare chest, leaving the pulsing cord intact and covering the pair quickly with multiple blankets.

Warmth, comfort, and prayers. There was little else they could give it. And yet . . .

Rose sucked in her lower lip and worried. "Fetch a reed from the swamp," she ordered suddenly. "It must be green and hollow, yea long, and as narrow as ye can find."

"Aye, me lady," agreed the men, and hurried to do her bidding.

She heated water and prayed during their absence. Only once had she seen this process done, and then the babe had died. But she had seen others die too, passing on from the sheer exhaustion of living, of trying to take enough nourishment to sustain life. For suckling took great energy—energy such a tiny infant often did not possess.

But if they could express the mother's milk and feed the babe through the reed . . .

Evening had come. Though the little hut felt hot as an oven, to Rose, the warmth seemed to comfort the babe, for he slept like a minute angel against his mother's breast.

"Thank ye, me lady." Eve's voice was husky, her eyes moist, but Rose shook her head.

"Do not thank me," she said softly, worry etched on her brow. "Thank the Lord. But I fear there is still danger. He is so tiny." She could not see the little bundle beneath the covers but remembered with clarity the deep wisdom on the infant's scrunched face. If he could but continue to take nourishment through the reed until he was strong enough to suckle, he would yet survive his early entry into the world. "I must gather some things from Glen Creag," she said finally, "but I will return this eventide if you do not mind my staying with you."

"Nay, lady," said John from behind her, his face earnest with gratitude. "Ye would do us great honor to stay, but I fear we already owe ye more than we can ever repay."

Rose opened the door and stepped out. The two men followed. "I ask no payment, John," she said as they closed the door behind them to hold the heat within the cottage. "I only ask that you keep the babe as warm as—"

From the sky came a soft whistle. A sickening

thud echoed through the glen as steel pierced
Rose's flesh. She gasped in shock and fell, the re-
verberating wooden shaft of an arrow embedded
deep within her chest.

Chapter 26

The black wolf had been slain, and Leith rode now to MacMartin's cottage but to find Rose. Maises saddle was empty as the mare raced toward him.

"Dear Jesu!" Leith whispered, his legs clamped hard against his stallion's sides. Riding at chilling speed was Roderic, bearing someone in his arms.

"Dunna let it be. Please!" Leith prayed, knowing with the bitter burn in his soul that Rose was hurt.

"Me liege," Roderic choked, pulling his mount to a halt before his brother. "I have failed ye."

For a moment weakness threatened to overcome Leith, but he drew himself up, fighting the numbing pain that crushed his heart. "Is she dead?" His tone was flat and as cold as stone. He made no attempt to touch her. Indeed, he did not even allow his gaze to drop to her.

Roderic's answer was no more than a whisper, his face pale and frantic above the lady's bright head. "She yet lives."

Hope! Painful in its stinging intensity! "What has happened?"

"Outside John MacMartin's hut. An arrow struck her." Roderic swallowed hard. "It passed within a hand's breadth of her heart."

Leith's gaze fell to her, drawn there against his will. "Give her to me."

She passed from hands to hands, her shoulder

and breast sticky with blood, her body limp, her face deadly pale.

Leith turned Beinn smoothly, then paused, not moving his gaze from her still form. "Who has done this?"

"I dunna ken," rasped Roderic, "but he will die."

"Come with me," Leith ordered.

"Me laird!" Roderic said, his tone harsh. "Ye would na let this crime go unpaid!"

"Hear me now," said Leith, his voice so low it was barely audible. "He who did this shall surely die a bloody death." His mouth twitched with the force of his emotion. "But for now we shall think only of saving me lady."

The drawbridge lowered on creaky pulleys. Their horses' hooves clattered across. The courtyard was nearly empty, but the hall was filled for the evening meal and the noise abounded.

The great door swung shut behind them. Faces turned, blearing in Leith's distress as he strode through the cavernous room, his grip tight about his small bundle.

"Me laird."

"Leith!"

Words and gasps accosted him, but he acknowledged none and stopped for nothing. His world lay wrapped in stillness in his arms.

He laid her upon the bed. Fresh blood seeped through the rend in her gown.

"She saved MacMartin's bairn," Roderic said softly. " 'Twas a miracle. A lad it is. Named Somerled."

"Ye got the arrow cleanly out?" Leith asked, ignoring his brother's words.

"Aye. It went straight through." Roderic said,

seeming to draw himself from a trance. "I broke it off and pulled it free."

Leith felt the pain rip through his own flesh. Sweet Jesu, if she should die . . . But nay. He gritted his teeth. He would not let it happen, even if he had to make a pact with the devil.

"Shall I fetch a priest, me laird?"

"Nay!" Leith bellowed, not knowing who asked the question or who answered in unison with him. "She willna die!" He rose like a towering mountain, his face contorted with rage. "Do ye hear? She willna!"

"Nay, Leith." Mabel's hands unclasped as she touched his rigid arm. "She willna. Judith, fetch warm water and clean cloths. The rest of ye, go out. She needs rest to heal."

Leith sank to the mattress beside Rose. They did not believe she would live, he knew, but he took her hand and gripped it in both of his. They thought she knocked even now at death's door, but she would not leave him. For he loved her.

Rose woke once during the night, speaking feverishly. Leith leaned close, wiping her brow with a wet cloth and whispering gentle words.

Dawn came in grim shades of gray. The day dragged toward noon and past, yet Leith sat, motionless and silent. A quiet rap sounded at the door, but he ignored it. He would not allow others to mourn her, for in truth, he could not bear their tears.

Sometime during the night he had slipped Rose's small wooden cross from about his neck and held it now, seeking solace from the rough-hewn symbol of forgiveness and peace.

His eyes felt dry and empty—as did his soul. There was the sound of shuffling in the hall and

Leith gritted his teeth, knowing Roman had bedded there, waiting to be admitted. But that was the face he could least bear to look upon, with those round, frightened eyes that mirrored his own panic with such perfect clarity.

He was Scots. He was Highlander. He was laird—strong, invincible. But without her he was nothing, only a shadow of a man who cared not whether he lived or died.

After all this time, it seemed he understood his sister and her lover. Eleanor had risked her pride and the pride of her people to be with Owen. And those who did not believe that he himself had killed Owen, believed the young man had taken his own life to be with *her*.

"Sweet Jesu!" For the first time Leith could pray for the lad's soul, for surely he had suffered enough here on this earth. Losing the woman he loved had surely caused him more pain than one man should have to bear.

His prayers continued into the night, through the dark hours, interrupted now and then by Rose's moans.

Gray light seeped slowly into the room. The rain had stopped. The burning pain in Leith's heart did not.

He stood, ignoring the stiffness in his back as he went to push open the window shutter.

"Silken!" he said in surprise.

The cat rose warily from his spot on the broad window ledge.

They stared at each other—feline and human, mere inches apart.

"She willna die," Leith vowed, as if the cat's presence there challenged his words.

Silken hunched his back slightly, his ears shifting.

"Why do ye come?" Leith whispered. "Stalking about as if to take her spirit from this world." Silence echoed around him, mocking him for his one-sided conversation. "Ye shall na have her." He drew himself straighter. "She is mine."

The cat eased onto his belly, watching, waiting.

"Damn ye," swore Leith, feeling the torturing lump of fear rising hopelessly. "No one will take her from me, for she is . . . " A strangled noise came from his throat. "Mine."

The single word slipped into the grayness of the morn, yet seemed to echo in his ears. *Mine. Mine.*

But she was not.

He covered his eyes with his hand, imagining the misery of a future without her.

Even now she was not truly his. Not by the words of a priest or a single vow from her lips.

But even if marriage vows had been spoken, would she belong to him alone?

Nay!

The truth came to him suddenly.

She was not his! She belonged to his people. To Roman and Roderic and Mabel. To wee Somerled just birthed, and Malcolm whom she had saved. And yes, perhaps she belonged even to Silken, who could not bear to be parted from her.

"Roman!" He yelled the name, startling Silken to his feet again, though he did not turn away. "Roman." Running to the door, Leith threw up the bar.

The boy was already there, camped at their door like a small, watchful angel, his narrow face shadowed below round eyes.

"Ye kept her safe before, lad." Leith gripped the boy's arms, lifting him from the floor and carrying him to Rose's bed. "Ye shall keep her safe again. Do ye hear me?" He shook Roman gently until the lad nodded. "Dunna let her leave us. Speak to her.

Call her back, lad, as ye did with yer dog," he pleaded, and then he was gone, running down the stairs, already shouting for Hannah.

The sun had come out!

The wagon rumbled along, bearing its precious burdens quickly toward Glen Creag. Again the drawbridge lowered. Again unshod hooves clattered across.

Leith threw his leg swiftly over Beinn's rump. "Here, John." He ran to where the man already lifted young Eve from the wagon. "Another blanket. Fiona Rose would never forgive me should yer bairn catch a chill."

"Aye, me laird." John nodded, but his face was strained, showing the same expression Leith had seen on the others.

They thought he had lost his sanity. But in fact, he had found it. And with it, Rose would live.

"Inside. Hurry now," he ordered and John went, carrying his wife who carried the tiny babe, still naked and clasped close to her breast beneath the blankets.

"Lass! Wee nun!" Leith called, taking the steps by threes. "Fiona!" For one horrendous, shuddering moment fear gripped him in dark hands and he stopped, his heart faltering as he stood immobile in the doorway.

"Me laird," Roman said, his round eyes catching Leith's. "I think—mayhap I saw her fingers move."

It was said with the blind, unquenchable faith of a child who has seen a lifetime's worth of pain, and yet dares to believe in the triumph of good.

Leith's heart thumped to life as he sped across the floor and clasped the boy to his chest in a crushing embrace. "Ye are surely sent from heaven, lad. Surely so.

"Come in. Come in," he called, setting the boy aside and motioning to John. "Put them under the blankets with me lady."

"Under . . . " John blanched at the words, terrified of placing his wife and son beside a woman who was surely dying, and abruptly shifting his gaze to the window ledge where Silken waited. But Leith only smiled and shook his head.

"Fear na, John. The lass willna die. For ye understand, she owes me a year, promised by her own lips, and she is a woman who will move heaven and earth to keep her vows." Putting his hand to his chest, he gripped the small cross beneath his shirt. "As God is me witness," he murmured huskily, "I willna be shortchanged."

Turning to the bed, his face stern, but his hands atremble, he reached out to shake the wounded girl.

"Fiona," he called, his tone harsh and loud. "Awake, lass."

She moaned once and turned her head, but he would not relent and shook her again.

"Awake, I say. Do ye think God has sent ye here for na purpose but to sleep? Think ye to wrest wee Somerled into this world then leave him with na care? Surely ye owe him more than that."

She moaned again, the sound anguished, and Roman reached out, grasping Leith's arm with both his small hands. "Nay!" he rasped, his lean face filled with terror. "Dunna hurt her."

"Quiet, lad," said Leith. "Dunna try to stop me, for I shall use any means to bring her back. Any means at all.

"Awake!" he ordered gruffly, shaking her again.

"Do ye na think Eve has suffered enough? Must she lose this bairn too because of yer lack of spirit?"

From midnight folds of deepest sleep, Rose saw a tiny face peering at her. It was wrinkled and reddened, with eyes of charcoal-blue and fists hugged close for comfort.

Somerled—that innocent babe, forced too soon into a world so wrought with hardships. He needed her. But she was tired. So very tired. She slipped back, called into the darkness.

But the voice came again and again, growing insistent and hoarse.

And there was crying—dry, heaving sobs from a child.

Roman.

She knew it suddenly. Roman—who had not shed a tear since coming to Glen Creag. Roman, with the unquenchable spirit and sunset-bright mop of hair, was crying. Weeping as if his heart would break. Dear Roman, who had suffered too much. She would comfort him, hold him until the tears stopped.

When her lids finally lifted, tiny dew-drops of empathy had already formed at the corners of her eyes.

"Roman." She lifted her right hand, touching the boy's bowed head. "Is it Dora?"

Roman's small, carrot-topped pate lifted slowly. His eyes were afloat with tears. "Me lady!" he choked, clutching her arm to his narrow chest as if he would hold her forever lest she escape again into a place where he could not follow. "Laird," he whispered, his liquid gaze not leaving her face, "she is returned."

"Indeed."

For the life of her, Rose could not read Leith's

tone. It sounded husky, and rather strained, as if he had been ill for a long while and had just now found the strength to speak.

"My laird?" She looked to him and noticed that his eyes too were moist. Indeed, she reasoned, he must have been very ill. Shame on her for leaving him to fend for himself. "Ye are well now?"

He took her left hand in his, lifting it ever so gently to his chest. "Verra well, wee lass," he said hoarsely. "Verra well now."

She relaxed somewhat, letting her gaze drift and seeing Dora scoot over the bed plaid toward her. The dog was well. Roman was fine. And it seemed Leith had recovered from his apparent illness.

Her lids fluttered downward. Darkness called.

"Nay!" Leith demanded, his tone so sharp it startled her to wakefulness. "Nay, lass." He gripped her hand harder, as if to hold her forever in his world. "Ye canna sleep. Wee Somerled is failing. And there is none other who can save him."

"Somerled?" Rose murmured.

"Aye. And . . . and yer cat has been worried."

"Silken?" Rose breathed, and managed to turn toward the window, where Silken's whiskered face peered warily around the frame.

"Aye. Silken has been waiting on the window's sill."

Rose's lids fluttered down.

"Fiona," Leith called urgently, startling her awake once more. " 'Tis unseemly that the cat sit there. 'Twill make any passersby think this place is enchanted."

"Enchanted, my laird?" she said softly.

"Aye." Leith nodded, feeling relief and hope like the stab of a dagger. "Call the cat forth, Fiona. For he loves ye."

Rose slowly drew her gaze from Leith's. "Silken." She lifted her right hand. "Come."

The cat moved with lithe caution, but he came. Miraculously, Dora remained as she was, comfortably pressed against Roman as Silken moved to the bedside and warily sniffed Rose's wounded shoulder. His eyes, golden as the first rays of morning sun, lifted to Rose's. For a moment absolute stillness held the room, and then he licked the torn fabric near her wound—just one quick swipe of his abrasive tongue before he settled himself onto his haunches to await her recovery.

Chapter 27

During the following weeks Rose rarely raised her own hands, though she did much to instruct others. And though Leith had spoken eloquently of wee Somerled, it was *her* wounds he had seen to first, tenderly and thoroughly performing whatever functions she proclaimed would cure her injuries.

He had done well, she mused now, lifting her left arm gingerly. Pain spurted through her shoulder and chest, but the limb was still mobile and her fever subdued.

Roman, with his gap-toothed smile and sudden need to hold her hand, had told her how Leith had never left her bedside except to fetch Eve and her babe.

And that babe . . . Rose smiled to herself. Wee Somerled—no bigger than a weanling pup—was already nursing on his own. It must be his stubborn Scottish blood that made him fight so to survive, she reasoned, easily dismissing her own efforts to save him—feeding the tiny lad through a softened and lubricated reed every few hours, waking painfully from those grasping folds of oblivion to Leith's tender voice and supportive hands, seeing his eyes fill with warmth and hope as she ministered to the bairn.

Aye, Leith was a strong laird and a good man, but he was no longer her lover. Each night he slept

beside her for a brief while, carefully avoiding
touching her except to tend her wounds, but then
he always removed himself to a nearby bedchamber, where he spent the remainder of the night. She
craved his more personal attention. Desired his caresses. His husky laughter. His . . . everything.
God's teeth, she loved him. More than life. But he
was being very difficult.

Laughter sounded from the next room. Rose
smiled, knowing Hannah was sitting by her sister's
bed, easing Eve's boredom as the new mother
warmed the baby with her own body's heat.

Life could be so good here, if only . . .

Footsteps trod softly in the hallway. Rose
glanced expectantly toward the door, but the foot-
falls passed. She sighed, closing her eyes and
searching for sleep again, only to wake to the
sound of Leith's voice coming from the hall. It was
low and harsh, the words barely audible.

"Ye slink about like a wolf on a scent," he hissed.
"What do ye want from her?"

Silence.

"Damn ye, Harlow!" Leith growled, his voice
trembling with rage. "Why are ye here?"

Hannah! Rose thought suddenly.

The image of the girl's lovely face flitted through
Rose's sleep-muddled mind like an autumn leaf in
the wind. Harlow was there because of his love for
Hannah.

Rose understood love now. It made people act
foolishly. It made *Harlow* act foolishly—risking his
laird's temper to be near the woman he adored, the
woman he would never be allowed to have because
of the boyish crimes of his past. The theft of Hannah's father's apples, if castle gossip was correct.

Stiffly pushing the blankets aside, Rose swung
her legs over the edge of the bed, wincing with the

movement. Beside her, Silken jumped from the mattress, then watched as she touched her bare feet to the floor and stood.

Daggers stabbed at Rose's chest, but she moved toward the door, her nightrail billowing behind her as she opened the portal. "Leith."

He stood with his fist clutched in Harlow's saffron shirt. Rose's gaze flitted from the lad's reddened face to Leith's hard expression.

"Leith," she repeated, clutching the doorjamb. "I feared there was something amiss."

"Nay." Leith loosened his grip, trying to soothe the anger from his face. He had done his best to keep Rose from worrying. "Nay, lass, I was only rankled that Harlow had left his duties. Nothing more." It was a poor lie, but it made no sense to worry her with his own suspicions that Harlow was involved in the attack on her.

Holy Jesu! How could it be that she had been pierced with an arrow and yet they could not determine the culprit? Or did he have the guilty one here by his shirtfront even now? "Ye should na be out of bed, lass," he said. "Ye will open the wound."

Leith was still angry and thought Harlow might be guilty of wounding her, Rose sensed easily. But ... She needed time to think, to figure things through before Leith did something which they would all regret. "I had a frightful dream," she said quietly. Her lie was no better than his, but she needed to draw on Leith's softness for her, to keep peace until facts became clear in her mind. "Might ye come sit with me for a spell?"

"Lass," he said gently, turning abruptly from Harlow, "there is naught to fear."

She sucked in her lower lip, seeing that warm

kindness in his eyes and remembering with aching clarity the times he had taken her in his arms. "There is nothing to fear," she whispered, "when you are near me."

Jesu, he loved her! Ached to lie beside her again.

"Harlow," he said, not looking to the lad, "go about yer business. I will speak with ye later."

Leith closed and barred the door behind them.

"Come to bed, lass," he said softly, taking her arm in his. "Ye should na be wandering about."

"I heard you in the hall."

"I will be sure to tread more quietly in the future," he said, his expression somber.

"Just stay beside me instead," she said, catching his eyes with her own.

In his was an emotion so intense it all but seared her heart, and she held her breath, waiting.

"I would stay by yer side forever if I could, lass," he murmured huskily. "But I have yet to avenge yer injury. And until that day comes, I canna rest."

She wanted to kiss him, to hold him in her arms and confess her love, to tell him not to worry, for all would be well. But he did worry, and there was a strong possibility that he might accuse the wrong man.

"About Harlow," she began, but Leith turned her toward the bed and pressed her gently onto the mattress. "Do not be too harsh with him," she advised.

A muscle jumped in Leith's jaw. "Dunna speak now, lass. Rest."

"Leith." She reached up with her hale arm, touching his sleeve. "The lad means no harm."

" 'Tis na for ye to worry on. Though I have failed ye in the past, I willna do so again." His face was tense, as was his tone. "Ranald guards yer door, and at every hour men watch the castle. Na one shall come in without me knowledge and permission. Ye are safe here."

"Safe?" She smiled, wanting to soften his mood, to feel his gentle hands on her, to hear his voice low and husky in her ear. "I never doubted that I was safe under your care."

Their eyes caught again, but he shook his head. "Ye forgive me failings too easily, lass."

"And you expect too much of yourself, as usual."

"Nay," Leith said. "For I am—"

"I know, you are laird."

"Aye. And I will keep ye safe. None will harm ye again, for ye will stay within these walls, where none shall come without me own permission."

Rose lifted her brows. "You plan to lock me away like a prisoner?"

"I but mean to keep ye safe. Ye will na be a—"

"Shh." Placing a finger gently to his lips, Rose smiled. "I do not mind being imprisoned for a time," she whispered, letting her fingers drift slowly down his broad throat to where the upper portions of his massive chest showed through the laced opening of his shirt. "So long as you are my jailer."

"Lass." He sucked in air through his teeth and closed his eyes. "Ye are tempting me."

"Am I?" She bit her lip, trying to look innocent. "'Tis a shame. But I . . ." She shrugged, pressing her right palm beneath his shirt and over his sensitive nipple. ". . . I am starved for companionship."

"Keep this up and ye shall get more than companionship," he vowed, his voice low as he caught her arm.

Her brows rose again. "Such as?"

"Ye know verra well."

"Show me," she whispered.

"Lass, ye have been sorely wounded, and I dunna wish to worsen the injury."

"You think I am so frail?"

"Aye," he admitted, nodding gravely. "That I do."

"Then I shall have to prove you wrong," she said, and, gripping his shirt, pulled herself closer to kiss him.

"Lass." His breath came hard as he struggled for control. "Ye know I canna resist ye."

"I hope not."

"Then let me go before I hurt ye."

"Leith," she entreated, but he pulled easily from her grasp and straightened with a scowl.

"Are ye certain ye were ever in a convent?"

"Aye." She nodded grumpily. "And for far too long. Come here."

"Nay, lass. I am concerned for yer well-being even if ye are na. And therefore I willna touch ye until ye are hale."

Their gazes caught again. But in a moment she grinned and shrugged. "We shall see."

Leith narrowed his eyes. "Why do ye smile?"

"No reason." Rose shifted her gaze to the windowsill, where Silken watched her with his golden stare.

"Ye think to seduce me," Leith guessed.

"I beg your pardon," gasped Rose, trying to sound offended.

"Dunna deny it. Ye plan to seduce me."

"I am shocked," she said, feeling disgruntled, and wishing he would move closer to the bed so that she could reach him again.

"But yer na going to, lass," Leith warned, "for until ye are healed I will sleep in the next room."

"You're being stubborn."

"Aye. Stubborn I am. But I ken me weakness." He watched her carefully, his russet eyes warm. "And ye, lass, are me weakness."

For just a moment longer their eyes held, and then he rose and strode to the hallway and beyond.

Chapter 28

Evil!
    Rose felt it! Tasted it! So near. Coming closer, suffocating her! She tried to run, to escape, but darkness held her immobile.

"No!" she whimpered, lifting an arm to ward off death, and suddenly the blackness of sleep was swept away.

It was a dream! She sat bolt upright, breathing hard and staring frantically past the here and now to the shadowed world still visible in her mind.

Danger! It was still there, still approaching, but suddenly the focus had shifted so that she seemed to look down at the scene from above. There was a velvet-draped bed with a still figure in its center, but it was not she.

"Father." She said the word aloud as goose bumps coursed over her. She was shaken by the intensity of the premonition as she yet gazed at the still form on the bed. It was Ian, deep in sleep, and danger was very near.

She must go to him! Save him!

Her hands trembled as she pulled a gown over her head. Pain echoed through her chest, but she laced up the garment and grabbed a plaid from the bed. Glancing momentarily at the door, Rose shifted her gaze to the window.

Silken was there, standing on the wide stone ledge, watching and waiting. Of course. She could

not go through the door for Ranald slept on the far
side and was sure to waken if she passed that way.
He would call Leith, and then all would be lost, for
Leith would not allow her departure. Nay. He
would not allow her to leave the castle, much less
go to MacAulay Hold, and she must go.

The stone window ledge felt cool against her
bare feet. Some five yards below, two soldiers
stood together, speaking Gaelic and laughing.

Her toes fit easily into the niches between the
stones. Her fingers found ready holds. It was not a
simple task to scale the wall directly behind the
soldiers' backs, but neither was it impossible, for
she had practiced much the same thing at St.
Mary's Abbey.

Silken waited until Rose squatted against the
moon-shadowed wall, and then he too descended,
jumping from window ledge to a lower window
ledge until he stood some forty feet off to the
guards' left.

Rose held her breath as the wildcat turned.
Moonlight glistened in his golden eyes. Their gazes
caught, transferring thoughts, and then he shifted
his attention to the soldiers. The sound that issued
from his throat was low and menacing, but loud
enough to startle the men from their talk.

Yanking out their claymores, the two pivoted toward Silken.

Quiet as the night, Rose slipped through the
shadows toward the stable, knowing Silken would
easily leave the two men behind.

No soldiers slept inside the barn tonight for it
was more comfortable out in the gentle breeze.
Maise nickered from her stall, and Rose shushed
her, lifting a hand to stroke her velvety muzzle. A
bridle hung from a peg nearby. Rose slipped the

bit between the mare's teeth and swung the door wide.

In a moment Maise was in the aisle, her hoofbeats muffled on the straw-strewn floor.

Outside, the breeze was fresh. The mare pricked her ears, watching as Silken approached, but at a word from Rose, she relaxed.

They were at Glen Creag's stone wall in a matter of minutes. It loomed dark and tall.

A movement! Shadowed and silent! Fear stabbed Rose with sharp spurs. The shadow shifted, swelled.

"Me lady!" Hannah gasped, barely visible in the lee of the towering wall. "Ye shouldna be out of bed. What be ye doing here so late at night?"

Rose swallowed a lump of fear and tried to soothe her nerves. "I might ask the same of you," she said quietly, noticing another shifting shadow behind the woman.

"I . . ." Hannah moved a nervous step backward. "I meant na harm, me lady."

Rose tightened her grip on the reins, glancing furtively about her. She was delaying too long, risking discovery with the sound of their voices. "I too mean no harm," she whispered. "Please, Hannah, let this be our secret. Just between us two."

"But Lady Fiona." Hannah came closer, and a frail moonbeam fell across her worried features and chestnut hair. "Where do ye go?"

"Please do not ask," begged Rose "For I must not say."

"But me lady, ye canna leave these grounds alone. 'Twould be unsafe."

Rose hurried away, praying for divine intervention. Leith must not awaken, for even if he trusted her instincts, he would not allow her to go. And if he sent an army, or went himself to MacAulay land . . . She shivered, seeing blood. No. She must go. And she must go alone.

"Please, me lady. Wait. Don't leave us," pleaded the maid. "There is danger. Harlow!" She turned abruptly, desperation making her voice wispy. "Harlow, do not let her go."

Rose stopped and stiffened. So she had been right. It was Harlow who was hidden in the shadows with the lovely Hannah. Harlow with the hard past and the flint eyes. Harlow who had accosted her by the river and been present at the rocky knoll where she'd felt the evil. And yet, was it *his* evil or was he simply a young man with too few prospects and a great love for a woman denied to him?

"If you stop me," Rose said firmly, "you will need to explain your presence here." Her gaze shifted to the shadow she knew to be Harlow and her tone softened. "Do not worry. There is but something I must do." She lifted the reins. "Keep silent, Hannah," she whispered, "and when I return on the morrow, I will ask our laird if there is not some way that you and Harlow might wed."

"Me lady," said Hannah, "how could ye ken me fondest desire?"

"Be silent now," Rose begged, and turned away again.

"I canna let ye go into danger to better me own life," Hannah whispered. "For I owe ye much already."

"You owe me nothing," countered Rose, hurrying toward the drawbridge.

" 'Tis na true."

From the darkness Silken called softly, startling a gasp from Hannah, but she grabbed Harlow's hand, dragging him along as she ran after the black mare. "I owe ye for wee Somerled's life. For sweet Roman's well-being. For Eve's happiness. I owe ye much already. Dunna go," she pleaded.

"I must. Please understand. I—"

"Auld William guards the drawbridge," said Harlow suddenly. "I will send him away and lower the bridge."

"No! Harlow!" Hannah gasped, but he was already striding off. "Please," pleaded the woman again, but Rose took her hand, shushing her softly. They stood together silently then, waiting until Harlow returned.

"I told him I'd keep his watch," he explained. He caught Rose's gaze with his own. "Ye have only a few minutes."

He turned away and she followed.

The crank complained softly as Harlow turned it. The drawbridge settled onto the land beyond the rushing river.

"Thank you," Rose whispered. "I shall not forget this."

She was across the bridge in a moment, and though it was not easy to mount bareback, she managed it somehow, and, leaning over the mare's neck, headed west, toward MacAulay Hold.

"Harlow," Hannah whispered, gripping her lover's sleeve with trembling hands, "what have we done?"

Most probably he had caused his own execution, Harlow reasoned grimly. "*We* have done nothing," he said, pulling her hands from his sleeve to take them in his own. "It is *I* and I alone who has aided her escape. Ye will claim na knowledge of it. Do ye hear me?"

"Nay, Harlow!" Hannah cried. "Why do ye do this?"

For a moment his eyes closed and when he turned his gaze to the west, there was no sight of the Lady Fiona, no sound of the black mare's hoofbeats in the darkness. "She could have seen me dead, Hannah," he answered. "She could have caused me death long since. For the laird thinks it is I who wounded her."

"Nay!" Hannah denied, her fingers tightening in his. "Nay. 'Tis na true."

"Aye, Hannah, me love," he said softly. "And he has reasons to think I wish her harm. And for that I am sorry. But I canna be sorry for granting her wish. She has saved me more than once from the Forbes' fury. I fear he thinks I stalk her, when in truth I only wish to be near ye. He thinks me lust for her so deep that I deny all good sense in me quest for her. He thinks me the greatest of fools."

Harlow's voice was filled with deep, quiet sorrow, an aching longing for respect.

"Harlow," Hannah whispered, "I dunna understand yer words, but I ken this. If the Lady Fiona should be harmed, the guilt shall be upon our heads, whether or na others know of our deeds. Please. If ye love me, go after her. Dunna let harm befall her."

In the darkness Harlow blanched. If he followed her, Leith would see his actions as proof of his guilt and would surely kill him. But if he did not . . . "I do love ye, lass. Dunna forget that," he implored, and, loosing her hands, hurried toward the stable and a swift mount.

Dermid chuckled to himself. So the lass had flown Glen Creag and now headed west toward MacAulay Hold.

Turning his horse, he followed her. He could kill

her quickly and soon, but how much better to wait until they reached MacAulay land and take his time with her!

Yes. He would follow her, anticipating the killing to come.

Chapter 29

"Me laird! Me laird!" Hannah pounded on the door of Leith's temporary bedchamber, her heart in her throat.

He appeared in an instant, a plaid clutched about his waist, his great chest heaving with panic, his sharp eyes gleaming in anticipation of her words. "Fiona?" he questioned, his mind scrambling to assemble thoughts. She had seemed to be recovering so well, but . . .

"Aye, me laird," said Hannah, but there was no time to say more for already he was rushing down the hall, one white-knuckled hand gripping the blanket at his hip.

Ranald still slept in the doorway. Leith vaulted over him in an instant, pushing the door inward. "Where is she?" he demanded, his gaze storming about the room.

"Gone, me laird."

"Gone?" The word was choked from his throat.

"Aye." Hannah squeezing her hands together, suddenly fearful of this man who ruled their lives. "She has flown. All alone. I could na stop her."

"Why?" He reviewed every word he had spoken to her, every detail that might give him a clue to her thoughts.

"She but said there was sommat she must do," Hannah exclaimed, wringing her hands.

"Sommat she must do?" Leith grabbed Hannah's arms. "What? What must she do?"

"I dunna know. She didna say, but insisted she must go. I begged her to stay, me laird, for she is na yet mended. Please . . . If anything should happen to her . . ." Hannah covered her face with splayed fingers. "Please—"

"Hannah!" Leith snapped, shaking her. "Where did she go? Which way?"

"I dunna ken," Hannah cried. "She rode the black horse. I couldna see her past—"

"Which way?" Leith roared, his face contorted with rage.

"West! West, I think. But I couldna see far for 'twas dark. She may have turned. I—"

"West," he said, his grip loosening. "Toward the MacAulays."

Hannah's jaw dropped as she shook her head in firm denial. "She is na a spy for the MacAulays," she insisted. "She loves us. She would na—"

"Hannah!" Leith shook her again, his tone flat. "Go to the stable. See that Beinn is saddled. Do ye hear?"

She swallowed hard, her face white, her body shaking.

"Do ye hear, lass?" he shouted.

"Aye." She nodded woodenly. "But me laird, I fear Harlow has . . . taken yer stallion."

"Harlow?" Within Leith's chest his heart stopped dead. "What say ye?"

"I begged him," she said. "I begged him to follow her. To keep her safe. He said yer stallion would follow her mare. That—"

"Brother!" called Roderic, running down the hall. "What is it?"

"Fiona! She is gone. See that a horse is readied," Leith ordered.

*   *   *

Rose had been riding for three hours or more. She winced, covering her wound with her right hand. Pain shook her with sharp tremors. But she could not stop. Perhaps she should have tried a straighter course toward the bridge that would take her to MacAulay Hold, but it had been dark as pitch when she'd started out, and she'd been uncertain she could find it without following the river.

But what if Creag Burn was not the watercourse that led to MacAulay land? What if the bridge she had traversed with Leith had been on another burn?

Doubt shook her resolve. Perhaps she was a fool to fly from the safety of Glen Creag on account of a fearsome dream. But . . . No. She closed her eyes for a moment, feeling the emotions again. Something drew her to the MacAulay's side. She was needed and she could not delay.

Maise tossed her head and pranced a bit. The movement sharpened the pain in Rose's shoulder, but she touched her heels to the mare's sides and hurried on.

Behind her the sky paled with the arrival of the sun. Birds tested their voices in their first morning songs as she urged Maise into a ground-eating trot.

Another ridge, another valley. Where was that damned bridge?

From far behind, Rose thought she heard the deep-throated trumpet of a stallion.

Someone followed. But who? It did not matter, for whoever it was, she must flee before it was too late.

The sun rose, sparkling off the dew below her mare's sweeping hooves. Down a steep grade now, and there—off to her right, just a quarter mile away—was the bridge. And past that, no more than a mile, would be MacAulay Hold.

Good God!

Harlow halted Beinn at the hill's crest.

Lady Fiona was headed toward the bridge to MacAulay Hold. But then, she was the old laird's daughter.

And yet he'd heard the tale of the old man's addled state. What MacAulay would care if she died? Mayhap she would be mistaken for just another Forbes. But no—not just another Forbes. The wife of *the* Forbes! The woman who would bear his heirs and therefore was a strong threat to them.

She would not be safe at MacAulay Hold. He must stop her.

But there! Off to the right! A man! Bow raised!

No! Not sweet Fiona! She must not die!

Harlow wrenched his bow from his shoulder to fit an arrow to the sinew.

"Jesu!" Leith breathed, astride his bay mount, seeing Harlow at the hill's crest, bow bent. *Nay, Jesu!* he pleaded, and, sweeping up his own bow, he set his arrow to flight just a heartbeat after Harlow's.

He saw it pierce the lad's side, saw the boy's body jerk, nearly falling from his horse. But Harlow did not fall. Instead he gripped Beinn's mane and turned to disappear below the hill.

"Nay!" Leith shrieked, his soul aching with the certainty of Harlow's quest to kill the lady he loved more than life. "Nay!" he railed again, kicking his mount into a gallop and thundering up the rise.

He saw Harlow for only a fleeting moment before he was hidden from sight again.

Beneath him, Leith's mount heaved for breath. Far ahead a black horse emerged from a copse. "Rose." He whispered her name. She was there, bent low over her mare's dark mane, her hair hidden beneath a Forbes plaid. She was alive. Still alive.

But there. Harlow rode on—following her like a hound with Beinn's great strides closing the distance.

Please, Jesu! Leith prayed, and took the downhill grade at a dead run. The bay stumbled, half-sliding down the slope.

To the right a movement caught Leith's eyes. What? A man? A large body teetered to its feet.

A wounded man? But who? How? Harlow's arrow?

No time to learn the truth! No time to stop.
Sweet Jesu, protect her!

She was a quarter mile ahead. No more. He had to stop her. He could not fail his Hannah. But the pain. It speared outward from the arrow, gripping Harlow in dark waves. He could not stop. Must save Fiona. Must prove his mettle. Beneath him the white stallion labored, his heart pounding, his great body lathered, his nostrils wide and flaring.

A rock ahead. The huge stallion swerved. Harlow swayed, his splayed hand cradling the arrow that pierced him, his fortitude slipping and suddenly he was gone, sliding beneath the animal's churning hooves.

Rose pulled Maise to a halt before the MacAulay's gate. Above the timbers a man heralded her.

"I must see Laird Ian MacAulay!" she called desperately.

"Nay," answered the man, canting his head in an attempt to see beneath the plaid that covered hers. "Na one sees the auld laird these days."

"Not even the laird's own?" she called, and, reaching up, she swept the shawl from her head.

"God!" gasped the man. Sunlight sparkled like unquenched flame from the woman's loosed hair. Her chin was uplifted, her voice strong and sure in the still morn. " 'Tis auld Ian's lady."

"Nay," breathed his partner, awe making his voice rasp. " 'Tis his daughter returned from afar."

"Or mayhap na kin atall, but a trickster sent from our enemies."

"Nay," said the other. "Ye canna look upon her face and deny that she came from any but Lady Elizabeth. For she is the exact image of the auld laird's first wife."

There was a moment of breathless silence before the gate swung open.

No hesitation. No delay, and Rose was through, her heart racing along with Maise's hoofbeats over the hard-packed earth. Past a small boy and his sister. She slid from the mare's back and in a moment was through the thick doors of the hall.

Faces turned to her. Jaws dropped, but she stopped for nothing, driven by the aching need that drew her toward Ian's chamber.

"MacAulay," she breathed, rushing on.

A man stepped before her, blocking her way, but she dodged him, hurrying across the floor and throwing open a door.

Ian MacAulay sat bolt upright in the midst of his velvet-draped bed.

"Father." Rose breathed the single word, forgetting the lies she had told. Forgetting everything but this one moment—her head filled with eerie sensations she could no longer deny.

Men streamed in behind her, reaching for her.

"Nay!" Ian said, lifting one hand and startling them with the strength of his voice. "Nay." He shook his head. "Leave us."

Ahead, Beinn stood with trailing reins. Harlow lay not far away, crumpled on the earth. But Leith had no time to stop, to question, to learn the truth, for the woman who held his soul was now inside MacAulay Hold.

Pressing the bay onward, Leith thundered up to the timber gate.

Huge hooves skidded to a halt, sliding in the churned earth.

"Let me enter," ordered Leith, his tone low and even, his expression somber and hard.

"Nay," returned the man who stood above the wall, his lance lowered toward Leith's chest. "I have told ye afore. Na Forbes is welcome here."

"Let me in." Beneath him the stallion lifted impatient hooves in a slow, cadenced dance.

"Nay," called the lance man. "I willna allow—"

But he never completed his sentence for Leith had no time to waste. He spurred his mount forward and with three mighty swipes of Leith's arm, the gate fell, severed and bent. With a roar, Leith pressed the bay on. The stallion reared, charging the break. Wood splintered, flying in all directions, and they were through, racing along the course Rose had taken only minutes before, but now there was another beside him—Roderic, his face a mask of determination "I am with ye, brother."

Vaulting from his mount's back, Leith flew to the door of the hall.

"Me lady!" He roared the words like a challenge. "If ye have harmed a hair on her head, me axe shall na be stilled till this keep floats in blood."

Warriors pivoted toward him, hands reaching for weapons.

"Hold!" commanded a wavering voice.

Heads turned.

Ian MacAulay stood in the doorway of his bed-chamber. And beside him, hale and straight and lovely, was Fiona Rose.

Relief sluiced through Leith's war-ready system, calming his fighting instincts, quieting the killing rage.

"I will have her back," he said, his voice barely audible, but his expression so dark his intent was obvious.

"He broke through the gate, me laird," announced the guard, rushing in.

"Then I shall see him out!" challenged another, drawing his blade.

"Nay!" called Ian in a stronger voice. "There shall be na Forbes blood shed here this day."

"Me laird." Dugald hurried down the steps toward them. "Ye have only just regained yer speech. Ye must save yer strength."

"Save it?" Ian smiled, though only one corner of his mouth lifted. "For what?" He paused, straightening his back and seeming to grow younger as they watched. "What could be more important than the return of me own daughter to MacAulay Hold?"

"With respect, me laird," Dugald said stiffly, his gaze shifting to Rose's face, "there is na proof that she be yer true daughter. Indeed, Murial swears that she is na."

"Murial." Ian nodded slowly. "I fear her hatred for the Forbes has infected ye with its poison, Dugald. Too long has she mourned her brother Owen's death. 'Tis past, and time to make a new future—a future where the Forbes and the MacAulays are again friends."

"Nay!" choked Dugald. "Too much has passed between us. There shall never be peace."

"Aye," said Ian, his expression somber. "For the sake of me daughter, Fiona, there shall be."

"We know na if she be indeed yer kin," spat Dugald. "But we do know that she is a Forbes—living with the verra man who kilt me brother by marriage!"

Leith tightened his grip on his axe. "I didna kill Owen," he said. "But the other is true. Fiona is indeed a Forbes now." It was far too late to back away from the lies now. "Though she was once a MacAulay."

"Lies!" Dugald shouted, fists clenched. "All lies from the mouth of a filthy—"

"Quiet!" Ian roared, then paled, looking weak as Rose gripped his arm to help him remain upright. "Dugald," he said finally, his tone softened, his head shaking sadly. "Have ye na eyes? Or be ye too young to recall the lass's mother?"

Dugald's gaze turned slowly to Rose, his expression hard, his jaw clenched.

Beneath his glare Rose refused to flinch. Reality had faded into a blur, so that she was no longer sure what was a lie and what was truth, but she had proclaimed herself to be the old laird's daughter, and now she must play out the game. Holding herself straight as a lance, her chin lifted, she spoke. "I *am* Fiona MacAulay, daughter to Elizabeth and Laird Ian."

"Nay!" Dugald snarled. "Ye are an imposter, brought here for Forbes' devious purposes. To—"

" 'Tis na true." Ian shook his head, his voice firm with conviction, stopping Dugald's words. "Forbes has brought her for *me* purposes. At me request."

"Me laird." Dugald took a short step backward, his tone baffled, his scowl dark. "Why?"

Ian's old eyes softened. "I could na afford to lose ye to this mission, Dugald," he said, "for me health was fast failing. I needed ye here with our people. Thus . . . " He shifted his gaze to Leith and shrugged. "I asked Forbes." He smiled, looking younger. "A test of sorts, mayhap, to judge how dearly he wished for peace between us. And indeed . . . " He motioned toward Rose, who stood as still as a statue. "He must have wanted it a great deal, for he has dared much to bring her to me."

The old eyes drifted to Leith. "Have ye not, Laird Forbes?"

Leith watched the MacAulay with narrow-eyed caution. How much did the old man know? How much did he guess? Though he had lost his ability to speak for a time, he was not a senile old fool, but a wizened, crafty bastard with something up his sleeve. Did he accept Rose as his daughter, or was he simply pretending that he did?

Dugald's gaze flew to Rose again. "Forbes searched far indeed, but mayhap he but searched for a woman who looked like yer lady of auld. One to trick even ye, knowing how ye longed for that child. He only tries now to make ye the fool, for there is na proof."

"Laird Forbes has found the jeweled brooch I gave the lass' mother. He brought it here to me along with the wee plaid the bairn was wrapped in when she was taken from this hold."

Dugald scowled, shaking his head. "The Forbes are a devious lot and could have found a way to deceive us. There is na proof."

So there was the truth. Laid bare—exactly as Leith saw it. He braced his feet, his heavy thighs taut, his right hand on the dark handle of his battle-axe.

But Ian's voice came, startling them all.

"Ah, there ye are wrong, young Dugald, for indeed—there is proof."

Rose swallowed a gasp, spinning her wide gaze to Leith.

"Proof?" Dugald took a step forward. "Proof, me laird?"

"Aye." Ian nodded, motioning Rose nearer. "And with the proof will come the beginning of a lasting peace between the Forbes and the MacAulays. Na more shall blood be shed. Na more shall we fear for our lives or the lives of our—"

"Nay!" screamed a woman, and suddenly she was behind Rose, her arm encircling her slim neck, her dirk poised at Rose's exposed throat.

Panic and shock surged through Rose like heady wine, weakening her knees, numbing her senses.

Death! She could feel it like a tangible thing.

"She shall die!" shrieked Murial, her knuckles white against the dirk's handle. "She shall die to avenge me brother's death! Me Owen." Her voice was hysterical. Her trembling hands were tight and hard against Rose's neck. "Ye killed him," she wailed at Leith.

"Nay." Leith kept his voice soft, placating, but his heart beat with painful strokes against his ribs. *Jesu, do not let her die,* he prayed. *Take me instead.* "I didna kill yer brother."

"Liar!"

He raised his empty hand, palm outward. "I dunna deny that I wished him dead, Lady Murial, for I thought he had defiled me sister. Indeed . . . " He nodded solemnly, a muscle jumping in his jaw. "I did wish him dead. In truth, I had me hands about his neck. But I didna kill him." He straightened slightly, flexing his hands. "Though he asked me to."

"Lies! All lies!" Murial shrieked, pulling Rose backward slightly. "Ye would have us believe he would shame us all with his death."

"Nay," denied Leith, daring one step forward. "I dunna ken how he died, only that I was na the cause. I could na." His voice was low, one hand outstretched. "For I knew then that his love for Eleanor was deep. I could na kill him—as ye canna kill Fiona."

"I shall!"

"Murial," Ian said, his face pale as he stood helplessly looking on, "ye canna . . ." For a moment he lost the necessary words, but they came to him in a moment. "Ye canna kill her, any more than ye could kill me last night."

Murial blanched, and though she stumbled backward a step, she dragged Rose with her, her hand still tight on the dirk and her wide gaze on Ian.

Silence settled in the hall as their eyes met.

"Aye," Ian said, his voice low. "I ken yer purpose in me room last night for I felt yer intent. As did me daughter. And thus her arrival here this morn."

"Nay," Murial whispered.

"Ye knew that if I fully recovered I would ensure peace between the Forbes and the MacAulays. Ye feared that, for ye know she is me daughter in truth."

"Nay."

"Aye. And that is why ye planned to kill me last night."

"I could na kill ye, me laird. But we canna have peace. Because of the Forbes, me Owen is gone. He must be avenged." Murial sobbed. "She will die!"

"I'll kill the lad!" Roderic's voice thundered

throughout the hall and suddenly he stepped forward, his own dirk pressed to the throat of a child who'd wandered too near.

"David!" cried Murial, her voice breaking.

" 'Tis na me way to harm an innocent," growled Roderic, his face hard above young David's fair head. "But for the lady's life, I will." He pressed the blade harder.

"No!" cried Rose. "Please, Roderic, I beg of you, let the boy go. He's done naught to deserve to die." Her face was pale and tilted painfully back away from Murial's dirk, but she managed the words. "Let this feud end with me."

Pain thudded hollowly in Leith's chest. Sweet Jesu! "No!"

Roderic tightened his grip, his gaze caught on Rose's wide eyes.

"Please," she whispered again.

Roderic's hands relaxed, letting the boy slip, unharmed, to his feet.

"Mama."

"David!" Murial gasped, and, dropping the dirk, she stumbled forward to embrace her son.

Rose gasped for breath, trying to still the tremor in her limbs.

Leith's heart bumped to life. Sweet Jesu, she was free. She was safe. But from behind him Silken snarled. He whirled to see Dermid, claymore in hand, ready to lunge.

Leith's axe flew, true and hard, plowing into Dermid's midsection with a sickening thud, forcing him back against the wall like a felled tree.

He lay there, half-upright with his back against the wall, his sword beside him, his bearded face twisted in a grimace of hate and pain. From his chest a broken arrow protruded. "I should have kilt the bitch that first time." He coughed, clutching his gut where the thick blade of Leith's axe was embedded. "Should've kilt her like I kilt yer sister." His eyes, hard and flinty, flitted to Leith. "That slut." He coughed again. "Saw her with the MacAulay lad." He chuckled, but the sound gurgled in his throat. "They paid to keep me from tellin'. But she tired of that . . . game. Threatened to tell ye." Bloody fingers curled spasmodically. "Strangled her, I did. Tossed her from the cliff.

"The lad," he gasped with a weak shake of his head. "He used to go there to mourn her. Besotted with the . . . bitch." His eyes rolled back for a moment, blood frothing at the corner of his mouth. "He accused me of her death." Coughing again, weaker now. "So I kilt him too. Fought—like a bastard MacAulay. But I bested him. Pushed him from the same cliff." A crazed grimace twisted his face. "Should have been . . . grateful . . . that I sent them off . . . to be . . . together." He chuckled, but the sound was horrible, ending in a garbled last gasp.

The hall was silent.

"Leith." It was Rose who spoke, stumbling into his arms.

He encircled her in his strength, pulling her close.

"I am sorry," she whispered, her cheek pressed to his chest. "So sorry. Poor Eleanor. Poor Owen."

"Nay, lass." He kissed her brow, his eyes closed, his great arms locked about her. "Nay, me love, dunna mourn her now, for the truth is out. She is at peace. We shall return home."

"This is her home." Murial MacAulay straightened, her son cradled in her arms. "She is Ian's daughter."

Dugald's face was pale and strained as he came forward to lay a broad hand on his son's small arm. "How do ye know this, wife?"

Her eyes were fixed on Rose. "I know. I knew her when she first came here, felt her spirit . . ." She lifted her hand toward her temple. "I knew she must die," Murial whispered. "I went to Forbes' land to kill her. She was picking flowers as I watched her. We draw each other, for she has the MacAulay gift. I could feel it like a strong wind. She came up the hill, but . . ." She shifted her gaze to the wildcat that stood in the hall's entrance. "The cat warned her of me presence, and . . . I couldna kill her anyhow. Na then. Na now."

"But Dermid could." Leith said the words quietly, still holding Rose tightly to his chest.

"Aye." Murial nodded once. "Dermid could. He has long been a spy for me, and promised to do the deed."

"Then it was he who pierced her with the arrow?" questioned Leith, his voice little more than a whisper as the enormity of his own actions settled in his mind. "And na Harlow."

"Aye," said Murial. "I felt her wound when the arrow pierced her flesh." She touched her own shoulder, wincing with the movement, then, drawing herself from her reverie, shrugged at the men's wary expressions. "We are kinswomen," she said softly. "In our blood, but more so in our souls." Her eyes lifted again to Rose's. "I dunna ask yer forgiveness." Her eyes were deep with sorrow. "For I loved Owen so."

Rose felt the woman's emotions like a stinging slap, knew the pain as if it were her own. "Eleanor loves him deeply," she whispered.

Murial smiled, her expression misty and wan. "Ye have strong sight indeed, to feel a woman's thoughts from beyond her grave."

"You know it is true," murmured Rose, the eerie

feelings so strong that she could no longer deny the forces that empowered her.

Murial closed her eyes, letting the need for revenge drain from her. "Aye," she said finally. "She loved him. As did we all."

"They would want peace," added Rose softly. "For the MacAulays. For the Forbes."

"Peace is a fragile thing," whispered Murial. "And hard it is to hold."

"But worth the effort if one can but find and nurture it."

"Aye," said Dugald. "Well worth the effort, is it na, me Murial?"

"Aye." She met his eyes over their son's head. "That it is."

Purest happiness sparked in old Ian's eyes. "Then let there be peace," he declared. "Peace between me daughter and me nephew's wife. Peace between our tribes. And now it seems . . . " He looked to Leith's wary face. "All that is left is to prove yer lady's identity." He lifted his hand, motioning to Rose again. "Lass, if ye will permit me to lift yer hair."

Rose felt as if her breath had long ago left her lungs and that her heart could not beat for the pressure in her chest. She raised her eyes to Leith, knowing fear showed in their depths.

"There is na longer need for a feud betwixt us, Ian," Leith said, his voice low, his embrace unrelenting. "The man responsible for our sorrow is dead. The lass is na needed to forge a peace."

Ian lifted his brows and his eyes twinkled. "Could it be ye doubt the lass?" he questioned, then motioned again. " 'Twould make me wonder if ye have tried to play me false."

Rose's grip was tight on Leith's arms, but Ian motioned again so that she stepped from the

Forbes' embrace to stand before the old man.

"Dunna fear, lass," he said softly, touching her arm with his open palm as he looked into her wide amethyst eyes. "Ye have the MacAulay spirit if na me blood. But come. Let me look." He smiled outright. "I dunna fear the outcome," he said softly, "for I too have some sight."

"Me bairn . . . " he said more loudly, addressing the crowd at large but most specifically Leith, who stood with every sinew taut, every muscle ready to launch himself into battle. "Me bairn had a patch of dark skin." He took Rose's hand, holding it gently. "The shape of a cloud, it was," he said, and, pulling her close, he gathered her heavy hair in both hands and pulled it aside, revealing the back of her slim, elegant neck—and the dark cloud that marred it.

Gasps echoed about the hall.

"What?" Rose asked.

Murmurs. Silence. More murmurs.

"What is it?" she demanded, her brow lifting in irritation as she twisted about in an attempt to look behind her.

Ian let her hair drop. "Ye have the beauty of yer dame, lass, and the temper of yer sire." He laughed, then bent to kiss her cheek. "Would that I could pity me son by marriage for what ye have inherited from birth."

Rose's jaw dropped slightly. Her head shook once. What of the accusations? The denials? "But-b . . . " she began, but Leith was across the room before her first word was out, gathering her in his arms and shushing her against his chest.

" 'Tis a miracle of God," he whispered, his own voice breathy with awe. " 'Tis a miracle. We can but accept—"

"Ye shall drop yer weapons, Forbes." The words rang from outside the hall.

"I but come to speak to me brothers," answered a voice Rose well remembered.

"Drop them," ordered the first man.

There was a clatter of steel and then the sound of hurrying feet.

"Leith!" Colin called, his gaze skimming the assemblage and settling on his liege. "Leith," he said again, with relief now. "And . . . me lady." He smiled at Rose, displaying every whit of that unforgettable charisma. "We have come as fast as ever we could."

Rose frowned in bewilderment.

Colin smiled, raising his brows as if challenging her to ask the questions she longed to voice. Before she uttered a word, however, he reached behind him and drew forth a bonny, dark-haired woman.

"Ye will remember me bride." He smiled crookedly. "Devona of Millshire."

"Devona," Rose said, blinking once and finding no other words.

"Yer bride?" questioned Leith, his expression somber, but a little more certain than Rose's.

"Aye." Colin shrugged, pulling his wife possessively to his chest. " 'Twas a long and slow journey to her homeland. There was little she could do but . . . " He paused, smiling wickedly as Devona's face pinkened and the crowd waited in silence. "But grow to love me," he finished matter-of-factly, then laughed. "Though she tried to do otherwise."

"Poor lass," commented Roderic, at which there were chuckles and amused nods.

"My lady," Devona said finally, stepping tentatively forward, her hand deep within the pocket of her gown. "I have something for you." She pulled a rolled note from her pocket. " 'Tis a message from the abbess."

"Message?" Rose could seem to make no sense of such a riotously unsteady world. "From the abbess?" The parchment was crisp in her hand and unrolled with a gentle crackling.

Rose's hands shook. The tiny, fair hairs along her forearms rose, bristling with the eerie feelings, and for a moment she could not read the script, could not look down or draw her eyes from Leith's deep gaze.

"Dunna fear," he murmured gently. "I am with ye."

She smiled ever so slightly, and then shifted her eyes to read. The words ran together, making no sense, and she read again and again, until she felt weak and drained with the news—the new knowledge that was not truly new at all, that her heart had perhaps known for all time.

"Lass?" Leith questioned, touching her pale face.

"The abbess," Rose began weakly. "It seems she knows the truth of my birth. It seems I arrived as an infant in my mother's arms. I was wrapped in a Scottish plaid, but my mother was very ill." Tears welled in her eyes as her voice dropped to a whisper. "Before she died of the fever she begged the abbess to keep my presence a secret, lest my father come to take me back. And so . . . " She shrugged in disbelief. "I was given to the Gunthers upon the death of their own daughter, who was buried in my place. And I am . . . " She shook her head slowly, feeling all reality crumble about her. "I am Fiona," she breathed, holding Leith's gaze in a desperate appeal for logic. "Fiona Rose MacAulay."

"Did I na say it was so?" Ian chuckled, his tone

light with pleasure, his eyes settling on Leith's stunned face as he finally laughed aloud. "But then, ye already knew that, did ye na, Laird Forbes?"

Chapter 30

Not only the hall was filled for the wedding, but also the courtyard beyond—crammed with milling Scots who had come to celebrate the uniting of Leith Forbes with Ian MacAulay's long-lost daughter.

Lifting her gaze to skim the crowd, Fiona Rose realized there were plaids of a great many hues, representing more sects and clans than she could name.

From the window in her bedchamber, Roman waved, his smile bright as he stroked Silken, who sat on the ledge.

"Me lady." Gregor MacGowan bent over her hand, drawing her gaze from Roman as he kissed her knuckles with courtly tenderness. He looked hale and hearty, she noticed, judging his hand and skull with a healer's eye. "'Tis a sad day indeed when I must give up me fondest dream to the laird of the Forbes." He straightened with a melodramatic sigh and a languid shake of his head. "Mayhap ye should have left me in the river for all eternity."

Fiona opened her mouth to speak, but in a moment Leith was behind her, resting his hand possessively on her waist.

"And mayhap 'tis na too late to throw ye back in, lad," he said, but his tone, Fiona noticed, was light and tolerant.

Gregor nodded with a lopsided smile. "Had I na seen yer bride meself, Laird Forbes, I might be offended by yer words. But . . . " He shrugged. "Alas, I ken yer wariness and dunna envy the battles ye will needs wage to keep others from her."

Leith's back was straight, his eyes slightly narrowed, but he nodded finally, accepting the man's words. "Then let there at least be peace between us," he suggested solemnly, "so that me wounds may be fewer."

"Aye." Gregor nodded in sober agreement. "For yer lady, the fairy princess, there shall be peace. But na only betwixt ye and me. Between all the MacGowans and the Forbes." He lifted her hand again, and, placing one more kiss to her knuckles, one last glance to her face, he turned to mingle with the crowd.

"He is right, of course," Leith said with a sigh. "Methinks I will needs fight off every lad with moss upon his cheek to keep ye from their greedy grasps."

Fiona turned in his arms, feeling a pleasant shock as her breasts rubbed sensuously against his fine red doublet. He was regally dressed today in his ceremonial plaid and his bejeweled sporran.

"And would ye fight for me, my laird?" she murmured softly. "Or in truth would ye let them take me?"

For just a moment Leith remembered the grinding fear of seeing her empty bed, of racing through the darkness in search of her. Against his will his arms tightened about her. "Would ye have me throw ye over me shoulder and carry ye to our room like a trophy of war, so that I might prove me feelings for ye there?"

"Nay, Leith," she murmured, embarrassed by the very thought. "I would not have ye act in such an unlordly manner. But truly . . . in the past I have often questioned your sentiments."

"I would challenge the demons of hell for ye," he vowed huskily. "As ye well ken."

"Nay," she denied, lowering her eyes and reaching up to straighten a fold of his plaid where it crossed his wide shoulder. With some irritation she remembered that he had flatly refused to sleep with her until after the wedding, insisting that she needed the extra time to mend.

She lifted her left eyebrow with unconscious impatience, and, coddling a bit of petty frustration, allowed her fingers to fall lower, touching his chest just where his doublet parted. She sensed the immediate tightening of his body and smiled sweetly up into his face. Mayhap this past week had not been so easy on his self-control either.

That thought brightened her already joyous mood. "In truth, I know not what ye'd do to keep me, my laird," she said, "for to my memory the only one ye have challenged is my father."

"As I have said," murmured Leith, grasping her seemingly innocent fingers in his own and drawing them abruptly from where they tormented his chest, "the demons of hell."

Her jaw dropped in a comic expression of offended shock. "Dare ye call my dear father a demon?"

"Aye," said Leith, his tone droll, "for even in his speechless state, the auld bastard knew I didna believe ye to be his kin. He knew I would do anything to bring peace between our clans."

"Even bring back an Englishwoman and claim her as his own flesh?" Fiona asked impishly, trying to pull her fingers away.

"Aye." Leith tightened his grip on her hand. "Even that. But in the end it didna matter, did it?

'Twas fate. I could na avoid getting the auld . . . ''
he stopped his words at his bride's stern expression, and found a more acceptable term for his
newly acquired father-in-law. "The auld . . . laird's
daughter."

Fiona shook her head, forgetting for a moment
her attempt to make him as frustrated as she. "Can
it all be true?"

Leith smiled down into her faraway expression,
loving her with an intensity that made his heart
ache. "Do ye call the abbess a liar?"

"Nay!" She said the word quickly, before she realized he but teased her. "Nay," she said more
softly, shaking her head at his dry wit. "I but marvel at the twist of events. Why did she never tell
me of my heritage?"

Leith pulled her close against his chest and gazed
over her bright coiled hair. "Yer mother begged her
na to, lass. An Englishwoman begging an Englishwoman to save her bairn from the awful Scots. Ye
canna blame her for trying to keep ye hid. Then
when the Gunthers lost their wee daughter, it must
have seemed like the divine will of God that they
give ye to them to raise." He paused, remembering
the fiery fairy princess by the lochan, the mesmerizing beauty who still haunted his nights, more
than ever this past week. "And mayhap it *was* the
Lord's will, lass."

Fiona raised her chin, looking into his strong, be-
loved face.

He shrugged. "Who is to say what would have
come about had ye been raised as a Scot. Mayhap,
if ye had not survived the fever that took yer
mother, ye would na have lived out the same dis-
ease that caused the Gunthers' deaths. And mayhap too," he said, "without the life ye had, ye

wouldna have grown into the woman who could steal me heart."

"And have I, my laird?" she whispered. "Stolen yer heart?"

"Aye," he answered without hesitation, "that ye have, lass. As I think mayhap the auld abbess knew ye would."

"Surely not," objected Fiona in disbelief. "Never would she have allowed me to leave the abbey had she thought I would be so tempted by yer... shameless advances."

He chuckled, the sound coming from deep in his throat. "Mayhap she knew what a poor nun ye would make, lass, and only wished to be rid of ye."

Fiona tried to look offended, but finding she had no talent for acting, let a grin lift one corner of her mouth. "Perhaps 'tis true. I was meant for other things." Their eyes caught, sparking on contact.

"Such as?"

"I canna guess," she answered breathily.

"I could na have lived if Dermid's arrow had taken yer life, lass. Knowing it was me own fault would surely have kilt me."

"Yer fault?" she questioned, still lost in his eyes.

"'Twas me fault ye were here in Scotland. I should have cared for ye better. Na have let ye—"

"Leith." She gave up the battle for her hand and lifted the other, placing it against the hard plane of his chest where she could feel her cross beneath his shirt. "Ye cannot do it all, for ye are only one man, and cannot expect to care for everyone—to know each child's needs."

He scowled, knowing the pain his mistakes had cost her, wee Roman, and Harlow. His jaw tightened. Without Harlow, Fiona would have died, lost her life beneath the evil of Dermid's weapons.

Poor, stubborn Harlow, always mistrusted, while his heart was strong and loyal.

"Too many mistakes," Leith muttered, shaking his head. "I canna afford the mis—"

"Leith," she reprimanded him, scowling up into his face. "Ye flay yerself unforgivingly. Why?"

"Because I am laird," he said, firmly. "Because they need me. And I must na fail them."

"Fail them?" She shook her head. "Hardly that, Forbes. No father could care more."

"Aye." He nodded. "I care. But 'tis na—"

"Shush," she commanded, catching a movement in the crowd and motioning wordlessly toward it. "I think there are others with different opinions."

From the sea of faces, Harlow came. He walked a bit stiffly up to them with young Hannah by his side.

Fiona felt Leith straighten slightly, a subtle indication of his guilt.

"Me lady." Hannah bobbed a curtsy, her bonny face alight with joy. "Me laird. We wish ye much happiness on this, yer wedding day. And to thank ye . . ." She paused, glancing up into her bridegroom's face. " . . . for yer words to me father."

Leith did not smile, but Fiona felt him relax somewhat. "I but told auld Evander the truth concerning Harlow," he admitted. "The theft of a few apples did na seem so terrible a crime to him when he realized the lad but wished for yer notice." He nodded solemnly. "In truth, I would have done far worse to get the attention of me Lady Fiona."

His eyes met with the lad's, whose gaze was dark and just as sober as his laird's.

"Loyalty and bravery grant their own rewards, lad." he said.

There was silence between the two men for a moment, then, "Ye have given me me fondest desire, me laird," said Harlow quietly, gently squeezing Hannah's hand but holding his gaze on Leith's. "I too wish to thank ye. And . . . " He lifted his chin slightly, as if finding it hard to use the words he'd so rarely said. "And ask forgiveness of yerself and yer lady for me . . . shameful conduct."

"Nay," Leith said softly. " 'Tis I who should apologize, for na seeing yer true mettle. For na finding ye a better home to foster in."

"But had things been different," said Harlow, "I may na have won bonny Hannah's heart. And so I thank ye. For her hand." He nodded once. "And for the post beneath the auld horse master."

For the first time Leith smiled. "Beinn willna let just any man ride him. Although I find he has a weakness for the lasses," he added, looking down at Fiona, "I knew ye had a special way with the steeds to ride him as ye did."

"Aye," Hannah said shyly. "He does that. He'll make a grand horse master himself someday."

"Hannah," her husband scolded. "We dunna know that I will be granted that position until—"

"Nay, lad. I doubt na yer ability, young Harlow. Nor yer loyalty," Leith said, thrusting forth his hand to have it grasped by the other.

"We owe ye much, me laird," murmured Harlow huskily.

"Nay," countered Leith, pulling Fiona slightly nearer and nestling her against his chest. " 'Tis I who owes ye—for the safekeeping of me heart."

"Harlow," Roman called, skipping through the crowd, Dora weaving behind him, "ye promised to . . . Oh!" He stopped, his small face alight, his mop of bright hair falling over one eye. "Me laird. And me lady." He reached out, gently touching Fiona's hand. "Ye look specially bonny today. Like a fairy princess."

Fiona smiled, turning her hand to hold his. "And ye look like a ray of sunshine, Roman," she said softly.

He laughed aloud, his face breaking into a gap-toothed smile. "There is much sunshine," he said, squeezing her hand with both of his now. "Since ye arrived."

"Aye," agreed Leith solemnly, but wee Roman had already had his fill of sentiment and was ready to be off.

"Will ye need me help in guarding her this day, me laird?" he asked.

"Nay, lad. I think I can manage this once. Take this time to play."

"Aye, me laird," he said happily, and, reaching out, took the hand Hannah offered and skipped off through the crowd with the young couple at his side.

Fiona turned to her husband with a joyous smile. "The lad will not lack for love."

Leith nodded. " 'Tis well past time he knew some happiness."

"And 'tis because of ye," she added quietly. "Because of yer great leadership."

"He would never have known such hardship had I been a better laird."

Fiona shook her head. "He would never have known such joy had ye not been such a *great* laird."

"But—"

"Nay." She placed a gentle finger to his lips. "Ye are but one man, Leith. With a large clan to care for. None could do it better. But I will try to help."

"Try?" he scoffed, shaking his head. "Ye have done more for this clan than any other. Healing their wounds, making them look to ye for comfort."

"There's nowhere I would rather be, Leith. By yer side, helping with yer burdens. But there are others as well. Colin, for instance, now that he is wed, wishes to take a larger part in the care of the tribe."

"Colin wed," said Leith, shaking his head. " 'Tis hard to believe."

"I am glad to know he is ready to help shoulder the responsibilities," Fiona said. "For ye will be a busy new father."

"Father?" Leith asked breathlessly.

"Aye." Fiona smiled into his eyes. "We have much to celebrate."

"There shall be a bairn?"

"Aye."

"And ye didna tell me?"

"In truth I have not known for long, but even if I had . . ." She paused, dropping her gaze. "You have avoided my bed long enough. I was quite certain such news would not hurry yer arrival there, since ye only bedded me to produce an heir."

"Ye ken that is na true," said Leith huskily.

"Do I?" she murmured, intentionally goading him. "Ye are a man of few words, and I am but a simple lass. How could I know yer reasons?"

"Would ye have me proclaim me love to the entire assemblage?" he asked.

"Aye, my laird," she replied, her newfound brogue soft and sweet. "That I would."

Their gazes met and held, then broke abruptly apart as he swept her from her feet and carried her in long strides to the top of the hall steps.

"Hear this, me people," he called, hugging her close to his chest as her face reddened with embarrassment. "This is me bride, the daughter of Ian

MacAulay. With this union the Forbes and the MacAulays will be kin—united in peace. But I say this also." For a moment he gazed into her eyes, finding there that special love that would hold him forever. " 'Tis na her heritage that made me wed her, nor 'tis it her heritage that makes me love her. 'Tis the woman herself. Whether she be MacAulay or Forbes. She is *ours!*"

A cheer went up—loud enough to rock the very foundations of Glen Creag.

Fiona's blush deepened as her name was roared and roared again.

"Well, hell," she muttered in discomfiture. "Ye might as well carry me to bed like that damned war trophy now."

"If ye insist." Leith grinned, and, turning, toted her up the stairs to their bed.